Heatherwilde Falls

Tillie Coldwater

ISBN-979-8-218-77523-0

Cover design by: Tillie Coldwater

Printed in the United States of America

This book is dedicated to my loving husband, my incredible son, and my wonderful nephews. Your love, support, wisdom, and encouragement inspire me.

To those who left us too soon, too unexpectedly—this book is also for you. Though you are no longer here, your names are woven into every chapter. This is my tribute to you: a place where your memory will never fade, where you continue to speak and to live on. May this book be a reminder that love doesn't end with death; it lives on in the hearts of those who remember, and in the pages that carry your names.

"Not everything that calls your name is a friend. Some voices are meant to lure you into darkness."
-UKNOWN

Table of Contents

PROLOGUE

Jamie Littlefield breathed in and slowly exhaled, lost in the moment. The sun was shining brightly, warming her skin. It was not a sticky, hot day, but a warm, sunny day with just a slight breeze blowing through occasionally. *Just perfect*, Jamie thought. She loved the sound of the water as it gently pushed up against her inflatable lounger, rhythmically rocking her to and fro. *This is great*, she thought as she floated, *it is just what I needed.* Around the pool, she glided, basking in the glorious moment. *This is the life.* Jamie was drifting through the pool, entirely immersed in the experience, unencumbered by the thought of paying bills or taking exams. She was blissfully relaxed, listening to the birds sing their happy songs and watching the leaves waving and dancing as the breeze gently moved through them. She heard a gull whining above and maybe someone whistling. Out of the corner of her eye, she thought she saw movement. Just as she turned to look, another sound pierced her eardrums. This sound was initially a slight, nagging sound, but it gradually grew in intensity and insistence. She looked left to right, trying to find the source. *What is that beeping sound*, she wondered. She looked all around, trying to find the source as the sound got louder and louder. Woosh! Without warning, Jamie was no longer on her lounger in the pool, but in new, unfamiliar surroundings. She was confused.

"No!! Where is my pool?! Where am I??" Jamie yelled aloud to only her big, fluffy black dog, Mr. Pickles.

As her mind started to clear, she realized the sound was her alarm clock. Home. She was in her bed at home.

"God Dammit!" she said as her arm stretched out from underneath her cozy cocoon of blankets. She slammed down on the incessantly beeping alarm clock. *Just five more minutes,* she thought grudgingly as she peeked out from under her warm cocoon of blankets to check the time.

"Oh SHIT!! How many times did I hit the snooze bar?" she yelled as she and Mr. Pickles jumped out of bed. "I overslept! Again!"

Jamie turned off her alarm clock, threw on her scrubs, and put her hair into a scrunchie, not caring how messy it looked. She rounded up all her textbooks and jammed them into her backpack. As she made her way to the front door, she grabbed a toaster pastry from the kitchen cupboard, stuffed her feet into a pair of sneakers she had tossed in the hallway late the night before, grabbed her bike, her keys, and hustled out the door. As she got to the end of her driveway, she stopped.

"Fuck! My phone! Oh God dammit, I am going to be late—again!!" she mumbled and huffed as she went back into her house and grabbed her phone off the counter. "I have got to quit doing this...."

She ran back outside, grabbed her bike, and swung her heavy backpack over one shoulder. She hoisted her leg onto the bike seat, sat down, and pedaled as fast as she could. She was glad the rainstorm forecast for the day hadn't arrived yet. The darkened sky suggested the storm was close. As Jamie moved through the streets on her way to work, she noticed something. Even though the wind was rushing past her quickly, the air felt oddly still that day. There was no rain or thunder. But the air was heavy and thick, and the scent of rain drifted through the town. It seemed like a quiet, dark, ominous fall day. She felt uneasy and disoriented, as if she were experiencing the sensation you get right before something bad is about to happen. Jamie shook her head, trying to clear her thoughts. She shrugged, thinking, *Get it together, girl. You didn't get enough sleep last night.* Still, something felt off to her. Nothing she could quite pinpoint. Just an unsettling feeling, like it was sitting right there on the tip of her tongue, waiting to be remembered. Again, she just brushed it aside and kept going to work.

Chapter One

Jamie pedaled her way to work, just as she had many times before. But because she was running behind that day, she was pedaling with ferocity, her legs pumping up and down rapidly. A small town meant little traffic, which was good because she weaved in and out of the cars as she rode. Jamie was usually a careful cyclist who conscientiously shared the road, but not on this occasion. A few horns honked at her. One man shook his fist and yelled, "Hey! Watch it!" A woman glared at Jamie and flipped her the bird as she peddled past her, squeezing in between cars.

Jamie didn't necessarily love the afternoon shift, but she did like the commute time. Living close to work did have its advantages. She loved watching families playing in the park. Their smiles and laughter were uplifting. She loved seeing owners playing with their dogs at the dog park. Every once in a while, if she left early enough, she would stop and chat with the owners, pet their dogs, and then continue on her way.

Even though summer was winding down, Jamie still saw a plethora of vehicles with kayaks strapped to their roofs, either headed to the water or returning from it. Heatherwilde Falls was blessed to have many lakes, rivers, and streams, for a wide range of outdoor activities. She felt fortunate to be surrounded by such beauty and loved swimming, tubing, and kayaking. She smiled, thinking she should get her sister Pam, her brother Albert, his friend Benji, and all her nieces and nephews out for at least one more kayaking adventure before the season was over.

During her rides, it was easy for Jamie to feel affection for the town she grew up in. Nestled in the forests and hills is where Heatherwilde Falls sat. It was a small town, but it had a great deal to offer. The shopping options were plentiful, from unique boutiques to box stores to organic co-ops. Because the town also tended to be a bit quirky and a little cheeky, many of its stores had unique and interesting names. Charlie's in Charge Daycare was one of them. Most people mistakenly thought it was a man who ran the facility, but Charlie, rather, Charlene (she hated that name), was a lovely woman who Jamie felt missed her calling as a teacher. The most unique and innovative business decision Charlie ever made was to share a building with PJ's Pet Rescue. Her husband, Patrick Jacob, was the town's only animal control personnel. He hated the idea of animals being housed in cold, unfriendly environments, so with town approval, he opened his pet rescue next to the daycare. It was a win-win situation because Charlie would often take the older kids over to help feed the animals or even play with them. The parents loved it because it taught responsibility while also providing some cuddle therapy for the anxious ones. It was mutualism at its finest. Often, one of the kids would leave with a new pet. The town agreed; Charlie was a phenomenal daycare provider. She even took older kids in during summer break, so they weren't home alone. She was truly a town gem.

The town also had stores, such as Quiet Things. That was the local bookstore and stationery supplier. It was the go-to place for all your invitation needs. Jamie loved that the owners, Marge and Clarence, treated it similarly to a library and asked people to support a more subdued tone of voice. It was a calming place. A soothing place. The couple was perfectly content having you stop by for a cup of coffee while sitting in one of their overstuffed chairs, reading a book. To encourage reading, they not only hosted a monthly book club but also kept a small lending library that their community could use. Before Jamie started her studies back up, Quiet Things was a place she frequented.

Heatherwilde Falls, whose beauty was unparalleled, also had a sense of humor. That was clear by the names of some of the town's other businesses. Butts & Guts, the local gym, was usually packed after the New Year but remained somewhat uncrowded throughout the spring and summer. You're Soaking in It was a local day spa that offered alternative therapies, including ice baths, saunas, infrared saunas, hot tubs, reiki, acupuncture, and more. As Jamie pedaled past, she made a mental note to call and schedule a massage, salt room session, and pedicure as soon as she graduated. She was ready for some relaxation.

Come to think of it, maybe I will call Josie and plan a vacation, she thought, as she pedaled by Josie's Vacation & Travel Agency. *I know I've earned it.* Jamie sighed, and a half smile appeared on her face as she thought of the dream, she had had that morning. *That is just the kind of vacation I need, lounging in the pool, basking in the sunlight.*

Jamie continued to pedal her way to work, getting lost in her own thoughts, thinking about what an upcoming vacation might look like. She was making a mental checklist of everything she wanted: sunlight and plenty of it, privacy, luxurious amenities, a private pool, access to the freshest fruit and vegetables available, and maybe even some yoga retreats. As she dreamily and longingly made her lists, she didn't notice the tow truck backing up out of their driveway. She came out of her trance when she heard someone holler, "LOOK OUT!!"

Jamie shook her head and saw the bright red tow truck right in front of her. She hit the brakes and veered right, doing everything she could to avoid colliding with the side of the truck. She had been pedaling at a decent speed, so her bike groaned, angry at the sudden deceleration. Jamie wobbled and tumbled into the shrubbery outside of J.J.'s Towing & Stowing. She picked herself up, brushing the dirt and leaves off as she did. Her face turned a deep shade of scarlet. *Oh my God! I haven't biffed on a bike since I was ten years old and thought I could do all those BMX tricks,* she thought, quite embarrassed.

She heard a truck door open and close, and a tall, thin guy ran over to her. It was J.J., whom she had known since first grade. She couldn't decide if falling in front of an old friend was better or worse. She figured it would be more embarrassing if it were a stranger. J.J. was a good guy, and she knew he wouldn't make a big deal out of it—that's just the kind of person he was. He was like that in school, too. An unassuming guy—kind, but capable of standing his ground if needed. Unfortunately, back in school, he often needed to. J.J.'s family moved to Heatherwilde Falls when he was six, which is why Jamie hadn't seen him in kindergarten, unlike the rest of her class. They moved from Astilbe Valley, a nearby town, for his mother's job. She became principal at Heatherwilde High, which wasn't always easy on J.J., given his real name, Jean Joseph. He was often bullied because people either thought his name was a girl's or mocked the French pronunciation. He then switched to J.J., and eventually, the teasing stopped. He went on to be class president and valedictorian.

"Jamie! Holy hell! You almost ran into me! Are you okay? Woman, you're too old to be crashing your bike. We aren't young anymore. We don't bounce like we did as kids." J.J. chuckled at the memory of riding bikes as kids.

"Hi J.J. Yeah, yeah...... I am ok....I think my pride is hurt more than my ass," Jamie said sheepishly, doing her best to laugh it off.

"Damn girl," J.J. said, chuckling as he plucked leaves and branches out of her hair. "Why are you riding your bike to work when a rainstorm is forecasted for today?"

Jamie's face turned a brighter shade of red; her cheeks felt like they were on fire. She shyly smiled and distracted herself by pretending to brush more dirt off her shoes and hands. That's when she noticed the blood. While falling, Jamie instinctively put her hands out to try to stop herself. She fell anyway and, on the way down, managed to grab the thorny shrubs, which shredded her hands and forearms. The cuts were not deep, but they felt like little paper cuts all over her arms and legs. She was peppered so the blood that had gathered at the injury sites trailed down her arms, dripped down her fingertips, and finally landed on the cement sidewalk below her. She looked down at the spot she was standing in, mortified that it was bespeckled with her blood. She had created her own mini horror scene right in front of her friend's store. Jamie groaned and covered her eyes. She peeked at J.J. to answer.

"Oh, uh, my car is currently over at Kellamy's Auto. Tiz is working on it. Good Lord. I'm a mess. I'm so sorry, J.J. Do you have a hose I can wash the blood off with?"

"I am not giving you a hose, Jamie. For cripes' sake. Come inside so we can wash up your hands, arms, and face."

"M..my face too?"

"'Fraid so. You look like you got into a tussle with a cat, and the cat won hands down. Hey, why didn't you bring me your vehicle? I would have helped you out. I mean, Tizzy is a great mechanic, but she's no J.J.," he said, winking and chuckling lightly.

Jamie, still embarrassed by the entire situation, moved her hands to her cheeks. She winced as her fingers hit one of the cuts. She pulled her hands away and nodded, knowing she could not brush this off. Back when she was a kid, she would have found a garden hose somewhere, rinsed herself off that way, and continued riding her bike. But as an adult nurse, she knew she couldn't show up at the hospital smeared with dirt and blood.

"Yeah, Yeah. But I figured you were probably too busy to work on my car. I know you have had your hands full with the girls these past few years..." Jamie trailed off.

She and J.J. had been friends for most of their lives. They had each attended the other's wedding. J.J. married one of her best friends, Daniella, who was a couple of years behind them in school. Jamie used to tease J.J. about being a cradle robber, but the truth was, Dani was the perfect person for him.

J.J. and Dani supported her when she discovered her then-husband, Tony, was cheating on her. They shared many late-night tears and ice cream sessions. They were by her side every step of the way during her divorce. Jamie was also there for every baby shower and birthday party they had, and she was even their girls' Godmother. When Dani passed away from a heart condition that went undetected for too long, Jamie did her best to support J.J. and the kids, but it wasn't the same. She knew that. Sometimes she felt like a reminder of what J.J. had lost, so she stepped back to give him space to grieve. She understood he needed to help his girls cope with the loss of their mother, and she didn't want to interfere with that process. She wasn't sure if that was right. Standing in front of J.J.'s store, she wondered if it might have been a mistake. She had never been able to have children herself, discovering her own health disorder too late in life. Endometriosis explained so much, but ultimately took away her ability to have her own kids. She often wondered if that contributed to Tony's betrayal. She would have happily adopted children, but her then-husband, Sean, said he couldn't love or raise children to whom he wasn't biologically related. Not being a mother herself, but having lost her own mother, she believed J.J. and Dani's kids needed their father during that time.

"Jamie, I am never too busy for a friend." J.J. looked at her with a kind but sad smile.

Jamie was tongue-tied. So many thoughts had filled her head. Instead of answering, she looked up at J.J., nodded, and followed him inside his business.

The office of the building wasn't large or fancy; it was just average size and unassuming. A front desk sat in the entrance, working like a dispatch center. Jamie saw two people sitting at the desks, taking calls and jotting down notes. They looked so young to her, almost too young to be working. They did a double-take as she walked by, covered in blood, leaves, and grime. Jamie lightly smiled, made a "ha ha" sound, and half waved as she continued to follow JJ. He led her to the employee breakroom and over to the sink. Next to that was what Jamie assumed was JJ.'s office. She could also see the door that led into the truck bay, which was bustling with activity. People were moving all over, machines were making noises, and guys were yelling at one another. Not only did JJ.'s provide towing in the area, but he also had a garage where he offered tire services, including repairs, sales, and the installation/removal of snow tires. He also stored locals' snow tires on site. JJ. was very successful and always busy.

"Here, let me help you clean up."

"JJ., I am a nurse. I am fully capable of cleaning my wounds. But thank you for-"

"Nonsense. You have blood all over. Just hold still," JJ. said as he went ahead and washed her scrapes.

Jamie looked at him and said, "I need to apologize to you. I think maybe.... Maybe I should have been around more. I didn't want you to think that I stayed away because of Dani's passing. I was trying to be a good friend. After I lost my parents, I was numb for a time. I threw myself into helping my brother and sister. It's not the same, but I just thought maybe you needed to do the same thing with Emerald, Dee Dee, and Rain. It can't be easy raising them on your own. And then I decided to go back to school. The past two years have been an utter blur. I am sorry for not being around as much."

J.J. held her hands but stopped cleaning them for a moment. He gazed intently into Jamie's eyes.

"You have nothing to apologize for. You didn't do anything wrong. You checked in periodically. I knew that if I needed anything at all, you would have been the first person to show up. You are right. I needed time with my girls. They were so young when they lost their mom. They were hurt and angry, and confused. Thank you for giving us the time we needed to work on becoming a new family unit. It's still lumpy, bumpy, and messy. I am always worried I am not doing a good enough job. Or I will somehow fail them."

"J.J., you are doing a fantastic job! Those girls are so smart, well-mannered, and just good kids. Don't you dare worry about failing them. You are an active parent. You show up every day. That's more than a lot of parents these days. But you know what? Call me on those days you start to worry. I will remind you that you are a phenomenal parent! And I promise, as soon as school is done, I will come around more often. Just two more semesters and then I graduate. Again!" Jamie said, sticking out her two thumbs and grinning.

"I will do that. Thank you for being a good friend to me and to Dani. Please give me a heads up about graduation. Dee Dee, Rain, Em, and I will cheer you on! Now let's get your hands dried off, ok?"

Jamie nodded and then glanced down. She had forgotten J.J. was still holding her hands. Her face burned with a light shade of pink creeping up her cheeks and ears as he grabbed a towel and dried her hands. When he was done, he handed her a wad of bandages. "I am not sure if these will work? They are all I've got."

"I don't need any bandages. But thank you, J.J. You went above and beyond, like always."

"I am just glad you didn't ride right into my truck. You could have really hurt it!" J.J. winked.

"Oh, thanks! Ha ha ha. Ooh, did I interrupt a run? I don't mean to keep you. I am running behind today and should get going myself."

"Nah. Don't worry about it. I was just heading over to Damn Fine Cookies to grab Dee Dee. The schools let out early, so she asked if she could go hang out with her friends for a bit. Kinda weird though. I didn't see anywhere in the school schedule that showed they had a half-day. It wasn't a snow day. Maybe it was a mechanical or electrical issue with the school. It's weird. But no, you are not keeping me from a run right now. Things just calmed down. It's been crazy today with the full mo—"

The front room suddenly burst into a cacophony of sounds all at once. Two people rushed into the office, one after another. The bell strung up at the top of the door was shaking wildly. At the same time, the phones started ringing loudly. J.J. had two main lines and a private back-office line. They were all ringing. Jamie and J.J. stared. The two people at the front desk hastily answered while simultaneously nodding to the people who had just come in. Bret, another classmate of theirs, came in from the truck bay and answered the office phone. Jamie and J.J. looked at each other wide-eyed, their jaws slack. Everyone was talking over one another.

"What in the hell?!" J.J. grumbled, his brows furrowed.

Jamie shrugged her shoulders and put her hands up. She noticed that the off feeling had intensified as soon as the phones began ringing. But now the hair was standing at attention on the back of her neck. She unconsciously shivered.

J.J. and Jamie walked out into the office area, where the employees and customers were all talking over one another. Everyone stopped and looked at J.J. They all started talking at once.

"Boss, there was an accident out on Old State Hospital Road. Sounds like a bad one. Multiple cars are involved. Several inoperable."

"Another one on Lilac Street. Two vehicles and a motorcycle. At least one car needs towing on that one."

"I need my flats fixed! It looks like someone slashed my tires!"

"I need my flats fixed as well. Same thing with my truck."

The two people stopped and looked at each other. They continued speaking to one another in loud voices.

"For real? Where were you parked? Was it near Punky's Brew Pub," the one customer asked.

"No, my dude. It's barely afternoon. Why would I be at the pub? Some of us *work*. I was parked over at Hank's Hunks of Cheese Shoppe picking up our office box lunches. As I went to put the order in my truck, I noticed all four of my tires were toast."

"Hey! Just a god damn minute here, little lady! First of all, it's late afternoon! Second, I *did* work! I am now reaping the rewards of my hard work and thoroughly enjoying my retirement. I did not put in my forty years of service just to be crapped on by a tattooed, entitled whiner like you!"

"Relaaaaax, guy. We are both here for the same thing. No one is telling you that you can't enjoy your retirement. Honestly, it's about time your generation left the workforce, so those of us trying to pay off our crippling student loan debt can get those good-paying jobs. I should be thanking you," the customer said in a thick, overly sweet tone.

"We all have debt. You just need to pull yourself up and work harder. If you can't make ends meet, get another job. It's not rocket science. Just try harder and—"

"Ok, Ok," J.J. deepened his voice and stared at the customers, "that's enough. If you can't be kind, I can't help either of you."

Both grumbling customers stopped arguing with each other and stared at J.J. He walked over to the counter, looking at his employees.

"Do we have any available trucks to send to those locations?"

Bret walked in from the back office, his face tight and lips pursed. He shook his head and headed over to J.J.

"Hey, boss. Uh, was Dee Dee on the bus today?"

"No. I dropped her off today. Why?"

"That was Frankie on the phone. Uh.... School let out early? I wasn't aware. It's just like my kids not to let me know., dammit. Anyway, all the buses should have been back in the bus garage by now, but Frankie received a call saying that someone had spotted what appeared to be a crushed bus at the end of a ravine off US 2. Frankie wasn't sure if it was one of our school buses or a tourist bus or what. She was heading over to check it out and wondered if you could tag along," Bret said, fidgeting as he stood.

J.J. looked at the employees again and said, "Jade, radio Jeremy and have him head over to the accident on Old State

Hospital Road. Anya, radio Joey, and have him head over to Lilac Street, please. I will go meet up with Frankie. Hopefully, it is nothing serious. I just need to make sure Dee Dee is home from Damn Fine Cookies. Things seem to be getting a little crazy. Must be the full moon."

"I am going to be riding near Damn Fine. Do you want me to check to see if Dee Dee is still there and send her home if she is?"

"If you don't mind, that would be very helpful. But you are on your way to work. I don't want to make you late."

"Oh, I am definitely going to be late," Jamie snorted. "I overslept again. But I am headed that way and don't mind. If she is still there, I will make sure she heads home. I would love to see her. It's been too long."

"Wait! Who will fix my tires?" asked the owner of the truck.

"Yeah! I need my tires repaired right away. I have places I need to be!" said the other customer.

"You just said you were retired," Jade said, looking at him with a raised eyebrow.

"Well, uh, yes.... But that doesn't mean I don't have places to be!"

"Riiiiiight."

"All right, all right, stop. Bret and some of the boys in the back can fix your tires. BOTH of you. Right, Bret?"

"You got it, boss. But is it ok if I call my kids to verify if they are home?"

"For sure!"

J.J. held the door for Jamie as she exited his store. She picked up her bike and brushed off the leaves and dirt.

J.J. turned to Jamie and said, "Gotta run. Sorry about that. Thanks for not hitting my truck, *Littlewierd*. I am very glad you weren't hurt worse. Would you like a ride to the hospital instead of riding your bike? I can drop you off on my way."

"Yeah, thanks, teacher's pet. Me too! No, thank you for the ride. I need to pick up 'sorry I am late' coffees for my coworkers. Besides, you just asked me to check on Dee Dee, remember?" Jamie asked, chuckling.

"Oh, my God. Duh!" J.J. said, smacking his head. "It's been a busy day, can you tell? Sorry."

"It's ok! It's a weird day, isn't it? And since it is starting to sprinkle, I would normally take you up on that. But like I said, I still need to head over to the bakery. Thank you, though," Jamie said, smiling at J.J.

"How are you going to carry coffee and donuts on your bike?" J.J. asked with his head cocked to one side and his right eyebrow raised.

"I have a basket on the front," Jamie said, grinning from ear to ear. "I came prepared!"

"For everything but a rainstorm, I see."

"That's not true! I brought my trusty rain jacket and a plastic bag. I can cover up the stuff after I put it in my basket. Plus, it's barely sprinkling right now. I'm good."

"Cool beans. Ok, I need to split. Listen, don't be a stranger, ok? I mean it. The girls would love to hang out with you. I get that you have a lot on your plate, but if you can squeeze in a visit, we would all love it."

"For sure. I promise I will holler as soon as my schedule calms down. I have tests this week, and then things chill out for a while. I promise to reach out. Good seeing you, J.J. Thanks again for fixing me up. I appreciate it. Sorry about your walkway."

Jamie shook her head and chuckled softly as she climbed onto her bike. She waved to J.J. and pedaled toward the café. As she headed to Last Drop Coffee Shop, she marveled at how, despite her small town's recent growth, everyone remained kind and friendly.

It was still a close-knit community where people were happy to lend a hand. They were fortunate to have farmers' markets all year round, along with community gardens that were always lively during the growing season. The town's only library hosted community events and story time for local children. There was just one school serving kindergarten through twelfth grade. For entertainment, options include a small community theater and a multiplex. Just outside town, there were a couple of manufacturing plants and a small college, the one she was attending again. Jamie had left Heatherwilde Falls to go to college elsewhere. She wanted to experience life outside where she grew up. Though she had some great experiences and made some wonderful friends, she didn't like the crowds and hustle of a bigger city, so she transferred from Trillium Hills University back to Heatherwilde Community College.

Each time Jamie rode her bike through town, she almost always saw someone she knew. She just loved the nods, smiles, and waves. It always made her feel welcome and safe, like a big family. But she didn't feel it that day. No one smiled or waved. People kept their heads straight while driving or down while walking. It made Jamie's skin crawl. It felt wrong. Jamie tried to shrug it off and continued pedaling as fast as she could. *People must be really busy today.* Or maybe they were preparing for the storm that was forecasted. Whatever the reason, Jamie wasn't going to obsess over it. She just needed to focus on getting to work on time, since the wipeout had delayed her more than she had planned. She decided she would add donuts to the coffee order she was going to place. *They won't be mad if their mouths are filled with glazed or jelly, right?* Jamie thought.

Jamie looked both ways and crossed the street. She leaned her bicycle against a tree outside Last Drop Coffee Shop and looked up to see Siobhan closing the shop door that had been propped open and walking away. Jamie looked quizzically, jogged over, and opened the door.

"Hi Siobhan! How are you? Too cold for the doors to be open today?"

Siobhan jumped at the sound of Jamie's voice, made a noise, and turned around wide-eyed. She looked visibly pale and shaken.

"Oh! Jamie! You startled me! Quick, get in here!!"

Siobhan walked past Jamie and over to the shop entrance. She pulled the blinds on the door windows and flipped the "open" sign to "closed". Her actions left Jamie scratching her head.

"Uh, Siobhan, you good?"

"Oh! Goodness! What are you doing here, Jamie? Haven't you heard?"

"I am on my way to work. I am running behind, so I wanted to pick up some coffee and donuts for the crew as a peace offering. Haven't I heard what?"

"You shouldn't be out riding your bike. Why aren't you driving your car with a murderer on the loose?!"

"Siobhan, what are you on about? What murderer? Who told you this? I was just over at JJ.'s, and he didn't mention it. My phone hasn't given me any notifications to stay inside. Why are you spreading rumors?"

"I am not spreading rumors! You heard the school let out early, right? *That's why!* A murderer is running around town!"

"Jesus. Ok. And who told you this?"

"Well....um...Esther told me. She told me when she stopped to get her coffee."

"And how did Esther get this intel when the rest of the town doesn't have it?"

"She said she heard it from Roman, who heard it from Pilar, who heard it from—"

"Siobhan, if that were true, it would be all over the news, don'tcha think? I mean, I haven't received any notifications."

This was the part of small-town life that Jamie did not enjoy. The rumor mill was always going. Tongues wagged all the time. If it wasn't who was dating whom, it was who was getting married or divorced or whose business was struggling. It was *always* something. Jamie experienced it firsthand after her divorce and again after her parents' passing. The local busybodies could not help themselves.

"I know for a fact that Roman had it on good authority! Now, if you will excuse me, I am closing the shop, going home, and locking all my doors and windows!"

Good grief, you old biddy. Jamie rolled her eyes. It's not that she truly disliked Siobhan. But after catching her in the act of gossiping about her parents, saying they were drunk and driving recklessly, she had little patience for Siobhan's rumors.

"Can I at least get coffee and some donuts before you go hide?"

"No!"

Siobhan put her hand on Jamie's back and forcefully escorted her toward the shop entrance. She hastily opened the door and gave Jamie a little shove through it. She looked directly at Jamie, shook her finger at her, and frowned.

"You would be better off just going home and calling in to work today. Mark my words!"

What in the actual fuck, Jamie thought as she climbed back on her bike. *The day keeps getting weirder.* She crossed the street and continued. *Well, I needed to stop by Damn Fine Cookies anyway.* Jamie shrugged at that thought and pedaled a little faster. *God, Siobhan can be such a pill sometimes!*

Jamie continued toward Damn Fine, grateful that the sprinkling rain had subsided for the time being. She didn't want to arrive at work soaking wet. As she made a right onto Main Street, she looked to the west. If the sky was any sign, she needed to hurry herself along. The sky was a grey green, mixed with various shades of dark blue. It looked like one hell of a storm off on the horizon. Jamie pedaled a little faster, her heart pounding in her chest. She finally saw the Damn Fine Cookies sign come into view.

She rolled up to the front of the store, quickly got off her bike, and leaned it against a tree. As she grabbed the handle and started to yank open the door, she heard someone call her name.

"Jamie!"

Jamie turned and saw Dee Dee headed toward her. She let go of the door and jogged over to her.

"Hey, kiddo, what are you still doing here? I just left your dad's, and he said you were supposed to be heading home."

"Yeah," Dee Dee said, brushing the curls out of her eyes as a gust of wind hit. "Don't worry about it. I'm going. I was hanging out with friends."

Dee Dee trailed off as a boy, about her age, walked out of the shop. The boy stopped and looked right through Jamie. He smiled at Dee Dee.

"Hey, are you going to Popcorn & Jellybeans next?" his voice cracking with a slight nervous tone. It was a popular snack and candy store where kids enjoyed hanging out.

Dee Dee blushed, smiled, and said, "Oh, I'm not sure. I want to." She looked at Jamie, her smile dropping as she did, and said, "Uh, no. I guess not. I have to get home...Maybe next time?"

"Ok. That sounds good! See ya," the boy said, smiling back at Dee Dee.

Dee Dee's face, which had been a light shade of red when the boy came out, was a few shades redder as he looked at her.

She put her head down shyly and smiled widely. She absent-mindedly kicked stones that sat on the sidewalk.

"Yeah! Uh.... See ya."

Jamie was expectantly waiting to be introduced to the boy, staring at Dee Dee and tilting her head toward her. Dee Dee's eyes followed the boy, and Jamie could tell it wasn't going to happen. The boy turned and walked away. Dee Dee giggled, but after noticing Jamie was watching her, she quickly became sullen.

"So. Who was *thaaaaat?*" Jamie asked in a sing-song voice.

"What? Huh? Uh, nobody..."

"Does 'nobody' have a name?"

"Oh, uh, yeah. His name is Faris. He's just a friend, Jamie," Dee Dee said very quickly.

"Uh-huh. I see. Ferris, eh? He's not trying to get you to ditch school, is he?" Jamie asked while laughing.

"What? No! Like I said, he's just a friend. School let out early, so we were hanging out," Dee Dee said. The red had crept back into her face as she spoke.

"Relax, dude. I was joking. It was a movie reference."

"Oh. I haven't seen a lot of those old people movies. Sorry."

"Wow! Harsh, kid. 'Old people movies'? I will have you know that it is a *classic!* Your mom and I would watch it over and over again during our sleepovers. Hey! We should make it a date: Godmother and Goddaughter Day. We'll binge on snacks and popcorn and watch a totally awesome movie! What do you say? I need to take my upcoming test, and then I'll be free. I can make some time for that."

"Yeah. I guess so......," Dee Dee trailed off.

"Hey, we don't have to. I know I haven't been around in a bit. And you are a teen now, with your own life."

"No, it's not that. I want to. I.... I guess I am just missing Mom a lot right now. Like today, for no reason. She's just on my mind. Does today feel weird to you? It feels weird to me. I can't explain it. Just.... I dunno... And then school let out early, but I don't know why. That's weird, too. Some of the kids are saying a murderer is on the loose, but come on, it's Heatherwilde Falls, the boringest city in the state."

"Yeah, this day has felt weird from the get-go. I am sure it's just the full moon and the upcoming storm. Things get weird sometimes. And your school probably closed early because of something simple like, uh, no heat, or plumbing. Or maybe the kitchen stoves went out. Try not to worry about it. And I miss her too, Dee. She was my best friend. I already told your dad earlier, and I also need to say it to your sisters; I need to apologize for not being around much. I wasn't trying to disappear from your life. I was trying to give you, your dad, and your sisters space to grieve and figure out who you all are now, without her. I know what a loss can do. I didn't want to insert myself into your lives while you put the pieces back together. I hope you can understand. I have missed you, girl. I got busy with school, but I am always here for you. Always! Call me day or night. We don't need to talk if you don't want to. If you need to cry, I will listen. If you want to scream on the phone about the unfairness of it all, I will scream with you. I got your back, kiddo."

Tears streamed down both of their faces. Dee Dee hurried over to Jamie, wrapped her arms around her, and hugged her tightly. Jamie reciprocated the hug and let her cry. Once Dee Dee calmed down, Jamie took a step back, held Dee Dee's face in her hands, and with bright, wet eyes, smiled wistfully.

"Your mom would be so proud of you. You know that, right?"

"Thank you, Jamie."

"Now, you'd better head home. Your dad wanted me to make sure you were on your way home. I was in the shop when a bunch of calls came in, so he's going to be busy for a while. Get home and make sure Emerald and Rain aren't causing trouble. They aren't home alone, are they?"

"No. Gammy Opal picked them up from school today. Pop said I could stop off here for a little while before I went home. But Gammy Opal wants to leave before the storm comes, so I'd better get going."

"Next time, you need to fill me in on 'Faris-Just-A-Friend'," she said, winking. "Reach out when you want to have a girls' night. And hey! You be very careful riding home, you got it? Text me when you arrive."

"I will, Jamie. I am glad I got to see you. I will also text you about that movie. See ya!"

Dee Dee hopped on her bike and headed down the road. When she was out of sight, Jamie turned toward Damn Fine Cookies and walked through the door. Her mouth watered as she thought about buying a dozen cookies and some coffee before heading to work. But the store was empty. That was unusual. It was usually a hub of activity most of the time. Teenagers and adults alike loved to gather there. It was rarely a quiet place and seldom empty. The owners, Wanda and Walt Anbrena, were always out sitting with customers when they weren't baking or taking orders.

The birth of the bakery was a funny story that they loved to tell everyone who hadn't heard it. It all started with Wanda losing her job as a researcher. To pass the time, while she searched for another job, she baked cookies. According to her factory-working husband, she made *a lot* of cookies. She gave them to family and friends, but eventually Walt started taking them to work with him to pass out to his coworkers. The story was that he had had enough one day and said, "Why don't you just open a cookie store?". Wanda thought about it but had trouble coming up with a name until one day, one of Walt's coworkers who was enjoying a cookie said, "Mmm mmm!

These are some damn fine cookies!" With that, Damn Fine Cookies was born, and the town loved it. They became so busy that Walt retired from his factory job and started working with his wife, which is why it was so weird that the store was currently empty.

"Helloooo? Wanda? Walt? You around?"

Jamie waited at the counter, leaning forward and trying to catch a glimpse of the kitchen. She checked her watch and realized she couldn't wait much longer; otherwise, she would be extremely late for work. She hollered one more time while leaning over the counter. She started to turn toward the door because she didn't have time to waste. She heard clamoring in the back kitchen, so she hollered again.

"Hey, Wanda? Walt? Can you come take an order?"

Still no answer. Jamie scrunched her face up in puzzlement and tentatively headed toward the door. Just as she grabbed the door handle, she thought, *If Wanda and Walt are back there, why weren't they answering? What could they be doing?*

Jamie looked at her watch again and couldn't believe what time it was. That was the deciding factor. She didn't have time to figure out what they were up to. She needed to get to work. She pushed the door open and went out. Jamie hopped back on her bike and headed toward the hospital. She decided to stop a few blocks over at Roasted Beans for coffee and hoped they had some muffins or something.

As Jamie furiously pumped the pedals up and down, lost in her own thoughts, she felt vibrations from her phone. Someone was calling her. *Oh dammit!* Jamie fumbled around in her pocket trying to find the phone, all while staying balanced on her bike. Jamie was in excellent shape for a middle-aged woman who hated exercising. But she loved to stay active, which helped. She particularly loved outdoor activities, such as riding her bicycle, hiking, and skiing, as well as any activity with her nieces and nephews. She liked staying busy. However, even the most active person would struggle to pedal their bike at that pace while trying to dig out a cell phone. She knew she should stop her bike to answer the phone, so she didn't fall again, but she was too stubborn.

Jamie was also a divorcee, but she had enough friends to keep a small social life. Since she didn't have children, that made things a bit easier. However, at her age, she didn't want to go out every night. Going back to school made it even less appealing. Still, Jamie couldn't help but wish she had her own children to hug and care for, children who would be home waiting for her after work and school instead of only being greeted by her overly friendly, slobbering big fuzz ball, Mr. Pickles, and an empty house. The idea of having children never completely left her, but she was incredibly blessed with many nieces and nephews to keep her busy and active. And she loved them all.

Jamie was always close to her siblings during her childhood. But they became very close after their parents passed away. They were a small family. Being the eldest of three, Jamie always felt responsible for her sister Pam and her brother, Albert. She still felt that even though they were all adults now. But since the loss of their parents about ten years ago, the younger siblings tended to go to her for advice more frequently. She didn't mind. She was glad to have them nearby. Albert was still in Heatherwilde Falls. Pam was in the next town over, but Astilbe Valley was only fifteen miles away.

Losing a parent, or parents in their case, changed their lives forever. It altered their perspectives. They always thought their parents would be around forever. They never even had that difficult talk about their parents' final wishes. No one liked talking about that, and like everyone else, Jamie and her siblings felt they had plenty of time to get that information. Their parents hadn't even retired. It was a horrible rainy night years ago, filled with bad choices by another person that took them away. On their way home from a date night, their parents were hit head-on by a drunk driver who had veered over into the wrong lane. Their dad was killed instantly, but their mom hung on for a few months. She had been put on life support.

They were told it was an open-and-shut case. They had apprehended the driver quickly. But something about it never sat right with Jamie. She was a nurse. Certain pieces never fit.

She questioned why her parents had taken a route home that they never drove, why they were each missing a finger, and why their midsections were sliced open. Sure, Jamie supposed that the accident could have caused that to one of her parents. But she wasn't sure how both could have been affected in the same way. She tried asking the coroner about it, but she was brushed aside as a bereaved daughter. Every time Jamie thought about it, all the questions would flood back.

One of the most challenging decisions Jamie ever had in her life was deciding to end life support. As a nurse, she knew her mother had no chance of recovery. The car accident nearly tore her apart. One horrible day, Jamie sat down with her siblings and thoroughly explained the situation. They all knew their mom would agree with their choice. In life, their mother was a busy, active woman. If it wasn't community outreach programs, it was the community garden, or their euchre club, or any outdoor activity.

As Jamie, Pam, and Albert mourned, so did their town. That was both a blessing and a curse. While trying to process their own grief, they found themselves having to comfort others. It often led Jamie to consider moving. It was one of the reasons she decided to go back to school. If she moved to another town, she could start over with a better career and a new outlook. She just wasn't sure she wanted to move away from her siblings, nieces, and nephews. Jamie wasn't even sure why she had been thinking about the accident after leaving Damn Fine Cookies. But it was fresh in her mind, like it had all just happened.

The phone kept ringing, jolting Jamie back to reality. She looked at her phone — it was her sister Pam. She thought it was a strange coincidence that she had just been thinking about the family when her sister called. She swiped up to answer, almost losing control of her bike. She wobbled briefly but then stabilized. *Good God, don't fall again on your way to work, girl. You'll never live it down.* Jamie made a face at the thought of the teasing she'd get from the other nurses. *Nope. Don't do that!* She straightened up and tried swiping again, this time successfully answering.

"H.... Hello," Jamie huffed into the phone.

"Good afternoon, my studious and favoritest seester! Oh Gawd! Did I interrupt *something* with someone...Or are you on your bike again?"

"Hi Pam. I am on my way to work! No! I am not with someone. Geez! Yes, I am on my bike. My car is in the shop again. Whyyyy? What's up?"

"You have sunk so much money into that car! Why do you continue to try to repair it? Why don't you trade it in for something new? That's nuts!"

"Well, I kinda can't afford a car payment right now, let alone the insurance. I have schooling to pay for. Send me a million bucks and I will consider it. But hey, this way I am staying healthy, right?" Jamie laughed wryly.

The cost of a new car was a partial reason for not buying a new one. The other part was her parents' accident. Even though it was years ago, because the accident was so gruesome, she still had issues with anxiety and nighttime driving. Daytime was not an issue, but nighttime, especially when a rain forecast was in place, was a huge issue. Jamie thought, *Why spend all that money on something I wouldn't be using while I'm on second shift?* Her bike was fine for a bit longer. She didn't live that far from the hospital, so if she had to bike home in the rain, she was ok with that.

"Yeah, yeah, whatever you say, sis. Soooooooo, I have a question. Do you think you could take Felix, Lily, and Tamileen, I mean *Millie*— I really wish she would stick to a name—tomorrow? You know how much you love them. And sis, get this, she is now 'Millie,' but she spells it m-i-l-ē-. I pointed out that her spelling will lead to mispronunciations, and she told me that was just my opinion. She said she wanted to be different, and if people couldn't pronounce her name correctly, that was on them. Lord help me, I am graying far faster than I should be!"

"Pammmmm! Nooo. I need to study. I told you I have a test coming up. And what do you mean, Millie? When did that happen? I just saw her last week."

"She announced it two days ago. She said she no longer *felt* like a Tamileen or a T or a Lee. From now on, she will be known as Millie. Teens, sis! Teens. I wasn't that bad, right?"

"Hmmm, let me think, Pam-Olive....I mean, Liv, Olive, Oli. *Weren't* you?"

"Yeah, ok. I had to try a few names on before I decided on Pam. But come on, who wouldn't? Mom couldn't settle on a more normal name like *Pamela,* so I got called the girl with two first names from kindergarten on. A lot of the kids said my name sounded like the dish soap brand, so they started calling me 'Dish Soap'. So, yeah, *Pam.* But what's wrong with Tamileen?!"

"Nothing is wrong with Tamileen. Although you did the same thing to her that mom did to you. You gave her two first names. But there is also nothing wrong with T, or Lee, or Millie—though I am gonna give her shit about the spelling—or even Tami. Bugg is just trying to figure out who she is, sis, just like you were. Be patient with her."

"I only gave her that name because we couldn't decide which nanna to name her after. She could have been Tamara or Eileen. Jamis and I just decided to combine them. It's a nice name! And yeah, yeah, yeah. I know you are right. Wow, you can be very wise sometimes."

Pam got quiet for a second. That was unusual for her. She was always the bubbly, constantly talking your ear off, social one in their family. She sighed quietly, but Jamie still heard her. Her tone changed, and she spoke more somberly.

"You should have had kids, you know that? I have absolutely no doubt in my mind that you would make an incredible mother."

Jamie knew Pam meant well. She knew it was a compliment. But that topic stung. Jamie wanted nothing more than to be a mother. She planned on adopting. But now that she was divorced, she wasn't sure she wanted to be a single mother.

"Pam, we have been through this. I can't have kids. My body wasn't having it. And I got to the point where I couldn't take another miscarriage. We eventually stopped trying, and then things just fell apart. Tony decided he didn't want to adopt, and then that asshole cheated. Ugh! Your heart is in the right place, but it's an excruciating subject for me. I would like it if you dropped it, ok?"

"Oh, Jame. I'm sorry. But it's still not out of the realm of possibilities, you know? You have so many options available, even for a single woman. Adoption, surrogacy, fostering...." Pam's voice trailed off.

"Pam, I know all of that. I am single *and* in school. I also work second shift right now, which wouldn't work. After I graduate from school, I hope to start my new career. It's just not in my cards, ok? Please drop it."

Pam heard the pain in Jamie's voice. She knew how much Jamie had wanted to be a mother. She only brought it up because she thought maybe it would help her with the healing process, knowing practical options existed. But as Pam learned from her therapist, you can't rush healing, and there is no time limit for grief. Even though she disagreed with Jamie's decision, she respected her sister enough to let it go.

"Ok. I'm sorry. So, back to this weekend. Was that a 'yes', I was about to hear? Come on, you want to see your favorite nieces and nephew."

"Pam-Olive! I don't have favorites! I love Albert and Kielson's kids just as much. Forrest, Benny, and Nalon are wonderful nephews. Just stop that!" Jamie laughed while pretending to scold her little sister.

"I love them too. But we both know Bertie is a weirdo! Ha ha ha. Jamie, *puh*-leeeeez? Please, oh please oh please? Come on! I just won tickets to see the play, "The Stars Are Aligned." You know how much Jamis loves theater! It would mean the world to both of us," Pam said, emphasizing her last sentence.

"Ugh. Yes. Ok, I can watch Boo, Bugg, and Tootie this weekend. But girl, you owe me big time! *Big Time*, you hear me?" Jamie laughed.

Her sister was always roping her into watching her nieces and nephew. Probably because she knew how much Jamie dearly loved those kids. Jamie watched them on her days off from the time they were infants, so she was very blessed to have a fantastic bond with them. She didn't mind at all. She loved Pam's family as if they were her own. But she still had to give her sister grief about it from time to time.

"Thank you, thank you, thank you!!! You are the best sister a gal could ever ask for!"

"Ha ha! I also happen to be your only sister. Listen, I have to get off the phone now, ok? I am just parking my bike in front of Roasted Beans. I will give you a call tomorrow after class. We can work out the details then."

"Why are you at Roasted Beans? Last Drop has the best coffee in town. I mean no disrespect to our cousin, Park. He has always had a nice shop, but he doesn't make his own baked goods, and his coffee options are limited. But I will let you go. James, you are the best. Hey, be careful today, ok? I got a weird feeling. It's leaving me...unsettled, I guess. I can't quite put my finger on it. Weird vibes? Sort of. Um, I think it's kind of like when you're waiting for the other shoe to drop, I guess? Kind of like that. But not exactly."

Jamie was so surprised that Pam had the same weird feeling while also trying to rush to get the coffee that she forgot to tell her the most bizarre part. The whole reason she was at Roasted Beans instead of Last Drop Coffee Shop was that Siobhan shoved her out the door and closed her shop. But as Pam was describing the feeling, Jamie became focused on that and neglected to mention the other.

"What? A weird feeling? You too? I have had it since I woke up this morning. I figured it was because I was rudely awakened by my alarm clock and yanked out of my blissful dream. That weird feeling has been here ever since. I even ran into J.J.'s truck because I was caught up in the weird vibes. It is very unsettling. Probably just the full moon or something. I have to go now, sis!"

"Ok, ok. But you'd better call me on break and tell me how you ran into a big tow truck! Remember, *this weekend*, not next weekend. Thank you again! Love you bunches!!"

"Yup, this weekend. Got it. Love you too."

Jamie hung up with her sister and jogged into Roasted Beans. She was extremely close to her cousin, Parker Dane (or "Park" as the town knew him), though he was around ten years her senior. He was already off to college when she was still in elementary school. They would hang out on weekends, and she always enjoyed seeing him. But once Jamie reached adulthood, she wasn't as good at catching up with him, other than at weddings, funerals, or birthdays. She made a mental note to fix that after she finished her degree.

"Hi, Park! I am running late again. I need to make this a quick trip."

Parker nodded and took Jamie's order. He put the coffees in the cup holders and took her money all without saying a word. Jamie looked at him, puzzled. She hoped her cousin wasn't offended. She wasn't trying to be rude. Jamie thought it seemed a little weird, but she didn't have time to question any more weirdness about the day. She hustled toward the door. She stopped dead in her tracks when she realized she had forgotten the muffins. She turned around and headed back to the counter, her arm full of commercially made muffins.

"Sorry, Park. I forgot these."

Parker nodded but again never uttered a word. Jamie stared at him. She noticed he was holding his left hand down by his side, which was odd because he was left-handed.

"Uh, are you ok? You seem quiet today."

"Yup, I am just fine," Parker stated a bit hoarsely. A bead of sweat ran down his forehead.

Jamie continued to stare at him. Not only was he her favorite cousin, but Jamie had also grown up going to Roasted Beans with her entire family. That store was like a second home. *Why was he so distant?* Jamie wondered. *Why was he sweating? Did he have a fever?* She was just about to ask him when her phone rang again. She glanced at Park sideways, wondering whether she should answer. He nodded. Jamie scooped everything up, hollered a thank you, and went out the door. She put the items in her bike's basket, covered them up, and pulled out her phone to answer it. But something about the interaction bothered her. She turned back, but Parker was no longer standing there, so Jamie shrugged and decided she would ask him about it later. Instead, she swiped on her phone to answer.

"Hello?"

"Woman, when are you getting to work? Cause I am scheduled to leave here soon, and I don't see you here yet."

"Hi, Ivy. I am on my way. I promise. I woke up late again. My car is in the shop, so I had to take my bike. I ran into a tow truck and got scraped up. That wasn't on my to-do list! Now, I have been trying to chase down some coffee for everyone."

"Well, please get your butt in here, 'Miss Can't Be On Time'. It's a full moon today. I am ready to go home and not deal with any more craziness!"

"Got it, Ivy. I will arrive as soon as I can. I am just leaving Roasted Beans. Did you want a specific coffee? I just paid, but I can go grab you–"

"No. I don't want any damn coffee. I *want* to go home. And what do you mean you ran into a tow truck?! Okay, never mind. I don't think I want to know after the day I had." Ivy's voice softened, "Just be careful, ok, Jamie. Things are weird today."

"You can say that again. I am getting on my bike now and will be right over!"

"I mean it, Jamie, be careful. No more running into things. I'll see you soon!"

"You got it, dude!"

Jamie hung up with Ivy, shoved the phone back in her pocket, and pedaled for all she was worth. The wind gusts were fighting her wildly as she moved, but that made her all the more determined. She wasn't worried about getting in trouble. The entire hospital staff was very understanding. They knew she had late nights with school. But Jamie was all too familiar with that feeling at the end of her shift. That time, that said, "home". And if the day had been crazy, Jamie was sure Ivy was feeling that.

Ivy was kind but stern. Jamie liked her. She was an excellent nurse who was probably nearing retirement. Ivy had moved to Heatherwilde Falls a few years ago, and although Jamie had worked with her briefly, she ended up moving to the second shift due to her college classes, and only saw her leaving as she was starting her shift. Jamie never had an issue with her, though. So out of respect for the job and *need* to go home, Jamie peddled as fast as she could.

She looked up and saw the hospital on the horizon. Just in time because the rain was starting to fall more heavily. Jamie zoomed into the hospital parking lot on her bike, trying not to drop or run into anything again. She was concentrating so much that she didn't see the ambulance leaving. She nearly collided with it. She wobbled again, tipped, caught herself this time, and stopped near the ambulance. The driver hit the horn, shaking his fist out the open window.

"Sorry! Sorry!" Jamie yelled as they hollered at her. She did a little wave with her hand as she rolled her bike up to them.

"Whoa there! You should be careful!" said the passenger in the ambulance.

"HEY! WHAT THE HELL?! WATCH OUT, Jamie! What's the matter with you? Trying to get out of work tonight? Hitting us won't do it. We would patch you up and send you back. Pay attention, little lady, or you'll end up with more than road rash. Now get to work! They neeeeeed you! *Especially* tonight," the driver said, sneering and snickering.

Jamie couldn't remember his name. Perhaps it was Brad or Thad, or something else. She never bothered to remember because he always acted like an ass. She didn't know how people tolerated him. He was good at his job...mostly. But something about him just oozed creep to her.

"Aren't you always late? I am surprised you still have a job. They must be desperate for help! Ooo, are those donuts? Hand me one," the voice boomed.

Jamie stared at him. *The dude just gave me shit about being late and then had the nerve to ask me for food? God, he is a total MFer!* Jamie thought as she smiled sweetly and extended her middle finger toward him. He just guffawed.

"Shut up, Mitch," the other rider remarked. "She has enough on her plate right now. She doesn't need your shit, either."

Mitch! Right! That was it. Jamie reached into her basket on her bike, dug out two muffins, and handed them to Andy. Even though Mitch didn't deserve a muffin, Andy did. Despite her feelings, Jamie knew how hard they both worked. They were both excellent at their job and were always on the go. It was the least she could do, even if she couldn't stand Mitch.

"No, Mitch, they are muffins. Here, Andy. I couldn't get any donuts or cookies. Siobhan shoved me out of Last Drop, and no one was in Damn's. It was weird. And thank you, Andy. I'll be—"

"I'm just sayin'! It's bad enough that it is a full moon, but a storm too? And now a murderer on the loose? Woooowie! She's gonna be busy!" Mitch interrupted. He took a bite of a muffin and laughed as he chewed, showing big chunks of food.

"Mitch, just shut up and drive." Andy shook his head and rolled his eyes. The look on his face suggested that he was not a fan of Mitch's either.

Andy shot Jamie an apologetic look and made the hand sign for "call me". She smiled and nodded. He was a nice guy. Jamie had started casually dating him a few months ago. They didn't want anyone to know, as work relationships could become messy. So, they kept a more professional tone while working.

Andy seemed to have a good head on his shoulders. He was several years younger, though, which felt a little weird to Jamie. He was kind, caring, and always willing to lend a hand. Jamie thought it was no wonder he ended up as a paramedic. He was just a great guy. But sometimes Jamie got the feeling they wanted different things. Andy brought up having children on several occasions. Jamie wasn't sure what to make of that. She had already told him that she was unable to have kids. She figured if he brought it up again, she would probably have to stop seeing him. It wouldn't be fair to stay if their lives were heading in different directions. But that wasn't something she wanted to talk about, let alone think about right then. She needed to get to work and study for her test. She was just about to peddle off when Mitch's comment sank in.

"Wait. What do you mean, murderer on the loose? Why is everyone saying that?" Jamie asked.

"Because there *is!*"

"Says who, Mitch? I know for a fact that Frankie is out checking on a potential bus accident. If a murderer is on the loose, wouldn't she issue a stay-at-home order? Like, come on, man. Be serious."

"There is a reason you couldn't get anything from Damn Fine Cooki—"

"What Mitch *means to say,*" Andy interrupted with a sigh, "is that we just brought in two people who appeared to be attacked. The police are involved. They haven't mentioned a murderer on the loose. Drea is with Levi. We don't know any more than that because *we left to do our job,* right, Mitch?" Andy asked, looking at Mitch for validation.

"We *did* do our job. They arrived at the hospital, didn't they? They sure didn't chop off their fingers and gut themselves, though. *Someone* did that to them."

"Fingers.... They were missing fingers? Who was it?"

"Jamie," Andy's voice became softer and quieter, "it was Walt and Wanda. It doesn't look good for Wanda. Walt was talking, but in and out of it. I'm sorry. You shouldn't be finding out like this. We aren't supposed to be talking about it right now, but Mitch obviously couldn't keep his mouth closed! Please don't share this information. Drea or Frankie will inform the public if or when they need to."

"Oh, my God. I was *just* there! I mean, *just* there. I wanted to bring everyone coffee and donuts. I thought it was weird that no one answered me. Oh my God! Did I miss something? Could I have helped or stopped it?"

"We don't know anything yet, Jamie. I doubt you could have done anything."

"That is just horrible. I guess I had better get inside. It sounds like they are going to need me."

Jamie made a slight frown; her eyes grew distant as her mind drifted back yet again to that terrible night when her parents had the accident. Missing fingers? Andy saw it in her face.

"They always need you. But remember, we don't know anything yet, so please try not to worry, Ok?"

Jamie tried to smile, but it looked more like a grimace. She let it fall and nodded to Andy.

"Bah ha ha! *Good luck*!!" Mitch said, and he guffawed as he shoved the rest of the muffin into his oversized mouth, chewing loudly. He was one of those people who was truly an asshole. The worst part was that he knew it. He didn't care.

Jamie glared at him. She flipped him the bird, got back on her bike, and peddled toward the hospital garage. As she rode away, she heard a call from inside the ambulance. She wasn't sure, but she thought she might have heard, "Roasted Beans". She was going to turn around to ask, but the ambulance sped off. She would have to call Andy a little later.

Jamie pulled into the garage and headed toward the bike rack area. She parked her bike and locked it up. *Walt and Wanda were attacked?* She wondered, shaking her head. *And is something going on at Roasted Beans? What the hell?* She looked at her watch and noticed it hadn't been that long since she had been inside Damn Fine Cookies, and even less since being in Roasted Beans. Jamie wondered how something like that could even happen. The missing finger thing was bothering her, too. It reminded her of her parents' accident. But she figured that must be purely coincidental. What Andy said did make her worry about Dee Dee, though. She picked up her phone and was just about to call Dee Dee when a text came through. It read, *Home. THNX. Movie next weekend?*

Jamie typed back, *Good. Stay inside tonight. Lock the doors and windows, ok? The storm is supposed to be bad. Stay safe. See you next weekend!* She waited for a response, hoping Dee Dee wouldn't ask any questions. She shouldn't have brought it up, but she wanted those kids to stay safe, no matter what was happening. She figured that telling her to lock the door because of the storm was a good cover. A few seconds later, Dee Dee texted back, *KK*. Jamie put her phone back in her pocket, grabbed the coffee and muffins, and headed inside. She wanted to call J.J. with the news, but she knew he was swamped. She also knew that all she had was rumors and gossip, not actual information, so she didn't see any point in calling him yet.

Jamie entered the building through a side employee entrance and made her way through the sea of people walking around. Because of the time of day, it was still a busy place. But Jamie knew it would die down in a couple of hours. It always did. She felt like a football player or soccer player as she walked through the lobby. She weaved in and out, dodging people to avoid being hit or hitting anyone while balancing the coffees and muffins.

She rechecked her watch. *Twenty minutes late! Those damn late nights.* Jamie had stayed up after her shift ended the night before, studying and trying to make sense of her homework, which led to her oversleeping later that day. Holding down a full-time job and attending college meant not getting much sleep. She thought the second shift kind of sucked, but it was necessary if she wanted to complete her degree. She often wondered if that was a good idea at her age. *Nothing like a middle-aged career change, I guess.*

As Jamie headed toward the elevator in the hospital to reach her floor, she realized the hospital seemed unusually busy. Almost too busy for Friday. *Must be the full moon,* she thought.

The first floor of the hospital consisted of the ER and waiting area, as well as some doctors' offices, a reception area, a cafeteria, and, behind the cafeteria, doors that led to their local mental health facility, Myers Mental Health Clinic. The hospital also had administration offices on that floor.

As Jamie neared the elevator, she peeked into the ER. It was a mess inside. She knew that Mitch and Andy had just dropped off Wanda and Walt, but it seemed like a lot of extra people were either being treated or waiting to be seen. *Well, that can't be good,* Jamie thought as the elevator doors opened. She stepped inside, pushed the up button, and waited. Jamie realized that the uneasy feeling from earlier had intensified. *Ugh,* she thought, *shake it off, girl. You need some sleep! Floating in that dream pool again might be nice.*

Chapter Two

The elevator ride seemed slower than usual, but that was probably because Jamie was late and in a hurry. As Jamie exited, she heard all kinds of sounds. Beeps from electronic things, ringing from the phone, bings from the call buttons, and people talking. So many people were talking. *Sounds just as busy up here.* But Jamie was used to that. Her floor was where the cardiac unit and ICU were. They also had some occasional geriatric rooms. Unfortunately, that meant her floor could be busy at times.

She balanced the coffee and muffins while she pulled out her cellphone, which her coworkers called 'outdated,' and attempted to clock in. She hated the app. It never worked right, and she always had to call to fix her timecards. The company kept telling her to update her phone to ensure the app worked properly, but she didn't want to buy a new one. She felt there was nothing wrong with the one she had. Jamie felt that updating tech was a never-ending process. She missed the days of an actual time clock, where you clocked in. The card with your name, the Ka-CHUNK of the machine stamping down. She felt it was so much simpler and easier. Even clocking in on a computer was preferable to the app; she hated that app.

She clocked in and walked down to the breakroom with the muffins and coffee still balanced in her arms. She placed them on one of the tables and was about to walk back to the nurses' station when something caught her eye. Up above the refrigerator, where the cupboard sat, was the most enormous spider Jamie had ever seen. It had to have been two and a half inches, she thought. It didn't look like the typical wolf or fishing spiders she usually saw. It stopped walking as she stood staring at it. Jamie swore it was looking her over. She muttered, "damn, dude! You're a big one," as she walked back out of the breakroom.

When Jamie got to her station, she sat down with a loud sigh. She placed her heavy backpack on the floor, pulled her long hair out of the scrunchie, and pulled out her homework, setting it in front of her. She had completed it, but with an upcoming test, she wanted to double-check her work. She was hoping for an easy night so she could study just a little bit more and maybe get a jump on her homework for the next day's class. This was the home stretch; she was so close to the finish line. *Just a few more months, and I will have my degree.* Jamie knew it would be worth it, but was also ready to be done with schooling.

"Hey, guys! Sorry, I am late. So sorry. Car is in the shop and it's, well, it's been a day." Jamie raised her voice to anyone listening.

"Bout time you showed up!! I was beginning to think you'd quit, boss," Keith said as he rushed past Jamie and disappeared into a room.

Keith and Jamie had been friends for years. He was a couple of years older than Jamie. She met him in college. He was a bit of a grouch at times. Many people referred to him as "grizzled." He was always giving someone shit about something. But the one thing Keith was not was a slacker. That man gave one hundred percent, no matter how he felt or how his patients behaved. He was a great employee and an exceptional nurse. Jamie enjoyed working with him because he was a straightforward guy with straightforward communication. She always knew where she stood. She loved that about him.

"Yeah, it's been a day! Good Lord. Still hard at it? How is school? Did class let out late today?" asked Kerrigan as Jamie was looking over her homework.

Kerrigan was one of the few nurses that Jamie felt had a real head on her shoulders. She worked hard, showed up on time every day, and was a quick thinker. She seemed to enjoy being a nurse. She cared about her patients and always tried to greet them with a smile, no

matter what was going on in her personal life or what the patient's mood was. She was just a good kid. Well, she wasn't a kid, but Jamie thought of anyone ten years younger than her as a kid. Jamie was sure Kerrigan would be a good fit as charge nurse after Jamie stepped down.

"No, I didn't have class today, thank God. I stayed up after my shift last night trying to make sense of my homework and study for the upcoming test. I went to bed later, which caused me to sleep through my alarm a few times. Sorry! But, yeah, I am still hard at it. Wash, rinse, repeat, seems to be my cycle of life right now." Jamie rolled her eyes and chuckled. "It was another late-night study session. I swear I am too old for this shit. Remind me again *why* I am doing this to myself??" She flopped a book down on the desk in front of her and opened it with a sigh, blowing her bangs that she had neglected for too long out of her face as she did.

"Because you're tired of the long hours and little pay? You're going for the big bucks?"

"Oh. Yeah. Riiiiight! Yup, going for the '*big bucks*'. Cause we all know this is where the money is at, right?" Jamie couldn't hold back the sarcasm.

She was in no way going to get a considerable salary increase with her new degree. But she was tired of scraping by on her little income. Even as a charge nurse, she wasn't making enough. Her area was known for lower wages for the nursing staff. In fact, they were trying to gain enough interest so they could unionize, but she wasn't sure that would happen. It was just one more reason for Jamie to consider moving. With her new degree, she could move to a new, better-paying area if she wanted. But truthfully, the biggest reason Jamie was in school was that she just wanted to have a little more control. She became a nurse because of her desire to help people. She genuinely enjoyed that. But she no longer wanted to wait for a doctor to handle a patient's needs. She often saw that patients were not being heard. They were being treated as transactions, with dollar signs, rather than as real people with real problems. Jamie didn't like that. She enjoyed listening to and trying to find solutions to their issues. Getting a big smile and hearing them thank her was what she loved the most, though. She didn't want to commit to becoming a doctor at her age. She figured that would be too much. But a nurse practitioner was a great choice. She was burnt out for sure. But she was in her final year of schooling. She just needed to be patient to reach it. *Good things, and all that,* she thought and chuckled to herself.

"Oh, hey, guys! Coffee and muffins are in the breakroom. Feel free to help yourself."

Jamie heard a few "Yays" and a couple of "Thank you's" from the nurses' station. However, everyone seemed too busy to retrieve them—all except one nurse.

"*Muffins*!?" Reid yelled excitedly.

Jamie hadn't even seen him sitting behind her. She jumped when he spoke. She gathered herself and hoped no one noticed. She did not like being so jumpy.

"Yes, MUFFINS," she chuckled and rolled her eyes at his enthusiasm. "I stopped by Roasted Beans on the way here. Help yourself."

"Don't mind if I do! But Roasted Beans? You know their coffee is inferior to Last Drop's."

"I do. However, Siobhan closed her shop today," Jamie said, shrugging.

"Huh. That's weird. Eh, free coffee is still good coffee!"

Reid leaped out of his chair and headed toward the breakroom. He was a very tall, freckly redhead who preferred socializing to working. He was constantly being reminded to focus on his job and the tasks at hand. It didn't seem to faze him, though. He never stopped talking. At least he was a good nurse. Most of the patients loved him. A few complained that he never listened—that was because they couldn't get a word in edgewise—but most enjoyed him because it was a bit like social hour when "Big Red" (as he was affectionately known) walked into a room. Reid was young and had time to learn. Jamie just wasn't sure he wanted to. He ran down to the breakroom and came back with two muffins and a coffee in his hands.

"Glad you decided to show up today, Jamie! I was starting to think I might have to step up as charge nurse!" Reid was smiling big and wide while eating a muffin and leaning over the counter to look at Jamie.

"Reid, *buddy*, we both know that wouldn't happen. Nothing would ever get done if you were in charge. That job would fall to Kerrigan or Charity or Keith." Jamie laughed, wagging her finger at him.

"Hey! I get stuff done...*most of the time*. It's not all work-related, that's all," Reid said, grinning mischievously. "Speaking of, I need to go check my patients."

He stood up, towering over everyone. His height and his bright red hair were the reasons he was called "Big Red". He sauntered down the hall to the breakroom to grab another muffin before going to a room. He walked past Jamie again, smiling and chewing. Jamie laughed. Reid was larger than life. Everyone on the floor could hear him talking, so he was often asked to lower his voice. Jamie didn't think he was capable of being quiet. She didn't know much about him other than he grew up with six other siblings, all boys, so she wasn't surprised by his loudness. She also knew that his family was part of the town's founders.

"So how crazy has it been today?" Jamie asked nobody in particular.

Ivy had walked up behind Jamie without her knowing, startling her again as she spoke. Jamie jumped and yelled. *Oh my God, what is wrong with me,* she thought. She wasn't normally skittish, but she was that day. Something about it left her thoughts racing and her body on edge.

"Oh, you know, a little of this, and a little of that," Ivy replied loudly. "Thank you for finally showing up! And thank God I get to go home! I have one more patient to check on, and then I am out of here. I won't have to deal with any more of the stupid full moon shenanigans."

Ivy was an excellent nurse. She had been a nurse for decades but remained hopeful and unjaded. She had plenty of nursing experience. She loved her job and her coworkers equally. She often hosted get-togethers with all the nurses, as she believed that fostering a strong coworker bond created a better, more cohesive unit and ultimately led to better overall nurses. In some ways, she may have been correct. Their nursing staff was one of the highest ranked in the hospital. And although Jamie didn't hang out with her co-workers all that much, she did enjoy Ivy's gatherings on occasion and did feel more connected to her co-workers, so maybe Ivy was right. It was no wonder that Ivy was also a charge nurse. She was smart with a great attitude. Nursing just came naturally to her. Jamie thought that when they first met, Ivy's height would be intimidating to her patients, but not a single one ever had a complaint about her. It helped that she was stunning and had an exceptional calming quality about herself. She had a stern side for sure, but anger rarely came out. When it did, it was best to nod and smile. None of Jamie's coworkers was afraid of her. They just never wanted to get on her bad side, either. Jamie didn't care either way. She would give as good as she got. But she respected Ivy, so she never had any issues with her.

"Oh fuuuuuudge! Has it been that bad? I saw Mitch on my way in, and he was trying to warn me about the full moon and—"

Jamie was going to ask if they had heard about weird things happening or if anyone else had that off feeling. But before she could finish her sentence, she was interrupted by another nurse who walked over, sipping on one of the coffees Jamie brought in.

"Heeeeeyyyyy.... like, it's all true! I read my horoscope today, and it said to like, be wary of strangers and stuff, and be cautious around heavy machinery, AND that during this full moon I should carefully weigh my options, so I am not held back from a future I deserve," stated a new, naive, and very young nurse named Tore.

She pronounced her name with the long "e" sound, like *Tori*, but kept spelling it like the word *tore*. People gave her shit about it all the time. Keith was the biggest offender, often calling her "Rip" or "Tear". She didn't care, though. She thought it was an interesting and unique way to spell her name, and people shouldn't "name shame" her.

None of the other nurses understood why Tore had decided on nursing as a career. Some gossiped that it was because she thought it would be easy. Others figured it was because her family, who were all successful white-collar professionals and prominent members of the town, told her to become a nurse after she flunked out of medical school. Tore told everyone her spirit guide told her it was the best profession for her because of her big heart, love of humanity, and desire to give back. She was an ok enough nurse. And patients did like her. So, Jamie thought maybe that was partly true.

"Je-zuss! Stop it, Tear. For God's sake, everyone should be wary of strangers and careful around heavy machinery! Horoscopes are just bullshit that gullible people swallow hook, line, and sinker," grumbled Keith, walking back to the nurses' station.

Keith had been a nurse for a long time. He was old enough to have seen the evolution of medical care over the years. It used to be that patients could discuss potential problems with their doctors and investigate them further. It used to be that patients could have their doctor prescribe things without issue. People used to be able to receive genuine, high-quality care. Now they had to prove that they needed specific tests, or they had to try many different medications or treatments before being allowed to follow what the doctor prescribed in the first place. It was like the poor patients were on trial or something. Those changes disheartened Keith. It left a bad taste in his mouth. He did admire Jamie for continuing her education. If he were going to do anything about his career, it would have been to get out of the medical field entirely. He didn't know what he would do, but it would not be nursing. *Life happens. Whatdya do?* Keith always thought. He was too busy taking care of his aging parents while simultaneously putting his kids through college to even entertain the idea of a new career. It wasn't that he was bitter. However, a midlife divorce took its toll on both his finances and his self-esteem. He was not anywhere near where he had planned on being at that age. Keith would have loved a change, but he figured that ship had sailed long ago, so he was planning to work until he died.

"Ok, like that is just not true. Horoscopes are sooooo accurate. Like, just quit being such a boomer," Tore said, both hurt and annoyed.

"Not a Boomer, dude. If I were, I would be happily retired right now instead of working my ass off. Good God!!"

Keith really hated being considered old. *I'm not THAT old,* he thought, shaking his head. *I will probably have to work until the day of my funeral, though. Retirement? Psshhht. That's not happening.* He smiled a sardonic smile, flipped Tore off, grabbed his stethoscope, and took off. He didn't care if he landed him in HR. That night, he felt it was worth it.

"Like, I didn't mean to upset him. But for real, horoscopes can save your life. You believe me, don't you, Jamie?"

Jamie panicked a little. She didn't believe in horoscopes at all. She was a no-nonsense, what-you-see-is-what-you-get kind of gal. But she also knew better than to hurt people's feelings.

Specifically, people who were kind enough to cover for her when she was late. Jamie knew Tore meant well. Sometimes she was a little much, though. That was one of those times.

"Yeah, what *do* you think, Jamie?" asked another male nurse who had just joined the station. "Also, these muffins kind of suck. Just sayin."

"Yo, dude. The complainer buys the next round!" Jamie pretended to glare at him.

"Yeah, no. That's not happening. I don't have the time or the money. Plus, I don't like you all that much." He laughed and laughed. "Come on, James, what gives? If you're going to bribe us, make sure to bring the good stuff next time. Why did you go to Roasted? No offense to Park, his coffee is tolerable; however, the muffins are the mass-produced kind. We desire the homemade ooey-gooey kind. Why didn't you get something from Last Drop or hell even Dick's Buns?" he asked in a very childlike whiny tone.

His name was Benjamin, but he preferred to be called Benji. He was easy-going enough with just the right amount of sass. He tended to greet all his patients with a smile, even those who were grumpy. But he would match energy when he needed to. He was an excellent nurse, loved by both patients and staff. Jamie loved him too. He could be a bit over the top at times, but Jamie was used to it.

"Dude! I tried to get the good stuff. It just wasn't happening. It's been a weird day, man. I woke up late. My car is in the shop, I was shoved out of Last Drop, Park acted like I was a stranger, and I nearly ran into a tow truck on my bike. So, you get what you get, and you don't throw a fit."

"Like, listen to Jamie, Benji. You are totally trying to harsh her vibes. All she was trying to do was like, do something *nice* for us, kay? So, quit being such a total bummer," Tore said protectively, trying to stick up for Jamie.

"You almost ran into a tow truck? What the hell, Jame? Are you ok?" Benji asked, concerned.

Everyone who was at the nurses' station now turned to Jamie. They all looked at her expectantly, wanting more information. It wasn't every day your coworker announced they hit a tow truck while riding a bike. They hoped it was a good story.

"I am fine, thanks. It was stupid. I got lost in my own thoughts and didn't see J.J. pulling out of his driveway. I nearly rode right into the side of his truck. As I tried to stop and steer away, I lost my balance and fell, along with my bike, into the shrubs. I was scraped up and bleeding, but J.J. helped me fix it. Not my proudest moment, and I'd rather not talk about it, okay? Like I said, it's just been a weird day. Don't you all have patients to tend to?" Jamie asked, raising one of her eyebrows.

"See? You should have read your horoscope, Jamie. It could have helped you! You believe me, right?" Tore asked imploringly.

No one had moved since mentioning the fall, so all eyes were still on Jamie. They were all curious about her answer. She sat quietly, trying to figure out a diplomatic way to say, "hell no".

"You *must* have something to say about it, right?" Benji asked teasingly, winking and egging her on.

Jamie glared at Benji, giving him a look that clearly said, *Stop it... You know I don't want to answer that*, which made him burst out laughing. He looked at her, waiting eagerly for her response. He was a good nurse and mostly a decent guy, but Jamie had known him for years and knew he liked to push buttons like nobody's business.

"Uh.... I... I am not too sure about that." Jamie was hoping that was diplomatic enough. "I mean, I know a lot of people enjoy reading them. They aren't for me, you know?" she added.

"Like OMG! That's probably because you haven't read any from the *real deal* astrologers!! I follow a lot of them on social media. But some are better than others." Tore grabbed Jamie's phone to look for a decent astrologer on TikTok or Instagram so she could show her. Instead, she got a weird look on her face.

"Um, what is wrong with your phone? Like, where are the apps?! Why can't I find—"

Benji snickered again. He knew Jamie's outlook on social media- it wasn't great, and she had a distaste for the ever-changing technology. Benji was Jamie's brother, Albert's best friend, so he knew her reasonably well. He knew she still owned and used a VCR and still used a record player. She told him they were classics and refused to give them up. She also told him it was just a never-ending ploy to spend money updating things that worked perfectly fine, and she refused to be a part of the technological waste society was creating at a rapid pace. Benji was younger. He grew up with technology and enjoyed its advancements, but he agreed that the waste was excessive.

"The only app I use is the stupid one for work. I don't use social media, so I don't have those apps," Jamie grumbled.

Tore just stared at Jamie with a puzzled look on her face. She couldn't believe it. *Like, are there people out there who don't use that stuff? I can't even,* she thought to herself. She grabbed her own phone out of her back pocket, while still holding Jamie's, and eagerly started typing things into it.

"Oh gosh! Let me find my favorite influencer..." Tore's fingers furiously swiped on the screen of her phone. "Ok, here, let me read yours for today. Let's see, you are a Taurus, right? Ok, here it is.... 'Today is a day filled with challenges. Rise and meet them head-on. Focus on stability and long-term goals. Consider career advancements. Try not to be overly stubborn, as it could negatively affect relationships. Not every smile is meant as a friendly gesture, so be sure to know who you are dealing with.' OMG, see? That is so freaking accurate! Like, Keith just smiled, and I am pretty sure it wasn't a friendly smile, and you are in school to advance your career, so that's just scary how good the astrologer is!!!"

Oh my God, Jamie thought. She had to bite her tongue and suck in her breath. *I'm not gonna say it...I'm not gonna say it.* She did her best not to make any negative response. She had already been sent to HR to discuss her "attitude" and had to take a sensitivity training course, even though all she had done was respond to someone with her typical sarcastic wit. She did not want to go through all of *that* again. It's not that she was rude. Jamie was cynical and blunt. And since re-entering school, she found her patience was wearing a little thinner and faster than usual. Jamie also preferred a strong separation between work and home life, which many of her younger coworkers did not. She was trying to work, not make friends. But times were changing. So, she smiled as kindly and as patiently as she could and mustered a, "Thank you, Tore. I appreciate that."

The call board quickly lit up. It was a sea of lights and a cacophony of sounds. It seemed like every patient needed help all at once. *Alrighty, here comes the full moon mania...* Jamie thought. One by one, each nurse grabbed their charts, files, or other miscellaneous items and headed to their patient's room.

Jamie grabbed her phone back from Tore, grabbed a sanitizing wipe, and cleaned it off. She then stuffed it into her pocket, trying not to seem put off by the entire encounter. Usually, she would immediately grab her phone back from the person, but Tore was so incredibly sensitive, and their shift was starting, that Jamie just let it go. She didn't want to spend the whole night calming Tore down. Instead, Jamie just gave Tore a look. Tore understood.

"Well, maybe there is something to this full moon, approaching storm thing after all!" Kerrigan said as she walked closer to Tore and Jamie, looking at the call board. "We are more lit up than a Christmas tree right now."

Kerrigan had been intentionally hanging back and was tactfully silent during Tore's enthusiastic exchange. She didn't necessarily believe in horoscopes either, but Tore seemed so passionate about the subject that she didn't want to hurt her feelings. Instead, she smiled at both ladies, grabbed a patient checklist, and headed off to her patient in need. Tore smiled back, grabbed her things, and headed off to check on patients.

Benji, who had also been standing at the station the entire time and had been intentionally silent, laughed, shook his head, and headed off to see a patient in need, greeting the person with a big enthusiastic, "HI! HI! HOW ARE WE DOING TODAY?"

"Holy Mother! What is going on with all the noise?" asked a nurse who had just walked up to the desk, coffee in one hand, muffin in the other.

Her name was Charity. She was petite, but you wouldn't know it. Charity carried herself in a way that showed she meant business, and she did not let her size affect her at all. Growing up small meant proving she was tough, so she was a bit of a hot head. If she felt pushed far enough, she could be a real fireball. That, at times, caused tension between her and her coworkers. She was okay with that because if she knew she was right, she wouldn't back down. If they could not manage a little spice, she felt that was their problem, not hers. Her job had little room for error, so she had no problems calling people out. Her husband, Donal, often called her his "little firecracker", which she pretended to hate but secretly loved. Charity was very bold in life. She greeted everything with passion and vigor. *Most* of her patients loved that. As the mother of two beautiful tweens, she also had a kind and caring side. The tweens made her perfectly equipped to handle a lot of complex patients. She was stern when necessary, but also very understanding and compassionate. She was just truly good at her job. Nursing was very demanding, and she was always ready for that.

"I think...I mean, I could be wrong here, but I *think* all the noise has something to do with patients in need." Jamie made a silly face, chuckled, and smirked.

"Well, no shit, Sherlock!" Charity blurted out. With a shocked look on her face, she covered her mouth when she realized what she had done. "I mean, yes, I know *that*. I was wondering why everyone needed help all at once!"

"That's the full moon, hun. Or maybe the upcoming storm. Hell, maybe both! Good luck tonight. I am glad my shift is over. What a weird day," said Ivy as she walked back up to the desk. She had a coffee and a couple of muffins in her hands. "Jamie, I know I told you I didn't want any coffee. But thank you for this. Next time, though, get to work on time because these commercially made muffins just aren't cutting it as an apology. If you are going to be late, at least bring us some of Damn Fine's best cookies!"

Ivy sounded mean, but she had a smile on her face. Jamie had worked with her long enough to know she was only irritated, not angry. She winked at Jamie. Jamie smiled back at her.

"Yes, of course! I tried to get some of Damn Fine's cookies, though. I couldn't because apparently—"

She was interrupted by more calls coming in. Jamie didn't get a chance to tell Ivy about Walt and Wanda. She wasn't going to say anything about the crime. She promised Andy she wouldn't. But she thought she should at least let them know that Walt and Wanda Anbrena were downstairs.

"I am on it," Charity said as she grabbed her checklist and headed off to a room.

"And that's also my cue!" Ivy smiled and headed toward the elevator. She put her hand in the air and waved. "You all have a *wonderful* night!!"

Ivy was grateful to be going home that day, e*xtremely* grateful. It wasn't that the day was excessively crazy. And she didn't have a bad day. The day was just filled with weirdness, odd requests, and things Ivy didn't usually see very often. She didn't generally think too much about the full moon or storm nonsense, but the day just felt a little different. It seemed off. She shuddered a little as she entered the elevator. As the doors closed around her, a hand shot out from somewhere in the elevator, covering Ivy's mouth tightly. Had someone been looking, they would have seen a look of pure terror on her face. She tried making noise. Instead, a small squeak came out of her, echoing ever so faintly just as the doors closed. Jamie looked down the hall, thinking she had heard Ivy say something, but the elevator doors were already closed. She watched the elevator floor lights move downward. She smiled enviously at the thought of Ivy at home, relaxing and unwinding. Her shift had barely begun, and Jamie was already ready to go home. Jamie was lost in thought when a sound jolted her back to reality. One of the desk phones was ringing. *Oh, what now,* Jamie wondered. She grabbed the handset.

"Hello, Third Floor. Jamie speak—"

Before she could say anything else, Rachelle, the ER nurse, started talking frantically. Her voice was filled with emotion, which wasn't like her. Jamie knew her to be a quick-thinking, levelheaded person, which made her the perfect fit for the emergency room. Jamie had known Rachelle for a long time. Rachelle was a few grades ahead of her, but they had had several classes together. Jamie knew that being emotional was quite out of character for her.

"Listen, we need some help down here. Do you have anyone that you can spare?" Rachelle asked rather urgently. She usually had the ER running like a well-oiled machine. The request was out of character for her.

"Is this about Walt and Wanda...?" Jamie asked tentatively.

"How did you hear about that? I have been keeping a tight lid on things down here."

"I ran into Andy and Mitch on the way inside. Rachelle, what is going on?" Jamie wasn't sure what answer she was hoping for. It was the emergency room, so that alone spoke to the severity of the situation. But Jamie was hoping for at least some kind of good news. She adored Wanda and Walt Anbrena. Everyone did. They were long-standing residents who were loved by their community. That one of them was hurt was horrible, but that both were hurt was heinous. And now there were enough people in the ER that Rachelle was asking for help.

"Hey, keep this to yourself, ok? Yes. It is bad. As for Walt and Wanda, we haven't been able to get in touch with their family yet, so I can't provide any information. That's all I am saying. But we just had five more drop-offs in the last thirty minutes. We could use some help down here if you can spare it?"

"Of course! Whatever you guys need! I will go find Benji and send him down, ok?"

"Thank you, Jamie. And please don't say anything to the others yet, ok? We need to get the family here first. Everyone will know soon enough. I gotta go. Thanks again!"

Rachelle hung up the phone before Jamie could ask about her cousin Park or who the other drop-offs were. But Jamie figured if their community were in danger, Frankie would let them all know. Jamie knew she needed to focus on her job and try to forget about the weird feelings. She shook her head, as if to shake off the bad vibes, and walked down the hallway looking for Benji. She found him just as he was headed into a patient's room.

"Benji, can you come here for a sec?" Jamie asked him quietly, motioning for him to walk over by the wall outside of the patient's earshot.

"What's up, James?" Benji asked as he walked toward Jamie.

"What do you have going on right now?"

"I was just about to head in to see Mr. Tichmand. You know he does not like to be kept waiting!" Benji chuckled.

"That I do. However, he will have to wait for a minute. Can you do me, I mean, Rachelle, a favor? Things are intense down in the ER right now. She called up asking if I could spare someone to help. Would you be willing to do that? I can go check on Mr. Tichmand for you, and we will cover your patients for as long as they need you."

"Of course. I am happy to help. But what's going on?"

"I am not entirely sure. Rachelle said they just had two more drop-offs in the last thirty minutes, and they need help. She seemed distraught."

"Okey Dokey. I will head right down."

"Thank you, Benj. You rock! Do you have your phone on you?"

"Yeah. Ok, don't give me crap about it! It's in my pocket and I clean it after I use it. I don't use it in front of the patients. You know that."

"Relax. I am glad you have it on you. For some reason, I think you might need it."

"What do you mean by that? What's going on, Jamie?"

"Nothing is going on. I just had a stupid, bad, ominous—pick a word, vibe today. My gut tells me you might want to have your phone with you. That's all."

"Ok. Don't worry. I have it. Try to relax, James. It's just a busy night, that's all. It's nothing we aren't used to or can't handle."

"Dude! Don't pep talk me. Just.... just be careful tonight, ok?"

"You got it, girl!" Benji grinned, back being his sassy self. He saluted Jamie, walked over to the elevator, pushed the button, and stepped inside. As the doors closed, he looked back at Jamie and said, "Today kinda feels extra heavy for some reason. Weird."

The elevator doors closed with a clunk, and the hallway was silent. Jamie turned around and headed in to check on Mr. Uriah Tichmand. He had a scowl as she entered the room. *Well, this is going to be fun,* Jamie thought as she mustered up her biggest smile and walked toward him. Fortunately, Mr. Tichmand was agreeable that night. Jamie explained that Benji had to fill in on a different floor, so she would be taking over his care for a while. She checked his vitals, gave him the water he had been waiting for, and then walked back to the nurses' station. Another call-light came on, though, causing Jamie to pick up her checklist again and head to the room in need. As she entered, she heard someone quietly crying. Jamie rushed over to Mrs. Arlene Makenin.

"Hi, Mrs. Makenin. What seems to be the problem?" Jamie asked softly.

"I don't want to be here anymore."

"Yeah, I can understand that. Are you missing home tonight?"

"Mmhmm. And Russell. I miss my Russ. Where is he? He was just here." Mrs. Makenin was usually such an easy-going, lovely woman, but at that moment, she seemed agitated.

Jamie knew Mr. Russell Makenin would sometimes stay with his wife when she was in the hospital, but Jamie hadn't seen him yet that night. She figured Arlene was just confused.

"You know, in all the years I have known you, I have never asked you. How did the two of you meet? Will you tell me about that while I check your vitals, Mrs. Makenin?"

Growing up and still living in a small town meant that Jamie knew most of the senior population. She had known the Makenins her entire life. They were good people. Jamie's parents were good friends of theirs. Arlene had the best temperament; she was as sweet as they came. Her husband, Russell, was a stoic but very kind fellow. The two were inseparable and made the most adorable couple. Jamie was surprised that Russell wasn't in the room with his wife. But the last thing she wanted to do was cause Arlene unnecessary anxiety. Jamie decided that distracting her until he came back was the best approach.

"Oh! Certainly! My Russ was the cutest boy in school. He was two years older, you know. I thought he was a jerk. But one

smiled at Monika. Jamie liked her. She was a quiet person. She was not shy; she was reserved and tended to keep things close to her chest.

"Oh, excellent! You are on the ball, Monika. Just like always," Jamie said, giving her a thumbs up. "I will get out of your hair. Mrs. Makenin, enjoy dinner. I will be back to check on you later. See you, Monika." Jamie nodded and headed toward the door to leave. Monika's question stopped her.

"Alrighty, Mrs. Makenin, let me get this food over to you. How are you doing this evening? Where is Mr. Makenin?"

Monika had also grown up in Heatherwilde Falls and had known Mr. and Mrs. Makenin her whole life. They were not next-door neighbors, but being only a block away, she often saw them when she rode her bike or walked to a friend's house. She adored them. They were just the kindest people you would ever meet.

Monika was one of the most dependable kitchen staff members the hospital had. She was a diligent worker who genuinely enjoyed interacting with people. She was a natural at making the patients feel valued and noticed. Often, people in the hospital ended up being nothing more than a number. Monika went out of her way to make sure that didn't happen, at least not from her. She wasn't delivering to room 310 that night; she was delivering to Arlene Makenin. It just felt right in her mind. It helped that their hospital wasn't large. Monika was sure that in a larger hospital, knowing everyone's name would probably be next to impossible. She appreciated small-town living and the advantages it brought.

"Oh, hello, Monika. How are you today, dear? Have you seen my Russ anywhere?"

"Uh, no, Mrs. Makenin. I haven't seen him since lunchtime today. Did he run home?"

"No. I mentioned that I wished I had a hot tea and some gelatin, so Russ went to find me some."

Jamie raised an eyebrow as she listened. She hadn't seen Russell all day, so she had just assumed he was home. She turned to Monika and motioned for her to step out into the hallway. Monika understood and nodded. She set up Arlene's tray and ensured she had everything she needed.

"Excuse us, ok, Mrs. Makenin?"

"Oh sure! Are you going to look for Russ?"

"We will see what we can do, ok?"

"Thank you, dear," Mrs. Makenin said as they stepped out the door.

When they were out of earshot, Jamie looked at Monika questioningly. She tried to keep the urgency out of her voice. She wasn't sure if it was the feeling of dread or the fact that stories were spreading about a supposed murderer on the loose, or the upcoming storm, or God knows what, but she still had an uneasy feeling. Even if none of those things were factored in, it was not a good idea to have a senior wandering around the hospital. Jamie needed to know if Russell had been with his wife.

"Did you see Russell at lunch? Was he here?"

"Yeah. I saw him. I also took some lunch up to him. I know I wasn't supposed to, but they are such sweet people. I didn't want him wandering around the hospital to get himself something to eat, you know? Why? What's going on?"

"MMmmm." Jamie's face scrunched up while she subconsciously bit her index finger, lost in thought.

Monika saw the distance in Jamie's face. She was starting to get concerned. She snapped her fingers in front of Jamie's face.

"Uh, Jamie? Heeelllooo?"

"Oh Good Lord. Sorry!" Jamie shook her head and patted her cheeks. "What is wrong with me today? I guess I didn't get enough sleep last night, huh? Yeah, a missing Russell isn't good. We need to find him. He is in his eighties. He could have fallen and hurt himself, or I don't know, had a stroke, heart attack, or something. I don't mean to lead with worst-case scenarios, but if Arlene doesn't know where he is, that is concerning. I hadn't seen him this evening, so I didn't know he was staying tonight. When you head back down to the kitchen, will you keep an eye out? I will let Bastian know. You know what? Will you also tell Glen on the first floor? Let's cover all bases. I will also call down and ask Rachelle if she has seen him. God forbid he fell or something and is one of the people in the ER."

Jamie went right into take-charge mode, forgetting that she had just dropped a bomb on poor Monika. She stopped talking when she saw the look on Monika's face.

"What? You think he could be hurt?"

"Oh, geez, no, I don't think so," Jamie said, putting her hand on Monika's arm, trying to reassure her. "Sorry! He probably just ran into someone he knew on the first floor and stayed to chat. I mean, it seemed excessively busy on the first floor, so it's possible. I just want to make sure he's ok."

Jamie wasn't about to share what Rachelle had told her. She didn't know what was happening or who was hurt. And since she had no real proof of anything Mitch had talked about, she wasn't going to talk about the potential murderer either. Jamie was doing her best to downplay the situation-whatever that situation was.

"Yeah, you are right. That man is a talker." Monika chuckled.

"Exactly! So, let's not jump the gun and frighten Arlene. Besides, I am sure that Rachelle would call if he were hurt and downstairs. I am just being a worrywart. But I will call her just in case. Let's try to find him and get him back to Arlene, ok?"

"Yeah, yeah, ok. For sure. Will you let me know when you find him? You have my number. I know I am not family, but I have known the Makenins for so long."

"I know. We all have. Yes, I will holler as soon as I find him. What time are you off tonight?"

"I have to clean up, and then I am headed home. Now that we know he isn't up here, I am sure we will find him before I go home. But just in case, feel free to text me anytime. I want to know that he is ok."

Monika was trying to keep the worry out of her head. Several years prior, one of her parents' neighbors had been hurt at home. She had had a stroke but couldn't get to the phone and lay on the floor for two days until Monika's parents showed up to check on her. That struck a chord with Monika. Since hearing about that tragic situation, she tried to check in on the Makenins at least twice a week. She didn't want anyone to go through what her parents' neighbor went through.

Jamie gave Monika a quick hug and told Arlene she would be back in a little while. She didn't mean to scare her. It just slipped out. She was glad she withheld the other information. She wasn't even sure if what Mitch mentioned was true. Pam would have called; Jamie was sure of that. And the news hadn't notified anyone either. *It was just Mitch being his usual dickhead self,* Jamie thought. Still, she couldn't shake that weird, uneasy feeling. She shook her head, smiled at Monika, turned, and headed back to the nurses' station so she could tell Bastian, their security guard, about Russell. As she was walking toward the desk, she spotted Bastian walking in the opposite direction.

"Bastian!" Jamie yelled.

He unfortunately did not hear her and continued down the hall. Jamie decided to jog over to him instead of yelling at the top of her lungs. She knew some of the patients were probably napping. Bastian was a big fellow, so Jamie had to hoof it. When she got close enough for him to hear her, she repeated his name.

"Hey, Bastian!"

Bastian stopped abruptly and turned around to face the voice. He had a pleasant half smile on his face.

"Oh, hey, Jamie. How are ya?"

"Livin' the dream?"

"You don't sound so sure of that," Bastian said, chuckling.

"Ha! Some days I wonder. I am okay. I just woke up with this dreadful feeling, you know, like when something is, I don't know... off. It's nothing, I'm sure. Too many late-night study sessions, I think. Listen, I need to ask you something. Have you seen Russell Makenin around tonight? I was just with Arlene, and she told me he left to get her tea. I think that was hours ago..." Jamie's voice trailed off, riddled with concern.

"Yeah, I saw him this afternoon over by the elevator. He was headed down to the lobby. He isn't back yet?"

"No. He isn't. Arlene is pretty concerned. Do you think you could check into it?"

"He said if the cafeteria didn't have Arlene's Earl Grey tea, he was going to walk down the street to Richard's Rolls. He probably just went there. However, since it's been a few hours, I will check with the lobby and cafeteria, okay? Don't worry. We will locate Russell."

"Thank you, Bastian. I appreciate that. I will let Arlene know. And I'll call over to Dick's Buns to see if they have seen Russell. Oh, hey, uh, can I ask you another question?" Jamie said in a hushed tone. She motioned, moving toward a wall and away from the people listening in.

Bastian nodded and walked with her. He had a puzzled look on his face.

"Sure, but, ah, 'Dick's Buns'? Where is that?"

"Sorry. Sorry." Jamie chuckled at the memory. "That's the old local's name. It's a funny story. It happened well before my time. My parents told me the story. Before Richard's Rolls existed, another café in town called Sandy's Sweet Synonym Rolls was the only bakery in town. Richard Yuleson and Sandy Yuleson-Shammly were siblings who worked together. Sandy was a schoolteacher who quit, pursuing a baking passion instead. She was proud of her clever name and was an excellent baker, I guess. Her shop was quite successful. The two squabbled sometimes, as siblings do. However, they managed to make it work most of the time and were very successful. Eventually, they had a major falling out, I guess. No one knows what the argument was about that was the final nail in the coffin, but Richard became angry enough to quit. He developed his own recipes and opened his café right across the street from his sister to compete with her. They argued nonstop, after that, I guess. The lore is that one particular day, things got very heated between Richard and Sandy. They were standing in the street yelling at each other's customers, trying to take business away from one another. As it happened in a small town, a crowd gathered. A few people tried to calm the siblings down and smooth things over. As they were being escorted to their respective sides of the street, Sandy turned back and yelled, 'Dick's buns aren't even that good! They are flat and stodgy!' The crowd that had gathered burst into laughter. Ever since then, the locals have all called it 'Dick's Buns'."

Jamie chuckled again. She seemed to be lost in her own thoughts. She had a distant look on her face. There was no way Bastian would know that talking about Dick's would stir up memories of Jamie's parents and their many trips to both cafés when she was younger.

"Jamie, are you *sure* you are, ok?"

Jamie shook her head to clear it. She didn't know why she was thinking about her parents at that moment. For a moment, she forgot all about their loss and was locked in those glorious, mundane memories of a complete family. *Grief is a funny thing,* Jamie thought. *You can be okay-ish for months, even years, and then, without any warning, it hits like a ton of bricks. In those times, it feels just as fresh and new.* She mustered a smile and nodded at Bastian.

"I think I just need sleep, man. Way too many late-night, early morning study sessions. Listen, not to change the subject, but back to my question. On my way in today, that asshole EMT, Mitch, told me something. He said a murderer is on the loose. That can't be true. I mean, it would be all over the news and crap, right?" Jamie asked, still half lost in her own thoughts. She continued, "We all know Mitch is a tool. So, I blew it off because he was warning me about it being a full moon, with an impending storm, and all that stuff. But then I started thinking that he was driving the ambulance, and they knew things before the rest of us. Plus, he got a call and had to leave right then, so it got me wondering. And when I was over at Last Drop earlier, Siobhan shoved me out of the door and closed her shop, saying a murderer was on the loose. I am getting a little concerned."

"I do know they are swamped in the ER for some reason this evening."

"Yeah, they are! Good. Thanks, Bastian. I will let you get back to work."

Jamie shook her head in disbelief, partially because she couldn't believe how she was acting and partially to clear those thoughts out. She figured she just needed to get back to focusing on work and finding Russell Makenin. As she turned to leave, she felt a hand gently touch her arm.

"Jamie.... wait. You are a good friend. I will level with you. But please keep this between us, ok? You have good reason to be concerned. Listen, this isn't public knowledge yet, but yes, it appears we *may* have a situation of some kind. Maybe an attacker? Who knows. Before you ask," Bastian raised his hand to stop Jamie from asking for more information, "I don't know any more than that. It has not been confirmed by Frankie, Drea, Lewis, or any of her staff. You know my husband, Harrison, right? He took the 911 call that dispatched Mitch and Andy. I don't know any other information. *I* wasn't even supposed to know. But Harrison was bothered since the victims were headed here soon, and wanted me to be on the lookout for anything strange. Russell not with Arlene isn't necessarily strange, but it's not typical either, if you get what I am saying."

"Ok. So, what do you want me to do?" Jamie asked, slipping into head nurse mode, taking charge, and getting it done.

"What you just did. Holler at me if you notice anything else out of the ordinary. I know you are discreet, but please do not breathe a word of this to anyone. And *definitely* not Tore. You know how she is. We do not need to rile up the patients when we don't know anything yet. I know Frankie will let us know if we need to be concerned. In the meantime, I will call down and speak to both the cafeteria and the lobby about Russell. I am sure someone saw him. But you go ahead and call Richard's Rolls just in case. We will get this figured out."

"Well, this evening can just take a flying leap, can't it?" Jamie asked, clenching her jaw while flipping off the air. She made fists and said, "Whatever is going on or whoever caused this had better not show up here. I am *not* in the mood. And yes, of course, I will keep it to myself. But please update me if and when you can, ok?"

"Will do. Hang in there, Jamie. The third shift will be here before you know it. And the craziness is bound to subside soon," Bastian said, crossing his fingers for Jamie to see.

Jamie was interrupted by a loud beeping noise. Someone was paging her. *Well, here we go again,* she thought. She turned and rushed to the room in need. By the time she was done helping Mr. Quinton Valamy, the thoughts about checking with Richard's Rolls, finding Russell Makenin, and a potential murderer on the loose had all slipped her mind. She was focused solely on doing her job: helping patients and keeping things running smoothly, like a well-oiled machine.

Chapter Three

Jamie and the rest of the nurses continued to answer calls nonstop. She didn't know whether it was the full moon or the storm, but it seemed excessively busy to her. After about two hours, the pace began to slow down. Patients were being taken care of. Emergencies were being treated. The noise was coming back down. And most importantly, the call board was quiet. Some of the nurses sat down at their stations, logging in their notes and shift information. This was probably their least favorite part of the job, but it did allow for some downtime.

"Do things seem a little off tonight? Or is it just me?" asked an orderly named Milton as he pushed a wheelchair down the hall and backed it against a wall.

Milton was a fantastic employee. Everyone at the hospital loved him. He was the first to help, first to stay late, and always seemed to go above and beyond. He was subdued, thinking and listening rather than talking. He was shy, which most people mistook for aloofness. The single women (and a few married) who worked with him all thought he was the handsome, boy-next-door kind of guy. He could have had a full social life if he chose to, but he either wasn't aware or didn't care. Jamie was surprised that he stopped to speak with them.

"You know, I have had that feeling since I left for work... well, no, back that up. I have had that feeling since I woke up. Even my dream was a little weird. Mitch warned me, saying it was going to be bad due to the full moon and the storm, but I had already had a feeling about it beforehand. Not a bad feeling. Just.... I don't know." Jamie shrugged.

"Off. Unsettling. Uneasy," said Hugh as he walked up to the counter. He was part of the hospital's janitorial crew. He was an easy-going guy who kept to himself a lot. Hugh always had a kind word for people or a joke to share, which helped lighten the mood. Not that night, though. That night, he seemed quite somber.

Hugh was highly intelligent. In school, most of his classmates and teachers thought he would become a physicist, engineer, land in I.T., or even become an inventor. His coworkers saw it too. He was always coming up with new, inventive, and innovative ways to do a job. And Hugh always did a fantastic job, whatever the task. So, no one knew why he chose to be a janitor, but they suspected it had to do with his family. They knew he had kids still in school and figured that might be part of it.

"Like OMG, you guys! You are really harshing my vibes. The only mood we need is like, *enthusiasm!*" Tore joyously proclaimed as she walked past the counter. "Like I am going to go grab one of those muffins Jamie brought in and work on washing away your negativity!"

Tore bounced her way down the hall in her lighthearted way and giggled as she headed into the newly renovated breakroom. Both Milton and Hugh just stared at her as she disappeared. They shook their heads in unison.

"That is one kooky kid," said Milton. "It's weird. She seems to be both dimly lit and also shining bright. I don't get it."

"That's called youthful ignorance if you ask me." Hugh laughed lightly and shook his head again. He looked at Jamie, "I have to leave early tonight, so if it is ok with you, I am going to start cleaning the bathrooms now."

"You don't have to ask permission, Hugh. Have at it! But thank you for checking. That was kind. So, hot date tonight?"

"I wish I could leave early!!" Reid exclaimed as he walked up to the desk, leaned down on the counter, and smiled.

"Big Red, you barely work as it is. How are you gonna survive leaving early?" Hugh asked him.

"Heeeeey! I am so offended! I *work*. Ok, yeah, maybe I *somewhat* resemble that remark. But I can't help it if I was blessed with the gift of gab."

"'Gift of Gab' my ass! You have diarrhea of the mouth, son." Keith could not help himself. He put a chart on the desk and sat down at a computer. The rest of the staff knew how he was, but half the time it looked like he was trying to get fired. He looked up at Reid and smiled. "Don't you have patients to check or paperwork to do?"

Big Red looked down at the floor sheepishly and grinned. "Well.... yes..." he sighed. He headed down the hall and entered the patient's room noisily.

Hugh chuckled, "That boy is something else. To answer your question, Jamie, yes, I have a date tonight. I am taking Jerriabeth to our first daddy-daughter dance."

Kerrigan and Jamie both placed their hands over their hearts and said, "Awwwwww."

"Yeah, it's kind of a big deal." Hugh grinned from ear to ear as he loaded his cleaning cart with supplies from the closet.

"That is awesome, Hugh. I hope you have a great time," Jamie said. When she saw him grabbing toilet paper, she laughed and pretended to scold him. "Hey, don't squeeze the toilet paper!"

"What?! How else is he going to carry it?" Kerrigan asked while Jamie snickered.

"Relax, Ms. Whipple, it is industrial. I can squeeze it." Hugh winked and squeezed the giant rolls. He put them on the cart, shaking his head and laughing. He hadn't thought about that old commercial for a long time. "Thanks for the laugh! See you all tomorrow."

"Hugh, have an excellent time at the dance tonight," Jamie patted his arm, and she smiled at him tenderly. She could tell by the excitement in his eyes that that was precisely what he was going to do.

day, when I tripped walking down the hallway and fell to the floor, he stopped to help me back up. He even picked up my schoolbooks. Before you knew it, we were dating. On our very first date, he told me that he had had a crush on me for over a year. Can you imagine that?! He is still as handsome and kind as ever, isn't he? And funny! He can always make me laugh. What are you doing?"

"I am just checking your lines, Mrs. Makenin," Jamie said. To keep her distracted, she asked, "So, you thought Mr. Makenin was a jerk at first, huh?"

"Oh yes," Arlene told Jamie. She had a distant, dreamy expression with a simple but lovely smile on her face. "He was so very handsome and incredibly popular. I just assumed he was putting on airs like some of the other people he hung out with. I am glad I was wrong. No one could believe it when he married plain ole me."

"Plain old you? Now what are you talking about? You are as beautiful as they come. Mr. Makenin is a lucky, lucky man. Well, that's it. Everything looks good. Did you order dinner yet? Or would you like some help with that?"

"It was already ordered and here!" Monika smiled as she pushed in the dinner cart. "Hello, Mrs. Makenin."

Jamie was startled by the sound of a new voice. She didn't hear anyone else enter the room, much less a kitchen cart. *God, why am I so jumpy today?* She recovered, turned around, and

Hugh nodded at everyone and headed down the hall to start cleaning. He knew people looked down on him for being a janitor. It wasn't the career he set out to have. He discovered that he was good at it, though. Very good. And the hours allowed him to be home with their kids while his wife was at work. Not having to pay for childcare was a godsend, but being home with their kids proved to be invaluable. That was a true blessing and Hugh's whole reason for being. So, while cleaning dirt from the floor and messes from toilets were not the career goals he had when he was younger, they were worth it in the long run. He was committed to his job, but leaving early that night was paramount. His youngest daughter was old enough for them to go to their very first daddy-daughter dance at her school. Excited didn't begin to describe it.

Milton was still standing at the counter, watching and listening. He couldn't put his finger on it. *Something just seems off.* He looked at Jamie, who appeared to be a million miles away. *She feels it too. I can see it.* "Are you ok?" he asked as he waved his hand in front of her face.

Ever since Milton brought up the off feeling, she couldn't stop thinking about it. It felt familiar. But not in a good way. *Why does this feeling remind me of something?* She was racking her brain, trying to figure it out, when she realized someone was saying something to her. She pulled herself back into reality.

"Huh? Oh jeez. Sorry. I'm a bit out of it today. What did you say?"

"I asked if you were, ok?"

"Yeah. Yes. I cannot shake this feeling.... It feels so familiar, but I can't quite put my finger on it." Jamie let her voice trail off.

"The feeling you get when you know something bad is going to happen, but you can't do a damn thing to stop it?" Keith asked as he looked over his glasses at them from the computer station. "Is that what you are talking about? Because that's what I have been feeling since I got here. I thought it was just me."

"*Come on*, you guys! You are all terrible. It's just a day. Nothing to do with the full moon. Nothing to do with the storm. It's just a day! I honestly can't believe you all." Kerrigan did not believe in any of that nonsense. She was not superstitious, didn't believe in old wives' tales, and didn't fall for the bad luck crap. She was a logical and practical thinker. She didn't have time for "weird feelings".

Charity walked up then and shook her head. She had seen her fair share of strange things on full moon shifts and stormy days, hell, even on Friday the 13th days. She did believe that weird stuff happened, particularly on those days. In fact, she believed it enough that she carried a lucky coin around with her, wherever she went. She was not going to take any chances. She gave them a look, touched the coin that was currently in the pocket of her sweater, and said, "Kerrigan! Careful there, girl.... Don't tempt fate like that."

Kerrigan just rolled her eyes and shook her head. She couldn't believe that such intelligent and wise people would fall for such utter nonsense. Dates and moon phases had zero bearing on the outcome of the day. That was such a silly notion. She was surprised by how deeply everyone seemed to be affected. Kerrigan thought it was downright dumb to believe such things.

"Guys!!" Tore yelled from the breakroom. "Did someone leave a phone in here or something? There has been ringing in here for like the last five minutes."

"Did you try *answering it*, Shredder?" Keith didn't even try to hide the disdain that was oozing out of his mouth at this point. He knew he should have apologized right away, but he was on edge, and his emotions were just frayed.

"Like, *there is nothing to ANSWER*, Keith! All we hear is ringing. We've looked everywhere, but like, there is no phone. Can someone else pu-leeze come in here? Oh, my gods, the ringing is driving me crazy."

"Who is 'we'? I thought you were alone?" Charity asked. She didn't know why, but she grabbed her coin a little tighter.

Reid popped his head out of the breakroom as well and smiled. Milton, who hadn't left yet, just stared at him, thinking,

How in the hell did he get into the breakroom? For being as tall as he was, Reid sure could be sneaky at times.

"Reid! What the actual FUCK, dude? How in the hell did you get into the breakroom without us seeing you? And *what* are you doing in there? You have paperwork you need to do!" Jamie raised her voice like a mom scolding her child.

"Ok, relax. I can explain. I um, uh, got thirsty after helping Mrs. Tonejati. So, while you were all chatting, I walked past you and went into the breakroom. My patients are all fine. My paperwork is caught up. Well, mostly. I needed a little break, ok?"

Jamie wondered how a 6-foot-6-inch guy could sneak past them. But she didn't see Milton waving his hand at first. She had almost run into the ambulance, and she nearly missed running into J.J. So, she guessed it was plausible. She could not shake that feeling. And judging by Milton's, Keith's, Kerrigan's, and Charity's faces, they couldn't either. *What is going on with me today?* Jamie wondered.

"Like, *hellooo?* Ringing?" Tore huffed, very annoyed that her coworkers were not listening to her. "It's still *ringing...*"

"Oh, for Christ's SAKE!" Keith yelled as he got up from the desk and wandered over to the breakroom, muttering under his breath the whole way. "Let's look together!"

"Uh, you guys go ahead. I have to *work*," Kerrigan declared, quite irritated. She raised one brow as if to say, *Am I the only one doing that tonight?*

"Someone probably accidentally left their phone behind. Shouldn't take but a minute. Because yes, we *all* have work to do," Jamie said, looking pointedly at Reid, who blushed a little.

Jamie, Milton, and Charity followed Keith into the breakroom. It wasn't a large room. But it was big enough. It looked like a typical breakroom with a refrigerator, stove, microwave, sink, and cupboard space to store snacks. A couple of tables sat in the center, and a small love seat-type chair was up against the wall. They even had a couple of laptops that could be used if anyone wanted. A largely unused item was the small vending machine, which offered a variety of unhealthy treats, including candy, chips, and snack cakes. Jamie wasn't even sure if they serviced the thing, so she never tried buying anything from it. She preferred to bring her snacks and drinks from home.

As soon as they entered the room, they all heard it. It sounded distant, but it was a phone ringing. They all looked at each other and started talking all at once.

"Did someone drop their phone?"

"Did you look here?"

"Where is the sound coming from?"

"Could it be something else?"

Tore, who had been standing with her arms crossed and tapping her fingers on her arms, looked at them exasperated and shouted, "Like, I don't know! That's why I was *asking!*" She spread her arms like a game show sweetheart, showing off a fantastic prize. "Like *I already looked all over!*"

"Ok, well obviously you didn't, did you, Slash, because it's still ringing." Keith was starting to lose what little patience he had. Jamie shot him an, *I know, I get it, but it's not worth it,* look. He shook his head and sighed.

"All right, all right, kiddies. Take a chill pill. Don't get your undies in a bunch. I am sure Tore and Big Red did a proper search. It must be hidden behind something. Or maybe it fell in the trash bin? Did you search the couch cushions?" Jamie was no stranger to playing *find the lost thing.* Every time her nieces and nephews came to visit, she had to hunt down her TV remote, stereo remote, DVDs, and even her shoes a couple of times. The younger nieces enjoyed playing dress-up. She didn't mind, but after they lost her favorite pair of earrings, she had put a stop to that. Jamie figured this would be no different. They just had to look in unexpected places to find the phone.

One by one, they all searched the breakroom for the source of the ringing. Keith checked behind the appliances. Charity looked in the cupboards and drawers. Tore and Reid pulled up the couch cushions again and checked behind the couch and chairs. Milton and Jamie searched the floor area. Again and again, their search yielded nothing.

Unable to find the source, Keith mumbled something like "fuck it, I have work to do" and walked out. He realized he was becoming less of a team player as he aged. He knew he should work on his patience, but right now, he didn't have it in him. Between his kids and his elderly parents, he was worn thin. He was tired and jaded. He knew he was edging on bitter, though he was trying not to be, for his kids' sake. *I just need a damn vacation. Something warm, relaxing, and well, free at this point. Because that's the only way I can afford it,* Keith thought as he walked back to the nurses' station.

Jamie stood in the center of the breakroom, listening. It was definitely a phone ringing. *Where in the hell is that coming from?* She slowly scanned the room, listening intently. She followed the sound up to where a set of cupboards would usually sit above the refrigerator. Well, she always thought they were cupboards. But as she looked closer, she realized they weren't. Or maybe they had been cupboards once, but at some point, they had been sealed up. Now, it was just a flat wall, but she saw vague outlines of what could have been cupboard openings. Jamie pulled a chair across the floor toward the refrigerator. She stood balanced on the chair and put her ear toward the weird wall space. Sure enough, behind the drywall, she could hear ringing. "It's coming from inside the wall!" she pointed, and they all looked up, puzzled. Everyone started talking at once again.

"I thought that was a cupboard?"

"Why is that boarded up?"

"WHY is it ringing?!"

"How do we get into it?"

Jamie stepped off the chair. "Milton, do you know where I can get a hammer?" She figured she could pound a hole in the wall and investigate the source of the noise. She knew she probably shouldn't destroy hospital property, but she didn't know who to call at that hour to obtain permission, and the situation seemed to require immediate attention.

"Like, I don't think you should do that! You are totally going to make a huge mess *and* wake up the patients. And that's not cool," Tore said. She was, at the heart of it, a very dedicated nurse.

Jamie was very proud of her at that moment. She looked at her and smiled. Tore was right. She did not need to be banging on a wall, waking people up. That wouldn't do.

Milton, who had looked a bit panicked at the thought of pounding through a wall, was relieved that Tore spoke up. "Uh, well, yeah. I do know where a hammer is. But we could use this." He held up his multitool that he always carried. It had a saw blade, albeit a small one. He figured they could cut a small chunk out and use a flashlight to see if they could find the source of the ringing. "It would cause less damage to the wall and be a little quieter."

"Right on. That's a much better idea! Thank you!" She smiled at Milton, and he shyly smiled back.

Jamie took the tool from him, got back up on the chair, and determinedly cut out a small square of drywall. The ringing was much louder, confirming that it was indeed in that space. Jamie couldn't see anything, though. The space was a dark, empty void. She took her old cell out of her pocket and tried using the frail light to search in the open area.

"Good Lord, woman! That little outdated pos isn't gonna shine on anything!" Charity laughed as she handed Jamie her phone with the flashlight on.

Jamie shone the light into the darkness. She didn't see anything at first. But then her eyes caught a strange sight. *Nah, it couldn't be. There's no way...* She had to cut again, making the opening larger so she could get a better look. By now, her hands were filthy with drywall dust, cobwebs, and dirt, which just added to her scratched and scraped arms from earlier. She shone the light again. This time, she followed the bright ray all the way back to the object. *No freaking way. Why is that up there? Better yet, why is it ringing?* Jamie stuck her arm in despite her coworkers' protests. She stood on her tiptoes and reached back as far as she could. She wobbled a bit, so Reid rushed in to spot her and steady the chair. Jamie pulled and pulled, busting out even more drywall. With a final tug, she managed to get it out from behind the weird wall. She could not believe what she was holding. Reid, Tore, Charity, and Milton all stared, mouths agape.

"OMG. Like, *what* is that?" Tore, the very young, very naïve Tore, couldn't figure out what Jamie was holding. She thought she might have seen something like it in a movie once or maybe at a museum.

"Holy Shit!" Milton gasped simultaneously. He embarrassedly covered his mouth when he realized he had said that aloud. He couldn't believe what he was looking at.

"It's a phone, dummy," said Charity. Her sass was starting to flare up.

"What in the hell is that doing in a boarded-up wall?" Jamie was holding it and still couldn't believe what she was seeing and hearing. As she cradled it in her arms, staring at it, the ringing stopped.

Everyone in the room was still. It was so quiet you could have heard a pin drop. The phone started to ring again. Being out from behind the wall made the ringing seem twice as loud and more unnerving. They all jumped at the sound.

"Are you going to answer it?" asked Reid. He was very, very curious. Unlike Tore, he did know what it was. He had just never used one before.

They all stood in disbelief, staring at an old, very outdated rotary phone. It was covered in dust and cobwebs, but the numbers on the dial were still visible. So many questions raced through their minds. Why was it up there? Who boarded it up? Did they know it was there? How did such an old phone stay hidden for so long? How in the hell was it still working? As Jamie held it, with everyone thinking about it, it continued to ring. Charity looked at Jamie expectantly and nodded, encouraging her to answer it.

"Uh, Hello?" Jamie tentatively said.

"H...h...hello...?"

Chapter Four

"Hello?" Jamie repeated.

"H..hello?" a faint, childlike voice said through the phone. "Hello? Are you there?"

Jamie had been holding the handset out so everyone could listen. They all looked at each other with surprised, wide-eyed, mouth-open expressions. They couldn't believe what they had just heard. There were so many questions racing through their minds: Why was an old phone hidden above the refrigerator? How was it still working? Whose child managed to connect to that line? No one even knew the number for that phone. The whole situation was incredibly strange.

"Like, is that a little girl talking?" Tore whispered. "Why would a little girl be calling an old phone? Where is sh—" Charity shot her a look and Tore shut up before she finished her sentence.

"Hello? Is someone there? Please. I need help..."

"Uh, yes, I'm here," Jamie said, just as puzzled as everyone else. She looked at the group and mouthed, *What is going on?* then asked the child, "Can I help you, sweetie? What do you need?"

"I need help!" Her voice changed to a whisper, barely audible to the group, and she continued, "It's dark in here."

Jamie, Milton, Reid, Charity, and Tore all looked at each other. Tore gasped, putting her hands over her mouth. Charity shot her another look, and Jamie shook her head and put her finger to her lips to make a *shhhh* sign. They all gathered in a circle around the phone. Jamie wanted to keep the little girl talking to gather more information. She considered calling the police, but Jamie didn't have enough details. They didn't know who the little girl was, where she was located, or if this was even a real call. It could have been a prank for all they knew. They needed to find out more.

"Sweetie, where are you? Where is here?" Jamie asked.

"Is this a prank call?" Milton wondered aloud.

"Where are you?" Reid asked.

"Like, do you have a name?" Tore innocently asked.

"Girl, this better not be a prank. We don't have time for that!" Charity said, irritated.

The little girl heard all the voices at once. Confused, she asked, "Who is there? Are there a lot of people?"

"Yes, I'm sorry. There are five of us here right now. Can you answer some questions for us?" Jamie wanted to keep talking to determine if it was just a prank or if the girl did need help.

"Five? Five is a good number...," the little girl said in a quiet voice, sounding a little older in that moment. "Maybe you could all help me?" she questioned, a little louder but still hushed and urgent.

"Of course, we can help. But we need some information, okay?"

"Y... yes...ok. I can try," she said, sounding more like a child again.

"What's your name?"

"My name...uh, it's Valentine. But you can call me, Val."

"Ok, hi Val." All the rest of the group muttered hellos as well. But they were too puzzled to say much else.

"Who are you?"

"My name is Jamie, Val. I am a charge nurse here at the hospital you are calling."

"My name is Reid. But everyone calls me Big Red," Reid said, hoping that by giving his nickname, it would make the weird situation a little lighter.

"Like my name is Tore. But it's Tore with an 'e' on the end, not an 'I' or a—"

"Tore! Stop. She doesn't care about the spelling of your damn name. Hi sweets. I am Charity," Charity said, interrupting Tore.

"Hi, I am Milton. Uh, where are you calling from?"

"I am calling a hospital? Are you all doctors and nurses?" Val was still quiet, but the shakiness had left her voice. There almost seemed to be a slight shift in tone.

"You sure are. Do you know where you are?" Jamie asked gently.

"I...uh....I don't know where I am. It's dark in here."

The group looked at each other, appearing to get more questions than answers. It was a peculiar situation that evoked an eerie sensation. *There's that feeling again...* Jamie thought. She covered the bottom part of the handset with her hand so Val couldn't hear them.

"Like, what are you doing? You should totally put that on mute, so she doesn't hear us," Tore innocently said.

Charity's sass was in full swing from the stress of the weird situation, so her mouth got ahead of her filter. "For God's sake, you Zoomer. It's an old rotary phone! It doesn't have a mute button!" She liked Tore. She knew Tore meant well and was a good nurse. And she always, *always* tried to give people the benefit of the doubt. But that girl had no common sense some days. *She must have lived a remarkably sheltered life, not knowing what an old phone is.*

Tore looked hurt. Her eyes started to well up. "Well, like, *excuse me*! Some of us have never seen that kind of phone before. I mean, I think my Nan had something like that, but her personal assistant always answered the calls."

Charity, Milton, and Jamie rolled their eyes at Tore this time. Reid smacked his forehead with his hand and shook his head. Tore was a good nurse. She was good at what she did. And she always tried to be kind. But she did not have a lot of what they considered real-life experience. She could be a bit naive at times and downright clueless at other times. That was one of those times. Jamie shushed them all.

"Listen, we can't all stand around here talking to this girl-"

"Valentine! But, like, she told us to call her Val," Tore interrupted with.

"OK! We can't *all* stand around here talking to Val. We still have work to do. Charity, if you can cover some of my patients, I will keep talking to Val and see what else I can find out. I don't want to call the police and waste their time on a hoax, you know? Milton, I know you have things to do as well, so go ahead. Tore, you too. Head out and check on your patients. Reid can stay here with me. It's not like he was busy." Jamie made a face and shot him a joking look.

"Hey! I work very hard! Sometimes. But, yeah, that's fine. I am happy to help you figure out what is going on."

Charity and Milton looked at each other, concerned. They figured it was a child speaking, so how bad could it be? They all still had that uneasy feeling, which seemed to intensify after the call. But it was just a weird call through an old phone, so Jamie thought it would be ok. A hidden phone ringing wasn't a regular occurrence, but it also wasn't necessarily a bad thing either. Jamie had Reid to help. And Jamie would call the police if she needed to. So, Charity gave her a look that said, *Let's keep checking in*, nodded, and then walked out. Milton followed. Tore smiled, patted Jamie's arm, and went back to work.

"Hello?? Are you there?" Val sounded vaguely more stern but also anxious.

"Yes, I'm still here. Sorry about that. What do you think, Val? Could you try to answer some questions for me?"

"I can try," she replied in the softest voice.

"Ok, great! First question. Do you know where you are?"

"Um...no. I don't know where I am. It's dark here."

"Ok. Hmmm. Can you turn on any lights?"

"I don't see any lights."

Reid was standing right beside Jamie now, so he could jot down notes as they talked. That way, he would have the correct information if they needed to call the police. He looked at Jamie as Val told her she didn't see any lights. He thought that seemed strange. In the digital age, everything emits some light. *How is she calling if she isn't using a cellphone?* he wondered. But before he could ask Jamie, she asked the little girl another question.

"Hm, well, what do you see? Can you describe your surroundings? What is around you?"

"Um.... I see metal round things. They are noisy! They look like big tanks or something. And pipes. I see lots of pipes."

"That's good! What else?" Jamie asked, coaxing the girl on.

"I see walls. Oh! I see a red sign. It says, E.X.I.T.... Exit! But there is no door. Why isn't there a door?" She was starting to get upset. "I also see another sign. It says....it says...I can't read it."

Jamie was worried that she would lose Val, so she spoke to her very gently. "It's ok. It's ok. We will figure this out." But the look she gave Reid suggested otherwise.

"Can you spell the sign to me?"

"Yes. It says, A.U.T.H.O.R.I.Z.E.D P.E.R.S.O.N.N.E.L. Under that, it says, 'only'."

Authorized Personnel Only? Where in the hell is she? Jamie was even more puzzled now. At first, she thought the call was a prank. But it was sounding more and more like Val was being serious.

"Oh! I hear something! It's so noisy here. It sounds like a motor. Or like a big fan."

It sounds like a motor or a fan? Where in hell was this girl? Jamie put her hand back over the phone's handset and turned to Reid, "Got any ideas?"

"Yeah. Actually, I do. What she is describing sounds like an old part of the hospital. Specifically, the back area of the mechanical room. I think she is hearing the boilers and the air handlers and seeing those pipes. It sounds like she is near the back part because they recently renovated it, but left an exit sign on the wall. I heard that one of the contractors thought it would be funny to leave it up after they walled off the tunnel."

Jamie just stared at Reid. *Just when you think you know a person.* She blinked several times and said, "How in the hell do you know all of that?" Before he could answer her, she nodded and said, "Riiiight. Gift of gab."

Reid smiled and shrugged. *Sometimes it pays to talk to anyone and everyone,* he thought. He learned a great deal of fascinating history about the hospital and persuaded the crews to let him see some of the renovations. He knew that the old asylum had an interesting history and was so much bigger back in the day.

A century ago, it had been an immense building that towered above the town. Several buildings had tunnels connecting them. As the town's size changed, so did the needs of the asylum. They couldn't support such a large facility anymore, so the town decided to demolish all but one of the buildings. The issue arose years later when it was discovered that local high school students were using the tunnels as a venue for parties and social gatherings. Sadly, it was also a place where people went to end their lives. So, the town boarded up all those tunnels as well. The rumor was that they missed boarding up a few of them, though, so the kids still hung out and partied there. However, no one could find any other openings, so town officials doubted the validity of the claim. The last known tunnel to be sealed off was down in the mechanical room.

Jamie pulled her hand off the handset and spoke to Val again. "Hey, kiddo? Nurse Reid thinks he might know where you are. But I need to know something. How are you calling us right now?"

"I... I am not sure. I found a phone plugged into a wall. I picked it up and heard it ringing, so I waited for someone to answer. Are you going to help me? It's so dark in here...."

Reid nodded. He had recently been in the mechanical room and knew that phones were still hanging on the walls. *I didn't think they would still be working, though.* He was about to mention that to Jamie when Milton and Charity came running into the room together.

"Oh my god, you are NOT going to believe this!!" Charity's eyes were open wide, and she looked visibly shaken. "My sister just texted me—"

"Two people were murdered just a few blocks from here tonight. Three others were critically injured. I guess they are all in the ER downstairs. Reporters stated it was a stabbing. But I spoke with Jerelle while I was in the ER, and she said she had never seen anything like it. She said it was like they had been mauled. She said one of the victims was missing a hand, one was missing a foot, and two others were missing fingers. They all looked like they had been bitten multiple times across the head and face by God knows what, if you can believe that. I only saw a quick glimpse as I was walking out, but one of them looked like a cartoon villain. You know, a slit across the face from the mouth to the ear? The police believe they were all attacked by the same person, who is currently at large. They are advising everyone at home to lock their doors and windows and stay inside until the suspect is caught," said Milton, interrupting Charity.

He paused to catch his breath. Jamie grabbed hold of the telephone handset and was going to cover the mouthpiece again. She didn't want the little girl to hear all of this and get more upset. But she decided to tell her to hold on for a second before she did.

"Val, I will be right back, ok? Something came up."

Jamie didn't wait for an answer. She needed to talk to her coworkers. As she began to pull the handset away from her face to cover the mouthpiece, she heard a noise. There was so much happening all at once that she struggled to focus. Yet, for a brief moment, Jamie thought she heard the little girl make a whistling sound followed by a giggle.

Jamie looked at Milton, shocked. *Three people injured and two dead? Five people in total? Who else was attacked besides Walt and Wanda,* Jamie wondered. The others mistook her reaction, thinking it was a response to the devastating news they had just received. But she had already known about two of the attacks. In an instant, Jamie thought about Mr. and Mrs. Makenin and Monika. *Oh my God! I never called Dick's Rolls.*

Shit! Just as Jamie was about to hand the old phone over to Reid and go call the bakery, Keith appeared at the threshold.

"Guys, I am not sure if you heard or ....n.ot..." Judging by their faces, Keith realized someone had already told them. "Ok, I guess so. Rachelle just called from downstairs. She was looking for you, Jamie. She didn't have time to wait or call your cell. She said she would try to call back as soon as she could. I was informed that we are not yet going into a full lockdown. But the entire hospital has been put on high alert. I spoke with Bastian, and he said they just called in a few more security guards for each floor to help out tonight. They should be here at any minute. To the best of our knowledge, we are not in any danger. This is *just* a precaution, ok?" They all nodded their heads as Keith continued, "keep doing your jobs and we will all be just fine," he said in full dad mode. "I already informed Kerrigan. She is still with her patients. Where is Tore with an 'e'? Has anyone told her yet? And where in the hell did you get that old thing, Jamie?" Keith just stared at the phone she was holding, one eyebrow raised. *I don't get paid enough to deal with all of this weird shit,* Keith thought.

"Tore was checking patients last I knew. I don't think she knows," said Reid.

At the same time, Jamie pointed to the space above the refrigerator. Not only was there now a gaping, telephone-sized hole, but the peeling paint chips and chunks of drywall were dangling. It was a mess. Keith looked up in the direction she was pointing and shook his head.

"No. Nope. No, thank you. Never mind, I don't even want to know. I am going to go find Tore."

Out the door, Keith went, still shaking his head and mumbling something about just wanting to do his fricking job. Milton, who had just been paged, followed behind. Both had concerned expressions on their faces as they left the break room.

"Do you think the murderer is here? And could the little girl be hiding from them?" Charity said, looking pale. Her hands trembled slightly. To her, this now seemed much less a hoax and much more a serious issue. "Are you sure we shouldn't call the police?"

"I don't know. Maybe? I hope not." Jamie was also starting to get concerned. It was one thing when she thought it was a prank. And another when she felt she was dealing with a lost kid. But potentially hiding from a murderer puts a whole new spin on things. "Reid thinks he knows where she is. But we *should* call the police and—"

"I doubt a murderer is hiding down in the hospital's mechanical room. He or she is probably long gone now. You heard Keith, we aren't even locked down. Hold off on calling them right now, ok? I am pretty sure I know where she is. Please just let me go down and check. She probably just wandered away from a room she was visiting, got turned around, and is now lost. I can even ask some of the other nurses in the PEDS ward to see if they are missing a patient named 'Val'. I can't imagine she could have sneaked past Ana, but you never know. I'll go grab her and bring her back. No big deal, right?" Reid asked, interrupting Jamie.

Reid was hoping Jamie would agree. He *did* enjoy being a nurse. He loved it when the patients wanted to visit. But it bored him at times. He absolutely detested the paperwork, which is mostly what he had to do for the next hour or so. Going down to the mechanical room would break up some of the night's monotony.

"Yeah, all right. If you are sure?" asked Jamie. Reid nodded, so she added, "Just be careful! You don't know what kind of situation you are walking into, ok? I will cover for you while you are trying to locate the girl. But take a flashlight and something you can protect yourself with."

"Jamie! Do you think that is a good idea? Maybe we should let security handle it. That's their job. Your job is nursing, Reid," Charity said, looking directly at him.

"I will be fiiiiiine, *mom*."

"Are you *sure* you want to do this, Reid?" Jamie was starting to doubt his decision.

"Yes. No point in bothering security right now."

Jamie groaned slightly, realizing she wasn't going to convince Reid to stay, and said, "Just be quick, ok? No stopping to chat. No wandering about the hospital. Go down and find the girl. If you don't find her in say, fifteen minutes, get your butt back up here and get back to work. Deal?"

"Yes, mother dear," Reid said with a little more attitude than he meant.

Jamie raised her eyebrow and walked closer to Reid. She crossed her arms and stared up at him. She didn't tolerate attitude from anyone, regardless of their height or size.

"Ex-squeeze me, kid?"

"Sorry!! That came out wrong. You know I am not like that. I am so sorry. I have a hard time being treated like I am too young or dumb to do something. Yes, I will go down and come right back either with or without this 'Val', ok?"

"Alrighty. Get to it, then. You have paperwork to complete when you return. Just be careful, ok? This day has just been weird as fuck."

"Jamie! Language! Reid, here, take this," Charity said as she dug something out of her pocket. It was a little pepper spray bottle.

"OMG! Like you are NOT supposed to have that in here and *especially* not on your person! That is SOOOOOO against the rules!" Tore huffed as she came in and saw what was in Charity's hand.

"Tore, did Keith find you?" Jamie asked.

"Yeah, he totally did. But like he actually said my name right. Should I be worried?"

"Let's just focus on our jobs and—" Jamie was interrupted by an upset Tore.

"Yes! Our *jobs!* Charity should not be carrying pepper spray! It totally said so in our handbook!! Like I'm sorry, Charity. I think you have a super fun and flowy energy about you, but I can't overlook you breaking the rules. Jamie, I want you to write her up!" Tore huffed in a serious tone.

"I am a woman working second shift. Do you think I would come here *without it?*" Charity exclaimed. "Besides, we all have this or something else, don't we, Jamie?"

"Uh, well, yeah. I often bike to work and school, and I work a second shift. I always have a whistle on my keychain, a can of bear spray in my backpack, and pepper spray with an alarm in my pocket." Jamie agreed. She knew she probably carried more than most women, but having dealt with a stalker situation several years ago, she kept what made her feel safe. The guy was apprehended eventually. But it had been downright frightening for several months.

"Well, yeah, ok. But like, you don't for real *need* any of that stuff, do you? That's for bigger cities and like gangs and bad people, right?" Tore innocently asked.

Jamie rolled her eyes so hard she was sure they would come flying out of her head. She could not believe how sheltered some people could be. She grew up in a time when boys and girls were separated during junior high gym class, allowing the girls to be educated on self-defense and safety protocols. Jamie never forgot. It's what inspired her to take a self-defense course in her twenties. And it proved handy while the stalking situation was taking place. She used that knowledge to defend herself against the guy. Two strangers who were walking on the opposite side of the street when the incident occurred ran over to help Jamie. They held him while she called the police. She was scared and bruised. She did have a couple of broken fingers. But Jamie knew she was incredibly lucky it worked out the way it did. It could have been so much worse. Since then, she never left without at least her personal pepper spray. She looked at Tore, and this time she couldn't hold back.

"Are you *kidding me*?! What would you do if an attacker walked up to you and grabbed you? For Christ's sake, girl! You should always be aware of your surroundings, keep your head up, be smart about things, and avoid burying your head in your phone. There is a reason we all go to the bathroom in groups! Safety in numbers, girl. Good God!"

Tore's eyes welled up. She looked both horrified and hurt. She wanted to be angry with Jamie and Charity for making her feel bad. But she was also grateful that two women whom she looked up to and admired took the time to educate her.

"OMG! I had NO idea! I totally thought we all went to the bathrooms in groups so, like, we could talk about our dates or help each other fix our makeup. But isn't that like old people's outdated information?" Tore asked.

Charity and Jamie looked at each other in disbelief. "No, Hun, it's not," they said in unison.

"I always tell my sister to be careful. She knows she can call me if she ever feels weird about a situation," Reid said, trying to make Tore feel a little better. "You can call me too."

"Oh, thank you, Big Red! You are so sweet. And like, your aura is just so beautiful, you know? I can see how kind and caring you are."

Reid had blushed a bit upon hearing that. Just then, they heard a whistling sound coming from the phone. All four of them had forgotten about it, even though Jamie was still holding it. They all looked down.

"Hello? Hello? Are you there? I am so hungry...," Val said in a quiet, strange voice. "Can someone please help me?"

Oh, good fucking Lord! How could I forget this poor child? Jamie pulled her hand off the handset and said, "Yes. A nice guy thinks he knows where you are. He is going to come down and get you, ok? Can you see anyone else down there with you?"

"No, I can't see anything. But I can hear things...Is it Reid who is coming down? Please help me," Val said again. "I'm hungry."

The entire situation seemed so outrageous to Jamie. So many things bothered her. Aside from the old phone and the fact that a little girl was lost in the hospital, she wondered why the little girl was so calm. She also wondered how Val remembered Reid's name after only just learning it. And she wondered why she kept hearing other faint sounds that she swore sounded like whistling and giggling. But mostly she wondered how that old phone was working. Nothing seemed to add up. She wasn't sure it was a good idea for Reid to go try to find the little girl. *But it will just be quick,* she thought.

"It sure is! I will be right down. You hold tight! Try to keep an eye out for me, ok?" Reid said.

"Stay safe, kid. I am going to hang up the phone now, ok?" Jamie asked.

"Ok, I understand. Can you please hurry? My tummy is so hungry."

"KK. I will be right there!" Reid said this with the same enthusiasm he had given everyone.

Jamie hung up the phone and placed it on top of the refrigerator. They all looked at each other. None of them believed it. Any of it. Murders a few blocks away, a girl lost in, maybe the mechanical room of the hospital, and potentially a murderer on the loose. *Man, good ole Mitch didn't know how accurate he was going to be!* Jamie thought, shaking her head.

"Here, like take these," Tore said, digging into her pocket and handing Reid a pile of candy and a broken but still wrapped granola bar. "Like, she said she's hungry. This should help!"

"Tore with an 'e'!" exclaimed Charity. "I cannot believe you have all that junk in your pocket! *You know* that's against policy. " Charity winked at her, shook her head, and went back to work.

Tore just smiled sheepishly and said, "Well, I get hungry when I am working..." She shrugged and shimmied out the door behind Charity.

"You had better head on down. I am going to ask you one more time, are you sure you want to do this? We could call the police. And before you say it, I am not mom-ing you. You have no idea what you are walking into," Jamie said, intently.

"No, no, no. It's all good. I need to stretch my long legs. I am sure I can find her and get her back to where she belongs. Easy peasy. Don't worry, Jamie," Reid said confidently.

"Ok. Just be careful. Like I said, we have no idea what is going on. And you never know with the suspect still not found."

"I will, Jamie. I promise!" And with that statement, the tall, lanky, Big Red headed out the door, down the hall, and into the elevator, and Jamie headed back to the nurses' station.

Chapter Five

Jamie didn't even have time to process the old phone when her cell unexpectedly rang. She had been so lost in thought, trying to process everything she had heard, that she jumped a little. Jamie fumbled to take the phone out of her pocket.

"Hello? Oh, hi Rachelle! How are y—"

Jamie's face fell as she continued to listen to Rachelle. She wasn't getting good news and didn't look forward to sharing it with the staff. Jamie braced herself for what was next. She called all the nurses into the breakroom. She chose that spot for two reasons. The first one was that she wanted to explain the telephone. Or at least *try* to explain what she could, of the weird old telephone. The second reason was that she did not want a single patient to discover what was happening. They were all in the hospital for a reason. She did not want to add more stress. After that, she needed to make good on her statement and call Dick's to check on Russell Makenin. Jamie looked at her watch and realized that Monika was already gone for the day. After she called Dick's, she would find Bastian again and see what he found out.

"Alrighty, ladies and gents.... You have all heard about the emergency situation that is currently happening downstairs. You have heard we are on high alert. Eiler and Robert just arrived here on our floor as added security. They also called in Tekonsha and Liatris for the second floor, and Wayne and John for the first floor. Again, this is *just* a precaution, ok? I got a call from Rachelle downstairs. She has asked if we can spare anyone else to help right now. Kerrigan, what do you think? Can you head down to the ER and see what you can do? We can cover your patients while you are helping Rachelle. You worked in the ER, so I think you would be a big help."

Jamie looked at them, Kerrigan, hoping she would say yes. She didn't think Tore would be able to handle the mess that was being described to her. And she wanted Charity and Keith with her in case things got a little out of hand.

"Yeah, of course I can help. I just finished my paperwork, so I will take off right now," Kerrigan said. "But I thought Benji was down helping out?"

"He is. They are slammed right now and need more help."

"Oh boy...Yup, I will head right down!"

Kerrigan was a stellar employee. She was usually the first to volunteer when needed, she always did everything without complaint, and she helped anyone who needed it. The hospital was lucky to have her, and Jamie knew and appreciated that.

Kerrigan walked out the door of the breakroom and headed toward the elevator to go downstairs. Jamie smacked her head with her palm. *Good lord, I forgot to tell them about the phone. Oh well, I can tell them later when things settle down. Reid should be back by then.* She then looked at Keith, Tore, and Charity.

"As you can see, I forgot to tell them about the phone call. But what the hell would I say because the entire situation is bizarre as hell."

"Well, like, they do need to know..." Tore said, trying to be helpful.

Charity rolled her eyes. Sometimes she did not get that girl. She turned to Jamie and said, "Did it ring again?"

"No, thank goodness. We have our hands full at the moment. We don't need to be dealing with—" Jamie motioned with her hands in a circle around the refrigerator, "—whatever the hell this is..."

"Uh, what phone call?" Keith asked. "Did that old phone you found actually *work*?!"

"Oh shit! I didn't tell you either, did I? Man, you aren't gonna believe this. I barely do. Yeah, the old antique rang. I answered it, and on the other end was what sounded like a little girl. She said she was lost and hungry......I don't know, though. Something about it feels so off," Jamie said, concerned.

"What?! I have so many questions. Did you find out where she was calling from? Did you get her name? Hang on, back it up. HOW was she calling an old line we didn't even know existed?! You're right, something seems hinky," Keith said, obviously very upset.

"We don't know. We did get her name. She said it was Valentine—" Jamie said as Tore interrupted her.

"Like she said, we should call her 'Val' for short, remember?"

Keith shot Tore a look and said, "I hardly think that is important right now."

"Well, like I am sorry. But that's what she told us," a hurt Tore said huffily.

"Tore, it's ok. We are all on our last nerve tonight, I think. Keith, I don't have any other information. Reid was headed down to the mechanical room to try to find her."

"Why the mechanical room? Is that where she is? How did our hospital lose a child? You should have let security handle that, or called the police," Keith said sternly.

"I wish I had those answers, dude. Reid said he would come right back if things seemed off or he couldn't find her. I am doing the best I can here, ok?" Jamie said, more than a little frustrated. "Reid was pretty confident he knew where she was. He insisted on going. He promised me he would get her back to PEDS, assuming she isn't a lost visitor, that is, as soon as he could. I know he can be a bit flighty at times, but I think he's got this. If, when he gets back here, he tells us he couldn't find her, then we will call the police. I held off on calling the police for the time being. It sounds like Frankie, and everyone has their hands full right now."

"Ok, alright. I didn't mean to sound like I was coming down on you. That sounds like a plan, Stan. Can we determine who needs what regarding Benji and Kerrigan's patients? We should get back to work. But let's all keep our eyes open, just in case. We don't need a murderer running around our facility," Keith said in the calmest voice he could muster.

The truth was, he was more than concerned. He had already called his parents and ensured they had locked their doors and windows, as they were in the habit of leaving everything unlocked. He then called to check on his kids. Everyone was fine, but the situation had him rattled. They all headed back to the nurses' station to review what needed to be done.

After the duties were divided, each nurse headed to their respective areas. They were busy again, but nothing they couldn't handle. Mrs.Viola Garcia needed a med check. She loved Benji, so when Jamie entered the room, she was greeted with a skeptical, "Who are you? Where is Benji?" She was a fiery little lady with a big personality. She had a wonderful laugh, a warm smile when she wanted to, and a fantastic attitude, even if it was spicy at times. Jamie loved her instantly.

"Hi, Mrs. Garcia! Benji had to help on a different floor for a while. I am Jamie, and I will be filling in, if that's ok with you? I'm no Benji, but I am going to take good care of you."

Viola raised one eyebrow and said, "I doubt you will be as good as Benji. He takes great care of me! He always knows what I need. And he is always so kind to me."

"He is very kind," Jamie said. "You know, I have known Benji for years. He is one of my brother's best friends. He can be a royal pain in the butt sometimes, but he is a stellar nurse, isn't he?" Because Benji was her brother Albert's best friend and she saw him so much, she just kind of adopted him as another brother. They got on each other's nerves at times, just like biological siblings. But they enjoyed each other's company enough that they would occasionally hang out.

Viola laughed and gave her the most beautiful smile. "Ah, you are alright! I like you. You tell it like it is, just like I do. You'll do. And between you and me," her voice lowered, "he can be a pain in the butt sometimes!" She laughed and laughed. She and Jamie spent the next few minutes chatting while Jamie worked.

Keith was not having as much luck as Jamie with the added patients. Most of them were grumbling that he wasn't as nice as Kerrigan. He was neither a rude nor an uncaring nurse. It was exactly the opposite. He was just more businesslike in his approach. He decided to try a different greeting to see if that would be more effective.

"Hello, Mr. Brown. How are you doing this fine even—"

"Who are you? Where is my regular nurse?!" Rusty grumbled, interrupting Keith.

"Unfortunately, Kerrigan had to go assist on a different floor for a while. My name is Keith, and I will be filling in."

"I don't want a damn male nurse! Go away!"

Keith was so ready for his break. He was over that night. However, he was determined to complete his task and persuade this gentleman to see the light. "So, how have you been feeling?" he said as cheerily as he could.

"I am in the damn hospital; how do you *think* I feel?" grumbled Rusty.

No one told Keith that Rusty was not the most cooperative or compliant patient. Kerrigan had to coax him into being agreeable enough to do her checks, and he was downright ornery when she had to give him pills. Rusty constantly threatened to leave the hospital, but thus far, he had not made good on that threat. He found out later in life that he was severely diabetic. He was angry about that. He was furious about the lifestyle changes they told him to make. He was angry that he couldn't eat or drink whatever he wanted anymore. Occasionally, he would try to sneak down to the vending machine to get a delicious sugary soda, but he always ended up being caught and sent back to his room with *water* or unsweetened iced tea. Sometimes he was so uncooperative that

Kerrigan had another nurse come in with her as a backup. She never needed it. But they were there, just in case.

Ok, this is my last patient before break. Just get the damn vitals, and you can relax in the breakroom for a while. By the time checks come around again, Kerrigan will be back. Just keep it together, Keith thought. He tried to smile at Rusty, but it looked more like a child who was just told to smile for a photo and did that weird, frozen, "*cheeeese*" face rather than an actual warm and friendly smile. Rusty looked taken aback, so Keith let his smile fall. He checked Rusty's blood pressure, heart rate, oxygen level, glucose level, and so on. He was on the last test. Things were going a little more smoothly. "Ok, Mr. Brown, if I can have you step into the bathroom and fill this for me. We just need this sample, and I will be out of your hair." Keith handed him the cup and went over to write down the information.

Rusty glared at Keith and swung his legs over the side of the bed, stepped down, and grabbed his IV stand. Keith was glad he was being so agreeable. That was a step in the right direction. He turned his back to continue writing. But instead of going into the restroom, Rusty wheeled around and took off from his room. Keith had been in the bathroom, turning the light on and placing the specimen cup, so he didn't notice until he heard someone holler. *Oh God fucking dammit! I really don't need this tonight!* He threw his pen and the cup down and went after

Rusty, thinking, *the last thing we need is him finding out about the murderer and a potential serious situation here at the hospital.*

Charity was doing just fine with the added patients. Most of them accepted the switch and were just grateful to have someone checking on them. Mr. Grigoriy Mockatavi, on the other hand, was an entirely different kind of handful.

"You aren't Kerrigan! Where is Kerrigan?!" Grigoriy demanded.

"Hello, Mr. Mockatavi! You are correct. I am indeed *not* Kerrigan. She had to go to help on another floor. I am Charity, and I am here to check your vitals, ok?"

"No! No, it's not ok! I want Kerrigan to do it!"

Grigoriy Mockatavi was a stubborn old man. He was the type of person who would complain about the smallest things. Everyone in the hospital recognized him. Most of the nurses tried to avoid him and would collectively groan when they found out he had been admitted. He was used to getting his way and would make anyone miserable who didn't cooperate. He lived by the saying, "the squeaky wheel gets the grease," so he complained about everything.

Charity was not in the mood for that. Not that night. She had too many things on her mind and was not going to listen to him complain all night long. Instead, she decided to match his energy.

"Oh. Ok. Well, *sure*. I can *go*. You can *wait*. And you can hope that your catheter bag isn't full and spilling by the time nurse Kerrigan makes it back up here. *Have a good niiiiight!*" Charity smiled a sickly-sweet smile, winked, and walked toward the doorway.

Grigoriy panicked. "Wait! Um, I mean, hold on now—just a minute. You don't have to be like that. I was *kidding*. I am sure you are almost as good as Kerrigan."

Grigoriy really couldn't help himself. But it was enough for Charity to stop, turn around, and say, "Sure, Mr. Mockatavi. Whatever you say......" as she walked over to him to check his vitals and catheter bag. *That's what I thought! Damn! WHY do people have to be like that when I am just doing my damn job? Good Lord.* Suddenly, she saw a man go by the door. She looked out to see Rusty streaking down the hallway. His hospital gown was flapping wildly against his legs as he and his visibly torn tighty whities hustled down the hall.

She hollered, "Whatcha doing, Mr. Brown?"

Rusty, who couldn't tell which room the voice came from, started showing his middle finger to every doorway he passed while continuing to head toward the elevator. Charity couldn't help but laugh. She knew who he was (the entire hospital did as well) and how difficult he could be. No one told Keith, though. She snickered. *You know, that man is pretty quick for his age. Color me impressed!* She considered helping, but figured Keith deserved a little of that. A few seconds later, Keith was high-tailing it down the hallway after his patient.

Tore was the one nurse who lucked out. She only had to cover two patients: one was Kerrigan's, and the other was Benji's. Ms. Nessa Featherstorm was a petite woman who never married. She said she never had time for such things. Tore loved her and told her so. She also told her that she had a beautiful aura and a nice spirit guide named Melvin who was trying to reach her. Agatha, on the other hand, was a very tall woman. If she could have stood straight up, she would have towered over Tore. Unfortunately, decades of untreated osteoporosis and years of rheumatoid arthritis had her back hunched over. Agatha was very self-conscious of it. All the nurses were aware that it was quite a touchy subject.

As Tore was humming while doing her checks, she turned to Agatha and said, "Mrs. Roop, like, you know, maybe if you let out some of your bottled-up negativity, your back would straighten up and you could walk better? Or maybe, like, maybe aligning your chakras would help? Oh! Like, wearing shades of blues and greens totally helps relieve pain and stress. Maybe try wearing more of those colors?" Tore shrugged, smiled, finished what she was doing, and said, "Ok, like buh-bye. You have a super night, m'kay?" and as she disappeared out the door and on to her regular patients, she watched an older man in nothing but his hospital gown and holey briefs, dragging his IV pole with him, go running down the hallway towards the elevator. "Wow! Like, slow down, sir. You shouldn't be doing that! Does your nurse know that you are running down the hall?"

Keith was farther back, yelling for Rusty to stop. But that did not stop him in the slightest. If anything, it seemed to make him speed up!

"Mr. Brown! MR. BROWN! STOP!"

Rusty did not stop. Instead, he held his arm high in the air, turned around, and flipped a middle finger at Keith. This action, however, caused him to get tangled up in his IV tubes and stumble forward. All three security guards had heard the commotion and had been walking toward them. Bastian, Eiler, and Robert all reached out and grabbed him at the same time, saving him from a terrible fall.

"Whoa. That could have been bad," Bastian said.

The other two nodded but were trying to hide the chuckles that were working their way up. It was a serious situation; the security guards were aware of this. But they couldn't help but snicker at the ridiculousness of it all.

"Hey! LET GO OF ME! What the hell are you doing?!" Mr. Brown yelled.

Eiler and Bastian helped stand him upright while Robert untangled the IV tubes. He was fortunate that nothing had been pulled out.

"It's a good thing we were here, Mr..." Robert said, waiting for the man to give him his name.

Rusty was obstinate to the end. He looked up at Robert and said, "Oh, fuck you and the horse you rode in on!" He gave him the middle finger and proceeded to double over in a coughing fit. All three of them looked at each other and rolled their eyes. Their faces looked like they were saying, *ok. so, it's going to be like that, is it?*

"Hey, hey, hey now. What did my horse ever do to you, huh?" Robert asked him. He looked down and, chuckling, said, "I see you are a briefs, not boxers kind of guy."

Rusty's face went red. He grabbed the back of his gown tightly and held it closed with one of his hands.

"Ok, I don't think that was necessary. If it weren't for us, you'd be a mess on the floor," said Eiler.

Eiler was a tall, unassuming guy who had a natural calming effect on people. He could have easily gone into another field, but he enjoyed being part of the security team. He got to witness some very crazy things. So, this guy was chump change, comparatively speaking. "You wouldn't want to be sprawled out on the floor, blood dripping from your ripped vein, while your personal items were hanging out of the lovely, ripped briefs, now, would you? Maybe we can try that again. Mr.....?"

"Brown. His name is Rusty Brown," Keith said, walking up to the group. "Thanks, guys. I appreciate the help. What do you say? Would handcuffs help our patient understand that he can't go running down the hallways at night?"

The three men just looked at him. "Your name is *Rusty Brown*? Like the color?" the three of them said in unison. They all chuckled.

"Whoa, whoa. Now wait just a fucking minute!" Rusty said, panicking, but also still with a bad attitude. "No need to resort to that. And don't call me Rusty, alright? It's an old family name, and I hate it. I prefer *Mr. Brown, thank you!*"

"Yeah, ok. Listen, will you willingly go back to your room with Keith?" asked Robert.

He was not as tall as Eiler but had a lot of muscle mass on his frame. He caught the attention of several nurses and some doctors. If push ever came to shove, he was the man you wanted for backup. He stared at Mr. Brown, letting the man size him up.

"Heyyyy, look, man, I wasn't trying to cause trouble. I—"

"That's a funny way of not causing trouble, bud," said Bastian, interrupting in his deep, low voice. His name was Sebastain, but he told people he didn't look like someone who should be named that, so he preferred Bastian. He was a huge guy. People used to tell him he was built like a brick shit house. They weren't wrong. He could handle trouble without an issue. He preferred not to do that. He enjoyed being a security guard, keeping people safe without having to use force. His mother used to tell him that he was a lover, not a fighter. But he could handle things if they needed him. He looked down at Rusty and said, "Isn't it?"

Rusty eventually realized he wasn't going to win. He sighed and nodded at Bastian. He put out his wrists, waiting to be cuffed. All three of the security guards chuckled and shook their heads.

"Dude, we aren't going to cuff you, ok? Just go back to your room peacefully," said Eiler.

"Give Keith a break, man. He is an excellent nurse. He is just doing his job. You need to *continue* to let him do his job, understand?" said Robert. He stared Rusty down. "Let's get you back to your room *now.*"

Rusty knew he couldn't win that fight. He relented. With a huge sigh, he turned around with his head hung low, one hand still tightly grasping his gown, and walked with Robert and Keith back to his room. Bastian and Eiler waved at him and said, "Good night, Rusty Brown." They chuckled again and shook their heads. Keith told the men Thank you as they walked away.

As Robert was leaving, he looked at Rusty and said, "Behave, and I won't have to come back down here." Rusty nodded sadly, took his cup, and headed into the bathroom to finally give Keith the sample.

Keith fist bumped Robert and said, "Thanks, man. It's been a night, hasn't it?"

"It sure has. How'd we get lucky enough to have a full moon on a stormy night AND have a murderer on the loose?" Robert said quietly.

"Luck of the draw? Dude, I have seen some crazy stuff and weird fricking behaviors, but nothing to this extent. Thanks for being here and having our backs."

"No thanks needed, Keith. I'm just doin' my job, man." Robert left the room.

Rusty crankily came out of the bathroom. He handed Keith the sample and then got back into bed. His face was a strange mix of anger, embarrassment, and exhaustion. Keith was glad. That meant he would probably quiet down and go to sleep soon.

"Have a good night. I am sure Kerrigan will be back to check on you next."

Keith had never been more ready for dinner break than he was at that moment. As he walked out of Mr. Brown's room, he caught up with Charity. Without saying a word, they both looked at each other, sighed, and nodded. They walked back to the nurses' station together in silence.

Jamie was completing her paperwork when Keith and Charity walked up. They both looked a little ragged and worn out. As Jamie was about to tell them both to head to dinner break, they heard the elevator open and close. Kerrigan was walking toward them, looking tired and haggard. At the same time, the phone rang. Jamie grabbed it and said, "Good evening, this is Jamie," but before she could get a word in, she got an earful. All Jamie could respond with were some "uh-huhs" and "Ok's" and a few "I will talk to her". She no sooner hung up the phone than it rang again. She answered and got another earful from a different patient. As she was placing the handset back down, she looked up and saw Tore flittering through the hallway. Jamie stood up and yelled, "TORE! PLEASE COME HERE!" Tore looked up, surprised, nodded, and headed towards the group standing at the station.

"Like, HI! I just finished up, and omg, I saw two of the cutest old—"

Jamie didn't let her finish. *Deep breaths. Remain calm. Talk to her sternly but rationally. No swearing, Jamie. No fucking swearing... well, not out loud at least.*

Jamie cleared her throat and tried saying as slowly and sweetly as she could, "Uh, *Tore?* Did you tell Agatha Roop that she needed to be more positive and balance her chakras, and her back would be cured? And did you also tell Nessa Featherstorm that her spirit guide Melvin, was yelling at her?!" Jamie's voice went up a little bit as she asked the second question.

"Well, like yeah. But also no. I told Ms. Featherstorm that Melvin was trying to *reach* her and, like I told Mrs. Roop, that she needed her chakras to be *aligned.* Why?"

"Tore. For the love of God. You cannot do that!"

"But like, why not? I am totally just trying to help. I tell all my patients that kind of stuff."

Tore smiled a very heartfelt, very innocent smile. She firmly believed she was following her own spirit guide's advice and was trying to help as many people as possible by being the best nurse she could be. In her mind, that meant being open, honest, and willing to say what others wouldn't, including offering alternative treatments to the patient.

"OH! For fuck's sake, girl! You can't suggest things like that! A, it can't be proved, and two, they aren't offered here at the hospital! You aren't a doctor. And you should never use the word '*cure*'! You are opening yourself and the hospital up to various lawsuits. Just fucking STOP!"

The stress and uncertainty of the night had taken a toll on Jamie. She didn't mean to snap. She didn't mean to swear. It just flew out of her mouth.

"I'm sorry. Like, I didn't know. I am just trying to be the best nurse I can," Tore said as she burst into tears. She ran into the breakroom and sat down. Everyone could hear her sobs. They all looked down at the counter, not wanting to make eye contact with Jamie. Each nurse had had their moment with Tore. But deep down, she was a very caring girl, and she did try to be the best nurse. She always had her patients' best interests in mind, but did not always say the best thing. As Tore continued to sob, one by one, they all lifted their eyes to Jamie to see how she would continue.

"Oh, Dammit! I am so sorry, guys. So sorry. This day, man. It's got me a little tense. And I took it out on poor Tore. Yeah, she can be a bit unconventional at times, but we all know she is a good nurse and always puts the patient's needs first. Ah, shit. I need to go talk to her."

Jamie started toward the breakroom. Keith reached out and put his hand on her shoulder to stop her. "No. Let me go talk to her first."

Everyone just stared at Keith. He was the first one to let Tore know she screwed up. He was always teasing her and messing up her name on purpose. None of them thought it was a good idea. They all started voicing their protests.

"Um, Keith, maybe sit this one out and let one of us talk to her," said Charity.

"I am happy to go sit down and explain why she can't do that and how to move forward," said the always levelheaded Kerrigan.

Keith wasn't having it. He turned to all of them and, in a somber, almost protective tone, said, "It's ok. I've got this." He walked into the breakroom and sat down beside Tore, who was still sobbing. Her head was resting on her folded arms, which were lying on the table. Keith gently put his hand on her shoulder. Tore looked up, cheeks wet with tears. Her eyes were now puffy and red, and her nose was running. Keith took a tissue box from one of the other tables, set it on their table, pulled out a tissue, and handed it to Tore.

"Listen, kiddo, Jamie didn't mean it. It's a tough night for all of us. I know she didn't mean to lose her cool. We all know you meant well," Keith said.

"Like, why are you being nice to me? You don't even like me." Tore started sobbing harder.

"No, that's not true. I tease you about your name, and I am harder on you, but not because I don't like you. You got me all wrong. I know you are a good nurse, Tore. We all do. It's just, you remind me of my daughter. You try too hard sometimes. Well, a lot of the time. Nursing isn't a popularity contest. It isn't about likes, followers, and subscribers like all the social media pages you follow. Nursing is about providing the best care possible to people going through difficult times in their lives. Sure, some patients remember us after they are discharged. But most of them simply continue with their lives. And that's ok. That's how it is supposed to be. You don't have to try so hard to make the patients and other staff like you. Just be you, do your job, and it will come naturally. You are a great kid with a big heart, you know that? Try to keep a lid on telling patients that they can be cured by anything—"

"But, like, alternative therapies *do* work! I saw it myself. When my Nan was diagnosed with cancer, she utilized other things. She had acupuncture and acupressure sessions. She had aromatherapists, relaxation therapists, and guided visualization sessions. My Nan was cured! Like, they DO work! They *do!*" said Tore passionately.

"It doesn't matter if the alternative therapies help. That's not our line of work. Your grandmother had conventional treatments as well, right? That's our area. Our job is to care for the patient's needs here at the hospital. We never give personal advice or discuss cures. We leave that up to the doctors, ok? Do I think alternative modalities can sometimes help a patient improve? I dunno. Maybe. Maybe not. The bottom line is that we are here to care for the patients at this hospital to the best of our ability, without making any promises. Just stick to that."

"Like, yeah, ok. I will try. My Auntie tells me that I try too hard too. It's just that, like, everyone in my family is *soooooo* successful. They often forget I exist. But if I *do* things for them, like, they kinda see me. Or...well... *use me,* I guess." Tore finished with a huge sigh. She blew her nose and looked at Keith, her big eyes still bright with tears. "Thanks, Keith. I guess you aren't the big meany I thought you were."

"Let's keep that between you and me, ok kid?" Keith smiled and chuckled. Tore did too. "I can't let the others find out I am just a big old teddy bear, can I?" Tore lifted an eyebrow at that sentiment. "Well, maybe I am more of a cuddly cactus." He laughed this time and then said, "For real, Tore. If you ever need someone to talk to, think of me as your work dad. Like I said, you remind me a lot of my daughter. She has a big heart as well and gets hurt frequently. I don't want that for either of you. Keep up the good work. You truly are a good nurse."

"Thank you. Like that means a lot to me. Ugh. Jamie must hate me right now. I didn't mean to cause trouble for her or the hospital."

"I know that, Tore with an 'e'," Jamie said as she walked into the breakroom, joining them at the table. "I let the stress of the day just take over. I am very sorry for losing my cool. I am the charge nurse; I know better. I try to treat everyone with respect and decency. I failed you tonight. I *did* not mean to cuss you out. You were only trying to help."

"Oh!" Tore gasped. "Like, you *don't* hate me? I am so relieved! I promise to do better! I promise to try harder!" Keith raised an eyebrow at Tore, so she smiled slightly and adjusted her words. "I mean, I will like, always try to be a good nurse. But I won't try to make people like me anymore. My job is to care for them, not make friends with them, right?"

"Right on, sister! Listen to Keith. He's old and quite wise." Jamie smiled and winked at Keith.

"Uh, how much did you hear?" Keith asked nervously.

"Enough. Don't worry. Your secret is safe with me, 'cuddly cactus'!"

"Well...damn...," Keith said. He hung his head and then laughed.

Jamie leaned over and hugged Tore. Keith patted Tore on the back. The other nurses had started entering the breakroom at that point to check on Tore. They all got along with her, even if she was exasperating at times. And they liked Jamie. They looked up to her as a nurse, and they admired her commitment to furthering her education. They needed to ensure everything was smoothed over because that odd feeling was still following them everywhere. One by one, they each hugged Tore and patted Jamie on the back. Jamie stood up.

"I am glad you are all in here. I want to say something to all of you. I lost my cool. I am sorry. We can agree the stress levels have been off the damn charts tonight, right? That is no excuse. I could blame it on a lot of things, but I won't. I will own my shit. That was very poor behavior. I apologized to Tore, and now I want to apologize to the rest of you. I am sorry for my outburst."

"It's ok, Jamie. We all have our days." Charity smiled and hugged her.

"You apologized. I think we can all move on." Kerrigan was always right to the point.

Keith just looked at Jamie and nodded. No words were needed. They were both old enough to know that blow-ups sometimes happened. They both did their best to keep their attitudes in check, but sometimes they slipped up.

"Someone needs to man the desk. I'll take my break in a few, ok Jamie?" Keith said. Jamie nodded. He got up, patted Tore again, and left the breakroom.

As he left, Kerrigan looked at Jamie. "Listen, I don't mean to break up a moment here, but we need to talk."

"Uh, yeah. Sure. Tore, Charity, excuse us for a minute, ok?" Jamie wasn't sure if Kerrigan wanted to talk about the outburst, the situation on the floors below, or something else entirely. They stepped out into the hallway, out of earshot of the others.

"Benji is still downstairs. It's a mess in the ER. Not only do they have the victims of the attack, but there was also a truck vs. SUV incident that left two dead and four in critical condition. There was a bus accident. A tree fell on top of the bus. No one was gravely injured, thank God, but about twenty people had cuts and abrasions. A couple of the kids had broken limbs, wrists, or fingers, but it could have been so much worse. Rachelle said she was going to call, but she was just too busy. I had to come up and get my bag, so I told her I would talk to you. Because things are so chaotic, she wondered if she could keep Benji and me for a little while longer? There are still emergency cases that have been tended to. They can't find Mark to transport patients or Taka to clean things up. And they are missing a nurse."

"Oh my God! That is awful," Jamie said, shaking her head. "Yes. Yes. Of course, she can keep you guys. Now that Rusty is calmed down, we got this."

"Had a runner, did you?" Kerrigan said, chuckling. "That man! You know, he is surprisingly quick for a man his age— I mean for, uh, yeah...You know what I mean!"

"Indeed. We oldies can move when we want to, can't we?"

"Sorry. What I meant was—"

"I know what you meant. It's ok. He's actually got several years on me. Tonight, though, I am extremely aware that I am middle-aged. I am feeling it. So, which nurse ditched work? Was it Cathy?"

"Uh, no. It was Skyler. It's weird. She went to take a quick break, and she never came back. I guess the stress of tonight just got to her. It surprised me, though. Skyler lived for those busy nights. Listen, I need to get back downstairs. As soon as we get everything under control, Benji and I will be back up."

"Ok, Kerrigan. Sounds good. Please keep us posted. And watch yourself, ok? We still haven't heard any more about the suspect. I mean, I am sure we are safe here at the hospital, with the added security, but be careful, ok?" Jamie still had that weird off feeling. She could not shake it. Before Kerrigan left, she decided to ask. She said, "Kerrigan, how are Walt and Wanda doing?"

"What? How did you know they were hurt?"

"Andy and Mitch told me. I spoke to Rachelle, who asked me to keep it to myself. But since you were seeing things firsthand, I just wondered if you could update me. They were like family to me."

"Jame, you know I am not supposed to. But it's bad. Walt is currently in surgery, fighting for his life. Um, did you also hear about your cousin, Parker?"

"Park? What's going on with him??"

"He's downstairs as well. He was attacked, too, Jame. I am so sorry."

"Oh my God! So, I did hear the ambulance call say, 'Roasted Beans'! What the actual fuck is going on? How is he? Jesus. He's in the hospital, so he's hurt. Duh! I mean, how *bad* is he hurt?" Jamie asked hurriedly and was more than a little concerned.

"Parker is going to make a full recovery. He fought his attacker off but has the wounds to show it. Jamie, did you see him earlier this afternoon?"

"Yeah, I stopped at Roasted Beans to pick up coffee and muffins for you guys. You know that. Why?"

"Right, right....it's just... well, he said that the attacker was there just before you were. I know if you had known, you would have helped him or called the cops. But did you see anything? Hear anything? Anything at all?"

"Oh my god, no! I didn't see or hear anyth— wait a minute. I *did* hear something. Just as I left, I thought I heard a woman laughing or whistling or something outside. But I figured it was someone on the other side of the street. Oh my God! That explains why he was acting so weird. Oh God! I can't believe I was *right there*! I will try to go see him. Has he been assigned a room yet?"

"No, he is being stitched up by. Dr. Tillcourt. He was damn lucky. He had some other cuts that needed bandages, and he's gonna have some hellacious bruises, but he is going to be ok. I can text you when he has a room, if you want?"

"Yes! Please do! Has his family been notified? Or should I call Aunt Lilligrove and Uncle Mel? Or his wife, Beamy?"

"He said he called his wife. He didn't want his parents to worry. Last I knew, she was on her way. However, with the current situation and the storm, who knows when she will arrive. He might like seeing a friendly face. I don't know if you have seen any weather reports lately or even looked out a window. The storm is getting worse. Some of Heatherwilde is currently without power. I should head back down. I will text you about your cousin, ok?"

"Thanks, Kerrigan. I appreciate it. Stay safe! You got it?!"

"I will. You too. See you as soon as things calm down," Kerrigan said as she grabbed her bag and headed toward the elevator.

When Kerrigan was in the elevator and out of sight, Jamie walked up to Keith at the counter. She looked around, noticing how quiet it seemed to be.

"I am going to regret saying this..."

"Then *don't*. No jinxes, ok?" Keith looked at Jamie. He knew she was going to say that things had finally calmed down. That was the last thing that needed to be said. "I am just going to head down to the cafeteria for a quick break and then be back."

"Keith, the cafeteria is *closed*. Oh! But that might work. Can you do me a favor?"

"It is. They are testing a new self-serve feature for the second and third shift employees. Not a ton of options, but it is better than that junky old vending machine up here. Handy too, since I was in a hurry today and forgot my damn lunch. Did you forget yours as well? I can see what they have and text you."

"Oh, sweet! I hadn't heard that. We have some of the best cooks. Ed makes some of the best foods I have ever had. I am glad they are making that a new option for us. Enjoy your break. And, uh, thanks again for talking to Tore. I appreciate that, dude. I am truly sorry for the blow-up." Jamie still felt bad about losing her cool. There is a time and a place, and that wasn't it. "And no, thank you. I don't want anything from the cafeteria. I wondered if you would keep an eye out for Russell Makenin? Arlene said he went down to get her some tea, but that was hours ago. He may be over at Dick's, though. I meant to call earlier, but got busy and forgot. I am going to give them a call in a minute."

"Don't sweat it, Jamie. It's all good. And I will keep an eye out for Russell. Those two are quite a pair, aren't they? You don't often see marriages like that anymore."
Keith trailed off, lost in the hurt and pain of his own divorce. He shook his head and continued, "God, do you feel extra tired today? Or is it just me? Maybe I *am* getting too old for this!"

"Oh, I don't think so, man, because if you are too old, *I* am too old!" Jamie crossed her arms and pretended to be offended. "*Maybe* if you hadn't been chasing Rusty Brown down the hallway, you wouldn't be so tired!" She laughed. "No. it's not just you. I could use a twelve-hour nap right about now. It's this day...... *something about this day.*"

Keith nodded, grabbed his phone, and headed down the hallway to the elevator. Jamie hollered after him, "Dude, be careful tonight, ok? Just be careful." Keith gave her the thumbs up and put his phone to his ear, talking to someone through it.

Before Jamie went back to peek on Tore and Charity, whom she had left in the breakroom, she needed to make good on calling Richard's Rolls to ask about Russell. As lifelong residents of Heatherwilde Falls, everyone knew them. That made things easier. Jamie pulled out her phone and dialed their number. She knew most people didn't bother memorizing numbers anymore, but her nephew was employed there and would call to chat when he was on break, so she was familiar with the number. She nervously twirled her hair absentmindedly as she waited for someone to answer. An old habit of Jamie's that she never lost was counting the rings. So, she knew by the eighth ring that it was strange that the bakery hadn't answered. She hung up and then hit redial. The phone just kept ringing. Something didn't feel right. Jamie was sure of it. As she went to find Charity and Tore so she could fill them in on Benji and Kerrigan, she kept her eyes peeled for Bastian as well. She needed to tell him about the bakery.

"Hey, guys," Jamie said as she entered the breakroom, "Listen. Keith just went on break, and Kerrigan just went down to help in the ER. Benji is still helping. They had a bus accident to deal with, plus a nurse is MIA. So, it's going to be just us again for a little while. If it gets too bad, I will call in a few third shift nurses to help. But this means dinner breaks are going to be altered." Jamie was hoping they would be understanding.

"Oh, like we totally both just ate, so we are ready to help!" Tore said enthusiastically.

"For real?! Which nurse?" Charity raised an eyebrow. "One was Cathy, right? I had a feeling about her. She seemed way too soft spoken and gentle for the emergency room."

"Uh, no. Surprisingly, it was Skyler—"

"Skyler? No. Uh uh. She *lives* for emergencies! Has anyone looked for her?"

"I guess so. But no one can find her. I don't know much. Evidently, Skyler went on break and never returned. It's not like her for sure. I will keep you posted. I know you two are friends. I am heading back to finish my paperwork. When you two are done cleaning up, can you meet me at the nurses' station to divvy up patients again?" Jamie asked. The women both nodded in response, and Jamie walked back out of the breakroom.

"I am going to try texting Skyler. Maybe she and Walker got into a fight again, and she is just hiding in the bathroom." Charity said, trying to be more hopeful than she was feeling at that point. She pulled out her phone and texted Skyler, *Hey, Girl! What's up? Wya?* She waited a few moments and then tucked her phone back into her front pocket. She shrugged and thought, *It's a busy night. I'll try again in a few minutes. She is probably just taking a breather.*

Tore and Charity got up from the table. Since they ate while talking, their breaks were over. They just had to clear the table and tidy up. Tore swept her hand across the table, sweeping the crumbs into her other waiting hand. She dumped them in the trash bin. Charity grabbed the little carpet sweeper, pulled out the chairs, and rolled around under the table. Suddenly, they heard a ringing. Tore and Charity looked at each other.

"That's a funny ringtone you have on your phone, Charity," Tore said.

"That's not my phone. My phone is right here. On silent."

They looked at each other and then up to the phone sitting on top of the refrigerator, in front of the broken wall. It was ringing again. Charity put the sweeper back in the corner, and they hesitantly walked up to the refrigerator together.

Without thinking, Tore reached up and grabbed the phone. She was surprised by how heavy it was. As she held it in her hands, marveling at the size of it, she picked up the handset, put it to her ear, and enthusiastically said, "Um, hellooo!"

"Hello? Hello, are you there?"

Chapter Six

Tore had the handset up to her ear, listening. *Wow! Like this is soooo cool,* she thought. The handset was heavy. Not at all what Tore was expecting, and certainly not what she was used to with her cell phone. She wasn't sure what she thought it would be like, but she didn't expect it to be so clunky. *Like I cannot imagine having to use a phone like this,* she thought. *Thank God I never had to!*

"Hello? Are..are you there?" Val said again.

"Like, HI THERE! Is this Val again?"

"Yes! Is this Tore?" Val said in a hushed, yet excited, voice.

"Like, yeah! You remembered my name? Wow, that's so awesome!"

Tore was thrilled; someone remembered her name for no reason and not because they were angry with her. Charity, however, was creeped out. They had only given their names once, during a stressful time. She didn't understand how a little girl could remember that.

"Oh yes, I remember. Can you help me? Please?"

"Like, of course I can! What do you need?" Tore was always eager to help.

Val's tone became slightly raspy as she spoke even more softly. "I am so hungry," she told Tore. A weird sound was made after she spoke. It was too faint to know for sure what it was. Charity heard it as well but had no idea what she was hearing. All she knew was that she was starting to get very creeped out. Tore did not need to be answering that phone right now. They had enough going on. Charity knew in her gut that this was a huge mistake. She grabbed the handset out of Tore's hand and covered the mouthpiece.

"Like HEY! What are you doing, Charity?!" Tore was just trying to help and hated when people took over, pushed her aside, or made her feel like she was doing something wrong. She was not a child and hated being treated like one.

"Tore, what the fuck is going on? We already spoke to this girl. Reid was supposed to find her and take her back to PEDS, remember?! Where is he? Why is she calling again? Better yet, *how* is she calling again? She should be back in her hospital bed or back with her parents. Something doesn't add up here." Charity was speaking in a hushed tone, but her voice was showing her irritation.

Tore looked at her with her wide eyes open even more. Her mouth was entirely agape. She had forgotten that Reid was supposed to find the girl. She told Charity, "Like you know, Reid. He probably got to chatting with someone and lost track of time. You know how he is. He loves to visit."

"That was hours ago, Tore," Charity said a little more urgently.

"OMG! Like, what!?" Tore preferred not to overthink anything. She liked simple things. She once read that happy thoughts lead to a happy life, so she glossed over the hard stuff. But this left her wondering. She looked at Charity and said, "Like, what do you want me to say?"

"Ask her about Reid!"

Tore took the handset back, put it back up to her ear, and said, "Um, Val? Didn't Reid find you? He was totally coming down to get you, remember?"

"Oh yes, I remember. He's not here. But there was a lot of noise here earlier. It sounded like fighting," Val said in a weird tone. Charity looked at Tore, trying to figure it out. *Was it anticipation... or something else? So weird!*

"Can you come find me, Tore? I am so hungry." Val said.

"Like yes! Of course I can!!" said Tore happily. The weirdness of the situation went right over her head. Instead, she was in helping mode. Charity looked at her, mouth wide open, her hands out, open-palmed in a *what in the hell* kind of stance. She smacked Tore across the arm.

"OW, Charity! That so completely violated my personal space!" Tore huffed. "I should totally make sure Jamie talks to you about abusing your coworkers. That was so not cool!"

Charity grabbed the handset out of Tore's hands and covered the mouthpiece again. She glared at Tore and said, "GO AHEAD! Report me. Whatever. But don't say you are going to help this....this.. *girl.* We have no clue what is going on. Why didn't Reid find her? Where is he? Where in the hell is she calling from? You can't just say *yes,* Tore! For fucks sake!"

"Charity, you don't need to be like, so mean and violent. I am only trying to help. Like, Reid is probably just talking with people downstairs and hasn't made it to Val yet."

"Except we have extra security right now because a potential murderer is on the loose! *Remember?!*"

Charity and Tore heard rustling on the other end of the phone call. They looked at each other, trying to figure out what they were hearing. It almost sounded to them like Val was struggling with something or someone. Tore grabbed the phone away from Charity.

"Val? Val? OMG! Are you ok? What's going on?"

"Yes, I am ok," the little girl said, sounding faintly out of breath.

Charity looked at Tore with one eyebrow raised. She had her arms crossed, and her face was filled with concern. She wasn't concerned about the little girl. She was worried about the bad feeling she was getting about the entire situation.

"Please, can someone come find me?" Val asked so softly they almost couldn't hear her.

Tore looked defiantly at Charity and answered, "Like, of course, Val. I will be right down to get you. For sure, don't worry, ok?"

"Oh, goodie," said Val. Again, her tone seemed off to Charity. She still couldn't quite figure it out. Charity swore it almost sounded like a hiss.

"Ok, so listen, it could be dangerous staying where you are, k? So, like, do you think you could step out into the hallway and wait for me? That will make it so much easier for me to find you. I sooo don't know the hospital the way that Reid does. And on the way back to PEDS, we will try to find Reid, Ok? Like, does that sound like something you can do?"

"Yes! I can do that," Val said enthusiastically. Tore and Charity heard a sudden click, and the line went dead. Tore put the handset back on the phone. Charity looked at Tore, pissed as hell at her.

"What in the hell are you doing, Tore?! We are short-staffed. Kerrigan and Benji are still downstairs. Skyler, Mark, and Taka are MIA, and Reid is missing. *And* our hospital is on high alert because a murderer is *on the loose*! Girl, what are you *thinking*?" Charity loved Tore, but some days that girl was more than half a bubble off. The fact that she would do that made Charity livid!

"Like, I don't think the murderer on the loose *is in the hospital,* or we would be locked down completely, Charity. Right? Like it'll be totally fine. I am just going to head down to the mechanical room. I am sure there are signs, k? Plus, I told her to wait out in the hallway so, like I could find her easier. It'll totally be easy," Tore said, obstinately. She was bound and determined to be the hero. She would find the girl *and* Reid. She would show everyone that she wasn't a child, but a dedicated and hardworking nurse.

Charity stared at Tore. "I don't think you should do that, Tore!"

"I am going, and you can't stop me, Charity!" She turned on her heels and went to head out the door. Charity followed her out of the breakroom and yelled at her, "If you insist on going to the mechanical room, take this!" Charity handed her pepper spray.

"Oh! You had *two*?!" Tore gasped. "That is like soooo against polic—"

"We have been over this, Tore. *Woman, second shifter* and all that....." Charity said, exasperated.

"Oh, riiiight." Tore said, taking the container from Charity. "Thank you," she said sheepishly. Tore tucked it in her pocket, walked down to the service elevator, and was gone without so much as a glance back.

Oh god dammit! Charity ran down the hall towards the nurses' station. She needed to let Jamie know what was going on. She couldn't believe Tore would be so reckless! Charity knew she was a dingbat at times, but Tore had never done anything so rash before.

While Tore and Charity were busy with the strange phone, Jamie was hurriedly trying to find Bastian. First, she walked down to Arlene's room and peeked in. Arlene had fallen asleep after her meal, which was a good thing. But Russell wasn't in the room either, which was bad. *Where in the hell could he be? And why didn't anyone answer at the bakery?* She turned around and headed down the hallway in a focused, intent manner. She was so lost in thought that she didn't watch where she was going and ran right into someone.

"Ooomph. Sorry! Sorry!" Jamie said as she stumbled backward. "That was on me!"

"Careful, Jamie. You gotta be more careful. You are gonna hurt yourself," said a very deep but calm-voiced man. He reached out to steady her.

Jamie looked up to see that she had walked right into Bastian. She was relieved to see him and needed to fill him in right away. She grabbed his hand and pulled him toward an empty hallway, away from patients and staff's listening ears.

"Bastian! I was looking for you! Did you have any luck finding Russell? I called over to Dick's, and no one answered. I tried twice. Unless they changed their hours, they should still be open. Last I knew, they were open until at least nine o'clock. It's weird and I don't like it. I have a bad feeling about that. Did you find anything out? Please tell me you did...." Jamie's tired voice trailed off. She looked up at Bastian with concern in her eyes.

"No. I called down to speak with Glen. He hadn't seen him at all. I even called the second floor. No luck. The cafeteria is closed, but I did try calling down to see if Jillie, Rhonda, or Corston might still be cleaning up. I think everyone cleared out early because of the storm, because I couldn't get an answer. Wait. What do you mean, no one answered?!"

"Yeah, no one answered. I called twice just to be sure."

"Well, that doesn't seem good...."

"That's what I thought. But I don't know. Is the storm getting intense? Maybe their phone line is down or something."

"Yeah, I think the winds have started to gust outside. So maybe. Wait, phone *lines*? Don't they have an internet phone like, well, everyone else?"

"No. Richard wanted no part of it. Hell, they still use the old swipe credit card readers sometimes. His family has tried to get him to switch over to electronic and digital, but he refuses. He's ninety-three. What do you do? You know, if the wind gusts are bad enough, maybe that knocked out their phones. I hope. It feels strange, though."

Just then, Bastian got a call. Jamie didn't know who it was. He didn't say much, but his face drained of all color. Whatever it was, it wasn't good news. Jamie clenched her jaw, preparing for bad news. Instead, Bastian said, "We will get to the bottom of it, Jamie. *And* we will find Russell. I am sure he is around here somewhere. I will keep my eye out for him. But I need to find Robert and Eiler. I can't talk right now. We will be back and watching the elevators and stairwells."

"Okaaay.... Thanks, Bastian. I assume all is not right in the world right now. Fill me in when you can. I will call the other floors again to see if anyone has seen Russell. Catch ya later."

With that, Bastian hurried down the hallway in the opposite direction. Jamie headed back up to the nurses' station. It was quiet at that moment so Jamie figured she would have time to call the other floors. *Someone must have seen him,* Jamie thought. She decided to try Dick's Buns again, figuring it couldn't hurt.

Chapter Seven

Jamie sat down in a chair at the desk. She put her hand out to pick up the handset of the phone when it rang. Jamie quickly answered and heard Jerelle speak. Jamie sat in the chair silently. She had no words for what she was hearing. She managed to mumble an "okay" as she dug around for the official paperwork. Jamie hung up the phone, stunned. She was trying to process what Jerelle had just told her when she heard footsteps rapidly approaching. She turned to look.

"Jamie, we have an issue," Charity said as she ran up to the counter.

"Yeah, we do." Jamie turned to her. She was pale and visibly shaken. "Me first. Here is the paperwork for emergency protocol. You can read it. I just did. I don't know about you, but I have been lucky enough never to need to know that information. We need it now, though. Here is the situation. Jerelle just called from the ER. While walking through the hallways, someone noticed fresh blood smears on a doorway and on some of the handrails along the walls. They *think*, lemme repeat, they *think* the murder suspect could be hiding in our hospital. To keep everyone safe, we are fully locked down. No one in or out. The police are on their way, but they have had their hands full this evening as well. The third shift was supposed to be here soon, but they won't be let in now. We are on our own. While the floors remain unlocked for the time being, they *are* asking us all to stay in our designated areas. I know you carry your cellphone. Make sure to put it on silent. We don't want the patients to find out right now. Bastian told me that he, Robert, and Eiler will be keeping a close eye on the stairwells and elevators. If you see anyone suspicious, hit the panic button on your key fob. But as I mentioned, the police were notified and are on their way. We do not tell the patients, and don't breathe a word to Rusty Brown. We tend to their needs as we normally would. It's nighttime, so most of our patients should be sleeping right now." Jamie was clearly trying to project an image of unconcern, but she was not doing a good job at it. Charity could see how worried she was. "So," Jamie said, "What was your news?"

"That damn phone rang again—"

"What?! What the hell! You didn't answer it, did you?"

"I didn't. But Tore did." Charity shook her head.

"Oh, good god. Please tell me that she did not leave the floor."

"Uh, yup. She spoke to that 'Val' again, and then she fricking took off. I tried to talk her out of it, but she wouldn't listen. I was able to give her my other pepper spray, though."

"Oh, what is that girl's damage? This is dangerous! Why is she being so reckless?" Jamie couldn't believe it. Or rather, she could because it was Tore. Tore, who always tried to help. Tore, who was young, naive, and trusting. Tore, who had the biggest and kindest heart of any of them. *Of course, she left. She is a great nurse. We all know it,* Jamie thought.

"Wait a minute. Where is Reid? He was supposed to get that Val and take her back to PEDS or her parents. Why didn't that happen? Where is he? Is this some prank after all? What in the hell is going on?"

Charity put her arms up, shrugged, and said, "We don't know. We asked Val, and all she told us was that he wasn't there. That's it. Oh, and that she was hungry. This whole thing is so weird, Jamie. It is starting to creep me out. At least the cops are coming. When do Kerrigan and Benji get back up here?"

"I don't know. I don't think they can right now. I will try to call down to the ER and get some information. Maybe Reid just got caught up talking again. Come to think of it, Keith didn't come back from his dinner break either……" Jamie looked at Charity, not even trying to conceal the concern at this point. "Oh, what the fuck? Russell Makenin is missing. Reid is missing. Keith hasn't come back from break yet. And now Tore took off? Fucking great." Jamie knew she should try to watch her language, but work manners were the last thing on her mind.

"Russell is missing?" Charity gasped.

"Well, maybe? I don't honestly know. We can't locate him. I didn't know he had been here. Bastian and Monika had seen him with Arlene earlier, but no one has seen him since, I guess," Jamie said.

Just then, the phone rang. Both women jumped. Charity gasped and grabbed her heart. Jamie made a fist with one hand and reached out to grab the phone with the other. She put the handset up to her ear. Charity couldn't hear who was speaking, but the look on Jamie's face said it wasn't good news.

"Hello, third-floor nurses' station, this is Jamie. Oh, Hi, Amber. They did? Ok. Yes, I can do that. Sure. What about— Yeah, sure. That works. Have her call first, ok? And use the service elevator. Keep me posted. Be safe! Wait! Amber, have you seen Russell Makenin? Or Reid? No? Uh, it's a long story. If you see them, have them come back up to the third floor asap, please? Great! Thanks, Amber."

Charity had been standing with her arms crossed. She was scanning and watching Jamie's body language, looking for clues. But she saw none. She looked expectantly at Jamie, wanting answers. Whatever the call was about, it couldn't have been good news. She could tell by the look on Jamie's face. Charity was trying to brace herself for it.

"Well, Amber just got a call from her wife, Drea."

"I know Drea. She's a good cop and a great person."

"She is. Drea wasn't supposed to say anything, but she was concerned for all of us, so she did. They have a lead on the suspect. His name is Valerian Manchester. He is five feet five inches tall, of a slender build, and has brown or black hair. His distinguishing characteristic is that he has a higher-pitched voice and a wide, weird smile. He was last seen heading towards the hospital. That was hours ago, I guess? Amber didn't know much more except that the police were looking for him as the suspect in the gruesome murders and attacks. I guess he is considered armed and very dangerous, which is why Andrea called to let her know. She asked us to please share the information with our coworkers, but not the patients. Frankie has already spoken with the security teams here, and they are aware. The police should be here very soon, and they will search the premises. Things have calmed down on her floor right now with the lockdown, so she is sending Kerrigan back up after she sends Tawny to dinner break. Skyler never did come back, so she asked if she could keep Benji for the time being. I told her that it was fine. We are quiet— no jinx— right now and are managing up here without him. Do you think you could help me make sure the patients are all sleeping? We need to make sure Rusty is asleep and not listening in, ok? The *last* thing we need is for him to be all riled up. It'll snowball. I can take one side of the hall if you can take the other?"

"Holy shit, Jamie. What the hell is with this night, huh? This is starting to really annoy me. Yeah, I can take one side and check on the patients. How are you, though? You alright?" She looked at Jamie's pale face with concern. She loved Jamie. They had worked together for decades. Charity viewed her as the big sister she never had. Seeing Jamie so shaken was something she wasn't used to.

Charity was doing her best to take in everything she had just heard, but she had a million thoughts running through her head. She wondered if her husband and kids were ok. She couldn't decide if she was more low-key angry or worried about Tore. That sound she heard from the little girl was eating at her, too. And to top it off, they potentially had a murderer in the hospital? *Ugh, this night can take a flying leap*, she thought as she waited for Jamie to respond.

Jamie groaned. All she wanted to do today was care for some patients, study some more, and then go home. This was not the kind of day she ever dreamed of having. It fit right in with the off and weird feeling everyone was getting. And she couldn't shake that nagging feeling that something about all of that was familiar. "Yeah, I am ok, I guess. After we are done, let's come back here so we can make a plan regarding Tore, ok?" Jamie knew not a lot could be done, but maybe if she started calling the other floors, she could locate Reid, Tore, and this Val person.

"Yup. Sounds like a plan."

"I will meet up with you in a second. I just need a minute, ok?" Jamie asked, sounding tired and defeated.

"You don't have to ask, sis. Take a breath. I will get started. I think most everyone is sleeping, so it should be a quick peek."

Jamie nodded and tried to smile. Instead, it ended up resembling a grimace. She put her head into her hands and leaned down on the desk, deep in thought. She was having a hard time wrapping her head around everything that had been going on. Her cousin was attacked. Walt and Wanda Anbrena were also attacked. Keith didn't come back from break. Skyler was missing. Mark and Taka were missing. Reid never came back after heading down to find the little girl. Tore did the same thing. Jamie was now highly suspicious of this Val person. She couldn't figure out how all the dots connected, but she felt they somehow did. Jamie shook her head. She needed to solve the only issue she could. She was now down several nurses. Even though it was nighttime, she knew that wouldn't do. That problem she could fix. She decided to call and see if she could borrow a nurse from the second floor. At least until the mess was over and the third shift was allowed in. Having a plan made Jamie feel better. She got up with determination and set off to peek in on her patients.

Chapter Eight

Jamie got back to the nurses' station first. It seemed like hours of nervousness waiting for Charity to arrive, but Jamie knew it was only minutes. She tried getting her books out to study, but she couldn't concentrate. Not with that nagging feeling. Jamie couldn't decide if it was Déjà vu or a familiarity or something else entirely. She absentmindedly stared at the computer screen in front of her while nervously tapping her nails on the desk when the phone rang. She jumped and grabbed the handset.

"Hello? Nurses' station, this is — Oh, hi, Kerrigan. Yes. I can do that. Oh really? Yeah, that would be awesome! Thank you! That saves me from having to make a call. Tell her I appreciate it. Alright. See you. Hey! Be careful!" Jamie hung the phone up, relieved that Kerrigan was on her way back up to their floor. She had a lot to catch up on. None of it was good. Jamie needed to find Charity and fill her in. As she turned, Charity approached the counter.

"Hey. How'd it go? Was everyone sleeping?"

"Uh, yeah, mostly," Charity nodded. "The few that were awake knew something was going on because an emergency broadcast went out for everyone to stay inside and lock their doors. That was all that was said. But that is bad enough. I dodged their questions the best I could."

"Ugh. Sorry. I don't know how any of this works," Jamie said to Charity, shaking her head. Just then, Bastian walked by.

"Hey, Bastian. Kerrigan is on her way back up here. She is bringing River up here to help us. They will both be using the service elevator. I just wanted to give you a heads up."

"Thank you for that. Are they on their way now? I can head down and escort them off, if they are," Bastian said. Jamie nodded.

"I will go get them. You gals be safe," Bastian said as he headed down the hallway to the elevator.

"River is coming up here? From the second floor? How'd you swing that?" Charity was looking at Jamie with a puzzled look on her face.

Jamie shrugged, "I didn't have to do anything. I was going to call when you got back here and beg Ana to borrow someone. Kerrigan ran into River while she was downstairs. Since Benji is staying in the ER to help out on the first floor, she took it upon herself to ask if we could borrow River. She followed him up to the second floor to ask Ana if he might be able to fill in here for a bit. That girl is always on the ball. And man am I grateful right now."

"Well, lucky us. River is an awesome nurse. I worked with him a few times when I filled in on the second floor. Ugh, poor Kerrigan. She has no idea what's been happening here...." Charity's voice trailed off.

Jamie heard the elevator bell ding down the hall. She was relieved they had finally arrived. She had been worrying about Kerrigan and Benji. Soon, Bastian, Kerrigan, and River appeared. They all smiled and nodded at each other.

"I am headed back down the other hall," Bastian said. He paused. After looking at Jamie, he said, "Are you doing ok?" She was not looking very well, which gave him concern. She looked tired and pale. And worried. Very worried. It wasn't like her.

Jamie looked up at Bastian and kind of gave a sort of nod while also putting her arms out in an *I don't know* kind of gesture and said, "Uh, yeah. I am ok. Or as good as it gets right now."

"Charity, you ok as well?" After seeing her nod her head yes, Bastian continued, "Robert, Eiler, and I are all right here. We are keeping a very watchful eye out, ok? If we see anything funny at all, you will know. And if you see something, you have your panic buttons, right?" Jamie and Charity nodded at him. So did Kerrigan and River, though River wasn't sure what was going on. "If you need *anything*, anything at all, you know where to find me." Bastian continued, "It's going to be ok. You are all going to be ok, all right?"

Bastian had such a calming quality about him. Jamie wondered why he had never pursued a different field. He would have been great as a therapist, guidance counselor, or even a psychiatrist. He had such a calm demeanor and soothing voice. He was a wonderful addition to their hospital, and she was so grateful he was on duty that night. She looked up at him and half attempted a smile.

"Thank you, Bastian. I appreciate that. You be careful, ok? I mean it, man. I'll be pissed if you aren't. And you won't like me when I am angry." Jamie chuckled and made a fist.

Bastian chuckled. Jamie was always stubborn, but he had grown accustomed to it. There he was trying to calm her down, and she was threatening him to be careful. She was an excellent nurse. He knew she would make a great nurse practitioner. She had a big heart and sincerely cared about others. But he also knew that she was not one to be pushed around or messed with. Bastian always told her that she had a heart of gold and fists of fury. She would laugh and laugh and then make a fist and say, "You won't like me when I am angry!" Bastian loved that about her. She was a very dear friend and coworker whom he respected greatly.

Bastian laughed. He looked directly at her and said, "I *will*, Jamie. I promise!" He turned around and headed down the hallway in the other direction.

Since Kerrigan had been downstairs with Tawny, Amber, Jerelle, Rachelle, Prue, and Cathy, she already knew some of the night's crises. But River knew nothing about what was happening. He stood looking a bit bewildered. He knew the hospital was on lockdown, but everything was hushed, especially on the second floor. It seemed more might be going on than he had been told. He looked expectantly at them both, waiting for more information.

"So, ah, what, what's going on? I know we are on lockdown. My floor is being extremely cautious. I heard there were murders and a suspect on the loose. That's about all I know. Care to share with the rest of the class?"

Jamie liked River. She had also worked with him several times when she had filled in on the second floor. He was younger than her, but by only a few years. Where she was sometimes rough around the edges, River had no edges. He was an all-around great guy. He was intelligent, kind, compassionate, and just loved being a nurse. Jamie was so glad to see him. Not only was he a good guy, but he was also quite tall and muscular with a solid frame. Coupled with his dark eyes and dark hair, he looked quite formidable. For that reason, it made her feel safer. She knew he wasn't security. And she knew, as big as he was, he was a giant teddy bear of a man. But he was big enough that Jamie figured his size alone might deter anyone from messing with them.

Charity looked at him and said, "That ain't the half of it."

Jamie shot her a look and made the zipped lips sign. She had decided to leave out the crazy phone calls for right now. She still didn't know what that was, and didn't need to worry people unnecessarily. She deemed it "need to know". For the time being, she decided that River didn't need to know.

Jamie continued to look at Kerrigan and River while she said, "ok, well, lots to talk about. Where should I start? You know the hospital is on lockdown. They found blood smeared on the first floor. I mean, the ER is on that floor, so it could be anything. But as a precaution, since the murder suspect was last seen near here, we went into lockdown. Third shifters can't come in right now. We are on our own, which is why I am so grateful to have you up here, River. Anyway, yeah, lockdown... It's uncharted territory for me."

Jamie was starting to lose her train of thought. She was tired and stressed. But her mind was preoccupied with the thought, *Who is that little girl who keeps calling? Is it a sick prank?* She shook her head, gathered her thoughts, and continued, "What we know so far is that there were multiple victims: some fatalities, some in critical condition. The police are aware and are en route. However, the storm has become intense. Trees and lines are down. And I have been told several accidents have occurred tonight. So, it could take some time for them to arrive. Now, what has not been shared with the rest of the class, but I will share with you, is that it appears the police have a name and description, and that he was, in fact, last spotted near the hospital. We all have added security. Tekonsha and Liatris should have joined Toby on your floor—"

"No. Tek came in tonight, and then he called Liatris in. Toby never showed up for his shift, I guess. Tek tried calling him a few times, but it just kept going to voicemail. It's just Liatris and Tek."

"What? We seem to have a lot of that going on around here. I guess Skyler, Mark, and Taka also went missing. And Keith—"

"Keith's not here?" Kerrigan said, eyes wide as she looked at Jamie.

"No. He said he was going to try out the new self-serve program the cafeteria had started and come back. I know he was worried about his parents. So maybe he stepped outside to call them before we went on lockdown..." Jamie's voice trailed off, knowing it didn't sound plausible. "Or. Or, you know, maybe they just won't let him back up on this floor. Kerrigan, you didn't see him when you were down in the ER, did you?"

"No. I didn't. So, Keith isn't here, and Toby never showed up? What in the hell is going on here tonight?" Kerrigan generally wasn't one to swear, so Jamie knew the usual levelheaded Kerrigan was starting to be concerned.

"Huh. Yeah, this *is* a weird night. We had a nurse not come back from break as well," River said.

"Who was that?" Jamie asked, trying to keep the concern out of her voice.

"Zephabelle. She said she was going on break, and we never saw her again. We assumed, since she was new here, that she had just walked off the job. I saw Arrow in the hall and asked him if he had seen her. He told me that as he was taking a patient down for X-rays, he thought he saw her headed down toward the cafeteria. We tried calling her phone, but it appeared to be shut off. What is going on here?"

"Honestly, I have no idea. But it doesn't seem good. Why was Arrow taking someone to X-ray? Where was Hunter?"

"Uh..We haven't seen Hunter in a while..." River said.

"What in the hell? I will see if I can get in touch with Rachelle and talk to her. River, can you man the desk while I talk to Kerrigan and Charity for a second?"

"Yeah, sure. No problem. Happy to help."

"Thank you. We will just be in the breakroom. Holler if things start to pick up, ok?"

River gave a thumbs up, so Jamie, Charity, and Kerrigan headed toward the breakroom. Kerrigan looked expectantly at the other two. She was really annoyed that Jamie would ask for help and then leave River alone. She wasn't sure she believed a murderer was on the loose in the hospital, but she also knew it was wise to be cautious. *She wanted help and then left River at the nurses' station. This had better be good*, she thought.

Before Jamie could even open her mouth, Charity blurted, "There is a weird phone that Jamie answered and spoke to a little girl on and Jamie thought it might be a prank but Reid went down to find her because he thought she wandered away from

PEDS or her parents but Reid never came back and the phone rang again and this time Tore answered and it was the little girl again but she said she never saw Reid so Tore went to go find her *and* Reid and now it's just a fucking mess and I am pissed as hell!" Charity stopped and gasped for breath.

"*WHAT?!*" Kerrigan stared at the two of them. She was so confused. She didn't know whether to be pissed or worried or a little of both. She was shocked and didn't know which part to focus on first. She was struggling to wrap her head around what Charity had just said. "What phone? What on earth are you talking about?"

Charity and Jamie pointed to the top of the refrigerator. Kerrigan's gaze followed their fingers, and on top of the fridge, sat the dirty, old rotary phone. It was dusty and had drywall dust fingerprints all over it. But there it sat. She turned to Jamie and said, "What the actual fuck?"

"Dude, I don't know, ok. I have no idea what is going on. Yeah, it's weird as hell, and it's pissing me off. At first, we thought it might be a prank. But then Reid said he pretty much knew where she was, so we figured she must have wandered away from the pediatric ward. Or maybe her parents or something. I don't know. Reid went to get her. That was hours ago. While Tore and Charity were in here having a dinner break, I guess it rang again. The little girl said her name was Valentine, Val for short. When she described her location, Reid thought it was the mechanical room because he saw an exit sign still hanging on a walled-up door. He knows this hospital inside and out, so he said he wanted to go get her." Jamie was back to making fists with her hands, but was now also kind of pacing. "I knew I should have trusted my gut and called the police! I knew it. God dammit. Now Keith and Tore are missing too." She fell into a chair, tears running down her cheeks. Typically, she was a calm, cool, and collected kind of person. But that was too much for Jamie. When she became extremely angry or frustrated, she would sometimes cry. Most of the time, Jamie fought that off, but not that night. Not in that moment. Charity sat down beside her, holding her hand while she silently cried.

Kerrigan had a hard time believing any of that. It sounded like a story someone made up. If she hadn't seen the phone with her own eyes and known the women so well, she never would have believed that. Some of it didn't quite add up. She had a lot of questions. Kerrigan was levelheaded and sensible. She liked dealing with facts and logic. She needed more information to figure everything out. She sat down in a chair directly across from them both and started asking.

"Firstly, *why* did you answer the phone?"

"Because it was *ringing?* What in the hell was I supposed to do?" Jamie snapped. She was getting a little perturbed. She didn't like feeling like she had done something wrong.

"Yeah, ok. Sorry. I would have done the same thing."

"Sorry. I didn't mean to bite your head off. We did talk about calling the police, but like I said, I didn't know if it was a prank or real or what, and I know the police have been busy," Jamie said defensively.

"I get it. I understand why you didn't. They seem to have their hands full tonight. When did all of this start?" Kerrigan asked them, unfazed by Jamie's attitude.

Charity and Jamie thought back. "It started right before we found out about the murders," Jamie said. Thinking back, the timeline was very close. "Do you remember Tore talking about the ringing she was hearing? It started then."

"Huh. A while ago. Okay, what was Val asking you to do? What made you think it was *not* a prank?"

"Well, I mean, I *did* think it was a prank at first. Who calls an old phone? Not to mention *how* does someone call it. I don't even know what number that phone is assigned. But the more I spoke to her, the more I began to believe her. She sounded—" Jamie gasped. She had always thought what she heard in Val's voice was nervousness and fear, but thinking back now, Jamie thought it was more like nervous excitement and anticipation. "Oh my god. Oh my god! What the ever-loving hell? That girl sounded *excited*."

Charity gasped. She became very pale. As pale as Jamie was. Charity knew Jamie was right. That was what had been bothering her. That and the strange noise.

Kerrigan said, "Ok, now we are getting somewhere." As the two other nurses looked at her, they were puzzled.

"How so?" Charity asked. She felt like she was pretty good at those whodunit games and books. She loved any true crime show. She knew she was intelligent, but she wasn't following Kerrigan's line of thinking.

"Well, if it sounded like excitement in her voice, then your first assumption was probably correct. She is playing a game. She is thrilled to have people looking for her. I have worked with people who would enjoy negative attention over no attention. This 'Val' must be desperately seeking to get the attention she craves. So, my next question.... Are you *sure* you are talking to a little girl?"

Both Jamie's and Charity's mouths fell open, and they looked at each other. They knew that voices could be difficult at times. When Jamie was young, she was often mistaken for her younger brother. It wasn't until after puberty, when Albert's voice became much lower, that it stopped. Now she had to think about Kerrigan's question. *She sounded like a little girl. Why didn't I question that? Why did I assume?*

Jamie looked at Kerrigan and said, "No, I'm not. I am not sure. I just assumed that because her voice sounded higher and lighter, it was a little girl. She also gave us a feminine-sounding name, 'Valetine'. So yeah, I guess I just jumped the gun. I should have asked. Where are you going with this? Do you think we are dealing with an adult? Wait a minute! The description of the suspect said the male had a higher-pitched voice. Are you talking about *him*?!"

"Oh my god. I just assumed she was a little girl as well. You guys," Charity said with worry in her voice now. "Tore and Reid went down to get that person."

"Uh, no. I don't think you are talking to a male with a higher voice, let alone some murder suspect. But I am thinking you are dealing with a very sick, *very adult* female. Whether she somehow took off from the psych ward or just wandered into the hospital, or was waiting to be seen, I think you are dealing with a young woman, not a child. This changes the dynamic. She could be armed and waiting for people to find her to try to take her back up to her room. Or she may be trying to avoid being committed. Or she may be playing some weird cat-and-mouse type of game. Like I said, getting attention might be the key. Either way, it isn't good. You said both Reid *and* Tore went down to get her? What about Keith? Did he go as well?"

Kerrigan was always so levelheaded. Jamie regretted not telling her everything before then. Maybe if she had, Tore, Reid, and Keith wouldn't be missing. She hung her head. She felt so off that night, and it was showing. She guessed that the Déjà vu feeling had impacted her more than she thought. She was forgetting things and making stupid decisions because she couldn't shake the familiarity of something. She made fists again and shook her head. *Get it together, girl. Quit being so daffy,* she thought. She looked at Kerrigan and continued.

"No, Keith went to the cafeteria for dinner. He didn't have anything to do with the calls. I told him about them, though. Christ, I can't believe I didn't even consider that she could be an adult. How fucking dumb. I am so sorry. As we sit here discussing this, everything you are saying makes sense. I clearly just assumed she was a child, and I shouldn't have done that. I should have considered all the options."

"Hey, it's ok. Don't beat yourself up, Jame. I, uh, happen to have experience with women with mental health issues. Um.." Kerrigan cleared her throat, clearly upset. "Yeah, so my mother when I was growing up was not mentally stable. She had ups and downs and everything in between. She was also a drunk. There were many times when she was so bad that my siblings and I hid from her in the cupboards or closets. She would giggle and use a soft sing-song voice, almost baby talk, trying to coax us out. One night, my younger sister decided to go to her. She left our hiding spot and went up to our sweet-talking, giggling mom, who instantly turned into a heinous being and beat her. She wouldn't stop. She said my sister needed to be punished for disobeying. My other sister and I had to tackle her. As we were trying to pull our sister away from her, she fell backward, hitting her head on the table as she went down."

Jamie and Charity sat quietly, still, completely stunned. They had no idea that Kerrigan had gone through so much. She was such an exceptional nurse—so kind, caring, and compassionate. She was always the first to offer help and handled anything that came her way. But she never talked about her personal life. They just assumed she was an extremely private person. It never occurred to them that there might be a very good reason why she kept to herself. As they tried to process what Kerrigan had just shared, she continued.

"When the police and ambulance arrived, we were taken to my aunt's house. My mother was treated at the hospital, and they ended up committing her. My aunt wasn't much better. I mean, she didn't drink, but she wasn't prepared to take three nieces in permanently. She traveled a lot for work. She was out of the country more than she was at home. So, I ended up raising my sisters. After I finished college and started working, I got us all an apartment. I never spoke to my aunt or mother again. My youngest sister still visits my aunt. And my middle sister goes to visit my mother. I just tried to start fresh, you know? What you are describing to me sounds very similar to what I dealt with growing up. Attention. Give them attention. They crave attention. For my mother, it didn't matter what kind. In her sick mind, if we yelled at her because we were angry, it meant we still cared enough to talk. But if we went silent while angry, she would chase us down, following us into our rooms, demanding that we forgive her, all while blaming us for being mad at something she had done. She would seem so kind and caring one minute and turn into the vilest thing a second later. It was a constant roller coaster. We never knew which mood she was going to be in, so we walked on eggshells all the time. It was such a twisted way to live. I am hoping that's not the case with that, Val, but it's just giving me such familiar vibes...."

Charity and Jamie each grabbed one of Kerrigan's hands that were tightly clasped together on the table. They squeezed her hands and just held them for a minute. No one needed to say anything. They just let Kerrigan be in that moment and get rid of whatever trauma she needed to. Jamie couldn't believe what poor Kerrigan had gone through. It was so awful. And yet out of something so horrible came a sweet, kind, and caring person that Jamie was so grateful to know. After a few minutes had passed, Jamie spoke up.

"You know you aren't alone, right? We are always here for you. You do not need to carry that burden anymore. Let us help you, ok? God, Kerrigan, I dearly love you. You are such an awesome person. It breaks my heart to think that you went through all of that. If you start to feel overwhelmed or stressed or whatever, come talk to me. Or Charity. We are here for you."

"For sure, girl. You know you can talk to me about anything. Sure, I can get sassy at times. But I mean well. And my bark is always worse than my bite. Well, *most* of the time..." Charity smiled and winked at Kerrigan, trying to lighten the mood a little. "For real, though, I am so sorry you went through all of that. Man, I thought I had it bad with a dad who took off when I was three. That wasn't anything. My momma managed just fine. I assume your dad must have taken off as well?"

"Yup. He said he had a business trip and never came back. I was five at the time. I spoke to him on the phone once, for my sixth birthday, asking when he was going to come home. He told me he couldn't deal with my mom. I found out years later that he had remarried and had a new family. I have zero interest in meeting any of them. He left me to deal with my crazy mother when I was little. I decided I could lead a perfectly happy life without either of them. And that's what I have been working on. It's why I enjoy being a nurse. I couldn't help my mother; I couldn't help my dad. But I *can* help our patients." Kerrigan paused, exhaled, and shook her head. "Wow! I apologize for dumping so much. I honestly had no idea that was all still floating around. I thought I had moved past it."

"Never apologize for what you are feeling or what you went through. Never. We are here for you and will listen anytime. Consider us your safe space." Jamie leaned over and hugged Kerrigan. Charity nodded and hugged her as well.

"Oh my god, you guys. You are going to make me cry, and I've shed enough tears over them already."

Kerrigan always had a tough exterior, but now that she was starting to open up, Charity and Jamie realized that she was quite gentle and sweet. She had just built up walls and armor after what she had gone through. The women thought it was nice to get to see the real Kerrigan. Just then, River stuck his head into the breakroom.

"Uh, guys? I hate to interrupt your meeting, but you have someone trying to sneak down the hall. I wasn't sure if you wanted me to call security or if you wanted me to take him back to his room?"

"Are his ripped tighty whities hangin' out?" Kerrigan asked.

"Yup, that's the guy. Should I escort him back? I'd be happy to," River said. He was such a kind and gentle nurse, and always tried to help.

Kerrigan couldn't have him deal with Rusty Brown. She couldn't do that to the poor guy. River was kind enough to help on their floor. He didn't need that. *Hell, no one needed that,* Kerrigan thought. She stood up, sighing heavily.

"No. I've got him. Thank you. You can go back to the desk. Trust me, you do not want to deal with whatever bee is in his bonnet this time," Kerrigan said as she left the breakroom.

"Hello, *Mr. Brown!*" They heard Kerrigan loudly say. They heard a surprised noise, followed by some grumbling. The voices kept getting louder, with more grumbling, until they all heard, "Do I need to call for Bastian, Robert, or Eiler? No?

That's what I thought." Their voices faded as they headed down the hallway and back toward his room. Charity and Jamie shook their heads. Just as River turned to go back to the desk, he looked up and noticed the rotary phone.

"Oh, cool! You guys found an old phone, too? What a weird coincidence."

"River, what do you mean, 'too'?" Jamie said, shocked.

"Yeah, have you seen one of these somewhere else in the hospital?" Whatever calm Charity had in that shared moment with Kerrigan was replaced by worry again.

"Well, yeah. It's funny. You don't see those anymore. And now I have seen two in one day. Someone found one on the second floor today. I think it was tucked inside an old drawer near PEDS. Why?"

"Did it ring?!" both women asked at the same time.

"I don't know. I had to check on a patient, so I didn't get to inspect it. Why? Does that old phone work? Sweet! You know, come to think of it, I heard a ringing as I was walking away. Zephabelle was the one sitting at that desk when I left. I don't know any more than that."

"Didn't you say Zephabelle never came back from break?"

"I did. Why? Do you think it is related?"

Jamie didn't want to worry the guy. He obviously knew nothing about the phone, and she wanted to keep it that way. Everyone who dealt with them ended up missing. She wasn't going to do that to him. But now she was very concerned. *How many of these damn phones are there? What in the hell is going on?* She decided it was best to keep her thoughts to herself, so she replied, "Oh, no. I am sure it is nothing like that."

"OK, cool. Well, if you need me, I will be back at the desk." River smiled and left the breakroom.

"What the actual fuck, Jamie? More than one? Does that one ring too? And why have people been going missing since that damn thing showed up?" Charity had moved past being concerned and was headfirst into a mix of anger and fear.

"I don't know. I really don't. But I am going to see if I can find out. Who is working on River's floor tonight, do you know?"

"No. But hang on...I can check the computer...." Charity sat down and scrolled through the computer. "It looks like River, Kosina, Ana, Shanleia, Arrow, and Zephabelle were scheduled for tonight. But River said that Zephabelle was missing..."

"Kosina is on tonight? Excellent. Let me call her from here so we don't worry, River." Jamie pulled out her cell and clicked on Kosina's number. While it was true that Jamie preferred a separation between work and home life, she broke that rule with Kosina. They had known each other back in high school, so Jamie was thrilled when she found out Kosina had started working on the floor below her. Jamie was so busy with school that she didn't have time for a real social life, but she and

Kosina did hang out on occasion and texted frequently. Kosina was a doll about sending encouraging or funny memes when she knew Jamie was stressing about life, school, work, and all of the above. Jamie was grateful they had reconnected. She told Kosina she owed her a big homemade dinner when she was done with school.

As the phone rang, she put it on speaker. She wanted Charity to hear as well. Just as Jamie was about to give up, she heard, "Hey, sis! Can't talk right now. Can I catch you late—"

"Hey, Kosina, sorry to interrupt, but this is important. Can you spare just a sec? I promise I will be quick. I know it's been a crazy night," Jamie said.

"Yeah, ok. But you had best be quick about it. Nurse Battle Ax—I mean Ana, is nearing meltdown status. What's up?"

"Ok, this is going to be a strange question, but just go with me on it."

"Yeah, ok. Sure," Kosina said, annoyed. She needed to get back to work. She loved Jamie, but she did not have time to play twenty questions.

"Uh, did you guys happen to find an old phone? Maybe a rotary phone, by any chance?"

"Indeed, we did. How in the hell did you know about that? Oh. Right. River is up, helping you guys out. Yeah, it's weird seeing a phone we grew up using, isn't it? I didn't think those things existed anywhere except antique stores now." Kosina chucked at the thought of her childhood being reduced to trinkets and memorabilia showcased in vintage shops.

"Hmm. Ok. How did you find it? Better yet, *who* found it?" Jamie said in a serious tone.

"Shanleia was the one who found it. She said she heard ringing coming from under an old desk. She had to get down on her hands and knees and look. All the way back behind the desk, on the floor, tucked under the drawers was the phone. Crazy! What's going on, J?"

Jamie disregarded Kosina's question and continued, "Is Shanleia available? Can I talk to her, please?" She was trying to sound calmer than she felt at that point.

Kosina got abnormally quiet. There was a significant pause before she answered. "Uh, here's the thing. We don't know where Shanleia went.... We haven't seen her in a while. *Why, J? What is going on?*"

"So Shanleia is missing and so is Zephabelle?"

"Yeah, I guess they are both gone. Well, I wouldn't say *gone*. Zephabelle said she had to check something, and that's the last time I saw her. Shanleia? Who the hell knows? You know her, Jame, she wanders. I am sure it is nothing. Why are you being so weird?" Kosina was trying to be patient, but the storm had everyone on edge, and her floor was quite busy, so she didn't have time to chit-chat with her friend.

There was no way Jamie could keep the information from her. It wouldn't be fair. So, she took a deep breath and said, "Ok, listen to me carefully, Kos, this is no joke, ok? I have some pretty wild things to tell you, and I need you to hear me out, ok?" She waited for Kosina to agree and then continued, "We have one of those phones up here, too. We found it walled up in what should have been a cupboard over the refrigerator. *I* answered it the first time—"

"*Yeah, ok.* It's just a phone, dude." Kosina was growing increasingly annoyed with Jamie and her overreaction to an old phone.

"KOS! Here's the thing: everyone who has been dealing with the phone has gone missing. Well, everyone but me, that is. Reid went to look for the person calling. Then Tore went to look for Reid and the person. Additionally, Keith never returned from break. Skyler is nowhere to be found. River said Toby never showed up for work. And now you are saying that Shanleia and Zephabelle, are missing. This is bad. Real bad," Jamie said, frazzled.

"Wait, are you *serious?* What the fuck, Jamie? *How* are those two things even related?" Kosina asked very bewilderedly.

Charity, who had been quietly listening the entire time, piped up, "We don't know. We just know that is what has been happening. I know it is difficult to believe, but it's true."

"Who is that?" Kosina asked.

"That's Charity. I have you on speaker, so we can all discuss this together. Sorry, I forgot to mention that. Listen, I need to tell you the rest of it, ok?"

"There's more? Yeah, ok. Sure. Whatever." Kosina was now losing her patience, but she also knew Jamie was not a bullshitter or prank puller, so she let her continue.

"So, the person I spoke to on the other end of the phone *sounded* like a little girl. I truly thought I was speaking to a little girl. We all did. She said she didn't know where she was. She was asking for help. Reid said he thought he knew where she was, so he went down to get her. We got busy and didn't realize he hadn't come back. The phone rang again, and this time Tore answered it, and you know Tore."

"Gotta help everyone and save the world? Yeah, I know, Tore."

"Yeah, *that's her.* So, while Tore and Charity were talking to the little girl or person, whatever, she asked for help again, and Tore took it upon herself to find her *and* Reid. Now she hasn't returned either. Benji and Kerrigan had been helping out with emergencies in the ER, so they didn't know any of this was happening. Benji still doesn't know. As we were filling Kerrigan in, she pointed out that the person might, in fact, be an adult rather than a child. The entire time, we just assumed it was a little girl. But as she reminded us, a young woman could use a baby talk voice." Jamie paused to catch her breath.

There was a pregnant pause on the other end. Kosina sucked in her breath and said, "*Oh, what the fuck, J!* What in the hell is going on? I also heard we have a murderer on the loose in the building? Is that true?!"

"That hasn't been confirmed—" Charity tried saying.

"The last thing that was said was that the suspect was near the area. Not that he was spotted *in* the hospital. But they did find blood..." Jamie's voice trailed off because even she wasn't believing herself at that point.

"Aw, the hell it hasn't been. He was last seen near here. We now have missing people. It's not rocket science. What the God damn fuck?" It was Kosina's turn to be worried. "I do *not* need this in my life right now. I just don't."

"Yeah, I know what you mean. Kerrigan thinks the person could be an adult with mental health issues. She could be playing some sick game just to get attention. We don't know. It's such a mess. Listen, do me a favor, sis. Don't answer that phone if it rings again, ok? Just ignore it. Hide it or break it. Do whatever. Just don't answer it and don't let anyone else either. Not until we figure this out," Jamie said with a little more emotion than she meant to have.

"Can do! I will take care of it right after I hang up with you two. I have a question for you, though. Where were Reid and Tore headed? Do you happen to know?"

"Well, after talking to Reid, he felt that the person was somewhere in the vicinity of the mechanical room. Why?"

"Just before Zephabelle went on break, I heard her ask our janitor, Mickey, if he knew which way the 'furnace room' was located...."

All three ladies got quiet. None of them knew what to say at that moment. They were tired. They were anxious. They were in a state of disbelief. They were trying to piece together an impossible puzzle. And, until the police arrived, they were on their own. Jamie broke the heavy silence. "Kosina? Get rid of that phone. Just, just get rid of that fucker. And for the love of God, do not let a single soul answer it, ok? Please?'

"You got it! I will do it right now. Thank you for letting us know, Jamie. We will get this figured out eventually, right? And then you can buy me some tacos, and we can have a few laughs over all of this nonsense, right? Right?" She repeated herself on purpose, but she wasn't sure if it was to convince Jamie and Charity or to convince herself.

"Dude, you got it! As many as you want!" Jamie's voice lowered into a hushed, serious tone, "Kos, please be careful. Promise me that you will *be careful.*"

"I will. I promise. Night, ladies." Kosina sighed and hung up.

Jamie had just hung up with Kosina when Kerrigan came walking back into the breakroom. She had Eiler in tow. She also had a look of determination, which worried Jamie greatly.

Anytime she looked like that, she was not taking no for an answer. Kerrigan looked at both women and said, "I am going down to the mechanical room."

"No! No! Absolutely NOT! Are you insane? You said it yourself; we have a murderer on the loose, and we have no idea who the person is on the other end of the line. No, Kerrigan. You are not doing that." Jamie was pissed at her for even considering it. There was no way in hell she was going to allow that to happen.

"Don't you even *think* about trying to stop me! Tore and Reid are our friends and coworkers. God knows what that woman wants! I am familiar with this type of behavior. I am sure I can help. Plus, Eiler said he would come with me. Right, Eiler?" Kerrigan, Jamie, and Charity all looked at him.

"Of course, I will escort Kerrigan down to" Eiler looked at Kerrigan questioningly.

"The mechanical room downstairs," Kerrigan said confidently.

"Yeah, of course I will. I don't understand why we are doing that. But if Kerrigan thinks it is that important, I insist on going with her. You guys will still have Robert and Bastian here. We will make it a quick trip and be back before anyone misses us, right, Kerrigan?" Eiler asked, still very confused.

Kerrigan didn't level with Eiler. She felt a little bad about that. But she wondered who would believe such a crazy story about an old rotary phone hidden in a wall randomly ringing. She hadn't heard it so she was struggling to wrap her head around it herself. All she knew was that her friends were potentially being harassed by a woman who needed mental health care. She wasn't going to let them go through what she did if she could help it. Going down to the mechanical room to find them was the only option Kerrigan saw. She looked at Eiler and nodded.

"Kerrigan, No! I am so not comfortable with this! We should call the police and—"

"The police are on their way, Jamie. It'll be ok. I promise to look after Kerrigan, ok?" Eiler interrupted in his calm and reassuring way.

"I am with Jamie on this, guys. It's too dangerous. We don't know the current situation. You shouldn't blindly walk into something. I think you should wait for the police." Charity knew Kerrigan wouldn't listen, but she had to say it.

"But you didn't hear the latest. I just–I mean, *we* just got off the phone with Kosina. Kerrigan, *there is a phone on that floor as well!*" Jamie said, almost whispering the last part.

"What? Are you serious!? Well, I don't care. I am going! Period. Our friends need us."

"God dammit, Kerrigan," Jamie sighed. "For the record, I do not approve of this, ok? I want you all to know that. But I know you, and you are just going to do it regardless of what I say. So, *please be careful. Please.* I am going to call Myers Mental Health Clinic to see if they are missing any of their patients. If they are, I will call you, ok? *And* if that is the case, you come straight back. We will have their orderlies deal with her. Otherwise, go try to find everyone. Eiler, watch her back, ok? Both of you, just be cautious. If something feels hinky, please come back immediately, and we will wait for the police to arrive. Which is what we should be doing anyway...." Jamie mumbled that last part. She knew better than to argue with Kerrigan when she got a bee in her bonnet about something. She didn't know why, but she grabbed Kerrigan and pulled her into a big hug. She then patted Eiler's shoulder and squeezed. "Ok, guys. Good luck."

Eiler and Kerrigan turned and headed down the hallway to the service elevator. Since the hospital was technically on lockdown, they were supposed to remain in place. Kerrigan and Eiler had to be sneaky. The service elevator was the easiest way. Additionally, Eiler had already radioed ahead to Wayne and Glen on the first floor to inform them that they would be coming down. Eiler wasn't worried. He trusted Kerrigan and believed she knew what she was doing. Just before they entered the elevator, Kerrigan turned to them and gave a quick wave. Eiler gave a thumbs up, and they stepped into the waiting space. The doors closed, and they were gone.

Jamie looked at Charity, her face filled with fear and worry. She grabbed Charity's hand and squeezed it. Charity squeezed back. Jamie sighed and nodded with a look that said, "I hope this is the right decision." Charity felt a lump in her throat. All she could do was nod. She didn't know where to cry or scream or both. Together, they left the breakroom and headed back to the nurses' station. As they arrived, River turned to them and said, "Guys, we have a problem."

Chapter Nine

While Charity and Jamie were talking to Kerrigan and Eiler, River had been seated at one of the desks at the nurses' station. It was a reasonably quiet moment, so he spent his downtime scrolling through social media on his phone. That time was short-lived as he was interrupted by a desk phone ringing. It startled him, which caused him to drop his cellphone. The screen shattered. As he picked it up, he muttered "dammit" and answered the desk phone.

"Good evening, third-floor nurses' station. This is River. How ca—" he was interrupted by someone on the other end. All he could do was listen and occasionally nod or shake his head, forgetting that they couldn't see him. As the person kept talking, the color started to leave River's face. He ended the call with, "ok, I understand. Thank you."

Just as River was hanging up the phone, Charity and Jamie came walking up to the counter. River turned to them and said, "Guys, we have a problem."

"Good God, *what now?*" Charity asked with her teeth clenched.

Jamie put her arm around Charity's shoulders. She pulled her into a kind of side hug and leaned her head against Charity. She looked at River and said, "Lay it on us."

"I just received a call from Frankie."

"You mean, like, the *Sheriff?* Frankie Goodweather? *That* Frankie?" Jamie's eyes got very wide.

Frankie knew everyone in town. If someone was new to Heatherwilde Falls, she made a point of meeting and welcoming them. Jamie loved that about her. She had known her her whole life. Frankie had been a big help when Jamie was dealing with the stalker. She was a laid-back, unassuming woman who just loved their town. She took protecting it seriously. Not much ever phased her, so if *she* was calling, it was serious.

"The one and only. So, it's a code silver. We are now on a *full* lockdown. No movement between floors, we are to stay put. Our security guards are now positioned by the elevators and entrances. The police should arrive here at any minute. The storm is quite bad now. The downed trees and lines have caused several accidents. They are doing their best, but another blocking accident has just occurred just a few blocks away. They need that cleared up to be able to get here. I guess more patients are headed to the ER. But we stay here. Looks like you are stuck with me a while longer."

"Code silver?" Charity was puzzled.

"Code silver? Are you kidding me? It means we have a situation— someone on the premises has a weapon. I guess the rumor about a murderer in the hospital is no longer a rumor...."

Jamie was grateful she had never experienced one before, but her auntie was a retired nurse from a bigger city. She told Jamie crazy stories about when her hospital had code silvers. It was downright terrifying. But this news left Jamie confused. She didn't understand how they could have a person with a weapon in the hospital when they had been on lockdown for the past hour or two.

"Ok, wait a minute. How did this happen? Did Frankie give you any more information?" Jamie asked River, trying to piece it together.

"No. But she sounded concerned," River said.

"Dammit. Ok, let's give Rachelle a call and see—"

"Oh, my *fucking* God, I am DONE with this night! Just done! You can't call Rachelle. River just said more people are headed to the ER. They will be too busy to answer. We can't leave our floor, which means it's just us now," Charity said. She was thinking about what hadn't been said yet. "Jamie, *Kerrigan just left and is now walking into God knows what!*" She blurted it out, nearly hysterical at this point.

"Charity. CHARITY! Stop! Breathe—breathe. Calm down. We don't know why we were put on code silver. We don't know anything yet. Just take some deep breaths while I call Rachelle. We will figure this out, ok?"

Charity was not easily upset or freaked out. She was a hot head at times, but that situation was making her nervous. Maybe even downright scared. She wasn't sure how much more she could take. She was worried about her husband. She was concerned about her kids. She was afraid for her momma and the rest of her family. She needed to know everyone was safe. Charity took a deep breath and looked at Jamie.

"I need to call Don! Please don't say I can't. Don't you dare try to stop me. I need to make sure Rik and Annise are safe!" Charity was in tears and almost sobbing.

Jamie was not a mother herself, but she knew how she felt about her nieces, nephews, and Godchildren. She also knew that when Charity went into mamma bear mode, nothing was changing her mind.

"Yes, yes, of course. Charity, look at me. You need to calm down first, ok? Be calm, for Don. They may not know what is going on, and we cannot have people rushing up here. Just talk to them, make sure they are safe, and leave it at that. I am going to try to call Rachelle to see what else I can find out. Maybe I can catch her before the other patients arrive."

Charity nodded, sat down in a chair, and pulled out her phone. She tapped on her husband's number, put the phone to her ear, and swiveled the chair so her back was to everyone. Jamie turned, saw River's face, and said, "River? River? Are you hanging in there, dude?"

River was such an easy-going guy that this was throwing him for a loop. He wasn't sure how to feel or what to do. He didn't even know how to respond to Jamie. He looked at her, searching for something, anything. Instead, he just shrugged and put up his hands. Jamie went and stood directly in front of him. She opened her arms wide, and River fell into them. The tears started to flow. Jamie just held him tighter. She concentrated on comforting him because she knew if she let herself feel anything else in that moment, she would freak out and bawl and not be a help to anyone. So, she bit her bottom lip and just held on to River. Eventually, his crying lessened. He pulled away from her and had an embarrassed look on his face.

"Oh my god. I am so sorry. I didn't mean to react like that."

"River, don't you *dare* apologize. Let it out, man. I am scared too. We have one hell of a situation here, and it is normal to feel overwhelmed by all of this. It's a shit-tastic thing here tonight. You got this. You are going to be ok. *We* are going to be ok, you hear me? Are you good if I try to call Rachelle? Or do you want me to sit down with you for a minute?"

"I..." River cleared his throat, "I'm ok. Thank you for that, Jamie. I truly appreciate you."

"I appreciate you as well, River. You know that. I think you are one hell of a super guy. And an amazing nurse. Try not to worry. We will get all this figured out. And like you said, the police will be here any minute." Jamie patted River's arm and attempted a smile. "I am going to call Rachelle now. Let's see what she knows."

River nodded. He thought about calling his parents, but they were most likely sleeping. He didn't want to worry them unnecessarily. So, he just sat at the desk, trying to process everything while he waited to see what Jamie found out.

Jamie picked up one of the phones sitting at the desk and dialed Rachelle's cell phone number. She could have used her cell phone, but she wanted to leave that open in case her sister or brother tried calling her. As the line was ringing, she thought to herself, *I hope Rachelle knows more and can fill me in.* The phone rang and rang and then it went to voicemail. Jamie thought that was odd, so she hung up and dialed again. This time it went straight to voicemail. *Now* Jamie was starting to be concerned. Rachelle should have answered her phone. It was very unlike her not to pick up at least to say that she was busy. She grabbed the directory and looked for the name of someone she could call. She didn't want to try Amber or Jerelle again because if the accident victims had arrived, they would have had their hands full. But she thought maybe she could get hold of someone else on the first floor. Jamie turned to River.

"River, can you do me a favor?"

"Yeah, yeah. Of course. What 'dya need?"

"Do you think you could try calling Ana? Rachelle isn't answering; it's going straight to voicemail. Maybe Ana would know something."

"You got it!"

He took his cell phone out of his back pocket and went to place the call. He promptly felt a burning pain in his fingers. He looked at his hand and saw that he had sliced his fingers. Shocked, he looked down at his phone. He had forgotten he had dropped it. The screen resembled a bizarre spider web. Cracks were everywhere. Blood was now dripping from a couple of his fingers. *No time for that,* he thought as he got up and walked down the hall to make his call.

Jamie sat pondering, trying to figure out who else she could call. She drummed her fingers on the desk, racking her brain. She had no idea where Keith, Reid, Tore, and Kerrigan were. Eiler was with Kerrigan, so she couldn't call him either. Benji! Maybe she could call Benji. Benji was still down helping in the ER, so Jamie thought perhaps he would know more. This time, she pulled out her cell phone to call him up directly. As the phone started ringing, she was absent-mindedly twirling her hair with her other hand. She had done that since she was a little girl. If she was stressed, afraid, or upset, she constantly twirled her hair around her fingers.

"Hello?" asked a hushed voice.

"Benji? Benj? Is that you?" Jamie always recognized his voice, but this time, she couldn't tell. She wasn't sure if it was her stress or the hushed tone of the voice that answered.

"Yes, it's me. Hi J. Listen, this isn't a good time," Benji said in almost a whisper.

"I know, I know. I am sorry. I am just trying to find out what is going on. Do you have any idea?"

"Uh, yeah, I do. I am obviously not coming back up any time soon. *I have to go.* But you know the murder suspect was last seen near our hospital, right? And the police were worried he might enter? Well, it looks like he got in somehow."

"*WHAT?*" Jamie held the phone tighter and asked, "Was he spotted? Why don't they have him detained?"

"Uh, no. No one that I have spoken to has seen the guy. It's just....well....we have another victim here we are working on."

"Who?" Jamie wasn't sure she wanted to know.

"Tawny. She left for her break, but she never showed back up. It turns out she had a run-in with the guy. Dr. Coleman found her. He said he heard a funny noise near the supply closet down the hall. He walked down the hallway and found Tawny lying on the floor in a pool of blood. Jamie, I saw her as they brought her in. She looked like someone had tried to rip her in half. It's a mess. Amber, Rachelle, Dr. Coleman, and everyone else are all doing their best, but it doesn't look good. She lost a lot of blood. They aren't sure, but it almost looked like someone was trying to cut out her kidneys and liver. Dr. Coleman also said he saw a trail of blood leading away from the area. He thought maybe toward the service elevator, but he wasn't sure. His main concern, of course, was getting Tawny care. It's bad. Look, I need to go. We have more car accident victims coming in, too."

"Wait! I know you have to work, but Benj, I need to know. Why do they think it's the murderer if he hasn't been seen? Could it be something else? Like, was Tawny headed down to the mechanical room, do you think?"

"Dude, I have no idea where Tawny was headed. But the reason they are sure the suspect is here is because...well, two reasons, I guess. One: she was missing some fingers, just like the other victims. Two: they found a bloody weapon. Dr. Coleman brought it back with him- in a bag- so we can give it to the police. *I have never seen anything like it.* It resembles a long, machete-type blade. But it is serrated like a saw. At the end of the handle is a hammer head with spikes sticking out. The hilt of the knife resembles a deer antler that has been filed down into sharp points. If he had this, God knows what else he had. Given the severity of injuries in the victims, we assume he had more than just that weapon.... J, I gotta go. I love ya. Be safe. Stay put. When this is over, let's grab dinner. Oh, ah, breakfast now, I guess."

"You stay safe too, Benj! I mean it. I will kick your ass if you don't. Love ya, kid."

Jamie could not believe what she had just listened to. Her mind was racing. *A murderer in the hospital? How? Why?*

Near the service elevator? "Oh my God!" she exclaimed. Her face was very pale as she realized something.

"What's going on?" River asked as he walked back to the desk and sat down.

Charity was off the phone, so she turned around to look at Jamie expectantly. Jamie had a look on her face that Charity had never seen before. Fear. Jamie was afraid. *If Jamie is worried, it's bad,* Charity thought.

"What is it? What's going on?" Charity asked as calmly as she could.

"I just spoke to Benji. They think the murderer is in the hospital. They found a weapon, and we had another victim. Hospital staff this time. It was Tawny."

"OH MY GOD! No! Is she ok? How is she? What happened?" Charity was freaking out now. She had worked with Tawny a few times, and they had started to become good friends. "Oh my god...."

"I don't know how she is. It's not good, Charity. But that's not the worst. They found her down past the supply closet somewhere. They found the weapon farther down, near the service elevator, cafeteria, or something. And there was a blood trail that headed back toward the service elevator area."

"Blood trail? Maybe that means Tawny was able to fight back! That's good, Jamie. When the police show up, they can use it to track him down. He's not going to be going very far,"

River said, trying to look on the bright side of a very dark situation. He always tried to be a perpetual optimist. But he was being challenged that night.

"No. It's not good. Kerrigan and Eiler are down there……"

River and Charity just stared at Jamie. Though River didn't know Kerrigan that well, he knew that heading in the direction of a killer was not good. Charity was good friends with Kerrigan, so she was starting to lose it. She wanted the stupid night to end already. Before anyone else could say anything, River spoke.

"Uh...So, I got in touch with Ana. She was in a mood. I guess being down nurses was getting on her nerves. She had no idea where Shanleia or Zephabelle were. But she wasn't bothered by that because we all knew she hated Shanleia and barely tolerated Zephabelle. She kinda hates everyone, I guess. She did have some information, though. She called down and spoke to Jerelle on the first floor, hoping to get some help."

"Uh, we are in a lockdown. How was she planning to do that?" Charity asked, interrupting him and rolling her eyes.

"Eh, you know Ana. The, I-don't-take-no-for-an-answer-always-find-a-way-to-make-it-work nurse. She was pretty pissed they disagreed with her request. But it's only Jerelle, Cathy, Prue, Amber, Benji, and Rachelle working the ER right now and they are expecting quite a few more patients. Oh, she also said that she saw Kosina smash that old phone I was telling you about. I guess Kosina borrowed a hammer from Mickey and just went to town, according to Ana," River said, shrugging.

"Good God! What is happening here? I am relieved that the phone was destroyed at least, and not surprised at all about Ana's attitude. There is a reason Kosina calls her 'Nurse Battle Ax'. Speaking of, what was Kosina up to? Did she sneak down to help in the ER?" Jamie asked.

"Um, no. That's why Ana is so pissed. I am up here, Zephabelle and Shanleia are all missing, and she hasn't seen Kosina. She wanted to know if I could go back down there now. She knows I am not supposed to, but she said she worked it out with Tekonsha. He would ride up in the elevator and get me. Are you guys good? I know it's night, but I hate leaving the kids without enough nurses. Dr. Grimdatter was there trying to help, but it's just Ana and Arrow there right now," River looked at Jamie imploringly.

"WHAT? Where is Kos? Oh my god! No. I told her to stay put!" Jamie was frantically looking for her phone so she could try calling Kosina again. She tapped her phone and waited. It went straight to voicemail. She groaned. Charity came over and rubbed her arm.

"It's going to be ok. You know Kos. She's a smart cookie. I am sure she is just fine. Let's not worry just yet," Charity said, trying to be reassuring.

"Yeah, ok. Maybe. Maybe she did end up going down to the ER. You are right. We have too many other things going on right now," Jamie said. She looked at River and continued, "Yeah, go ahead, River. Those kids need their nurses. Would you do me a favor, though? If you see Kos, would you please have her call me as soon as possible?"

Before River could answer, Robert and Bastian came hustling up to the counter. They looked quite concerned. Both seemed like the color had drained from their faces.

"Are you guys ok?" Bastian asked hurriedly.

"Are any of you in trouble? Have you seen anything strange?" Robert said intensely.

Jamie, Charity, and River looked at the security guards, stunned at their intensity. They knew if Bastian and Robert were concerned, *they* should be concerned. The three nurses stared at the security guards.

"We are ok," Jamie said, "why?"

"We found a small trail of blood leading back here. I don't want to cause alarm, but I think—"

"*What!?* Oh my god! Yeah, ok, what do you want us—" Charity interrupted Bastian.

"Guys? Guys!" River yelled. He was trying to get their attention before the group descended into full panic. "That's my blood. I am so sorry to cause a scare. That's all my blood. I cut my fingers on my phone. Look." He showed them his bandaged fingers.

Robert grabbed River's hand and closely inspected it. "Oh, good effing lord, that is a relief! It didn't seem like enough blood for what we were told to be on the lookout for. Um, maybe call Hugh to see if he can clean it up?" Robert asked.

"Hugh left for the night—daddy-daughter dance. I'll get it. No worries. Thank God it was just your fingers bleeding, River. Well, you know what I mean. I am sorry you cut yourself, but glad it wasn't something else, you know?" Jamie said.

"Nah, it's all good. I get it. I cut my fingers on my broken screen trying to call Ana. I didn't want to disturb you and Charity while you two were making your calls, so I walked down the hall and got some bandages from a cupboard. Sorry, guys!"

"Don't worry about it. Sorry about your cuts, man. Hey, isn't Tekonsha coming up for you?" Bastian asked him.

"Yeah, he is supposed to be here any—"

A sound interrupted River. They all turned around at the sound of the elevator. Even though he was supposed to use the service elevator, they looked down the hall, expecting to see Tekonsha exit. But he didn't. No one did. That made them feel even more uneasy. Bastian and Robert rushed over to the elevator. The doors were closed. With Bastian at the ready, Robert pressed the button to open the doors. They didn't move. Robert noticed the down arrow was lit up. As he was looking at that, something else caught his eye. He crouched down and looked closely. He looked up at Bastian and pointed. They looked at each other and nodded, backing away from the elevator.

"Hey, River...did you also walk over here while your fingers were bleeding?" Robert asked, concerned.

"No. I went the other direction. Why?" River asked while walking towards them.

"Stop!" Both men said as they jumped up, blocking River.

River jumped, startled by their intense response. Charity and Jamie also jumped at their raised voices. They also tried walking toward the men.

"Guys? What's going on? Everything ok?" Jamie asked them as she noticed the intense look on their faces.

"Ladies, River, please go back to the nurses' station, ok? Just go back there while we check this out," Robert said in a profoundly serious tone.

Jamie didn't like the sound of that one bit. She nodded ok to Robert, put one arm around River and one around Charity, and they rapidly walked back to their stations. As they sat down, Jamie absent-mindedly fiddled with her name tag with the panic button on it. River had already grabbed his and had it ready. Charity reached down and grabbed her heavy golf umbrella. Having her hand on it made her feel a little safer, even though it wouldn't be helpful if she had to swing it at someone.

Robert and Bastian stood in front of the elevator doors, tense and ready for whatever might be in there. They had their batons out, listening as the elevator made noise while it moved toward them. It came to a stop, and the doors creaked open. They both waited. Nothing happened. They moved cautiously closer, trying to assess the space. It appeared empty, so they entered. The elevator was indeed empty, but a small blood trail was visible inside. The number panel also had blood. The button for the first floor was the most covered. They exited the elevator and walked toward the group, who were nervously waiting at the nurses' station.

"It's empty," Bastian said. He shrugged his large shoulders.

"It *is* empty. But there was a blood trail inside. And the first-floor button was covered in it. For now, stay away from that area. I am going to give Glen, Wayne, and John a heads-up. It appears someone is headed their way," Robert said. For the first time that night, he had concern in his voice. "If you all will excuse me...." his voice trailing off as he started walking away.

"That's it! Kerrigan needs to get back here! I don't care if she did or didn't find Tore, Reid, and Keith. I don't care if she thinks she can handle some little girl, or mentally ill woman, or whoever. She needs to get back here now!" Charity said very heatedly.

"I agree with you, Charity. Let's call—*Call?* Aw, hell's bells. I never called Myers Mental Health Clinic to see if they were missing a patient. God dammit. Charity, will you reach out to Kerrigan? Bastian, can you try Eiler? I will call over to MMHC to check in with them. River, can you let Ana know it's going to be a few minutes?" Jamie looked expectantly at the group.

Everyone nodded and took out their phones. Everyone but River. He sat down in a chair and picked up a desk phone to use. He didn't need any more sliced fingers, and he certainly didn't need to be leaving any more blood trails. He knew Ana was not going to be happy with the delay and was not looking forward to the earful he was going to get. As he suspected, when she answered, River had to hold the handset away from his ear because of her yelling.

Jamie sat down in a chair and clicked the computer screen to life. She searched until she found the number for Myers Mental Health Clinic, picked up a desk phone, and dialed them up. It seemed to ring for what Jamie thought was an eternity until someone picked up.

"Yeah, hello," said an unpleasant voice.

"Hey, hi! This is Jamie Littlefield calling from Memorial Medical Center. Listen, I have a strange question. I was wondering if you might be missing any patients? Specifically, female patients?"

"Who is this? I can't give out any patient information," said the person on the other end of the phone. She sounded downright snotty now.

"Yeah, I am not asking for patient information. Who am I speaking with?" Jamie asked as politely as she could. But she was struggling to keep things kind.

"This is Marguerite. Who are you?" she said in a very clipped tone.

"As I said, *my name is Jamie,* and I am not trying to get patient information. I am trying to find out if you had a patient potentially wander over to the hospital?"

"I very much doubt it! Erica, the night nurse, never showed up for work, so I am swamped with calls and paperwork right now—"

"What do you mean your night nurse never showed up?" Jamie asked, alarmed.

"Yeah, she was due here hours ago. She said she was stopping off at the cafeteria in the hospital first so she could grab some food. She never showed up. We tried calling her cell, but it went straight to voicemail. Listen, I am sorry to be so short. I apologize if I sounded snotty. It's a full moon here tonight. You know how it goes. The storm isn't helping either! Things have been getting bonkers. Couple that with a no-show employee, and a lockdown, and things are downright intense at the moment."

As Marguerite finished speaking, Jamie heard mumbling. That was followed by Marguerite telling someone to go back to their room. And that was followed by yelling and the sound of something being knocked over.

"Hey! You can go back on your own, or our security guard, Chad, can assist you! That's what I thought. Yeah, yeah... Good night! Hey, *super* sorry, Janie. Like I said, intense. I am not sure about any missing patients. I highly doubt it. I would have seen them. But to make you feel more comfortable, how about I put you through to Dr. Prouty? He's here and may be able to answer your questions."

"It's Jamie... uh, sure. Thanks." Jamie could tell she wasn't going to be able to get answers from Marguerite. She seemed to have her hands full.

Jamie heard the click of being put on hold, or so she thought. It turned into a dial tone. The nurse had hung up on her. She wasn't sure if that was accidental or intentional. Marguerite wasn't overly helpful, so instead of trying her again, Jamie felt the best option was to call Dr. Prouty directly. She didn't know that much about him. He was new to their small town. But she had run into him a few times downstairs in the cafeteria and knew some of her patients who went to see him for therapy. Everyone always had nice things to say about him so Jamie hoped he would be pleasant to her and maybe be able to help. She searched the directory again, scrolling through a sea of names until she found his number. She determinedly punched the numbers into the phone and waited. After the seventh ring, someone picked up.

"H—He—Hel—" said a whispered voice. It was followed by soft giggling.

"Hello?" Jamie said back. "Uh, Dr. Prouty?"

"Uhn...oooo.... unh!'

"Ah, helloo? I am Jamie Littlefield, a nurse over at Memorial Medical Center. I work in the cardiac unit. I know you aren't part of the hospital, but a hallway connects our buildings. Listen, I was wondering if you uh, well, this is going to sound odd, but I wondered if you had any patients go missing tonight? Specifically, a female patient?"

Jamie was nervous about his reply. She wasn't sure whether she was hoping for a "yes" or a "no." A "yes" meant Kerrigan was in way over her head. A "no" meant that there actually was a little girl, lost in the hospital somewhere, needing help. She bit her bottom lip while she waited for him to answer.

"Ah, hello? Are you there, Dr. Prouty?"

"He..he.... unh.... unh... hel"

Dr. Prouty wasn't making much sense. She realized it was a long night, and they were all on edge from the lockdown, but she was perturbed that he wasn't answering her. Jamie listened intently, trying to figure out what Dr. Prouty was trying to say. Very faintly, she heard what sounded like a female voice in the background and heard a giggle again. Jamie could hear a rhythmic movement along with the grunting. *Oh God!* Her eyes opened wide, and her mouth gaped open. It sounded to Jamie like two people having sex. She couldn't believe that two people would be going at it right then. Jamie wasn't sure if she should call them out, cuss them out, or hang up. She decided to hang up. *People are going to be people, appropriate or not,* Jamie figured. As she started to place the handset back on the phone, she thought she heard another sound. It was so faint she wasn't sure.

".... hel...hel..."

Jamie put the handset back up to her ear. There was nothing there but a dial tone. She looked at the phone for a minute, puzzled. She put the handset back down on the phone and spun around in the chair. Everyone was off their phones and looking expectantly at her.

"No luck. I mean, their nurse Marguerite said they had a night nurse no call no show, but she didn't think they had any patients missing from MMHC. Get this! She suggested I call Dr. Prouty to double-check with him, which was fine because she was not at all helpful. I called him directly, and when the call picked up, all I heard were two people, uh, well, potentially engaging in adult activities, maybe. I am not a prude. But like *now?! Now* is the time for that? Christ. Anyway, Charity, did you get a hold of Kerrigan?"

"Oh, for real? Two people having sexy time during a lockdown? Whatever floats your goat, I guess. But, *hello.... lockdown.... murderer.* Jeez, man. And no. I heard Kerrigan's line pick up. I said 'hello,' and I thought I heard her talking back, but it also sounded like her phone had fallen. I hollered 'Hello' again, but never got a response, so I hung up and immediately called back. This time it went straight to her voicemail. Jamie, I am worried about her! God, this whole situation is pissing me off!" Charity grumbled.

"Me too, Char. Bastian, did you have any luck reaching Eiler?" Jamie was hoping for better news.

"Yes, I did. I know he was supposed to be with Kerrigan, but on the way down, he ran into John and Milton, who were going to be escorting one of the kiddos from the accident earlier up to PEDS. Kerrigan, being Kerrigan, told him it was stupid for John to leave his post when Eiler could do it. Eiler said he didn't want to, but Kerrigan said it made more sense. You know how she loves to be logical. She said that after he escorted Milton and the patient to PEDS, he could return to the first floor. Kerrigan said she would be waiting for him there. So, he grudgingly did it. You know Kerrigan. There is no arguing with that girl when she thinks she's right. After he got Milton and the patient safely to the second floor, he was heading back down to the first floor. That's how they left it," Bastian said with furrowed brows. He didn't get a good feeling about any of it.

"River, did you get a hold of Ana? Will she let you stay a little longer?" Jamie didn't think he would have much luck getting her to be understanding.

"I did. She needs me. Dr. Grimdatter isn't much help, and the kids are arriving from the car accident. I am sorry, Jamie. But I need to go help her."

"No, I get it. I knew it was a long shot. Help her and the kids. I am grateful you were able to help us tonight. Hey, do me a favor? If you see Kosina, will you please have her text me? I am worried about her," Jamie said. She patted him on the arm and smiled gently. "I always enjoy working with you. Next time, let's have a normal day and a normal shift, though, right?"

"For sure!" River nodded vigorously.

Just then, the group heard the elevator ding. They all tensed up, and held their breath while looking down the hallway, hoping to see Tekonsha exiting to escort River back to the second floor. Bastian turned, hand on his baton, and hurried down the hall. The group then heard talking. Charity, River, and Jamie looked at each other with concern on their faces. They huddled closer to one another. As the voices got louder and closer, the group of nurses all breathed a sigh of relief.

"Milton! I am so glad to see you! Where have you been? Are you ok? What's going on?" Charity asked, running over and hugging him.

"Hi, guys. This is insane. I was down helping in the ER. What a mess they have. It quieted down for a while, but with the recent accident, it's bad. Plus, a couple of our own are wounded—"

"What do you mean, a *couple* of our own are wounded?" Jamie felt a lump in her throat. They knew about Tawny, but she didn't know who else was hurt. She wasn't sure she was ready for the answer.

"I am sorry to break the news to you. It's Prue and Tawny. Um, it's not looking good for Tawny. It was a bloody mess. Last I knew, Tawny's surgery was almost done. Prue fared a little better. She fought the person off, but she was wounded. Her finger was cut, and she had a huge gash across her abdomen, but they were able to stitch her up. Prue went to clean up the blood after Dr. Coleman found Tawny. She said she kept hearing weird noises. She thought it sounded like whistling or humming. But it sounded peculiar, and it creeped her out, so she started to head back to the ER. As she did, someone tried grabbing her from behind, slicing her. While she was trying to turn around and defend herself, her finger was cut. At that point, I guess she pulled the pepper spray she kept in her pocket out and gave her attacker a healthy dose. She was able to break free at that point and crawl toward the ER. She was able to make it just outside the doors before she collapsed. Eiler had been heading over to talk to Glen, John, and Wayne about our current situation and see if they had any updates before coming back up here when he found Prue and brought her in. I haven't spoken to Prue, only to Cathy. But I guess Prue described the person as having short stature, a higher-pitched voice, and carrying at least one large knife. Cathy said Prue kept mumbling something like *friends*. They had no idea what that meant. Tawny is almost ready to be transferred to the ICU. I saw Benji on the first floor, and he mentioned that you were short-staffed, so I wanted to give you a heads-up. Also, Ana caught up with me and told me to make sure to get you, River. I guess Tekonsha went down to help bring another child up to PEDS, so he can't come up here. Can someone else escort us?"

Everyone just stared at Milton. They were all taking time to process what he had just said. They knew they were on lockdown. Sure. But hearing that not one but two of their coworkers were harmed was more than unnerving. It was downright terrifying. Just then, they heard two voices approaching from the other direction. Robert and Eiler appeared. Jamie ran over and gave Eiler a big hug. As she backed away, she noticed she now had blood all over her lab coat.

"Oh my God! Are you ok? Are you hurt? What about Kerrigan? Where is she?"

"I don't know, Jamie. I told Bastian I was going back down to get her, but she wasn't anywhere to be found. I looked for her as

I headed over toward Wayne. On my way there I saw Prue crawling on the floor outside the ER. She was covered in blood. I picked her up and carried her into the ER. I am not hurt. That is Prue's blood, not mine."

"What can we do?" Charity asked, visibly shaken.

"There isn't much you can do. Eiler is going to escort River back to the second floor. I called down and spoke to Glen. He let me know what was going on, and I let him know about the blood trail. At this point, the murderer is certainly loose in our facility. We all need to be vigilant and prepared. Glen, Wayne, and John are watching the elevator, entrances, and stairwells on the first floor. Bastian, you will be down that hallway and I will be down the other. Eiler, since Toby is missing from the second floor, I would like you to help Tekonsha and Liatris. Let's make PEDS a priority. You can take River with you," Robert said.

Robert's tone was very intense and serious. His face was drained of color. He had seen a lot of things in his time as a security guard, but he had never seen anything this grisly. He was more than a little concerned, and he wasn't one to be easily rattled.

"Sounds good, boss. River, let's roll," Eiler said as he unconsciously let the palm of his hand rest on the holster at his side.

Robert nodded to Eiler. "Stay safe," he said. He turned and walked down the hallway back to the elevator.

"River, thank you so much for all your help. You are awesome. Stay safe! And please have Kosina get a hold of me, ok?" Jamie said as she gave River a side hug.

"No problem, Jamie. You know that. You all stay safe as well, Charity, Bastian, Robert," River nodded at each of them. He then looked at Eiler and said, "Ok, let's head down to floor two."

"Well, ladies. I am sorry, but I also need to get going. I need to bring Tawny up here. Dr. Grimdatter will be up to check on her. I will take Prue to floor two once I get Tawny here. Eiler, could I tag along?" Milton asked.

"I insist," Eiler said in a serious tone.

"Milton, please be careful, ok? Let's catch up in a couple of days when all this madness has ended," Jamie said, resting her hand on his shoulder.

"That sounds like an excellent plan, Jamie. You be careful as well. Catch you later," Milton said, squeezing her hand just before he turned to leave with River and Eiler.

As the three of them walked toward the elevator, Jamie had a sinking feeling. She wasn't sure why. And it was different than the off feeling she had had all day long. She shivered a little and crossed her arms. Charity looked at her concerned.

"You, ok?"

"I am lightyears from ok."

"Yeah...." Charity frowned, "I get it."

The women watched the men walk down the hallway and out of sight. Jamie sighed. She really wanted the night to end. She turned and looked at Charity and Bastian.

"Bastian, I assume you will be headed down the hall now as well?"

"Yes. Remember, Robert is just down the other hallway by the elevator. You two have your panic buttons. Do NOT hesitate to use them. *Anything* funny, and you push it. I am sure I know the answer to this, but do you both have pepper spray?"

"Yeah, of course we—"

"Oh, fuck me! Jamie, I gave mine to Reid and Tore, remember?" Charity interrupted, very upset.

Charity started to tear up when she mentioned the names of her coworkers. She was still very worried about both of them. She wanted to know where they were. Especially with a murderer on the loose.

Jamie reached over and patted her hand. She nodded and said, "I know. I am worried about them too. We will figure out where they all are, ok? Now is not the time, though. We need to check on our patients and prepare the room for Tawny. I have a can of bear spray in my bag; you can use it if needed. Does that work, Bastian?"

"It sure does. Keep it close. I'll be back when I can," Bastian said. He turned and went back down the hallway.

"Alright, girl. You heard him, keep it close. Don't be a hothead, Charity. I mean it. Keep your little sassy spicy self safe!" Jamie said, attempting to be playful, but it didn't come out that way. She cleared her throat and said, "Promise me?"

"Yes. This time, I promise one hundred percent. I am not dyin' in this damn hospital!"

Jamie and Charity looked at each other, a mix of exhaustion, determination, and concern on their faces. They grabbed each other's hands and squeezed. They both nodded simultaneously.

"So....uh...which one of us is taking Rusty?" Charity asked slowly. She looked slyly at Jamie. Before Jamie could even respond, Charity started to back away and said, "*NOT IT!*"

"Oh god dammit. *Fine,* I will be the one to check on him. I hate you. You know this, right? I just hate you," Jamie said, chuckling for real that time.

"*No, you don't,*" Charity said in a singsong voice while twisting side to side, smiling. "You love me, and you know it!" She winked at Jamie.

Jamie smiled and walked over to Charity. She put her arm around Charity's shoulders and said, "Indeed, I do," and the two walked down the hallway together.

Jamie decided to check on Rusty last. She didn't need any more stress. Most of her patients were sleeping. She was glad about that. Agatha wanted help getting to the bathroom. Viola wanted more water. Uriah was only partially awake and asked for five more minutes before getting up to go to school. Jamie chuckled at that. Uriah Tichmand was well into his sixties. Elio Shajane, one of Keith's patients and an absolute sweetheart, simply wanted an extra blanket. As she placed the blanket down on him, he looked up at Jamie and smiled.

"Thank you. I appreciate you being so kind to an ancient old man."

"Oh, Mr. Shajane, you are not an ancient old man," Jamie said, patting his shoulder lightly. She smiled at him.

"No? My great-grandchildren say otherwise. But they can be a bit sassy." He chuckled at that thought.

"Well, I don't think you are ancient at all. Your grandchildren and great-grandchildren are very blessed. We will get you fixed up so you can get back to those sassy kids, OK?"

He smiled at Jamie and closed his eyes. She gave his arm a pat, straightened the blankets for him, and left.

Jamie had one more patient, Rusty Brown. She was begging the universe that he would be asleep, but he was such a busybody, she wouldn't be surprised to find him up watching TV again. She lightly knocked on the door and entered. She was looking down at papers and not paying attention to anything else until she stepped fully into the room. She looked at the bed, puzzled. It was empty. *He must be using the bathroom,* Jamie thought. She went to that door and knocked. As she did, the door opened. She peeked in and saw that it was empty. *Oh, what in the absolute hell?* Jamie was pissed. Rusty was always threatening to leave the hospital or trying to sneak out for food or smokes. As she walked toward the door to see Charity, Jamie noticed something on the floor. She squatted down and looked closer. Blood. Small droplets of blood on the floor. Small enough that she hadn't seen before. She followed the blood trail out of his room and down the hallway. She followed it all the way to the elevator. The same blood Robert had seen. *Unbelievable! This man is fricking unbelievable!!*

Jamie sprinted down the other hallway. She found Charity in Tawny's room. Milton had gone down to the O.R. and brought her up to the ICU. Charity was sitting in a chair next to Tawny, holding her hand and quietly singing a song as tears slid down her cheeks. Seeing that stopped Jamie in her tracks. It was quite a shock to see her coworker hooked up to so many machines, barely alive. Charity looked up. She stopped singing and wiped her eyes.

"Sorry. I know this isn't professional. I couldn't help it. I saw Milton bring her up as I was headed back to the nurses' station. She is in bad shape, Jamie. They aren't sure she is going to make it through the night."

"It's just awful," Jamie said, her voice filled with emotion as she walked up, grabbed Charity's other hand, and squeezed it.

She just stood there looking at Tawny. She was pale and lifeless. *How could someone do that to her? Who could do something like that?* Jamie was so upset that she nearly forgot about Rusty.

"Charity? We have another problem."

Charity's face fell. She looked at Jamie expectantly, waiting for the bad news. She wasn't sure how much more she could take.

"Rusty Brown is not in his room."

Charity just stared at Jamie. She was trying to process what Jamie just said. She opened her mouth to say something, but before she could, Jamie continued.

"Wait, it gets better... You know that trail of blood Robert had found by the elevator? That trail led back to Rusty's room. It's faint. But it does go back to his room...." Jamie let her voice fade.

"Oh, what the god damn hell is wrong with that man?! Wait! Was it his blood? Or....oh my god, could the murderer be up here?" Charity's wet eyes were now wide with concern.

"I don't know. I don't think so. But we'd better find Bastian or Robert and let them know."

Chapter Ten

Earlier that evening, when Rusty had first been escorted back to his room by that male nurse and security guard, all he could think about was sneaking out for a smoke. Or getting something good to eat. He hated the hospital and thought it was all a money-making scheme.

All Rusty ever thought about was smoking and eating. Earlier in the day, he had overheard a couple of nurses discussing the new self-service station located in the cafeteria. That was just what he wanted. He just needed to get to it. *That guy nurse ruined my plans. But not this time*, thought Rusty.

Rusty was a heavy smoker with COPD and a bad heart. They called him a frequent flyer at Memorial Medical Center because he neglected to take care of himself. He was currently back, awaiting heart surgery. Rusty was an angry patient, resentful of the restrictions and what he called 'mothering.' He was also recently diagnosed with severe diabetes, but he never bothered checking his blood sugar, lowering his sugar intake, or exercising. He told the nurses and the doctors that he enjoyed booze, cigarettes, and snacking, in that order. He resented being told what he could and couldn't eat, drink, or do. He felt that it was his body, so he could do what he wanted. *I am not going to eat a low-sodium, low-fat, low-sugar diet*, Rusty thought. *I might as well eat cardboard!*

He climbed out of the bed, grabbed his IV stand, and ambled toward the door. He peeked his head out and looked around. He was thrilled that he didn't see anyone, particularly not any of those big security guards. Rusty was sure he could take those guys, but didn't think he should prove it. He slowly and methodically made his way down the hallway. He froze as soon as he saw a security guard's back. He flattened himself against the wall and held his breath. *Oh shit! I am going to be caught*, he thought as he waited with bated breath. But miraculously, the security guard turned and went in the other direction. *Hot damn! I am golden.*

Rusty put his hand back around the IV stand and continued walking toward the elevator. As he got closer, he could see the nurses' station. A different male nurse was sitting there. Rusty stopped dead in his tracks and waited. All it would take was one glance in his direction, and he would be caught. The nurse walked toward another room, away from Rusty. He could not believe his luck! He turned, stepped up his pace, and shuffled toward the elevator. *This is it. I am good to go*, he thought. As he took another step, he was startled by a voice.

"Hello, Mr. Brown!" he heard Kerrigan loudly say behind him.

It surprised him so much he yelped a bit. He didn't like that. It made him angry. When he turned to look at Kerrigan, he glared at her.

"What? Can't a guy go out for a smoke?" Rusty asked angrily.

"As a matter of fact, *no. No, you cannot go out for a smoke,* Mr. Brown. This is the CCU and ICU floor. You most certainly may not go smoke!" Kerrigan was pissed at him. She put up with a lot, but he could be too much at times.

"I can do whatever I want! *You* work for *Me. I know my rights!*" Rusty was doubling down on his bad attitude.

"Mr. Brown, what are you here for? What were you admitted for?"

"Nothing. This is all bullshit my doctor made up to keep me here," Rusty grumbled, knowing it wasn't true, but he wasn't going to back down.

"That's not true, and you know it. Dr. Murgonia is going to be performing a bypass on you tomorrow. It is not made up. You are supposed to follow his restrictions, both dietary and health related. Get your butt back down in your room right now. If you need something, use the call button. But NO cigarettes!"

"You can't tell me what to do," Rusty said, getting crankier and more defiant by the moment.

"*Mr. Brown,* do I need to call for security?"

Rusty's eyes got wider. He looked around to see if those big security guards were near him. He turned back to Kerrigan. His head fell as he shook it. He knew he would have to go back to his room.

"No? That's what I thought." Their voices faded as they headed down the hallway and back into his room.

Kerrigan escorted Rusty back to his room this time. She made sure he got back into his bed. Since she was there, she checked his vitals and made some notes. Kerrigan loved being a nurse, but that man truly tested her patience. She got him some extra ice and water for his room and placed those next to his bed, in case he needed them. Though she was hoping he would just fall asleep.

"Do I need to sit in here with you all night? Do you need a babysitter?" Kerrigan asked in a huffier tone than she meant to.

"*No, I do not need a babysitter.* I am in my sixties; do I look like a child to you?!"

"Nope, not even a little bit! But you sure *act* like one! You had better stay put this time. Robert, Bastian, and Eiler have enough to deal with right now, ok? Just go to sleep. It's getting late."

"What do you mean, they have enough to deal with? What's going on?"

Kerrigan was so tired that she accidentally slipped up. The *last* thing any of them needed was Rusty finding out what was going on and causing a scene, or worse, freaking out and taking all the other patients with him.

"Nothing that concerns you. A bus accident caused the ER to become overwhelmed. They all went down to help transport patients to the proper floors, that's all."

Kerrigan knew that was a lie, but she needed Rusty in bed, not trying to sneak out while a potential murderer was nearby. She continued, "They need to help with the emergencies, got it? Full moons tend to make things a little more hectic. They have got it covered. But they don't need to be escorting your butt back to your room all night long. So, please, MR. BROWN, just go to sleep."

"Was the accident bad? Who were the people involved? Why are *they* getting special treatment while I am left up here all alone?"

"Ok, first off, I can't give you any patient information. You know that. Secondly, they are not getting special treatment; they are getting the expected treatment, just as you would if you had been down in the ER. Third, you *aren't* alone! Please, Mr. Brown, call it a night, Ok?" Kerrigan said, exasperated.

"Yeah, yeah, sure. Whatever you say."

"*Thank you*," Kerrigan said as she breathed in a sigh of relief.

Kerrigan adjusted his pillows and blankets. She made sure the water was nearby and that he had access to his TV remote, as well as the call button, although she regretted giving him the latter. She looked over his lines one more time, making sure he hadn't ripped anything out. She was trying to hide it, but all she kept thinking about while dealing with the angry, obstinate Rusty was poor Tore and Reid. The more she thought about some woman calling and coaxing them down to her, the angrier she got. As she fluffed Rusty's pillow one last time, she patted it a little more forcefully than she meant. She smoothed it back out, looked at him, and smiled as sweetly as she could muster. She turned and headed toward the door. With every step, she became increasingly determined. She knew what she needed to do. She was going down to the mechanical room to get Tore and Reid. And she was getting the psych patient back where they belonged. Jamie was just going to have to deal with it because she wasn't going to take no for an answer. *I should probably take someone with me, though,* Kerrigan thought. *Jamie will never let me go on my own.* She turned back to give Rusty one last smile, was delighted to see that he was already asleep, and marched out the door with newfound determination.

Rusty, who had lain in bed with his eyes closed pretending to be asleep so Kerrigan would leave, sat up in bed as soon as he heard the door close. As he sat there, he heard his stomach growl. He knew the kitchen was closed. He got up and searched in the pockets of his clothing, looking for something, anything to snack on. All he found were empty snack cake wrappers and a sucker that had fallen out of its wrapper and was covered in fuzz and dirt from his pocket. He shrugged, rinsed the sucker off in the bathroom faucet, and promptly stuck it in his mouth. It wasn't there very long before he crunched down on it. His stomach growled louder this time. He knew it was risky, but he was going to get down to that cafeteria self-serve no matter what. He was tired of being cooped up and

being fed tasteless, bland food and water. He wanted real food. Or what he considered real food. He wanted sandwiches, chips, soda pop, snack cakes, or a big juicy burger with a side of fries. He had no intention of following the guidelines Dr. Murgonia set. *Screw that diet!* Rusty thought angrily.

He wasn't sure how late it was. He never bothered checking the time. It all seemed to blur together, so why would he bother? He was hoping it wasn't time for the night shift to come because he didn't want to get caught by them. He remembered Kerrigan saying that the security guards were down in the ER. That was excellent news. If his timing was right and they were still down there, Rusty thought he would have had a chance to sneak down and get some real food.

He made his way back to his clothing to grab his wallet. As he stuffed his hand down in his pocket, he felt a sting. He had caught his IV on part of the pocket lining. He yanked out his hand and the wallet, wincing in pain. Rusty shook it off. He was in a hurry. He wasn't sure how a self-serve kitchen worked, but he had cash and his card to pay for it. He decided to leave his phone. He saw no point in taking it since he only carried it to make or receive calls. Anything else was unnecessary in Rusty's mind.

With his wallet in one hand and the IV pole in his other hand, he quietly shuffled his way to the door. He peeked his head out and saw that the coast was clear. Slowly and deliberately, he made his way down the hall. Most of the other patients on his side of the floor were sleeping. He was grateful for that. *First, an accident to distract those security guards, and then sleeping patients? I am in the clear*, Rusty thought, rather confidently. He had no sooner thought that when he heard a throat clear. He stopped dead in his tracks and turned around. Standing in the threshold of a room was another patient, Mr. Vemdeirjay. He had one of his grey bushy eyebrows raised as he leaned on the doorframe.

"Where do you think *you* are going, Rusty?"

"I think I am going to— *none of your damn business*, Bert!"

"My name is Bernt, you dickhead. What are you doing out of your room?"

"I told you, that's my business! What's it to you?"

Bernt sighed and said, "Hmm. Guess what I found out?" looking pointedly at Rusty Brown.

"*What did you find out?*" Rusty asked, not even trying to hide the disdain in his voice.

"I found out that my call button reaches all the way over here."

Bernt smiled as he held up his call button, gleefully giving it a little shake as he showed it to Rusty. It was stretched taut, but that didn't matter. Both men knew that it would still work.

"Ok. Hey, now. Wait a minute. You don't need the call button, do you?"

"Don't I?" Bernt asked with one eyebrow raised.

"Hey, hey, hey, listen, bub…. I am sure we can work something out here. I am not doing anything wrong, ok? I am starving, and the kitchen closed hours ago. I am just going down to the cafeteria to grab a snack. It's no big deal."

"Why don't you call your nurse to get you something like you are supposed to?" Bernt raised his eyebrow again as he asked.

"Well….well..because," Rusty sputtered, trying to come up with something. "Kerrigan told me that there was a bus accident tonight, so everyone is helping out down in the ER right now. I don't want to be a bother, do I? I would *never* distract the nurses from their *important duties.* So, I am just going to slip down to the cafeteria and be right back. That way, I don't have to interfere and cause more stress. Or worse, have to wait for them to get me something to eat."

"Man, you are such an asshole. Why do you have to be, well, you? Wait a minute. What accident? What do you *think* you know? My granddaughter was supposed to be coming home from a basketball game tonight."

Bernt went from pissed at Rusty to concerned. He and his granddaughter were very close. Logically, he knew his daughter and son-in-law would call if something had happened, but maybe they didn't want him to worry because he was in the hospital. Bernt decided he needed more information.

"They won't give that info out. All Kerrigan said was that there was a bus accident tonight, so everyone was busy trying to help out."

Rusty could see the concern on Bernt's face and decided to use it to his advantage. He thought about it for a minute. He smiled slowly and looked slyly at Bernt.

"I tell ya what, though. You put that call button away and let me go downstairs. On my way to the cafeteria, I will swing by the ER. I am sure I can find out about the bus crash. Would that work for you?" Rusty had almost an evil grin now. He was always a master manipulator.

Bernt didn't want to agree. He hated Rusty. They had grown up together, attended school together, and still lived in the same town. He wasn't aware of anyone who wanted to live in the same town as their school bully. Rusty had tormented Bernt when he was younger, and there he was in the hospital, causing trouble again.

Bernt Vemdeirjay regretted never having moved away and exploring the world. He had always wanted to live in at least one different state and maybe travel to a few other countries. That was always the plan. But when his wife was offered the chance of a lifetime —to take over the local veterinarian's office, right there in their hometown —they jumped at the chance. He let go of the moving dreams and instead focused on his family and his own career. He enjoyed being a business owner. He enjoyed art even more, which made his little art supply store, Brush with Destiny, his pride and joy. He and his wife Karenia had a fantastic life with a beautiful grown daughter, a wonderful son-in-law, an adventurous grown son, a smart-as-a-whip granddaughter, and another grandchild on the way. Their lives were always busy and filled with love and laughter. He only slowed down after he had a heart attack. His surgery went well, and he was healing up nicely. He had one more day in the hospital, and then he could go home. He didn't want to deal with Rusty anymore. He preferred to hand him over to the nurses or security, but if there was a bus accident, he didn't want to add to their stress. So, after some consideration, he decided Dawnetta was far more important than giving Rusty some just dessert.

"Fine. Go see what you can find out."

Rusty's smile unfurled slowly and evilly. He knew Bernt would agree to it. He knew how to manipulate that guy. It brought him back to their school years. *Ah, those were the days,*

Rusty thought. He chuckled, thinking about all the money he took from Bernt growing up.

"Hey, you got it, *bud*. Will do!"

As Rusty started to shuffle off down the hallway again, he thought he heard Bernt say something. He turned around and looked.

"What's that?"

Bernt had mumbled "asshat" under his breath. But it wasn't as quiet as he had thought because Rusty turned around. He played it off like he had said nothing and just walked back into his room. Inside, away from view, he gave Rusty double middle fingers. Bernt detested the guy. *How does someone not grow up? How do they act just like they are still in school?* Bernt didn't get it. But he would be leaving soon and wouldn't have to see Rusty's ugly face anymore.

Rusty flipped off Bernt's room and slowly and methodically made his way down the hallway towards the elevator. He was pleased to see that the security guards were still busy helping with the bus accident. He hoped they stayed down there just a bit longer. He just had a few more rooms to sneak past, and then he would be at the elevator. As he neared another room, a light clicked on, and the hallway was illuminated. He stopped. Out came a tall, thin, middle-aged woman. Rusty knew her. She had been several grades behind him in school, but that didn't stop him from picking on her as well.

"Hey, Rusty. What's up?" she said in a sleepy voice.

"Oh, uh, hey George. How's it hanging?"

"Rusty, you know my name is Georgina. Why are you always like that? You are one ornery old dude. What are you doing out of your room?"

"Oh, mind your business, you wrinkly old busy body! I got business to tend to!"

"What kind of business happens in a hospital when people are supposed to be sleeping? Are you selling drugs?"

"No. I am not selling drugs, you biddy. I am running an errand, that's all. Like I said, mind your business. Seems like you ought to be paying more attention to yourself. You have aged kind of hard, haven't you?"

Georgina Plattworth (or Georgie to her friends and family) was a beautiful woman. Her tall, slender build, with her jet-black hair, was quite a sight to behold. But Georgie's height had always worked against her. If people like Rusty weren't bullying her, she was sitting alone at dances because none of the boys wanted to feel short. Eventually, she learned to accept and appreciate her height. She modeled briefly during high school and a few years afterward. It was primarily local work, so she eventually went to college, earned a degree in marketing, and started an advertising agency called Ad-venturous Ideas. She kept her agency small, mainly because it was a small town, but also because she loved all aspects of the job.

She met a wide range of interesting people in her line of work. One of those people ended up becoming her husband. Nathaniel was a local artist looking to grow his following. They hit it off immediately, spending a lot of time together. Eventually, Nathaniel started working there. He loved the steady work and creativity. Soon after, they fell in love. They tried having kids of their own for years to no avail. They saved up and spent all kinds of money on IVF. Nothing worked. They waited for years on an adoption list. Just as Georgie and Nathaniel were about to give up hope of becoming parents, the adoption agency called. They became the parents of beautiful fraternal twins, Todrick and Cynthia.

Georgie felt that she had a very blessed life. She loved her job. She loved her kids. She loved her husband. But being middle-aged and raising teenagers was not easy. Her agency had slowed down a bit, so Nathaniel was taking on extra art commissions to help. Stress got the best of Georgie. At least she was convinced it was just a result of stress. Her heart had started acting funny a few months ago. First, it was just butterflies, but it turned into a racing heart rate. It would subside rather rapidly, so she knew she was stressing herself out. But when she couldn't get the racing to stop, they admitted her to Memorial Medical Center. She hated being there, hooked up to a monitor. Doctor Murgonia and the nurses kept using words like Afib, Vfib, tachycardia, and cardiomyopathy. She didn't understand any of it. She just wanted to feel better. Heart issues ran in her family, so she hoped they would figure it out soon. She wanted to be out of the hospital. She missed her home filled with the laughter of her kids and her husband. She missed work too. Dr. Murgonia had scheduled another series of tests for the morning, which made her nervous. She couldn't sleep, even though she needed it. Instead, she was up talking to Rusty, of all people, the bully from school. He was just a jerk who never grew up.

"Aw, don't be jealous, sweetie. Not everyone grows out of their awkward stage. Hell, you didn't even *grow*, did you?" Georgie smiled widely. He may have bullied her in the past, but he no longer bothered her in the slightest.

"HEY! Just because I didn't become a...a..." Rusty struggled with an insult and ended up settling on, "*giraffe*, doesn't mean I am jealous of you, you fugly duckling."

"Oooo. *Really?* Well, maybe I should call the nurse to come help you back to your room..." Georgie trailed off, letting her words sink in.

"Heyyyyy, I was just playing around. No need to call the nurses. Look, I am just going down to the first floor to see if I can get some information, ok?"

"What information?"

"Well, see, I heard there was a bus accident tonight. It's why everyone is so busy. I need to find out if my cousin's daughter was on the bus, that's all."

"Yes, there was a bus accident. Nathaniel called to tell me about it. Our kids were not on the bus, thank goodness. They rode home with their father. Why don't you call your cousin? Why all the cloak and dagger?"

"I tried," Rusty lied. "He didn't pick up, which has me concerned. It's late, but he always answers my calls."

Georgie doubted Rusty's cousin always took his calls. She doubted anyone would want to talk to him. However, she did understand the worry about family, particularly when an accident was involved.

"You are aware they won't give out patient information to you, right? What do you think you are going to accomplish?"

"I *know* that! But if my cousin's daughter is hurt, he will be in the waiting room, won't he?" Rusty said snottily.

"Ok, I won't call the nurses IF you are just going to get information and come right back up. If I don't see you back up here in a few minutes, I am calling the nurses!"

"Yeah, yeah. That won't be necessary. I told you, I am just going to see about the accident."

Georgie lifted her arm and shooed him away like a gnat. She disliked that man immensely. But if she were in the same situation, she would also want information. She was banking on him getting caught and being escorted back up. *Good riddance,* she thought as she went back into her room.

Rusty breathed a sigh of relief. He wasn't sure if Georgie would be agreeable or not. She was always such a goodie two-shoes in school. He grabbed his IV pole and continued towards the elevator. Just a few more yards and he was golden. As the nurses' station came into view, he saw the same male nurse sitting at one of the desks scrolling on his phone. He stopped dead in his tracks. He scooted over to the side of the hallway against the wall, hoping the low lighting would help conceal him. He watched and waited, trying not to make a sound. *Who is that nurse? I saw him earlier. I don't recognize him. Where are all the regular nurses?* He thought that was weird.

As he stood with anxious anticipation, his stomach growled. He put his hand over his midsection and looked up, expecting to be busted. Instead, the desk phone rang. The nurse that Rusty had never met jumped as it rang, and his cellphone fell to the floor. As he bent down and picked up his phone, Rusty took his shot. He hurriedly started across the hallway. In his haste to get to the elevator undetected, he accidentally jerked his hand, dislodging his IV even more. *Bah, who cares? I don't need the damn thing anyway. It's just holding me back.* He pulled the needle the rest of the way out and left the pole (with the tube and needle dangling) standing near the wall.

He shuffled as fast as he could to the elevator around the corner. Rusty looked over his shoulder and saw that the nurses were now gathering around the counter. He needed to be quick.

He pushed the arrow down button and waited for the doors to open. He stepped inside and reached out to push the first-floor button. As he did, he saw a big smear of blood on the panel. He pulled his hand back in disgust, just for a second, thinking, *they should do a better job of cleaning this place! Someone should lose their job for leaving blood all over the elevator. I will report this as soon as I get back to my room.* Rusty's stomach growled again, so he pushed the button despite the blood. It was then that he noticed he was bleeding. There were blood droplets on a trail on the floor of the elevator. Some looked dried. Some looked fresh. Rusty looked down at his arm and saw the blood dripping from the site where his IV had been. *Oh well,* he thought as his stomach moaned, *time for some food.* As the elevator started descending, he smiled at the thought of his escape.

The nurses and security guards, who were now all standing at the desk with their backs to the elevator, heard it ding as Rusty got into the elevator and left the third floor. They all turned around expectantly at the sound. The group thought Tekonsha was finally there for River. They waited for someone to exit, but no one did.

Chapter Eleven

Rusty stood in the elevator, thoroughly elated. He had done it! He successfully managed to sneak out of his hospital room. His stomach noisily cheered with encouragement as he slowly descended. His mouth watered in anticipation of some wonderfully delicious sugary treat.

He was pretty sure that as the group was gathering around the counter of the nurses' station, they were too busy to notice him. He never heard any yelling or commotion, so he figured he was in the clear. Just to be safe, he wouldn't waste any time waiting to be caught. He was going to get to that cafeteria as fast as possible.

The elevator slowed to a stop, giving a slight bounce as it came to a rest. Rusty noticed a corner of one of the panels bounce as well. *Man, this hospital is falling apart,* he thought. *Eh, who cares? I need to eat!* Rusty couldn't wait to get his hands on some junk food, though he was also considering going out for a smoke after he had had his fill of food.

He was sure there wasn't an accident. He knew the nurse and Georgina just said that to keep him in his room. He felt confident in that. But he was now curious. Rusty decided to make the ER his first stop. He knew he could peek through the windows of the doors and get a good idea about what was going on.

As the elevator door opened, he was greeted with silence, which surprised him. It made him both thrilled and apprehensive. No one around made it easier for him to get where he wanted to go, but it was also unusual. He knew that. The admissions area was dark. Not a single person was there. He knew it was after hours, but there was usually someone there to answer the phone. Rusty didn't like that.

He steadily made his way down the hallway towards the front of the hospital. As he got closer, he could hear all kinds of noise coming from the ER. *Huh, maybe those dummies were right. Maybe there was an accident.*

Rusty inched his way closer to the ER doors. It was noisier there. Things were beeping, people were yelling. There were clangs and bangs, and then more people yelling. He peered through the window of the doors to see what was happening. He wasn't sure whether it was a bus accident or not, but there were all kinds of people in the ER. Some of them looked severely hurt. The nurses looked frantic and tense as people rushed around. Rusty wasn't sure what was going on, but it looked serious.

"Get out of the way!"

Rusty was peering in, but he was shoved aside. He fell to the floor. Someone carrying a very bloody woman pushed past him, unlocked the doors, and rushed her into the ER. Inside the room, Rusty heard gasping and crying. He peeked through the window again. The person had set the woman down, and people were rushing to her aid. Bloody as they were, Rusty could tell that she was wearing scrubs, so he knew she must have been someone who worked at the hospital. Whatever was going on, he wanted no part of it. He didn't care. It wasn't his business. *Better them than me*, Rusty thought. And then his stomach reminded him of why he was down there in the first place.

Rusty looked around the first floor. He thought it seemed darker than usual. But he had never been down there at night. Maybe it was always that way. He didn't have time to figure it out. He needed to get some food and go back to his room before the nurses noticed he was gone. Or worse, before one of his hospital neighbors ratted him out.

Other than the ER, everything down there seemed eerily quiet. He knew that visiting hours were over and the kitchen was closed. But it seemed off. Rusty shook his head. *Oh my god, quit being a wuss*, he thought.

Rusty's stomach made angry sounds, so he turned in the direction of the cafeteria and shuffled toward it. As he looked down at the floor, he noticed something. He bent down as far as he could to get a better look. Rusty's oversized belly kept him from getting close, so he stuck his finger in it. *Blood? Why is there blood all over the floor?* Then he remembered how the wounded employee looked as the man pushed him out of the way. She was covered in blood. He wasn't sure, but he thought he saw a huge cut on her. Rusty shuddered at that thought. He shook his head, stood back up, and continued toward the cafeteria. He watched the blood trail as he walked.

He was about halfway there when he heard a noise. He wasn't sure what it sounded like, and he wasn't sure where it was coming from. First, it sounded like it was in front of him. Then it sounded like it was to the left of him. And then it switched again, sounding like it was coming from his right. The noise changed, too. Rusty wasn't sure if it was a giggle, a whistle, a growl, or a weird combination of sounds, but it made the hair on the back of his neck stand up. He didn't like that one bit. For a millisecond, he considered going back to the elevator. But he was so hungry his stomach hurt, and he didn't go all that way for nothing, so he shook his head and continued toward the cafeteria.

Rusty kept looking at the blood trail as he walked. There was a lot of it. *How could someone bleed so much?* As Rusty was thinking about that, he noticed the trail had abruptly turned to the left. He thought about it. *That's a lot of blood. What if the person who hurt that nurse was at the end of the trail? I don't want any trouble. Besides, nothing I can do to help. It's none of my business.* He nodded, reassuring himself. Since it didn't concern him, he continued toward the cafeteria. Strangely, though, the blood trail had started again. It was directly in front of him again. He followed it as he walked.

Rusty made it as far as the doors near the supply closet when he had to stop and rest. He was winded and needed to catch his breath. He bent over into a coughing fit. When it subsided, he stood up and leaned against the wall, panting. Then he heard a noise again. This one was different. It sounded like a whistling sort of thing. Rusty looked around but couldn't see anything. *That's it,* he thought, *I don't need snacks that badly. There must be another elevator around here somewhere......*

Rusty made his way toward where he thought an elevator might be and heard yet another sound. This sounded like a low guttural growl. A sound you might hear a large cat or maybe a big, angry human make. Rusty wasn't sure, but he didn't like it. He couldn't tell which direction it came from, but he was sure it wasn't from the same place the whistle and high-pitched sounds had come from. The hair on the back of his neck was at full attention now. He didn't want to be down here anymore. He wanted to be back up in his room. He shuffled as fast as he could down the hallway, desperately trying to find another elevator. He stopped briefly to catch his breath. As he stood, he noticed a shadowy figure approaching him. He thought it might be the person who hurt the nurse. Rusty panicked, closed his eyes, and froze. A hand reached out and grabbed his arm. Rusty screamed. His scream wasn't just any scream. His scream was something akin to a woman in a horror show. It was piercing and high-pitched.

"Good God, Mr. Brown! Stop screaming," Kerrigan yelled as she covered her ears.

Rusty stopped screaming. He opened his eyes and saw Kerrigan standing in front of him, scowling at him. He grabbed his arm back from her and cleared his throat.

"Uh, I wasn't scared!"

"Yeah, ok. You greet everyone with a blood-curdling scream, do you?"

"No! I uh, I was ah, just...a little startled..yeah, a little startled, ok?"

"Yeah, riiiiight. What the actual fuck, Rusty? How did you get down here?" Kerrigan said. She was beyond pissed that he was out of his room.

"Oh, ha ha ha, well, you see—"

More sounds cut him off. His eyes got very wide. He looked at Kerrigan, trying to see if she heard them as well. She must have because she turned to look in the direction of the sound.

"Hey, you know what? I should probably get back up to my room. I need to find the closest elevator. I'll see you back up—"

"The closest elevator is the service elevator, over there," Kerrigan said, pointing down the hallway behind her. "It is for staff. And right now, it's locked. You can't open it; you need an escort."

"Well, then, escort me!" Rusty tried to sound in control, but he was getting nervous, and it was showing.

"I am down here for a reason. When Eiler gets here, we will all ride back up together. He was helping transport a patient to the second floor. You didn't see him, did you? I was supposed to wait right by the elevator, but I heard noises in the restrooms and went to investigate. God, Mr. Brown, you are a pain in the—nope, never mind. I am just going to call Eiler and let him know you are with me. The sooner we get you back to the third floor, the better!"

"What do you mean the elevators are locked?! What in the hell kind of hospital is this? You guys are locking people in now? I'm gonna sue you all for every penny you have! Why I—"

Rusty abruptly fell over into another coughing fit. As it subsided, he righted himself, though he was queasy and shaky this time. He looked at Kerrigan, pointed his finger, and was about to continue yelling at her when she spoke up.

"Rusty, *shut up*! God, you are so damn rude! It is no wonder you end up here so much. You are mean, ornery, and unhealthy. Did you even notice that you were bleeding? I am not kidding! You need to go back upstairs. We are getting you back to your room!"

Kerrigan pulled out her phone, but just as she was about to dial, it rang. As she swiped to answer it and say hello, Rusty's hand batted the phone down to the ground. He did not want to be taken back up to the third floor by security. He just wanted to go home. As they stared at the phone on the floor, they both heard a voice.

"Hello? Kerrigan?" Charity asked.

At that exact moment, Rusty and Kerrigan heard a sound. It was louder that time. First, it sounded like a whistle, then a giggle, but then it became raspy, almost like another growl. Kerrigan looked at Rusty questioningly, wondering if he had heard the same things. She shook her head, thinking she must be hearing things. She moved to reach for her phone, but before she could get it, Rusty took one of his dirty socked feet and slammed his heel down onto Kerrigan's phone.

"What the actual fuck, *Rusty*? Why would you break my phone? That was Charity. I don't know why she was calling me. Maybe she needed something! Plus, she could have sent someone down to get you and—"

"Exactly. You were going to have someone come down and pick me up. I am NOT going back to my room. If I do anything, it is to check out of this worthless place. But not before I get some snacks. And you better believe I will be calling my lawyer first thing in the morning!"

"Rusty, just shut the fuck up. I have really had enough of you right now."

"Kerrigan? Is that you?" a voice asked from down the hallway, back towards the ER.

"Yeah. Prue?"

"Yeah. What are you doing down here? You should be back on your floor. It's dangerous here right now."

"What do you mean it's 'dangerous'?" asked a now very concerned Rusty.

Prue came into their view. She was pushing a cleaning cart with a mop bucket. Kerrigan noticed that she did not seem to be her usual perky self. She walked over to Prue, ignoring Rusty entirely. As Kerrigan got closer, she could see tears had been running down Prue's face.

"Hey, what's going on? Are you ok?"

"You don't know, do you?"

"Know what?" Kerrigan asked, now very concerned.

"It's...it's..," Prue said while holding back sobs, "It's Tawny, Ker. She isn't doing well."

Rusty, who had been listening to every detail, decided he needed more information. He walked over to Prue.

"Is that the bloody nurse I just saw being carried into the ER?"

"WHAT?!" Kerrigan yelled.

Tears were now freely flowing down Prue's face. She could no longer hold anything back. Her face looked scared, exhausted, and utterly grief-stricken. She turned to Rusty.

"Yes," Prue said.

She shook her head a bit, as if to shake some of the emotion out with it. She wiped away her tears and tried to refocus her mind, returning to nurse mode and setting the personal aspect aside.

"Ker, it was bad. I will leave it at that for now. Dr. Coleman found Tawny down in this area, I think. He carried her into the ER. There wasn't much that could be done. She was sent up to surgery. She will head to the ICU on your floor after that. The prognosis is grim."

"Oh my GOD! What can I do?"

"Nothing. Tawny's already up in surgery right now. Dr. Murgonia is operating. You know she's one of the best. Are you aware of the lockdown? Why are you down here with a patient?"

"Hey, listen, lady, she is not down here with me! I came down here to get something and then leave, ok?"

"Well, you sure picked a hell of a night to do that! You *should* be in your room. You aren't going anywhere right now. No one in or out of this hospital. You might as well go get comfortable in your room."

"*If it's locked down, why are YOU down here?*" Rusty asked, not trying to hide his snotty tone.

"*I* am down here cleaning up the blood from the floors! See the cleaning cart? You might have noticed the blood trail while you were roaming around. It needs to be cleaned up."

"Wait a minute, Prue, why isn't Taka cleaning it up? You still haven't seen him?"

"No. We still have no idea where he is. And we couldn't just leave it. Benji is still helping out in the ER, so I stepped away long enough to clean this up. But Kerrigan, what are *you* doing down here? Didn't you go back up to your floor?"

"I did. But uh, I had to check on something, so Eiler came down with me. Except we ran into Arrow. He said he needed to transport a patient to two, and I told Eiler to assist with that and then come back down here for me. While I was waiting, I heard noises coming from the restrooms, so I went in there. I didn't find anything, though. When I came out, I heard more noises, so I followed those and ran into him," Kerrigan said, pointing a thumb at Rusty.

Before anyone could say anything, they all heard a whistle sound, followed by a weird giggle that turned raspy and was reminiscent of a growl. They looked at each other.

"You guys heard that right?" Rusty asked.

"Yeah, I did. That isn't the first time tonight either," Kerrigan said.

"I heard it too," Prue said.

They all stopped talking so they could listen. Nothing. Everything was silent. Normally, that wouldn't bother them, but on that night, it made the situation feel creepier.

"Prue, can you tell me what happened to Tawny?"

"She was fortunate that Dr. Coleman had to retrieve some items from one of the supply closets. He heard noises farther down the hall, saw blood, followed the trail, and it led to Tawny. He scooped her up and ran down to the ER with her in his arms. She was obviously attacked. We will learn more if— I mean *when* she wakes up...."

"Attacked? That's it! I am getting the hell out of here. You all can't stop me!"

"No, we can't. But Wayne, Glen, or John can. They are all posted at the entrances. The third shift can't even come in right now. You aren't going anywhere. You aren't supposed to be out of your room, are you?! The police are on their way. I have full confidence that they will resolve this entire situation. In the meantime, let's get you back up to your floor, shall we, Mr. Brown?" Prue asked pointedly.

"How do you know who I am?" Rusty asked, crossing his arms while scowling at her.

"Dude, the whole hospital staff knows who you are! We have a pool going on when you will be admitted again!" Kerrigan glared at him as she replied.

"Aw, that is bullshit. You probably just told her or someth—"

Rusty was interrupted by a sound. Puzzled, all three of them looked at each other. Prue leaned her head to one side, listening intently.

"Y..you heard that, right?" Rusty asked nervously.

"Yeah, I did. It sounded like whistling," said Prue.

"No, it sounded like a higher-pitched growl," said Kerrigan.

"No. It was a laughing sound. And it came from over there," Rusty said, pointing to the mechanical room doors.

Looking at the room reminded Kerrigan of why she was down there in the first place. She had to find out more from Prue.

"Prue, you mentioned it looked like someone attacked Tawny, right? This might sound like a strange question, but please bear with me. Did Tawny or anyone else happen to receive a strange call from a female tonight?"

"I have no idea. Why?"

"Well, the third floor got a couple of strange phone calls tonight. I only recently learned about them from Jamie and Charity. They thought it might be a child because the voice was higher-pitched, asking for help, but after speaking to them, I didn't agree. It's why I am down here. I think there might be an adult female who needs a psych eval, or one of the patients wandered out of Myers Mental Health Clinic. Eiler was going to go with me into the mechanical room to retrieve the person. At least, that's where we think she is. "

"Whoa. Uh, ok. No calls from any females that I have heard of. But we have been pretty busy with the accidents and the murderer on the loose thing, so I couldn't say for certain."

"WHAT MURDERER ON THE LOOSE?" Rusty yelled.

"Shhhhh! Good God, man. Hush. We haven't told the patients yet because we didn't want anyone to worry. The police are on their way. We have extra security. But it's also why you should have stayed in your room!" Kerrigan said, not even trying to hide her anger.

Kerrigan did not like Rusty. No one did. But it was excruciatingly challenging to tolerate him at that moment. She had one task on her mind, and he came down and screwed it all up. Kerrigan decided she would get him out of there so she could do what she came downstairs for.

"Listen, why don't we go wait down by the service elevator and get out of your hair, Prue. That way, you can get this cleaned up, and I can get this guy back up to his room, where he *should* be."

"You aren't in my hair, but I do need to run back to one of the other supply closets for some more cleaner. I ran out just as I arrived at this area. You sure you don't need any help with this one?" Prue asked while pointing at Rusty.

"Nope. I can handle this old codger."

"HEY! I don't have to take that kind of—"

"Ooookay, *Mr. Brown*, settle down. Ker, I will leave you to it. I wish you well with *him*," Prue said back in nurse mode. She nodded at Kerrigan, turned on her heels, and headed off to a supply closet.

"Well, Rusty, since you smashed my phone, let's head back toward the service elevator and wait for Eiler, ok? You *will* be replacing my phone, by the way. I will make certain of that."

"....Yeah...ok...fine," Rusty said in a defeated tone. His head was still reeling from all the news.

Kerrigan and Rusty turned and headed to the back of the building, toward the service elevator. They had only gone a few yards when they heard some clanging coming from the hallway that led to the mechanical room.

"That's it! I am going in there for a look around," Kerrigan said, walking down the hallway toward the mechanical room. Rusty followed her but was continually looking back over his shoulder. Kerrigan looked at him and said, "Go ahead and wait down by the service elevator. Explain to Eiler that he needs to escort you back up to your room. I am sure this is a wild goose chase or something I can handle. I will meet him back at the elevator after I look around in there."

"No! I, uh, I mean, nah. I don't want to walk down there by myself-I mean, I don't want to leave you down here all by yourself. I will wait for you right here."

"Ok, suit yourself. Remember, there is a murderer on the loose...." Kerrigan said as she headed into the mechanical room.

As Rusty stood there, he heard another sound back in the direction they had come from. He wasn't sure what it was, but it was all the motivation he needed. He nervously opened the mechanical room doors and entered the room after her.

"Don't you leave me out here by myself!" he hollered as he stepped down into the noise room. The doors closed behind him with a slam.

Chapter Twelve

Back upstairs on the third floor, after it was discovered that Rusty was missing, Jamie and Charity ran out of Tawny's room and down the hallway, looking for Bastian or Robert. They found Robert walking past the nurses' station.

"Ladies.... everything ok? You two look a little pale."

"You know that blood you and Bastian found on the elevator buttons? We think it might be Rusty Brown's blood!" Charity said shrilly to Robert.

"What do you mean it's Rusty's blood? How is that possible?"

"Yeah, so I went in to check on him because he has been such a royal pain tonight, right? The room was quiet. I thought he was finally sleeping. I peeked in and found an empty room. I went in and checked the bathroom. He wasn't there. As I turned around to leave, I noticed tiny drops of blood starting in his room and continuing down the hallway. It was barely visible at first. The blood droplets didn't get big until they were farther down the hallway, closer to the elevator. I found his IV pole and bag up against the wall, needle and tape just hanging, so that would explain the bigger droplets of blood. However, I am not sure if Rusty did that to himself or if someone did it to him," Jamie said.

"Have you seen him since you found that?"

"No. I haven't."

"I will call Wayne to see if he has seen good old Rusty."

As Robert pulled out his phone, he turned to Jamie and said, "Show me the IV pole and blood trail, will you?"

"Of course!"

Together, the three of them walked over to the hallway where Jamie found Rusty's IV pole. She gestured with her hands and then pointed to the floor. They all looked down and saw blood droplets. The group walked across the hallway, following the trail. Sure enough, it ended in front of the elevator. Robert pushed the button, waited for the doors to open, and peeked inside.

"Well, it appears that someone was bleeding when they got into the elevator. But there is something strange.... Some of the blood looks older and dried. Those blood spots are also larger. The smaller droplets are fresh. There are some smears on the buttons that look dried as well," Robert said, puzzled.

"Well, what does that mean exactly?" Charity asked a little more hostility than she meant.

"I'm not sure. Maybe two bleeding people used this elevator? You said the trail started in Rusty's room, right, Jamie?" When she nodded her head, Robert continued, "Maybe he had company in the elevator? Are there any other patients missing from their rooms?"

"Well, shit. I didn't even think about checking that. God, I am tired. Char, let's do a quick, quiet check, ok?"

"Yup. You take one side; I will take the other."

"Ok, I am going to go call Wayne and go get Bastian. Maybe he saw Rusty and is trying to get him back up here.... Let's meet back at the nurses' station, ok?"

"Yup. You got it," Jamie said.

Jamie, Charity, and Robert all nodded to each other, and proceeded down the hall. As the women walked, they each had unconsciously placed their hands on their panic buttons. They started at the far end of the hallway and worked towards the front. One by one, they quietly peeked into the rooms. The patients were all asleep, so they didn't need to explain anything. Just as the nurses met up near the last rooms, a light came on. Georgina Plattworth came to the doorway. She looked at the nurses with a raised eyebrow.

"Are you looking for that crusty old Rusty Brown?" she asked.

"Uh, yes. We are. You didn't see him by any chance, did you?" Jamie asked her.

"I did. He said he was worried about his cousin's daughter since there was a bus accident tonight. He wanted to check if she was in the ER. He said he was coming right back up. Doesn't surprise me at all that he didn't keep his word. Excuse me for saying so, but that man is a jerk," Georgina said. She always tried to be polite, even when she didn't like someone, because being respectful was important to her. But she could not hide her disdain for Rusty right then. She continued, "He acts like he always has a bee in his bonnet, and everyone else is to blame for it. I am sorry I didn't try to stop him. Is he ok?"

"Oh, Mrs. Plattworth, you do not have anything at all to apologize for! We are all familiar with Mr. Brown's poor attitude. We need to find him and return him to his room. Try not to worry," Charity said, trying to console her.

"Oh, please call me Georgie. You aren't that much younger than I am. The 'Mrs..' makes me feel old. Have you heard if the phones are down? I couldn't reach Nathaniel a moment ago."

"I am not sure. I am wondering if some of the phone lines and towers are being affected by the storm because I couldn't get a hold of Richard's Rolls either," Jamie said.

"Yeah, that must be it...." Georgina said, worriedly.

"While we are both here, can we get you anything? Are you doing ok?"

"No, no, I don't need anything. I've been having trouble sleeping tonight. It must be the storm. I don't need anything. Thank you."

"Would you like something to help you sleep?" Charity asked.

"Goodness no! I'll be ok. Thank you, though," Georgina said, yawning.

"Ok, Mrs. Plattworth— Georgie. I hope you get some rest. We will be back in to check on you in a few hours. Good night," Jamie said.

"Good night, you two. Stay safe!"

Jamie and Charity looked at each other. As far as they knew, none of the patients knew about the lockdown, added security, or the murderer on the loose. They were shocked Georgina would say that. Jamie looked questioningly at her.

"Uh.... Stay safe?"

"Well, yes, if the storm is that bad and we end up losing power, you two are going to have your hands full with Rusty Brown roaming around. Honestly, *that man*! I hope you find him and get him back in his room soon. Good luck with that."

"Oh, yeah. That's true. Thank you, Georgie. Good night. Get some rest. I am sure your tests tomorrow will go smoothly, so try not to worry," Jamie said, smiling at her reassuringly.

It was Georgina's turn to be surprised. She thought she had put the upcoming tests out of her mind, but even her nurses saw the worry. She just needed to get some sleep and deal with the tests in the morning. She smiled, nodded, and walked back into her room.

Jamie and Charity smiled and walked away. When they returned to the desk, they saw that Robert and Bastian were engaged in an intense discussion by the elevator. They both walked over to the security guards.

"Hi, guys. What's going on? Did you find Rusty?" Jamie asked the men, who had solemn looks on their faces.

"We did not. Wayne hadn't seen him either, but they had been dealing with a lot down there. We were checking out the blood trail and smears in the elevator again," Robert said in quite a serious tone. "You think this was the work of Rusty?"

"Yes. He tried sneaking out twice tonight. When I went to check on him, I found an empty room, but there were blood droplets. I followed the trail, and that's when I discovered his IV pole up against the wall," Jamie said.

"Had he been in the elevator prior? Or did anyone else with a bleeding wound use this elevator earlier?" Bastian asked.

"Not to my knowledge. I didn't see any blood when I came up in the elevator. Why?"

"Like I said, some of the blood looks older. The smaller droplets look fresher. But the larger smears are dried. Which means two people in the elevator were bleeding," Robert said with a concerned look on his face.

"Oh my god! *Do you think the murderer was in the elevator*?!" Charity yelled.

"Shhh!" Jamie hissed; her eyes were as big as saucers.

"Sorry... sorry," Charity said sheepishly.

"I have no idea, Charity. I am no expert. I am just going by what I am seeing. I have no idea what it means. But I am pretty sure two people bled in the elevator," Robert said calmly. "We'll look around and see what else we can find. You two go back to the nurses' station. Bastian will go by the service elevator. Unfortunately, there is not much more we can do until the police catch the suspect."

"Yeah, you are right. Sorry. We don't want to interfere. We will head back to the desk and ride out the storm. Hopefully, the police arrive soon and get the guy who hurt Tawny and Prue," Jamie said. She put her arm around Charity's shoulders and continued, "Come on, girl, let's get back to the desk. Not sure about you, but I need to take a seat for a bit."

Charity nodded, staring intently at the blood drops on the floor and the ones smeared inside the elevator. The whole situation had her on edge. But missing staff, missing patients, and now blood smears were almost too much for her. She breathed out slowly. A tear silently rolled down her face. She turned and followed Jamie back to their workstations. They pulled out a couple of chairs and sat down. Both women were used to being on their feet, but they needed the break. Charity and Jamie sat there in silence. A loud rumble broke their respite.

"What in the hell was that?" Charity yelled looking around wildly.

"Oh my god. That was me. Sorry," Jamie said with a very red face. The noise rumbled again. Jamie put her hand over her stomach.

"Uh, you good over there? 'Cause that did not sound normal!"

"With everything going on tonight and worrying about everyone else's breaks, I forgot to take mine. I am famished!" And as if on cue, Jamie's stomach growled even louder, expressing its complaint.

"Good lord, James! Go eat before your stomach wakes up the patients," Charity said, laughing. "I can handle things while you are in the breakroom. We don't have checks again for a while, and the guys are keeping watch. Please go feed your poor, angry stomach."

"I don't feel hungry right now, but I will at least eat a granola bar or cheese stick or something." Jamie's stomach growled and grumbled as if responding to her. Her face was very red as she got up out of the chair and headed to the breakroom.

Jamie made her way down the hallway slowly. She knew that Robert and Bastian were attentively watching their floor. But Jamie still felt uneasy. As she got closer to the breakroom, she heard sounds coming from inside. She stopped dead in her tracks and listened. It sounded like people talking. Or maybe it sounded like singing. Jamie wasn't sure. The next sound made the hair on her arms stand up. Jamie was sure the sound was a child laughing. Without thinking about finding one of the security guards, Jamie grabbed her pepper spray and stormed into the breakroom, arms out, ready to douse whoever was in there. The yelp and protesting made her stop just before she pushed down on the canister in her hand.

"Whoa! Whoa! JAMIE! It's me! It's just me. Sorry," said a visibly shaken Hugh. The phone he had been holding in his hand dropped down on the table in front of him.

"Hugh! Oh my god! I am so sorry! I almost sprayed you! Wait. What are you doing here? And why did I hear a little girl laughing?" Jamie asked, looking frantically around the room.

"I am here because the daddy-daughter dance was canceled. With the hospital locked down, the second floor was extremely busy, so I offered to stay there and help out. But I left my lunchbox up here, so I asked Liatris if she would bring me up. I should have called you all. I am sorry. It's just been such a bizarre night. The dance cancellation and my daughter's disappointment were on my mind. I was missing her and the dance, so I sat watching a video she had made for me. That's why you heard a girl laughing. See? It's Jerriabeth," Hugh said as he picked up his phone to show Jamie.

Jamie's face was red again. She was mortified about storming in on Hugh and nearly spraying him. She always made an effort to be prepared and alert. But that night, she was jumpy and on edge. It was unnatural for her and made her feel off kilter and out of whack. She shook her head as if to shake out cobwebs and smacked her own cheeks a bit. She walked over and sat down next to Hugh. He picked up his phone and showed her the video.

"Aw. Look at her. She is so beautiful. When did she get so big? I think the last time I saw her, she was starting school. You and Novi must keep busy. How old are Marcola and Vine now?" Jamie said, smiling softly as she looked at Hugh's phone.

"Thank you. Jerriabeth takes after her mother and not me, thank God," Hugh said, chuckling. "She just started third grade. She was looking forward to the dance. She had been practicing for weeks. That's why she made the video for me. And the other two? They keep their mother and me on our toes. Nothing like two teenagers in the house, right? Marcola just started her sophomore year, and Vine just started seventh grade. Between sports and choir and the playhouse and every other extracurricular activity they can do, we are always running around, it seems."

"Wait, I thought you and Novi homeschooled? Did you stop doing that?"

"No, not exactly. The kids participate in the hybrid program at Living & Learning Institute. They have in-person classes two days a week, and I help them with online learning and lessons the other three days. It works out well because they can participate in all the school's functions and extracurricular activities, while also learning at their own pace. That's why I am grateful to work the second shift. It allows me to be a very active parent and take part in most of their activities. I wouldn't trade that for the world," Hugh said, smiling.

"Aw, you two must be so proud of them. I mean, look at them helping their little sister in the video. Gosh, where did the time go?" Jamie asked.

"It sure does go by too fast..."

"I have been meaning to stop by High Anxie-Tea and visit with Novi. Things have been incredibly busy with classes and work. Her tea blends are amazing, and the CBD muscle rub is out of this world! Perfect for my raggedy old body," Jamie said, chuckling at the thought of not only tea and CBD being her ways to destress but also that she could get both at the same store. It was a far cry from her youthful days of smoking weed or drinking wine coolers. "How do you two do it? You two work such different schedules. How do you make time for each other?"

"Oh, you just do. My marriage and my kids are my priorities. That makes it a little easier, I suppose."

"I honestly wish I had that, Hugh," Jamie said wistfully. "But those days are long passed now."

Hugh stood up from the chair and patted Jamie on the shoulder. He smiled at her and said, "Oh, you never know, Jamie. You just never know... Never in a million years did I think I would be in my fifties with teenagers and an elementary-aged child. But that's what happens when you are ten years older than your wife, I guess. So don't count yourself out yet. Life is a strange and wondrous thing," Hugh said with a huge smile now.

"Hmm, I am not too sure about that, Hugh. But I tell you what. I will leave myself open to possibilities. How's that?"

"I think that is a good idea! You would be a fabulous mother, Jamie. I am certain. Now, please excuse me. I am going to make myself useful. Since I am stuck here for a while, I might as well get some more work done. Good talking to you. Try to stop by High Anxie-Tea soon. Novi would love it," Hugh said as he walked out of the breakroom.

Jamie sat alone in the breakroom, thinking about what Hugh said. She wanted nothing more than to be a mother. That feeling never left, even after the miscarriages, failed marriage, and hysterectomy. She didn't share Hugh's outlook, though. After what she had been through, she decided that focusing on the life she had was the most important thing. And Jamie was ok with her life. Even though she was overworked and overloaded with school, she did enjoy it. As if to remind Jamie that part of living was eating, her stomach let out a giant rumble in protest. She patted her belly and said, "Sorry, tummy. I will feed you something now."

She stood up to grab a yogurt out of the refrigerator when a sound stopped her dead in her tracks. The hair on the back of her neck and her arms stood at attention. She held her breath, waiting to see if she would hear it again. She did. The old phone was ringing again. Jamie's panic turned into rage. She was tired. She was unsettled. She was sick of the weird night and everything that was going on. She was worried about her friends and coworkers and was going to get to the bottom of it. She reached up to the top of the refrigerator and pulled the clunky old phone down. With her face twisted in anger, she answered it.

"Hello!!" Jamie yelled into the phone,

"He..hello? Are you there?" said a little girl's voice.

"Oh, knock it off! I know damn well you aren't a little girl! Who is this? Who are you?"

"Wha..what? What are you talking about? This is Val..." the little girl's voice said again.

"Come off it! You *are not* a little girl, so quit pretending!" Jamie said, fuming. She kept clenching and unclenching her fists.

"Well, that's not very kind....is it?" said a mildly deeper voice. She no longer sounded like the little girl who had been calling all night. The change made the hair on Jamie's neck stand up again. She thought she heard a slight growl mixed in as well.

"WHO AM I SPEAKING TO?!"

"I told you, this is *Val*," the voice on the other end said a little deeper and in a singsong way.

Jamie was both fearful and enraged. She was angry at herself for not just calling the police the moment the phone rang the first time. She felt guilty for agreeing to let Reid find her. She felt angry that Tore and Kerrigan also went down there after her. And she was livid that she had been taken advantage of. It was clear that Kerrigan had been right; there was no little girl. Jamie was speaking to a woman.

"Listen, you crazy psycho, I am *done* playing around! Who are you and where are my friends!?" Jamie demanded rather than asked. She hoped the woman would give up and admit the truth. But Jamie wasn't prepared for what she heard next. The woman started whistling. And then she began to giggle and giggle. Though Jamie swore she also heard a sort of guttural growl. Jamie gripped the phone handset with both hands and yelled into the phone, "WHAT IS SO FUNNY?"

"Why *you* are, Jamie. You think you have it all figured out, don't you?"

"What don't I have figured out, huh? You are a patient of Myers Mental Health Clinic who escaped her room and is now playing some sick and twisted game, calling people on this old phone, pretending to be a little girl who needs help. Is that what you think I don't understand?"

"This isn't the first time we have spoken to one another......"

"Yeah. I'm aware. You called early, pretending to be a lost little girl. I remember."

"Mmmm, correct. But that wasn't the first time either. Think, Jamie. Think back..." Val giggled again.

"What are you talking about..." Jamie trailed off, recalling a very vague and fuzzy memory. The day after her parents' passing, there was a strange call on their landline. Pam and Bertie were each talking to relatives on their cell phones, so Jamie answered the call. She was quiet as she thought back.

"Ah... Are you remembering now?" asked the voice, hissed in a pleased tone. Jamie wasn't sure, but it almost sounded like the woman was whistling again.

Jamie thought back to that day. It was right after her parents' accident. She was standing in their kitchen when the landline phone rang. She was distraught at the time, so the memory wasn't vivid. But she did remember hearing a voice that sounded like a young girl... *It was a little girl's voice asking for help.* Jamie had been so out of it, dumbstruck with grief, that she told the little girl she had the wrong number and hung up on her. It rang again, but so did Jamie's cell phone. Her aunt was calling her, and she chose to answer the cellphone, ignoring the house phone. *That call could not have been from the woman. There is no way!* Jamie thought now, a bit panicked. She continued to think back and realized why things seemed familiar to her. Both of her parents had missing fingers. They also had huge gashes and looked like they had nearly been cut in half, which had been attributed to the accident. But Jamie always questioned that. *Those sound like the wounds of the current murder victims. I got a strange call the day after they had died. And I am getting a peculiar call now. What in the actual fuck? Could this woman or the murder suspects have had something to do with my parents' accident?!*

She felt sick. Tears started to form in her eyes. As one slid down her cheek, she said, "I only remember one call like that ten years ago. That call could not possibly have been you. Quit playing games, you lunatic!"

"I know you were going through a lot—the untimely death of your parents and all—but surely you remember my call," Val said in the sweetest, sickliest voice Jamie had ever heard. Again, she swore she heard faint whistling, but she also heard giggling. *Is there someone else with this crazy bitch? And how does she have information about my parents' accident,* Jamie wondered.

She had to hold the counter to steady herself. She couldn't process what was being said. It could not possibly be true. And at the same time, it felt like it was correct. *How could that be? How could that woman/little girl have called years ago? How could she have known Bertie, Pam, and I lost our parents?* None of it made sense to Jamie. She was now shaking with anger and probably some fear mixed in as well.

"Listen, *Val,* or whoever you are, I am done playing games. Quit dicking around and tell me where you are," Jamie said, trying to sound determined, but her voice wavered just a bit.

"Quit playing games? But we're just getting started, dear Jamie. I have been trying to get your attention for a very long time, you see......"

"What in the hell do you mean, you have been trying to get my attention for a long time? What does that even mean? I told you, I have no idea who you are. I have never spoken to you before tonight. You have more than a few screws loose." Jamie could not believe that woman. She didn't care what Myers Mental Health Clinic said, she was sure they were missing a patient!

"As I said, that isn't a very kind way to speak to me, is it? You may not want to remember. Maybe your mind won't let you remember. But this is not the first time we have spoken to each other. We even saw each other. Tell me, didn't you have a situation with a stalker?"

All the color drained from Jamie's face. Not many people knew she went through that. She rarely spoke about that time in her life. *Did I mention that during the first call, and she overheard? No. I am sure I didn't! But that would mean she was talking to...* "Am I speaking to a man? Are you the person who stalked me?!" Jamie asked, astonished, in almost a whisper. Strangers helped rescue her and stayed with her while the police arrested the man. Eventually, he was convicted and went to jail. She stopped keeping tabs on him, but she knew he had been out for years. *Could he be involved in this somehow,* Jamie wondered.

The voice on the other end of the phone laughed. It wasn't a pleasant sound. It sounded sinister and diabolical. It made Jamie queasy and unsteady. She heard whistling again. And more giggling. Jamie had had it! She didn't care if she was afraid, or if the person on the other end of the phone was a man *or* woman; she was going to find them and get them back to the mental health facility.

"I am done with you. I am done with this. Tell me where you are! You need help," Jamie growled.

"Come find me..." the voice said before the line went dead.

Jamie slammed down the handset. She couldn't stop shaking. But she was done with the games from the little girl or woman or man or whoever it was that kept calling. Fueled purely by rage and adrenaline, Jamie stormed out of the breakroom toward the nurses' station. Charity turned around at the sound of her stomping down the hallway.

"Oh, good. Did you feed your stom—"

"That fucking phone rang again, Char. I am over it. Done. I am going to find that woman. Or man. Whatever! I am taking them back to Myers'! Where the hell is my bear spray?" Jamie growled while rifling through her bag. She was tossing things all around in complete frustration and ended up just dumping her bag and backpack out on the floor, still searching.

It was Charity's turn to have the color drained from her face. Her mouth hung open. She stared at Jamie, trying to process what she had just heard.

"Stop. Jamie! Stop. You gave it to me to hold on to, remember? Here. What do you mean that phone rang again? What the hell? *How?* The phones are out right now. Wait a minute. What do you mean by *woman or man?*? We all thought she was a little girl. Kerrigan explained how she could be a grown woman. Now you are thinking the voice could be a man?!"

"Thank you," Jamie said as she took the bear spray from Charity. "How? I have no fucking clue. But he or she or whoever knew personal things about me that they shouldn't, Char. The voice mentioned the stalker I had in my *twenties*. Not many people knew about it. But there was no woman involved. My stalker was a *man*, not a woman. Didn't they say the murderer was a small-statured man with a higher-pitched voice?"

Charity gasped, "Yeah! They did! Was your stalker like that?"

"I am not sure about his voice. He never spoke to me. But he was shorter for sure. When I was being followed, I often heard whistling and giggling. Just like on the phone tonight. So maybe it's him...I have no damn idea."

"Jesus, Jamie. You need to find Bastian or Robert. Let *them* handle it!"

"No. I don't. I need to end this once and for all!" Jamie snarled. "I am done. I am all out of bubble gum!"

"Bubble gum? What the hell does that even mean?" Charity asked, puzzled.

Jamie wasn't going to stay and answer Charity. She was infuriated. She didn't care who was calling; she was going to get them back to Myers Mental Health Clinic, security, or even the police. She held the bear spray tightly in one hand and grabbed the pepper spray with the other, and tried to march towards the elevator. Bastian had heard Jamie start yelling and had been walking toward the women when he heard the last part of their conversation. He shook his head. The last thing he needed was Jamie going off on a tear. Bastian walked over to Jamie and blocked her.

"It's a movie quote, Charity. It means Jamie thinks she is going to kick someone's ass. But that's not going to happen, Jamie," Bastian said firmly.

"Bastian, I adore you. But you need to get the hell out of my way. You have no idea what's been going on here tonight. I do. And I am putting an end to it. They fuck around; they find out!" Jamie said, trying to push past Bastian.

Bastian didn't move or flinch. He stood firmly in place, trying to calm her down. He had known Jamie for a long time and knew that when she got riled up, it was best to try to defuse the situation. His attempts were futile. Jamie wasn't hearing him. She was sputtering and muttering. As her anger grew from being blocked, she tried to dash past Bastian. As she did, he grabbed her around the waist and twirled her around while she kicked and cussed. He set her down but did not let go of her. Instead, he kept her in a bear hug.

"Bastian! Let me go! I swear to God I am going to...I am going to... to..." Jamie stopped. She realized she was going to threaten a coworker whom she dearly loved. She whimpered and fell to the floor in tears. "I am so sorry, Bastian. But you don't know what that damn woman—man—whatever has put us through tonight. It needs to stop," Jamie said, utterly exhausted.

"This crazy night just got the better of you. Maybe it's time you filled me in, huh? What calls? How are you getting calls anyway? The landlines and most cellphones are all out right now."

"I have no clue. Maybe they called right before service went out? Or maybe internal calls work differently. No idea. But yeah, I guess I need to fill you in. Aren't you supposed to be watching the elevator, though?"

"It'll be ok. Just before I walked over here, Wayne radioed to me that Frankie had arrived. Lewis, Drea, Bryan, and Levi are here, as well as a few more officers. The rest will arrive as soon as possible. They still had accidents that needed attention.

Hopefully, they will find the guy soon, so we can all go home. In the meantime, you need to explain why you are so angry," Bastian said in his calming way.

Jamie took a deep breath in and said, "Ok. But be prepared. If I hadn't experienced it, *I* wouldn't have believed it!"

Charity nodded and said, "That's for sure!"

Jamie and Charity told him about the very first call from the old phone. They told him what Val had said and how Reid thought he knew where she was. Charity told him about the next call and how Tore was determined to help her. They both told him about Kerrigan, explaining how her mother used to play scary games with Kerrigan and her siblings when she was drunk, and that perhaps the caller was a grown woman in need of mental care. They explained that Kerrigan chose to go down there quickly, check it out with Eiler, and return. Jamie told him about the last call, questioning if the caller was male or female and how they said it wasn't the first time they had spoken to her, and how they were aware of her stalker. At that point, Bastian, who had been listening intently, asked a question.

"What stalker, Jamie? When did that happen?"

"Oh, I was twenty-something at the time. I noticed I was being followed around a lot. I blew it off at first. But after about a week, I noticed that it was becoming intense. I tried to confront him a few times and tell him to leave me alone, but he always ran. I went to the police and attempted to obtain a restraining order. It didn't work, of course. The guy ultimately got brave and tried to attack me. Two strangers happened to see what was going on from across the street and were able to help rescue me. They were also helpful in court. So, ah, yeah, that's it," Jamie said, shrugging her shoulders. "The weird part, though? When I was being stalked, whether he was in the store or on the street, I often heard giggling or whistling. I just remembered that tonight, while talking to Val. I always thought it was other people around me and never gave it a second thought. But now I wonder if it is somehow connected."

"I am so sorry you went through that. That is scary. You both just said you thought it was a woman who might have gotten out of Myers' or maybe came in for some mental care, though. So how could it be your stalker? I am confused," Bastian said gently.

"You and me both, dude. The *only* thing I can tie together is that my stalker was a shorter-statured guy, which fits the description of the murd—"

"Suspect. We don't have any other information yet, so he is a suspect," Bastian reminded her.

"Yes. *Suspect.* I never heard the stalker guy speak because he never said a word in court. But maybe he had a higher-pitched voice that might be mistaken for a woman, just as the *suspect* is described as having. Honestly, Bastian, nothing makes sense. I am grasping at straws here. But we need to find that person and get them help or..or..something."

"Things are not adding up. None of it makes sense. I believe you. Neither one of you would make something like this up. But something seems off. Jamie, I think we need to find Frankie. You need to tell her what you told me. You are not going after the person yourself. I will not allow that. But together, we can go talk to Frankie."

"Yeah. Ok. That's a better plan, I suppose. Frankie helped me with the stalker situation. She might have an idea what is going on. But, Charity, will you be ok here for a minute? I shouldn't have said I was going to leave before. I was just livid and reacted. Poorly at that. I don't want to leave you up here all by yourself," Jamie said.

"Firstly, I am not alone. Hugh is still here. He was down the hall last I knew. And Robert is still here. We already checked the patients. So that is taken care of for now. And if Frankie is here, that means this nightmare of a night will be over soon, and third shift can finally come in and help. I will be ok. Bastian is right. You need to tell her what has been going on."

"It's a plan then. Let me go fill Robert in, and we will go find Frankie, ok?"

"Ok, Bastian. I will clean up the mess I made and see you back here in a few. I assume we are taking that elevator and not the service one down the hall?" Jamie said questioningly.

"Yup. That way, Wayne, John, or Glen can escort us to Frankie. I will be right back." Bastian nodded to both women and walked away toward the other hallway, where Robert was.

Jamie turned to Charity, very embarrassed. She was not usually such an emotional person. She tended to compartmentalize a lot. She knew she let the phone call get to her, and her reaction was intense. She sighed deeply and looked directly into Charity's eyes.

"Char, I am so sorry. That was completely uncalled for."

"Stop. Just stop."

"I should not have responded that way. I apologize."

"Jame, you have *nothing* to apologize for. Tonight, has been the shittiest of shitty nights. The person who called seems to be very good at saying just the right things. If it had been me, I wouldn't have even remembered to grab the spray. I would have just gone down there in a blind rage. I get it. Do not apologize. Let's get this person back to where they need to be." Charity gave Jamie a slight smile and squeezed her hand. Her eyes started to well up. She continued, "I am just so over this night. So please, tell Frankie everything, and let's hope she can find the person from the phone *and* the murderer. Or, if they are the same, I hope she finds that person, I guess. I am tired. I want to go home and see my family...." Charity said, her voice thick with emotion.

"Aw, Charity. God, I love you. Yeah, I am ready for this night to be over as well. Here, keep the bear spray just in case. I still have my little one," Jamie said, patting the pocket of her scrubs and handing the bear spray back to Charity. "Shit! I have a quiz tomorrow, and I didn't even study. Whatever. Ta hell with studying for the quiz. I want a hot shower and my bed. Anyway, thank you for being so understanding, thoughtful, kind—"

"Oh, *stop!*" Charity said, chuckling. "No, no, never mind. Go on...."

Jamie laughed that time, albeit a tired and exhausted sounding one. "I am serious, Char. I love ya girl!" She grabbed Charity and gave her a big hug.

"Hang on a minute." Charity dug around in her pocket, brought her hand back out, and handed something to Jamie. "Stick this in your pocket with the spray. It's my lucky coin. Not that I think you need luck! It's just, well, just give it back to me after you talk to Frankie, ok?"

"*Charity*, God, I really adore you, you know that? Thank you. I will keep it safe and return it soon." She hugged Charity again tightly.

"I don't mean to break up your moment, but Jamie, we should get going. I radioed ahead. Glen is aware we are headed down. Wayne was trying to find Frankie to tell her we needed to speak to her. Are you ready?" Bastian asked as he walked back up to the nurses' station.

"As good as it gets. Be back in a few, Charity. Stay safe," Jamie said as she let go of Charity. She walked over to Bastian and said, "Let's do it."

"Bastian, Jamie, you both be safe! You hear me? STAY SAFE!"

"We are just going down to talk to Frankie. We'll be fine," Jamie said.

"We will be careful, Charity. Robert is just down the other hallway. Do not hesitate to use your panic button if needed. We should be right back up. And for the love of it all, *don't answer that phone anymore!*" Bastian said, looking sternly at Charity.

Charity nodded vigorously and said, "I will not answer that damn thing. You have my word. See you in a few, guys."

Jamie looked at Bastian, and he looked down at her. They nodded and headed to the elevator. Jamie subconsciously clasped her small canister of pepper spray tightly in one hand. Her other hand played with the panic button on her key fob. Together, they got into the same elevator that Rusty Brown had sneaked into. The blood droplets, as well as the smears, were still there. Hugh had been told to leave them so the police could examine them.

Jamie looked around the elevator. As she turned around facing the back, she saw something else. It didn't seem right. She moved closer and peered down.

"Bastian? Hey Bastian. Look at this! Something is wrong here."

"What?"

"Look at that panel right there. The edges don't match up. It appears to have popped out of place. And there is blood on it."

"Hmmmm," Bastian mumbled as he pushed the panel with his baton. It wobbled and fell forward, leaving an open space where they could watch the elevator move downward. On the back of the panel, there was even more blood.

"Bastian, that is way too much blood to be Rusty's." Jamie gripped her spray even tighter.

"I agree. That doesn't seem like a very good sign, does it? I will ask Glen about it when we get to the first floor."

Bastian finished his sentence just as the elevator stopped with a clunk. It bounced ever so slightly, causing the panel to fall the rest of the way to the floor. Behind the panel, instead of where the wall should have been, was a gaping hole. Bastian and Jamie let the elevator doors open and then close as they stood there staring. They bent down to peer into the black hole. Bastian grabbed his flashlight and pointed it into the pitch-black abyss. Neither person could believe what they were seeing.

"That's a tunnel! What is a tunnel doing here?" Bastian asked Jamie, quite puzzled.

"Huh. I didn't realize one used to run through here."

"What do you mean?"

"Back when this area was the asylum, it was a ginormous place. There were multiple buildings and even some lodging. Funny. Reid was talking about this earlier. Due to our seasonal weather, tunnels were constructed to make transporting the patients back and forth easier. It kept people dry or out of the snow. When they demolished most of the asylum and added on to the remaining building to make it the town's hospital, they supposedly blocked off the tunnels. They didn't, though. There were some great parties in them back in the day. After some unfortunate events occurred, the town did its best to block all the tunnels. Looks like they missed one. Wait...Bastian, is that *blood?!*" Jamie asked, horrified.

Bastian moved forward to get a closer look. The floor and sides of the tunnel were covered in blood. It was smeared down the walkway like a weird and disgusting red carpet. Bastian's eyes got very wide. He turned to Jamie and said, "I think we had better tell Frank—" but before he could finish his thought, he was interrupted by a horrible sound. It was a sound that nightmares were made of. Deep from the depths of the darkness, they heard a guttural groan echoing from somewhere in the tunnel. An intense plea followed it. It sounded far away.

"......h...he...help...meee....."

Jamie didn't even think. She went right into nurse mode. Her job was to save people. Help people. She pushed past Bastian, ducked down through the opening, and out into the tunnel on the other side. The sharp metal tore through her coat, cutting the skin beneath. She ignored it. Upon entering the tunnel, Jamie was able to stand up straight, which was a good thing. As she went to run down the walkway, a hand grabbed her wrist.

"Jamie, *wait.*"

"No, Bastian. Not a chance. Someone is hurt down there. I need to try to help them. Get Frankie if you want, but I am helping that person. It's my job," Jamie said, trying to push Bastian's big hand off her wrist. He wasn't budging.

They heard the plea again, and Bastian sighed heavily. He let go of her wrist. He knew there was no trying to argue or change Jamie's mind. She had a clenched jaw, fierce eyes, and a determined look. Everyone who worked with her knew that once she had an idea in her head, they all needed to stay out of her way. But she was an excellent nurse, and everyone knew it. So instead of wasting time trying to convince her to stay, he bent down and squeezed his large body through the empty elevator wall. It was a very tight squeeze, but he managed to get through. The tunnel smelled like stale, old air with a metallic scent. With the flashlight on the other side, they were able to get a clear view of the walls. Blood was smeared and splattered everywhere. It looked like a scene from a slasher horror movie. They looked at each other in shock and disbelief.

"Ok, let's go. But be cautious. And I will go first. Try to avoid as much blood as possible. We have no idea where it came from and shouldn't compromise any potential crime scenes. I will be bringing one of the officers back down here as soon as we help the person," Bastian said tensely.

"Yeah, ok. Hey, don't get too far ahead of me, and please don't tell Tore I said this, but maybe I *do* need to upgrade my phone. This little light of mine; it definitely does not shine."

"I think it is best if we stick close together. We have no idea what we are walking into down here."

Cautiously and methodically, Bastian and Jamie made their way down the tunnel. Now and again, they heard the same plea for help. It was getting weaker by the minute. The sense of urgency Jamie felt intensified drastically. If the person crying out was getting quieter, that meant they were critically hurt. She wanted to run down the tunnel. But with all the blood and nearly complete darkness, she knew Bastian was right. They needed to be careful.

"Jamie? Are we going downhill? You said you were familiar with the tunnels. Is this one going downward?" Bastian's question echoed through the darkness.

"I have never been in this tunnel. But yes, it does feel like we are headed downhill. Kinda weird."

"Weird is one word for it. Hang on, we need to turn right...." Bastian slowly inched around the corner, his flashlight leading the way. His other hand, which had been on his holster since they entered the tunnel, tightened its grip.

Down they went. They traveled a short distance and had to turn right again. To Jamie and Bastian, it felt like they were going in a circle. They followed the tunnel in silence. Both were listening, watching, and cautiously traversing the eerie darkness that tried to engulf them. The echo was disorienting, so silence was easier.

They didn't have to go very far when the tunnel abruptly stopped. Jamie and Bastian were now standing in a small room of some kind. Ahead of them was a broken, dilapidated door. Bastian took his flashlight and shone it all around, trying to figure out where they were. They both heard a groan again, although it was not as strong as before. But they could hear it more clearly, which meant someone else was in the room with them. Bastian snapped into action. He put himself directly in front of Jamie and slowly and deliberately pointed his flashlight at every nook and cranny in the run-down room. While he did that, Jamie listened, hoping she could figure out which direction the groan was coming from. They waited until they heard it again. When they did, they both spun around with Bastian's flashlight landing on a pile of what looked like old hospital bedding and gowns. Bastian still had his other hand on his holster, and as he was getting ready to unholster his weapon, Jamie whispered.

"*Bastian!* That's a shoe sticking out of that pile of— what is that? Is that bloody laundry?"

Bastian didn't have time to investigate for Jamie. She had already run over to the pile and was uncovering the shoe. That led to a leg, which led to another, which led to a torso... There was so much blood. The heaviest concentration of blood was on the person lying there. Another faint groan sounded again from beneath the pile. Jamie saw wounds all over the body. Some cuts were deep. Both hands were bloody and cut. There was also a massive gash across the abdomen. Jamie continued removing the fabric, and as she uncovered the person's head, she gasped.

"Oh my God! Oh my God! Hey....hey...hang in there. You are going to be ok! We will get you back inside the hospital. Just hang on!" Jamie frantically looked around for something to use to slow the bleeding down.

"Who is that, Jamie?" Bastian asked as he bent down for a closer look. He sucked in his breath.

"Oh god, Tek. Hang in there, ok?" Jamie pleaded. "Bastian, can you find me a gurney, or a wheelchair, or *something,* anything that we can put him on and take him to the ER in?"

"I don't see anything in here, Jamie. I will have to go through the doors and check. Will you be all right while I do that?" Bastian asked Jamie with great concern in his voice.

"Yes, yes, of course. Just see what you can find. Anything with wheels at this point. Hell, maybe even an old laundry cart."

"I will see what I can do. Sit tight."

Jamie busied herself trying to tear pieces of fabric to tie around Tekonsha's wounds. She grabbed whatever she could and either piled it on him or wrapped it around him. He was very weak and in and out of consciousness. Jamie was mainly talking to herself, but was also trying to keep Tekonsha with her.

"Who did this to you, Tek? What happened? How did you get here? Where in the hell are we? Hang in there. Just hang in there..." Jamie wiped a tear from her cheek and continued, "Bastian is going to find something that we can use to get you up to the ER. Just hang on."

After what seemed like hours but in reality was only a minute or two, the door burst open. Bastian walked in, pushing a gurney. Though there wasn't much light, Jamie saw that the color had left his face. She braced herself for whatever was next.

"Do you know where we ended up, Jamie?" When she shook her head no, he continued, "We are in the basement of the hospital down by the laundry room and the morgue. I took a gurney from the morgue. Jame? Uh, I am not sure how to say this delicately, but it's...ah...it's bad out there. I think I just found several of our missing coworkers...."

"*What?! What do you mean?*"

"There are bodies all over the morgue, J," Bastian said as he stopped the gurney right in front of her and Tekonsha.

"Well, it is a morgue. There are going to be bodies," Jamie said, only half paying attention as she piled more material on Tek to try to stop the bleeding.

"Not like this. Not... like this. Forgive me for being gruesome, but they are missing fingers and feet, and a lot of them seem to have one missing eye, and their intestines are lying in piles. Some of the pieces are piled on top of each other. There is so much blood. It isn't good, Jamie. I am not a squeamish guy. Things don't usually bother me. This is wrong on so many levels. It is very clear that the murderer was down here."

"Ok. I will take a look on our way out. Now help me get Tek up on this thing, will you?"

"Yes, of course. But I don't think you'll want to look, Jamie. It might be better left for Frankie and the rest of the police."

"I am a nurse, Bastian. I can handle it," Jamie said confidently.

Together, Jamie and Bastian lifted Tekonsha onto the gurney. They did their best to be delicate and inflict as little pain as possible. But he was in bad shape, so as they laid him down, he let out a huge groan.

"Yes, yeah, Tek. I am so sorry. That was it. You did it. Hang in there while we get you up to the ER. Just hang in there, bud,"

Jamie said, very concerned. She hoped she did a good enough job masking it so that Tekonsha couldn't tell.

Tekonsha was in and out of consciousness. His breathing was labored, and he had a thready pulse. He had lost a lot of blood, and he was in a tremendous amount of pain. It took everything in him to open his eyes. He looked at Jamie, staring down with such concern in her eyes. He needed to find a way to tell her. He needed to make his body function. They needed to recognize the danger they were all in. He attempted to grab Jamie's arm, but he was just too weak. Instead, to Jamie, it looked like he was twitching. Jamie rubbed his shoulder, trying to console him. He lifted his head as much as he could and stared at Jamie.

"T...t.. two.." was all Tekonsha got out before he passed out again.

"What did he just say?" Bastian asked.

"He said *too*. Maybe others are hurt too. Or maybe he meant number two because he works on the second floor. I don't know. Let's get him up to the ER as fast as we can, ok?"

"Copy that! Let's go."

Jamie and Bastian cautiously but briskly pushed the gurney through the narrow door and into a room that looked old and forgotten. Jamie had been down to the morgue a few times, but she had never seen that room before. As they pushed Tekonsha forward, her eyes scanned the dimly lit walls, searching for a light switch. Over by another door, she saw one. She ran ahead and flicked them on. The room looked like an old office left over from the asylum. There were dusty and rusty filing cabinets, old, moldy books, and papers that were yellowed and crumbling with time.

"What a weird room. Where in the hell did this come from?" Jamie said, wondering aloud as she kept pressure on the wounds while pushing Tekonsha.

"I was wondering the same thing. It looks like it was frozen in time."

"I will have to ask Reid when I find him. I bet he will have that information," Jamie said. Though she had way too many things on her mind, finding Reid had not left it.

"The morgue is on the other side of that door. We can grab the service elevator from there and get Tekonsha up to the ER. You hear that, Tek? Hang in there. We are almost there," Bastian said, trying to encourage himself just as much as his coworker.

As they pushed through the door and out into the enormous morgue, Jamie scanned the room, looking for a light switch. Over on another wall, she found one and flicked it on. The room was engulfed in bright light, revealing the kind of horror scene they were standing in. The floor was covered in blood. It almost glowed and shimmered under the artificial lights. There were gnawed fingers and torn out eyes in various spots, piles of what looked like chewed on feet and intestines. And lined up against the wall were bodies. They were staged, sitting to appear relaxed, and leaning back against the wall. The most grotesque thing was that each person had been made to look like they were smiling. Their lips were pulled up and back, showing their teeth, and they were covered in blood like some macabre lipstick. It was the most disturbing thing Jamie and Bastian had ever seen.

Jamie quietly muttered, "Oh my god," as she stepped closer. Even though she was a nurse and had seen a lot, that was too much. Bastian was right. It was the most horrific thing she had ever seen. But Jamie needed to see who was sitting there. She had to find out. She moved closer still, being careful not to step on any body parts or disturb the scene. The first person she saw made her burst into tears. There, up against the wall with a deformed smile, sat Ivy.

"Oh my god. Oh my god. How? Ivy left work *hours* ago. What is she doing down here? How did she get down here? Oh, Ivy...." Jamie cried.

She continued to look down the wall. There was Mark, the missing first-floor orderly. Next was Taka, the first-floor janitor, followed by Toby, the second-floor security guard who never showed up for work. Hunter, the second-floor orderly, was also there. The last person Jamie recognized, sitting and propped against the wall, was Dr. Prouty.

Jamie gasped. "Bastian. Oh god. I spoke to Dr. Prouty, or at least I tried to. He was making weird grunting and groaning noises over the phone. I thought I heard a woman's voice as well, so I thought he was having sex! But he was being attacked?! Oh my god! Why? Who would do this?"

As Jamie turned her back on the bodies, her coworkers, propped against the wall, looked at Bastian for an answer, and turned her attention back on Tekonsha. She didn't notice what was happening behind her. Bastian, who had been standing on the other side of the gurney applying pressure on Tekonsha's wounds, saw it all transpire. Two of the bodies (Jamie hadn't recognized them) that had been sitting up against the wall, with their gruesome smiles, quietly and slowly rose from the slumped positions they had been in. There was a male and a female who were both covered from head to toe in blood. The male had irritated, bloodshot eyes that he blinked rapidly. The female kept licking her lips. With the crazed smiles on their faces, they lifted their arms to reveal huge, very odd-looking knives. They lifted their weapons high above their heads, ready to strike.

Bastian stood horrified as he was applying pressure to Tekonsha's wounds. He looked at Jamie and yelled, "Look out!!"

Jamie spun around and, without looking, pressed the button on her pepper spray, aiming it at whomever Bastian had warned her about. The man, who had been closer to her, cried out, covering his eyes. He stumbled backward, growling and rubbing his eyes, as the woman, who had been behind him, smiled a wider, deranged smile and said, "I *knew* you would try to come find us," as she continued toward Jamie. She had a look of pure madness in her eyes. "We have been after you for a while now..." She looked directly at Jamie and giggled.

Before Bastian could do anything else, two things happened simultaneously. The service elevator door dinged open, with Lewis, Frankie, and Drea standing inside, weapons drawn, and Tekonsha attempting to point. He was unable to lift his hand to a significant height, but as he pointed, he whispered, "two" again as the crazed people continued toward Jamie. One person was smiling maniacally as her tongue ran over her upper lip, while the other was blinking furiously, squinting through his burning, watery eyes.

Lewis saw what was happening and yelled, "Get down, Jamie!!" She dropped instantly. The next thing she heard was explosive sounds followed by cries of pain and then the sounds of people falling to the bloodied floor. She put her hands over her ringing ears and looked up. Bastain was standing frozen, staring at the bodies on the floor. Lewis, Frankie, and Drea were all looking in the same direction. Jamie followed their gaze and saw the two people on the floor, blood oozing out from gunshot wounds. She instinctively walked toward the male. She wanted to check if that was her old stalker. Frankie yelled at her to stop, but it was too late. The male weakly grabbed his knife and struck Jamie in the arm, slicing through her bicep. As the knife came down, it bounced off the coin Charity had given her, cutting through her uniform. She was grabbing for her spray again when Lewis bellowed, "Down!" She ran and ducked down under the gurney, and Lewis shot the man again. Slowly and cautiously, Frankie and Lewis walked over to the two strangers. They each kicked the weirdly shaped knives away. Then they knelt and checked the people. Lewis nodded to Frankie, and Frankie nodded to Bastian. Bastian let out a long exhale.

Jamie was in a state of shock. Her mind couldn't process all that had just taken place. She wondered where the strangers came from. She didn't understand how Lewis, Drea, and Frankie knew to go down to the morgue. She snapped out of it when she faintly heard Tekonsha groan again. None of that mattered at that point. Tekonsha was their number one priority. She looked at him and then at everyone else, shouting, "We have got to get him up to the ER right now!"

Drea reopened the elevator and held the doors open for them. Frankie and Bastian helped push the gurney as Jamie took over, keeping the material on Tek's wounds and applying pressure. They all piled into the elevator: everyone but Lewis.

"I think I should stay down here, boss," Lewis said in his deep voice, looking at Frankie.

"I agree. I will radio Bryan and have him come down here to help you secure the area," Frankie said in an exhausted tone. They nodded to one another again, and the elevator doors shut.

Inside the elevator, Jamie's mind was reeling. She was trying to put the pieces together. She did not understand any of it, and she wanted answers. She looked at the two officers and one security guard.

"What in the fuck just happened?" Jamie asked a little too loudly. Her ears were still ringing from the gunshots.

"Which part?" Drea asked.

"All of it!" Jamie grumbled, trying to lower her voice to a normal tone.

Frankie spoke up then. "Glen had been expecting you two. When you didn't show up, he knew something was off and informed us as we walked up. We opened the doors, went in, and saw the tunnel. We weren't sure where it went and didn't want to go in blind, so we started asking around. John was the one who had heard about an old tunnel that led to the morgue and guessed it might be that one. We ran to the end of the hallway and rode the service elevator down, hoping to find you. When the doors opened, we saw you bending down toward Tekonsha and Bastian standing on the other side of the gurney. What *you* didn't see while your back was turned was two people who had been seated against the wall, rise and come toward you with weapons held above their heads. There was one male and one female. We had no idea there was a female until we spoke to Walt and Parker. We had been looking for them all night. They left quite a trail in their wake. Anyway, as the woman started toward you, Lewis and I fired at them." She put up her finger, indicating to wait a minute, and took out her radio. "Bryan, please respond." When he did, she continued, "Please meet me at the service elevator. Suspects have been located. Both are deceased. I need you to go help Lewis secure the area." Frankie heard an "affirmative" from Bryan and then continued, "We had to act fast. We didn't need them getting you and Bastian as well."

Jamie looked at Frankie, trying to make sense of everything. *Two murderers? So, I was talking to a male AND a female? The man didn't look like my stalker. What is going on?* But before Jamie had a chance to ask anything, Tekonsha groaned again. She looked down and said urgently, "Hang in there, Tek. Hang in there. We are almost there," just as the elevator doors opened. Standing outside of it was Bryan. He nodded to everyone.

"What's going on, boss?" He asked.

"Lewis will fill you in. Never mind, I will fill you in on the way down. I need to go check something out. Let's go. Drea, help these two get him to the ER, ok?"

Drea nodded as she, Bastian, and Jamie stepped out of the elevator. The doors closed, and the elevator headed back down to the morgue. Just then, Tekonsha's arm fell to the side. Jamie checked his pulse. It was faint. His breathing became shallow. She looked at everyone and yelled, "He's going into shock. Let's move!"

Bastian didn't need to be told twice. He and Tekonsha were not just coworkers; they were also good friends. Bastian always tried to be sensible in any situation, but seeing his friend hurt so badly was challenging his calm demeanor. He responded more loudly than usual with "OK!" He grabbed hold of the front of the gurney and started to run.

Jamie had trouble keeping up. She hollered, "Hold on. Slow it down a bit. I can't run and hold those over his wounds."

Drea's radio went off then. She stopped running to answer it. She looked at Jamie and Bastian and yelled, "Frankie wants me to go back down to the morgue. You guys got this?" When they both nodded yes, Drea jogged back to the service elevator and got on.

The commotion in the hallway by the service elevator caught the attention of some others who, unbeknownst to them, had been in the vicinity. A group that had been hiding in the cafeteria came running out armed and ready, expecting to see their attackers. Instead, they saw Bastian and Jamie running a person on a gurney down the hall. They dropped their sprays, makeshift clubs, and other various things and ran alongside.

"What do we have?" Keith panted alongside the group.

"Oh my god!! Keith!" Jamie said, crying. As she looked at him, her face filled with a multitude of thoughts and emotions, Keith interrupted.

"I know, Jamie. Me too. We'll talk later. What's going on?"

"It's bad. I can barely find a pulse. We have to get him to the ER now!"

"Got it," huffed the bruised and cut-up Keith.

"Like omg! Is that Tek?"

Jamie looked up again, still crying at the sight of Keith. She gasped and said, "Tore? Tore! You are ok!!!"

By this time, Jamie was panting a lot. Keith put his hands over the makeshift bandages and nodded to Jamie. She let go, stopped running, and crumpled to the floor. She lay her head on her knees, sobbing. Two people walked over to her and sat beside her. They were patting and rubbing her back. Jamie turned her head to see who stayed behind with her. She stared in disbelief. Looking back at her were the very dirty and obviously hurt Tore and Monika.

"Like, it's going to be ok, Jamie. Shhhh. You are totally ok," Tore said soothingly.

Jamie sobbed harder. After her coworkers disappeared, she feared the worst. She didn't want to admit it, let alone show Charity how concerned she was. So, she had pushed it way back in her mind. But seeing Tore and Monika brought it to the forefront. She opened her arms and hugged both women tightly.

She was sweaty, bloody, and dirty from the tunnel and from running, but she didn't care. She was so thrilled to see them.

"Oh my god. I am so glad to see you two! Where have you been? What happened? Monika, shouldn't you be home? I see blood. How hurt are you two?" Jamie asked, leaning back to observe them.

"Like, we are ok. I mean, we should totally head to the ER to get our cuts taken care of, but it's not urgent, urgent. I'm so happy to see you, Jamie! Guess what? It like, totally worked!" Tore said, quite proud.

"What worked, Tore?"

"The pepper spray stuff Charity gave me! Like it really worked!"

"Why did you need pepper spray? Where have you been?"

"Ok, so like, that weird phone rang again, right? I came down here to find Val *and* Reid. But like, when I got down here, I didn't see them anywhere. I was walking down the hallway toward the cafeteria, and I felt something pull my hair! Ew! I turned around, and a short man was standing there. He gave me like, super 'ick' vibes. And I was right because he totally tried to grab me, Jamie! Can you believe it? So, I remembered what you and Charity said. I got out that spray and shot it right in his eyes! I so totally did it!" Tore said gleefully. She continued, "While he was screaming and flailing around, Keith and Monika came out from where they had been hiding and totally took me with them.

We were hiding in the meal carts until we heard you guys. Like, what happened to Tek, Jamie? He did not look good."

"I have no idea, Tore. We found him down in the tunnel behind a weird office in the morgue. I found him under a pile of laundry. His hands were cut, he had wounds all over his body, and his middle was nearly sawn in half. I believe I saw a head wound as well. When Bastian and I were in the elevator, a panel fell off that led to a tunnel. I am guessing the murderers snuck through there, attacked Tek, and dragged him down through the tunnel. He was supposed to go up to the third floor and escort River back, but he never made it. I guess we found the reason. Dr. Coleman will help him. It's out of our hands now."

"Thank God, you found him, Jamie," Monika said. She asked, "Did you ever find Mr. Makenin?"

"No, we never found him. But we got a little sidetracked with the phone and—"

Tore interrupted, "Like, did you find Val? Did you get her back to safety? I *still* don't know where Reid went."

"No, Tore. Um....it appears that there was never a little girl who needed help. It was the murder suspect. *Suspects.* There were two: a male *and* a female. Kerrigan was the one who figured out it was an adult. I received the last call, and the person was aware of my stalker situation more than twenty-five years ago. I rarely talk about that. It could have only been a male speaking at that point. So, no. There was no little girl to find.

We were all being manipulated. Oh god! Have you seen Kerrigan? She came down here to find the woman and you and Reid. That was a while ago."

"Well, no. But like, we were hiding. We weren't sure when it would be safe to come out. We only did because Keith thought he heard you, and we totally heard the police radio. He thought it would be safe. But we weren't sure, so we came armed."

"I am so grateful the two of you are safe. But you are bleeding. It's time for you to go to the ER and get treated. Monika, that slice on your arm looks like it could use a couple of stitches. And Tore, your head is bleeding something awful. Head down to the ER. I will follow. I need a minute, ok? It's been a very long night," Jamie said thickly, holding back tears. She was physically exhausted and mentally drained. She needed to pause for a moment.

"Are you sure? We can stay until you are ready," said Monika.

"Monika, you are always so kind. Yes, I am. Get your injuries taken care of. I will head down there and get fixed up, too. I won't be long. I promise. I need a minute to rest. It's been one hell of a night. But it's finally over, thank God."

"It sure has been. Ok, Tore and I will head down to the ER if you are sure?" Monika said tentatively.

Jamie nodded slowly and said, "I am sure. I need a second to breathe, ok?"

The women nodded in agreement. Tore gave Jamie another hug. Monika did the same. Both women got up and slowly headed down the hallway towards the ER. They looked back a couple of times. Each time Jamie nodded, reassuring them that it was ok. She continued to sit on the floor, dazed by all that had transpired that night. She leaned her head down on her knees and just rested. A strange sound disrupted her moment. It sounded to Jamie like a door banging open or closed. She got up from the floor and followed the sound down a small hallway. At the end of the hall was the mechanical room. *The room that started it all,* Jamie thought. The door was slightly ajar. She cautiously pushed it open and hollered, "Helloooo." There was no response. Jamie turned around to head back towards the ER to check on her friends. As she took a step forward, she heard a small voice.

"H...hello," she said softly. "Are you there?"

"Hello?" Jamie said again, completely shocked while standing outside the doorway, speaking into the darkness.

Out of the shadows stepped a little girl. She had long brown hair, very big, round, dark eyes, and a petite frame. Jamie couldn't believe it. *There was actually a little girl?* After all that had happened that night, she was certain those calls had come from the murderers. *Could the little girl have been calling as well? Could there have been three different callers? Was that possible? How in the hell did she get all the way down here?*

Jamie's head was flooded with questions. She shook the thoughts out of her head and looked at the little girl.

"Oh my gosh! How did you get all the way down here?"

"I don't know....I am lost. Can you help me?" the little girl asked, holding her hand out for Jamie to take.

"Are you.... Val?" Jamie said, trepidatiously reaching her hand towards the little girl's.

"Jamie! There you are. I have been looking for you everywhere," a voice said, walking down the little hallway.

Jamie looked up, saw the familiar face, and smiled. "Hi Kevin! Boy, you are a sight for sore eyes," Jamie said as she walked over and hugged him. "What are you doing here?"

"It's an 'all hands on deck' kind of night, Littlefoot," Kevin said, using his long-time nickname for Jamie. "Jeff and Rook are here too."

Jamie had known Kevin, Jeff, and Rook for decades. Small-town living was like that. Kevin had been a few grades ahead of her in school, but they bonded more in college. He had been in the pre-med program when Jamie was attending Trillium Hills University. They had many career choice talks during that time. Jamie was present the day Kevin decided to drop out of college and become a firefighter instead. She saw the relief in his face that day. They remained friends, and when Kevin finished his firefighter training, Jamie saw the spark in his eyes and knew that he had made the right choice.

"Oh, yeah. I guess that makes sense. Sorry. I am fried. Hey, can you help me? This little girl is lost. We need to get her to safety." Jamie gestured to the little girl, who flashed Jamie a dark look for just a moment.

Kevin looked down at the little girl. "Hi there! I'm Kevin!" She smiled at him innocently and held out her hand. He grabbed it and said, "Let's go find out who you belong to, little lady." He turned to Jamie, put his arm around her, and said, "What a night, huh? I am glad you are safe, old friend."

They all walked down the hallway and back toward the ER. Though it was late into the night, edging on early morning, the hospital was bustling with activity. Emergency personnel were everywhere. The third shift workers who had waited, were finally allowed inside. There were police officers, firefighters, and EMTs. Jamie nodded to Andy and shot Mitch a dirty look. Kevin waved to two people who were having an intense conversation. He motioned for them to come over.

"Kevin," the man said, nodding at him.

"Hi," Kevin said, nodding back. He turned to Jamie and said, "This is Agent Bevic Torianson with the FBI. And of course you remember, Chiselle. Chiselle, do you think you can help this little girl? She said she is lost. I need to speak with Jamie and Agent Torianson for a minute."

"Of course I can. Hi, sweetie, why don't you come with me? Let's see about finding your family." She reached out, waiting for the little girl to grab hold.

The little girl smiled and sweetly said, "Ok." As she and Chiselle started to walk away, the little girl turned around, looked directly at Jamie, and said in a different tone, "See you, Jamie..." Her smile faltered, and a dark look flashed on her face for a split second as she finished her sentence. She then turned and followed the officer out of the chaotic hospital lobby.

The hair on Jamie's neck bristled again. Goosebumps covered her arms. She stared at the back of the little girl. *She said my name. She heard it from Kevin, right?* She was just about to chase after them when Agent Torianson spoke to her.

"I hear you have a lot to tell me about tonight?" he said with a touch of arrogance.

"I do? Uh, yeah. Sure. Probably," Jamie said, distracted by her thoughts about the little girl. She tried to take a step forward, wanting to catch up and ask the girl some questions, but Kevin stopped her by putting his hand on her shoulder.

"Jamie? Are you alright? You look like you have seen a ghost."

"Huh?" Jamie said, turning around. Her heart was beating faster. She shook her head. "Yeah, yeah, I am ok. Sorry, Agent, uh, Torbanson. What was your question?"

"Torianson. I wondered if you knew either of the suspects. Sheriff Goodweather and a security guard named Bastian Willowhill said you had information regarding the suspects? Is that correct? Did you know Valerian Manchester or Valencia Herbfeld? Had you seen them before tonight or had any connection to them?"

"What? No. I have no idea who they are. Wait a minute. Valerian and Valencia...? Val's?" Jamie almost whispered. She looked at the agent. "Did either one of them go by Val?" Jamie asked urgently. The agent stared at her, quizzically. He seemed more annoyed that she wasn't answering his questions. Jamie distractedly said, "Hang on. I need to go check on something!"

Jamie jogged away from the men, leaving them with puzzled looks on their faces. She weaved in and out of the crowds of people toward the entrance. She pushed through the front door, looking around wildly. The storm was still intense, so she squinted through the sheets of rain. She eventually saw Levi and went jogging over to him.

"Levi! Hey Levi!"

"Oh, hey, Jamie. What are you doing out here? It's raining cats and dogs. You should be inside. Frankie wants to talk to you. Bastian told her you had information for her."

"Oh, yeah, I guess maybe I do. Tonight has been crazy. Listen, have you seen Chiselle? Maybe a little girl, too?" Jamie said, trying not to sound too frantic.

"Yeah, they are just leaving. Chiselle and Hakka are going to drive her home. The phones were out, so they couldn't call her parents. But I guess Val said she could show them where she lived. See? There they are," Levi said, pointing to a patrol car.

"Val? She said her name was Val?" Jamie said, now in a complete state of panic. She took off after the car. She hollered and waved her arms wildly while the rain pelted her, trying to get either officer's attention. They didn't hear or see her and kept driving. Someone in the car saw her, though. The little girl, Val, turned around slowly. She watched Jamie running after the car. She waved, gave Jamie a big, wide smile, winked, and turned back around.

Jamie stopped dead in her tracks. She thought she was losing her mind. *What did I see? What did I just see? Am I going crazy?* The hair on her neck and arms was standing at attention. What her brain couldn't process (or maybe it wouldn't allow her to process) was the smile Val gave her. When Val's lips had turned upward to smile, they seemed to extend farther than usual. The smile was oversized, wicked, sinister, cold, and absolutely blood chilling. Behind the smile sat the craziest teeth. They looked like rows and rows of long, very narrow, sharp, needle-like teeth. Jamie wasn't sure what she was seeing. If she had been able to fully comprehend it, she would have seen the blood dripping off some of them.

Oh my God, Jamie thought, standing there. She snapped out of it and into action. She ran as fast as she could back to the hospital. People were hollering for her, trying to get her attention. She didn't bother to acknowledge any of them until she saw Lewis and Bryan. She grabbed each one by their wrists and said, "You need to come with me," while continuing to run to the back of the hospital. She led them back down the small hallway, where the mechanical room was located.

"Jamie, what is this all about? What is the meaning of this?" Lewis asked.

"Are you ok?" Bryan asked.

"No, I am not ok. Not even a little bit. I have an awful feeling about this. But we need to go in here," she said, gesturing toward the mechanical room door.

Both men took what she said very seriously. They knew Jamie and knew she wasn't the dramatic type. They didn't hesitate. They unholstered their weapons and cautiously entered. Bryan turned to Jamie and said, "Stay behind us."

The room was dark. There was a cacophony of noises jumbling around. Lewis used his flashlight until he found the light switch. He flicked it on, and the room flooded with light. It took a second or two for their eyes to adjust to the sudden brightness.

When they could see clearly, the two men sucked in their breath. Jamie groaned and started to sob. She held the door, so she didn't fall. Bryan turned around and helped to steady her. Together they all stared into the room, shocked and in disbelief. The room looked like a slaughterhouse. Blood painted the floor and walls. It was dripping off pipes and machinery, making plopping sounds as it hit the scarlet pools below. Body parts were strewn about: feet, eyes, fingers, toes, hands, and even bits of scalp. Flesh was mangled and tossed here and there. Right in the center of the room, atop the blood and carnage, there was a pile of blood-spattered hospital badges. Jamie squinted through her tears at the pile. The top badge read, "Kerrigan."

Chapter Thirteen

After Lewis, Bryan, and Jamie discovered the horrific scene in the mechanical room, they immediately informed Frankie and the other officers. Frankie tried to make sense of the ghastly scene. In all her years as a police officer and sheriff, she had never seen anything so gruesome and vile. It was a bloody butchery mess, she thought looked like something that would come straight out of a horror movie. Frankie had already wanted to speak with Jamie after the morgue situation. But seeing that, she knew she really needed to talk to her. She wondered how Jamie could have known to go to the mechanical room. She also wondered why Jamie seemed so enmeshed in the entire situation. After she secured the crime scene, Frankie went back to speak with her. She knew Jamie was in shock, but she needed more information. Frankie was having a hard time understanding it all.

Jamie sat in one of the offices on the main floor of the hospital. She was shivering uncontrollably, but she wasn't cold. The tears had stopped, replaced by a blank stare. Jamie had been so distraught that Bastian brought her into one of the unoccupied offices to calm down. Frankie put her hand on Jamie's shoulder. Jamie jumped.

"Sorry, hun. I didn't mean to startle you. But I have some questions," Frankie said gently. "Why did you go down to the mechanical room?"

"Val.....The little girl who called..." Jamie said exhaustedly.

"Called? Who called? What does that have to do with the mechanical room? I don't follow."

"Reid. Reid was the one who figured out she was calling from the mechanical room...oh... poor Reid...that stupid fucking phone..." Jamie said, crying again.

"I am trying to follow here. Uh, can you please tell me about the phone again?"

Jamie didn't answer Frankie. She was just too out of it. Frankie decided a different approach might be better.

"Bastian, let's go up to the third floor. I am sure Jamie needs to get her things. We can look at the phone and discuss things there. Help me get her up, would you?"

Bastian nodded. He, too, was unusually silent. They had all lost friends and coworkers that night. It was almost too much to bear. He walked over and coaxed Jamie out of the chair. The three of them headed to the back of the hospital, towards the service entrance, and away from the crowds. As they passed by the hallway to the mechanical room, Jamie's shivering intensified. Bastian and Frankie flanked Jamie and hurried her past that spot. Just before they got to the elevator, they heard someone call out.

"Jamie! JAMES!!"

Jamie turned around, staring blankly and unable to focus. The person was running towards her. She was waving her arms frantically. Another person was running alongside her, also waving. Jamie blinked to clear her eyes. She blinked again and gasped. The two people ran over and gave Jamie the biggest hug she had ever had. She started crying again.

"Jamie! I am so glad you are okay!! I was so worried!" Rachelle said, squeezing Jamie harder.

"Oh, my freaking God, Jame! Don't ever scare me like that again!" Kosina hollered.

"Me?! *I* scared *you*? You were missing Kos!" Jamie said, coming back into focus.

"What? When was I missing? Ooooh. Yeah, right. You tried to call me. Sorry. I was walking down the hallway and heard someone talking in the bathroom. I went in, looking for the source of the sound, pushing each stall door open. I found the cause in the last stall, which turned out to be Hugh's phone. He had been helping us out with cleaning and left his phone in there with a video playing while he went to get some supplies. You called while I was still in there. You had me so creeped out and on edge about that old phone story that when I took my phone out to answer, a huge clap of thunder hit, startling me. I jumped and threw my phone, which landed in the toilet. It took me a minute to find some gloves to fish the damn thing out. It's still sitting in a specimen bag. I tried calling you back from River's broken phone, but the call wouldn't go through. I went to a desk phone and called the nurses' station instead, and Charity told me you and Bastian had come down here to find Frankie. That's just about when the shit hit the fan, I guess. We had cops and security all over the place."

"I took Tek up to surgery on two. I found Kosina and informed her. We have been looking for you since," Rachelle said.

Jamie inhaled sharply at the mention of Tek. "How is he, Rachelle?" Jamie asked softly.

"It's not good. He is still in surgery. They will put him up near Tawny when he is out. Time will tell. He wouldn't have had a snowball's chance if you and Bastian hadn't found him. He is very fortunate. Let's hope the blessings continue, eh? Have you been seen? You are cut and bloody. Haven't you noticed?"

Jamie looked down at her arms and torn clothes. Nothing was registering with her. She said flatly, "Oh....I am alright. I will have Benji or Tore take care of me later."

Both women looked at Jamie, their eyes instantly welled up with tears. Jamie swallowed hard and asked, "What's wrong?"

"Oh, Jame....Uh, Benji....Well, we hadn't seen him in a long time. I am sorry to inform you of this. Um...so they found his hospital badge in the pile on the mechanical room floor....He....

He's gone. I am so sorry," Rachelle said, rubbing Jamie's good arm, trying to comfort her.

Jamie was confused. Benji was helping in the ER. *How did he end up in the mechanical room?* She looked at Rachelle and asked, "Did he answer an old phone? Did he answer an old rotary phone and then leave? Is that what happened? What about Amber? Is she ok??"

"Amber is okay. She already went home. Ah, no, I don't think Benji answered a rotary phone. Kosina was trying to tell me about them, though. Strange. No, the last time I saw Benji, he said he had to help a little girl. I watched him walk out the back doors of the ER into the hallway, where he took a little girl's hand and headed back toward the cafeteria."

"Oh my god...." Jamie groaned and leaned against Bastian.

He protectively put his arm around her and said softly, "I know, J."

Frankie was worried about Jamie and wanted to get the information as soon as possible. She looked at both of the ladies and said, "Why don't you ride up with us. Jamie is going to show us the phone. Kosina, you said your floor has one as well?"

"I have to stay down here and help out. Third shifters are allowed in now, but since it is nearing dawn, first shift will be here soon, too. It's going to be a fuster cluck. I need to go sort that out. Hang in there, Jamie. Come see me before you go home so I can patch you up, ok?"

Jamie was too exhausted to speak. She nodded to Rachelle before they all got into the elevator. Once they were all situated, Frankie started talking again.

"So, Kosina, the second floor also has a phone? Can someone help me understand how that factors into any of tonight's events?"

"I am not entirely sure. I didn't have anything to do with the phone. That was Zephabelle and Shanleia. Jamie is the one who told me about it. I mean, I borrowed a hammer from Mickey and smashed the hell out of it like Jamie told me to do. But I never heard it ring, never spoke to anyone, never even picked the handset up," Kosina said.

Frankie turned to Jamie and said, "So you knew about the phones first? How?"

"Shortly after my shift started, Tore heard ringing. We all went into the breakroom to listen. The sound was coming from above the refrigerator, like in those cupboards that are usually above it. Except this one was boarded over. I was able to punch a hole in the wall, and I pulled out an old rotary phone. It was still ringing when I pulled it out, so I answered it. *Why did I answer it?*" Jamie cried out, sobbing again. "Why? Why?"

"Jamie, this has to be very difficult, but I need you to continue...."

"Yeah, fine. Ok," Jamie said, wiping her tears and taking a deep breath. "So, the caller *sounded* like a little girl. She asked for help. Reid thought the place she described seemed like it was the mechanical room, so he went down to find her. At that point, we weren't sure if it was a prank or if a little girl had somehow managed to get down to the first floor from pediatrics, or if she had wandered out the back of the ER, or what. We didn't call you all because I already knew how busy you were. And we honestly thought it was an easy, peasy thing. Reid was supposed to get her back to wherever she belonged, whether that was her parents, ER, or PEDS, and come back up to here. We got busy, and well, out of sight, out of mind. Until the damn thing rang again, this time it was Charity and Tore who spoke to her. I guess she said the same thing; she needed help. Tore took it upon herself to go down this time. We all figured Reid got to talking— he likes to chat. So, Tore was going to find Reid and the girl. While Tore was gone, Kerrigan came back up from the ER. She and Benji had been down helping them. We filled her in on what had been going on. She pretty much convinced us that it was a woman playing sick games. And it made complete sense. She thought it was probably someone from MMHC. I called over, and the nurse said no one was missing except their nurse, Erica. Oh, and I think the doctor over there was being killed as I was talking to him. So, there's that," Jamie said, wryly. She continued, "Frankie, if you didn't check that building, you might want to send people over there. There could be more injured or killed. Dr. Prouty was in the morgue, but it's possible that more were harmed. Kerrigan made up her mind that she was going to find the woman and take her back to Myers'. There was no talking her out of it. To be safer, she was supposed to go with Eiler, but that became a debacle. The phone rang once more. This time I answered it. The caller sounded like the same little girl... at first. When I called her out and said I knew she was a grown woman, her entire voice and demeanor changed. She no longer sounded young and innocent. And she had personal information. She said it wasn't the first time we had spoken to one another. She claimed she called right after my parents' accident. I cannot understand how she knew about my parents. And I don't see how any of that is possible. She then claimed to have seen me and knew about the stalking incident. *She knew about the stalking incident, Frankie.* How is *that* possible? I didn't even tell my parents! At that point, I was pissed. I decided to go down there and get the person the hell out of our hospital. Bastian calmed me down and talked me into telling you about it. So that was the plan. We headed down in the elevator and, well, you are all caught up. Charity said the murderer, well, one of them, I guess, was described as a smaller-statured man with a higher voice. Was he the one calling me, Frankie? I looked at him after Lewis shot him. He appeared too young to be my stalker. But could he have been a nephew or son or something....?" Jamie's voice trailed off. She looked at Frankie imploringly.

"I put your stalker away. That wasn't him. Could Valerian have known him? It's possible, I guess. I am not sure about him or Valencia at this point. But it appears that everyone who went down to the mechanical room has perished. I need to see these phones you are talking about. That part still doesn't make any sense," Frankie said. She kept rubbing her temples and shaking her head slowly from side to side.

"Um, so, here's the thing," Kosina said as they all stepped off the elevator together. "The one on our floor wasn't hooked up. When I smashed it, I pulled the cord, and it wasn't attached to anything. I am not saying you all are making it up, Jamie. I am just saying there is no way it could have been ringing- at least not on my floor."

"No. Kos, that is impossible! *Impossible*! I answered the phone *because* it was ringing. How else would I have known where to find it? It rang! I heard it two different times! And I wasn't the only one who heard it ring. Maybe, uh, maybe you pulled yours out of the wall while you were destroying it?" Jamie asked as they all walked toward the third-floor breakroom.

"I guess that could have happened. I never heard it ring. You told me to destroy it, so I did. But I never heard it ring, Jame."

The three women and Bastian stepped into the third-floor breakroom. Keith, Tore, Hugh, and Charity were all there.

They all jumped up at the sight of Jamie. They walked over, circled her, and gave her a big hug, their eyes red and glistening. They all lost so much more than their coworkers; they lost their friends that night. Despite the pain and grief, they were so relieved to see her.

"Jamie! OMG! You still need to be looked at. You have like cuts and blood all over you. Come on, let's go down to an empty room so I can get you taken care of," Tore said, concerned as she saw Jamie's wounds still bleeding.

"In a minute, Tor. Frankie wants to see the phone," Jamie said, as she pulled back from the group and walked over to the refrigerator. She reached up and grabbed the old phone and said, "See? *This* is the cause of everything tonight. *This* is the reason my friends are gone!"

Frankie pulled the phone closer. She turned it over and over. She picked up the handset and listened. There was no dial tone, no voice, no nothing. She tugged at the cord, and it came tumbling out of the space in the wall and onto the floor. She held up a frayed end for everyone to see.

"Jamie, hun, there is no way this phone rang. It's not even connected," Frankie said, looking at her, confused.

"WHAT?!" Charity, Tore, and Jamie yelled. All three of them walked over for a closer look.

"That must have happened after you got mad at the woman...man...whatever. Right Jamie? You said you were livid.

Did you pull the phone cord out of the wall, maybe?" Charity asked.

"I have no idea, Char. I don't know anything anymore..." Jamie was utterly drained. Her head throbbed with pain, her cuts were really starting to hurt, and her middle-aged body complained about all the physical trauma it had gone through, aching in every possible spot.

"Like Sheriff Frankie, ma'am? The phone absolutely totally rang. I heard it twice. I even answered it once. It for sure really worked," Tore said.

"Forgive me here. I am having a hard time understanding how an old phone that isn't hooked up could work. You are all certain that it rang, and you spoke to... a woman, you all said? Bastian, did you hear it ring or speak to anyone?"

"No, ma'am. But I believe them. Jamie, Tore, and Charity are not people to make things up. Especially things like that," Bastian said.

"We all thought it was a little girl at first. Kerrigan thought it was a woman. But Kerrigan was wrong because I *saw* the little girl. She asked me for help. Ask Kevin. He helped me take her back to the front of the hospital from the mechanical room area. She was probably waiting for me to come inside the room so she could kill me, too."

"Oh my god! *You saw the little girl?*" Charity squeaked.

Tore gasped. "Val? You found her?"

"I do believe *she* found *me*... And I would have been next if it hadn't been for Kevin coming to find me. Oh." Jamie dug down in her pocket and pulled out Charity's coin, handing it back to her. "Here. *Thank you.* This helped more than you know."

"Hang on. You all are trying to say that a *little girl* caused that horrific scene in the mechanical room? That's a little far-fetched, isn't it? I realize it has been a very long and appalling night, but to say a little girl was responsible for that...that *carnage* is a bit much. Where is this little girl now?" Frankie asked. She was tired as well. She had been trying to catch those murderers all night. Now she had to piece together another massacre. Never in her career had she dealt with something so god awful. Her own frustration and exhaustion made her more than a bit temperamental at that moment.

"Maybe she wasn't a little girl at all? Maybe she was a short woman who dressed like a little girl...." Charity said, shrugging and hoping that it was true.

"I didn't speak to anyone on the phone tonight. But they told me about it. I can tell you with absolute certainty that I heard whistling and giggling when we were all hiding in the cafeteria. It sounded like more than two people out there. Were the murderers working with the little girl? I mean, it's inconceivable to think a little girl could be involved, but these women don't make things up. Maybe it's like Charity said, and she's actually a grown woman? I don't know. Or maybe it's like Bastian said, none of them are prone to storytelling or embellishing. If they say the phone rang, it did. If they think a little girl was involved, impossible as it sounds, maybe she was. This has been kind of an impossible night. A heinous night. What if they are right? Can't you check? Where did the little girl go after Jamie found her? You should be looking into that as well," Keith said rather sternly to Frankie. Jamie smiled ever so faintly. She knew she could always count on Keith to have her back.

Before Jamie could tell Keith about Val leaving, Hugh, who had been quietly taking everything in, watching and listening intently, finally spoke up. "I saw one of those phones when I was downstairs. Zephabelle told me about the one she found on the second floor. And when I was down on the first floor, Dr. Kantivoric showed me one. She said the same thing Jamie is saying, Sheriff. Dr. Kantivoric told me a little girl had asked for help, and she was going to help her find the little girl's family," he said. Everyone stared at Hugh. He continued, "And as I was walking out of this room tonight, I heard an old telephone ring. I thought it was Jamie's cell phone. Some people use those ringtones. But I heard an old phone. If it wasn't Jamie's phone and she said that one rang, I'd believe her."

"Eyden? Eyden Kantivoric? Where is she? We can talk to her about the phone and the little girl," Kosina said.

Frankie checked her notepad and gently said, "Uh, no. I don't think we can. Her badge was also found in the pile on the mechanical room floor..."

"Well, like if you only found her badge, maybe she is still in the hospital somewhere," said a very innocent Tore. She had not seen the monstrosities in that room, so she still held out hope that people were ok.

Jamie took her hand, looked her in the eyes, and sadly said, "No, Tore, it's just not possible."

"Yeah, but—"

"You have to trust me, Tore. It's not possible," Jamie said brokenheartedly.

"They are still cleaning up down there. Until everything can get sorted and people can be identified, all we have to go on are those badges. However, Jamie is correct; it simply isn't possible. I am sorry," said Frankie.

"Oh no," Kosina cried.

"Ok. But what about the two officers, Chiselle and Hakka, who took Val home? Can't they bring her back here so we can figure out what is going on?" Jamie asked. She involuntarily shuddered, thinking about the little girl leaving. Jamie had been in shock, so the memory was fuzzy. But something about it gave her the chills, nonetheless.

"There has been so much going on here tonight. I wasn't aware that some of my officers took a little girl home. Let me radio them and check. I will also send some people over to Myers', just in case. Be right back." Frankie picked up her radio, stepped out into the hallway, and walked out of earshot.

Bastian got up from the table as well and said, "I need to go make a call as well. I need to check in with Harrison. Excuse me, everyone." He nodded to them all and went out the door.

Tore got up and escorted Jamie back over to the table where Hugh was still sitting. Kosina, Charity, and Keith all followed. Tore retrieved the emergency supplies from one of the cabinets and set them down in front of Jamie. She began to clean up the wounds tenderly. A few were superficial, but a couple were deep enough that Tore thought they needed to be stitched.

"Like, let me go get the supplies, and I will totally stitch those two up," Tore said, pointing to Jamie's arm.

Jamie hadn't noticed that there were two cuts on her upper arm. She thought the guy only got her arm once and then her thigh. Then she remembered cutting herself as she entered the tunnel. She hadn't even bothered to look when it happened. She shook her head and exhaustedly said, "No, Tore. No stitches, please. Just butterfly them or zip strip them or something, ok?"

"Jamie, like, you don't make a very good patient, do you?"

"Aw, give her a break, Tore with an 'e'. We've all had a night, haven't we?" Keith said. He patted Tore and said, "I am sure Jamie appreciates all your care and concern, though. You are a good nurse, kiddo."

"Awwwwww! Keith. Like, you are going to make me cry more. Thank you," Tore said, her eyes welling up as she finished putting the bandages on Jamie.

"It's true, Tore. You are an excellent nurse. You found your calling. Just keep the spirit guides talk out of things now, ok?" Jamie said, smiling weakly.

Kosina, who had been lost in her own thoughts, turned to Tore and said, "What? 'Spirit guides'? What does that even mean?"

Charity and Keith laughed. Hugh chuckled. And Tore had a sheepish look on her face.

"Don't ask," Jamie said, shaking her head.

"No, seriously, Tore. What are 'spirit guides'?" Kosina asked.

"Oh, now you've done it...." Charity said, rolling her eyes and shaking her head.

"Like OMG! You don't know about spirit guides? Let's talk!" Tore plopped down in the seat next to Kosina, and they started a conversation about spirit guides, Melvin, and anything to keep their minds off the night's terrors. Keith and Charity rolled their eyes, Hugh chuckled, and Jamie just shook her head.

The conversation slowed. They all sat in silence. Each one of them was in pain. For some, it was physical pain. For all of them, it was an emotional upheaval. Many good people were lost that night. They were all having difficulty processing that. Tore ended the silence.

"I can't believe Benji, Ivy, Reid, and Kerrigan are gone. Like, I just can't believe it.... I am just going to say this now, ok? I love you guys. All of you. Even you, Keith," Tore said while crying softly.

Keith smiled genuinely, looked at Tore, and said, "I always have your back, kiddo. Remember that."

"We all love you, Tore. Ivy, Benji, Reid, and Kerrigan did too. And we loved them. They will be greatly missed. But I am so glad you, Kos, Charity, Keith, Hugh, and everyone else are all ok. What a *fucking* night...." Jamie shook her head. Her tears slid down her cheeks.

The group all turned to the doorway as Frankie came back into the breakroom. The color had drained from her face, and she had an expression on it that Jamie had never once seen her have. It was fear. For the first time, Frankie looked afraid. They motioned for her to sit down, but she shook her head. She continued to stand, using the countertop to help keep her balanced.

"Jamie, are you *sure* you saw a little girl riding in the back of the patrol car with Chiselle and Hakka?"

"I wasn't aware the other person was, Hakka. But yes. One thousand percent certain, Frankie. I chased after the vehicle, trying to get their attention. *Why?*"

"The patrol car was found about two miles down the road from the hospital. The back door was open, which is odd because it can only be opened from the outside. The...ah, the two officers in the front of the car were mangled in their seats. There was so much blood they couldn't even see into the front of the patrol car. All the windows were covered. It was only when they opened the doors that they saw their bodies, in pieces. Bodycam footage doesn't show much. But....um... very briefly, I guess it looked like—I am not sure I understand how to explain this, but a mouth full of narrow needle-like teeth biting down on Chiselle. That's the only video we have. It stopped recording after that. There was no footage from Hakka's camera at all."

Everyone at the table stared at Frankie. Tore gasped and lay her head down on her arms on the table, crying softly. Hugh's eyes were wide open in disbelief. Kosina's jaw had dropped. Keith and Charity just stared at each other. And Jamie groaned and propped her head up with her hand on the table.

Frankie shook her head and continued. "There is no sign of a little girl. There is a video of a girl walking out with the officers. So, we knew she was in the vehicle. That has been confirmed. But she is no longer in it. In fact, no one has seen the little girl since. Like I said, the door was open..... the backseat was empty. I....I..ah am honestly not sure what to make of it. Or what it means. I also had officers visit Myers Mental Health Clinic. Marguerite confirmed what you said, Jamie. Dr. Prouty and Erica were not there. Dr. Prouty is in the morgue. Marguerite said that when she was searching for Erica, she found an old phone with the handset lying on the floor. When she put the handset back on the cradle, she said it started to ring. She was short-staffed, dealing with riled-up patients due to the storm, and lacking patience, so she angerly grabbed the ringing phone and tossed it out the front door. We have people looking for it now, though I'm not sure what good that will do. We also picked up the one you smashed, Kosina. Hugh, could you please show me where the one on the first floor is?" When Hugh nodded yes, she continued, "The last bit of news I must deliver is very unpleasant. They finished cleaning off the pile of badges in the mechanical room. They found the following: Kerrigan Mahoney, Benjamin Summerleaf, Shanleia Bounpradeng, Zephabelle Miner, Skyler Trufant, Dr. Eyden Kantivoric, Reid Heatherwide, Erica Grimm, and a patient's wristband with the name Rusty Brown. In the morgue, along with the perpetrators, Valerian Manchester and Valencia Herbfeld, they also found: Ivy Allouez, Mark Sorinas, Taka Sharvan, Hunter Butte, Toby Brea, and Dr. Lidion Prouty."

Frankie sighed heavily as she finished. Never, in all her career, had she dealt with something so truly deplorable.

Frankie waited a minute to gather her thoughts. That night was not easy for any of them. She knew that. The news was hitting her hard as well. Frankie had taken pride in the fact that she had never lost an officer during her career as Sheriff. The recent news was devastating, and she was struggling. But she also wanted answers. She took a deep breath and continued.

"I have other news. Reenia Kestbell, a teacher at the high school, was killed today. That's why school let out early. Jamie, when I spoke to Park, he mentioned seeing you. Where else did you go today?"

"I don't understand the relevance, but I stopped by a few places on my way to work this afternoon. I was trying to get coffee for everyone here because I woke up late again. I tried going to Last Drop, but Siobhan wouldn't let me buy anything. In fact, she told me to go home because there was a murderer on the loose," Jamie said, shaking her head. "Wait! Scratch that. First, I ran into J.J., *then* I saw Siobhan. After that, I saw Dee Dee at Damn Fine. But Walt and Wanda weren't there. So, I ended up going to Roasted, where I saw Park. Why does any of this matter?" Jamie asked.

"And you are certain you didn't ever encounter either of the suspects?" Frankie asked tensely.

"I am. Again, *why?*" Jamie asked, very puzzled.

"It appears the suspects—one or both— may have been following you today. Siobhan Kennedy was also killed today. Walt and Wanda Anbrena were attacked. Unfortunately, Wanda didn't make it. And Park was attacked as well. The suspects were at nearly all the same places you were in today. It almost seems like they were following you."

"Oh my God! Are Dee Dee and J.J. ok? And what do you mean by, following? I would have noticed someone like that following me. You know me; I've become hyper-vigilant since that incident years ago. I didn't see anyone."

"I haven't spoken to J.J. since the accident earlier today. I am sure he is fine," Frankie said, brushing Jamie's concern aside. She continued, "I knew you stopped in to Damn Fine Cookies because Walt heard you. He couldn't answer you, but he *did* hear you. And like I said, Park told me he saw you today. He said one of the suspects, the woman, was in the shop just before you walked in. He had been fighting off her attacks when they heard you outside. The female fled on foot. Park said he waited to call 911 until after you left. He told me he didn't say a word to you because he didn't want to worry or scare you. It is just a really weird coincidence that the suspects were in the same places you were today," Frankie said, shaking her head in confusion.

They all sat at the table in complete silence. They were filled with disbelief, shock, and grief. None of that made sense, not to any of them. They were hurting from the losses of their coworkers. The news of their community's losses was almost too much to bear. They were emotionally exhausted and physically drained from the events of that night. Suddenly, a sound filled the quiet room, making everyone jump, Frankie included.

"Sorry. Sorry. Phones seem to be back up. That's my wife. Sheriff, can I tell her I will be home soon?" Hugh said.

"Yes. Go ahead. Hey, Hugh, on second thought, just head home. Be sure to stop by the station tomorrow, though, ok?"

Hugh nodded and stepped out of the breakroom to answer his wife's call. Even with everything that had happened and everything they had all been through, his coworkers could hear him trying to comfort and reassure his wife. That was just Hugh.

"Sheriff, I need to head back to the second floor and get my things. Is that, ok?" Kosina asked.

Frankie nodded, looked at everyone at the table, and said, "In fact, why don't you all head home. It has been a *very* long night. Go home. Clean up. Get some sleep. But I will need you all to come to the station, ok? We have a lot to discuss with that phone and the little girl situation. Agent Torianson was only concerned about Valerian Manchester and Valencia Herbfeld. *I* am concerned about all of it, though. I lost some good officers, and I am having a hard time understanding and making sense of it."

"You and me both, sister," Jamie said out loud. Jamie had known Frankie for a long, long time. Nearly her entire life. But she always tried to maintain a professional demeanor when Frankie was working. She realized her casual internal thought had slipped out and said, "I mean, me too, Sheriff. Me too."

"It's ok, kiddo. Don't sweat it. We are all tired. Fuck formalities, right?"

Tore gasped and covered her mouth, "Sheriff Frankie!"

They all looked at Tore and laughed. And as they listened to that sound, they laughed more. It was a welcome noise. They laughed at the silliness of Tore's being offended by a word, after the savagery their night held. They laughed that Tore always had that innocent way about her. They laughed that even with all they had been through, Tore *still* had some of that purity. It warmed their hearts. Tore's cheeks reddened a little, knowing how she had just sounded.

"Like, I'm sorry. You are totally right! Um, fudge formalities," Tore said sheepishly. Which was greeted with more laughter.

One by one, they all got up from the table. They gave each other hugs. Every single person there couldn't wait to get home. Keith wanted to hug his kids and call his parents. Tore wanted to proudly tell her judgmental family how she fought off an attacker, cared for a coworker, and made lifelong bonds that night. Charity needed to kiss her kids and lie in her husband's arms. Hugh, who had already left, was looking forward to having his family around him. Kosina was going to draw a long bath, call her mother, and rethink her career choice. Jamie wasn't sure what she wanted. She wasn't looking forward to being alone, but she also didn't want to deal with her siblings at that moment. She knew they would be frantic and worried about her, and when she eventually told them about Benji, they would be grieving him. Jamie just needed some peace and quiet.

As they were all filing out of the room, Charity said, "I can't believe Rusty is gone as well."

"It is horrible. Why didn't that man stay in his room?" Jamie asked sadly, looking at Charity.

"I mean, we all know he was a jerk, but he didn't deserve that," Charity said.

Jamie nodded and said, "I wholeheartedly agree. No one deserved that."

"Ok, all, I need to get home to my kids and Don," Charity said heavily. "Everyone, get some sleep, K? Love you all." She didn't wait for anyone to respond; she just turned and headed to the service elevator.

"Rusty went down to the first floor? When did that happen?" Keith asked.

"We aren't sure when he snuck down there. You didn't hear him, did you?" Jamie said, looking at Keith.

"No, but we were hiding. The only reason we heard you was because you were yelling as you came down the hallway. I recognized your voice and wasn't sure if you needed help, protection, or something," Keith said. His voice was thick and heavy. His brows furrowed as he shook his head, "That man...."

"Like, I didn't see Mr. Brown, but that's so totally awful. Also, Jamie, like please make sure to take care of those wounds, mkay? You are bleeding again and totally should have been stitched," Tore said with concern.

"Yes, for sure. I will be ok, Tore. I promise. Go get some sleep," Jamie said gently. As Tore turned to walk away, Jamie said louder, "I am proud of you, Tore, with an e. You are a damn fine nurse and a wonderfully kindhearted person."

Tore started crying again and said, "Oh, Jamie. Thank you. That totally means so much coming from you."

Keith put his arm around Tore and said, "Come on, kiddo. I will walk you to your car. Night, Jamie. Get some rest." He reached out his hand to squeeze Jamie's as he said that.

She squeezed back, nodded, and walked toward the nurses' station. She grabbed the rest of the things that she had tossed on the floor earlier and stuffed them in her backpack and purse. She picked everything up and readied herself to walk down to the service elevator when she heard a gentleman's voice call her name. She looked up and saw Russel Makenin.

"Mr. Makenin! Oh, thank God! Where have you been? Your wife was so worried about you!" Jamie said as she rushed over to him.

"Oh no! I didn't mean to worry my poor Ar. I went to get her some tea. The cafeteria was out of her favorite kind, and she loves the tea from High Anxie-Tea, so I walked over there. I was chatting with Novi for a little while—maybe more than a little while," he said, chuckling. "I lost track of time, and then the power went out. I was going to run back to the hospital, but the storm got worse. Novi was worried about me being out in that, so she had me stay with her until the worst of it passed. The phones were out, so I couldn't call Arlene. When I finally walked back to the hospital, they had us all locked out. I heard you all had quite a scary night. I am so glad to see you safe. What a tragedy. If you need to talk, find us. We loved your parents and miss them very much. We would welcome a visit from you," Russel said. His face showed he was sincere. He continued, "And stop calling us Mr. and Mrs. We are Arlene and Russel. Period."

"I know. But I grew up calling you Mr. and Mrs. It's a hard habit to break at my age. I will do my best. I'm so happy you are here. Please give Mrs. M— *Arlene* a hug for me. I am so glad you are back! And *I* am headed home. Finally," Jamie said, her voice weighed down with emotions.

"Will do. You take care, Jamie," he smiled and walked down the hallway toward his wife.

Seeing him made some of the heaviness of the night lift for Jamie. She slung her backpack over her good shoulder and headed toward the service elevator. After finding the tunnel in the main elevator, she decided she was in no hurry to be in that again, even if the police officers were there escorting people. As she neared the breakroom, she saw that Frankie was still in there and was talking to Bastian. Their conversation looked intense. When Bastian saw Jamie, he got up and ran over to her. He picked her up in a big hug, not thinking about her wounds. She winced slightly but didn't care.

"Go get some rest. Listen, if you need to talk about anything, anything at all, please don't hesitate to call me. We went through one hell of a night. There is a lot to work through. Harrison and I are both here for you," Bastian said. His voice filled with concern for Jamie.

"Hey, the same goes for you. You can call me too. It's not every day you deal with a couple of murderers and a little gi...ah...um... *monster* is a sufficient word, I guess. Right?" Jamie said, still in disbelief with everything that had transpired.

"Indeed. Monster seems more precise. Now go home and take care of yourself."

"Thank you, Bastian. For *everything*." Jamie hugged him again, waved at Frankie, and continued to the elevator. As she approached it, Eiler and Robert, who had just come from there, walked up to her.

"Jamie, how are you doing? Quite a night," Robert said his face filled with concern.

"Are you holding up, ok?" Eiler gently asked.

Jamie always liked those two men. She generally got along with everyone. But at that moment, she realized how blessed she was to have those security guards around. They were great at their job, but it was their compassion that made them invaluable. Jamie teared up again.

"Yes. As good as I can be, I think. Thank you, both. I am just going to go home, clean up, and pass out. I do believe my bed is calling my name. Ta hell with class. I am fried."

"Class should be the last thing on your mind right now. Do you have someone to stay with you? You shouldn't be alone," Robert asked, concerned.

"I will figure it out. I can call my brother or sister. In fact, I need to call Bertie. He is going to be so heartbroken. Oh, I don't want him to stay with me and deal with that. Ugh. I will figure it out. No worries."

"Call if you need company. Either of us is available," Eiler said. Robert nodded in agreement.

"Thanks, guys. I mean it. Now, if you will excuse me, I need to get the fuck out of here," Jamie said, completely depleted of all energy.

They each hugged her and walked away from her toward the breakroom. Jamie felt doubly blessed to have such kind and caring coworkers. She walked up to the elevator and pushed the down button. She shivered a little bit, said to herself, "fuck this", grabbed her badge, and opened the door to the stairwell instead. She had had enough of the elevators right then. As she descended, enjoying the silence, she heard someone climbing in her direction. Jamie stopped and waited. Soon enough, a third shift nurse appeared. Jamie gave her a faint smile.

"Hi, Jamie. Long night, huh?" Viki gently asked, looking at Jamie with great concern.

"You can say that again, sister," Jamie said, looking at her watch. "It won't be long before the first shift arrives."

"Yeah. Some of the third shifters went home when we were told we couldn't get in. I knew something bad must have happened, so I stuck around to see if I could help. I figured you all might need it," Viki said.

Viki was a couple of years younger. But since she was Jerelle's sister, Jamie saw her all the time. They bonded during nursing school. Viki was entering as Jamie was graduating. Jamie always knew Viki had picked the right career. She was the perfect nurse. She cared deeply for the patients, could be stern when necessary, and genuinely wanted to help people. Jamie was glad to run into her.

"Uh, yeah. Everyone is going to need a lot of help. Thank you for doing that."

"Jamie, are you ok? They didn't tell us much, but the rumors are flying around, like always..."

"No. Not even a little bit," Jamie said with tears in her eyes. "But I will be. Thank you for asking. I do need to get home, though. I need outta here."

"Oh, Jamie. I am so sorry," Viki said as she gave Jamie a quick hug. "Call me any time for anything! I mean it! Oh, since you are heading downstairs, could you do me a favor? Would you ask my sister to call me before she leaves? I want to check in with her. I tried calling, but the phones went out. And then things got so crazy. I just came up here instead of bugging her in the ER. Plus, you all needed help," Viki said.

"You got it, girly. I will pass the message along. Be safe, ok?"

"Definitely. Get some rest, my friend." Viki nodded to her and continued up the stairs.

Jamie continued down the stairs. When she got down to the second floor, the stairwell door opened. Kosina came through the door. She smiled at Jamie.

"I see you had the same idea. *Are* you ok? I mean, I get you aren't, given our night. But that little girl thing has me freaked. Do you want me to come over? I will. Plus, you owe me tacos," Kosina said, smiling weakly.

"Eating is the *last* thing on my mind. I will make good on my promise soon. I need a minute. I promise not to stay home alone, but I need to decompress, ok? The little girl thing has me a bit unraveled as well," Jamie said, as her eyes welled up and her face filled with sorrow.

They were talking as they were walking through the door to the first floor. They both walked faster past the hallway that led to the mechanical room. Jamie involuntarily shivered.

Kosina put her arm around Jamie and said, "I understand, sis. Can I at least walk you out?"

"Aw, thanks. But I am going to the ER to check on my cousin, Park. I want to make sure he's doing ok."

"Ok. Tell him hello and wish him a speedy recovery for me. I haven't been to his shop in forever. I need to get over there."

"I will. See ya, Kos," Jamie said as she hugged her.

They parted ways in the lobby. Kosina headed to the parking lot. Jamie headed to the back doors of the ER. Before going in, she called her brother, Albert, to break the news about Benji. She kept the call short because it was just too much for her to deal with her brother's grief after the night she had. She was not up to talking to her sister, so she just texted her, *I'm ok. Will text more soon. Call Bertie. He needs you. I need sleep. Lova ya.* She put her phone away, opened the doors, and walked into the ER. As she searched around, looking for her cousin, Jerelle, who was also still there, came over to her.

"Hey, Jamie. Looking for something?"

"Oh, hi, Jerelle. Some*one*, actually. Have you seen Park? I wanted to check in on him."

"Sure have. He's over in room four. I think Beamy is in there with him," she said, pointing to a room. "Hey, you doing, ok?" Jerelle looked at Jamie, concerned.

"Boy, a lot of people have been asking me that. Do I look like hell warmed over or something?" Jamie said, sounding a little more annoyed than she meant to. She quickly added, "I'm sorry, Jerelle. You only ask because you care. It's just been a hell of a long night. I am ready for my bed."

"Yup. It certainly was an epically shit-tastic night. It's ok. I understand. I am a little snarky and over it as well. I am on my way home. Call or text me if you need anything, even if you want me to come over and sit with you. I am happy to. When things calm down, let's catch up. Since you started school, it's been a minute since we hung out."

"I will. I promise. I appreciate that. I am sure that in the coming days, I will be venting a lot. Right now, I am still processing it all, I guess. And you are correct. I started school and fell off the face of the planet, didn't I? We really need to hang out and catch up! Hey, I meant to ask earlier, before I left for the third floor, how are Prue and Tawny?"

"Prue is stable. They think she will make a full recovery. But, oh Jamie…. Tawny didn't make it, Jame. She didn't make it,"

Jerelle said softly. "She just passed a few minutes ago..." Jerelle said with tears streaming down her face.

Jamie chucked her backpack and other belongings to the floor and put Jerelle in a gigantic hug, then just held on. Together, the women let out their grief and anger. When the crying slowed down, Jamie let go of her embrace. That's when she heard someone clear their throat. Jerelle, who was looking behind Jamie, smiled and said, "Call me later, ok? Love ya, girl."

"Jerelle. I almost forgot! Viki would like you to give her a call, ok? She's upstairs working right now, but she wants to hear from you."

"Got it. I will call her. Thanks, Jamie. Night."

Jamie turned around to see who was behind her. She was amazed and concerned to see J.J. standing there after all that had transpired through the night; her first thought was of her godchildren. Jamie panicked.

"J.J.! Why are you here? What's going on? Are the kids ok? Dee Dee texted me that she was home. Was that a lie?" she asked frantically, looking around the ER.

"Jamie. JAMIE. Slow down. Everything is fine. The kids are ok," J.J. said with his hands on Jamie's shoulders. He looked down into her eyes and said, "They are fine. I promise. Their grandmother is with them right now. I am here because a tree fell on Jeremy's truck while he was out helping with an accident.

Unfortunately, he was inside." Before Jamie could ask, J.J. continued, "It missed him. But some of the branches roughed him up a bit. He has a scratched cornea, some cuts and bruises, and a broken wrist. Thank God it wasn't worse."

"Oh my God. That's terrible. But I am glad he is going to be ok!"

"How about you? You look terrible. Did you know you are bleeding? Are you ok? Sounds like a grisly night here."

"How could you have possibly heard about it? Did it make the news already?"

"Small town living, J. There have been bits and pieces floating around all night. Plus, I ran into Frankie. *Are* you ok?" J.J. asked, looking directly into Jamie's eyes.

Because J.J. was her oldest and dearest friend and they knew each other well, she couldn't hide it from him. And she didn't want to. He was the one person she didn't need to be tough or strong around. And right then, she required stability, familiarity, and comfort. She looked up at J.J., her eyes welling up, shook her head "no", and just fell into his arms. They stood like that for a long time. J.J. didn't try to say he understood. He didn't try to see the bright side or make light of the situation. He just let her be. He let her express and get out what she needed to. When her sobs lessened and Jamie tried to pull back, J.J. brought her close again.

"It's ok. I've got you."

Jamie sobbed until she couldn't anymore. Her eyes were swollen and puffy. Her head was pounding. The adrenaline had long gone and was replaced by various aches and pains from the injuries she had sustained. She pulled back from J.J. and rubbed her arm gently. The bleeding had intensified.

Rachelle came around the corner and saw the blood coming through Jamie's bandage. Without saying a word, she led Jamie over to an empty bed so she could stitch her up properly. When she was done, she gave Jamie the tightest, longest hug she could.

"As my beautiful, strong yet soft, tough yet gentle, amazingly wonderful friend Jamie would say, 'what a fucking night', huh?"

Despite their sorrow for all their lost loved ones, despite the grief for their fallen coworkers, despite the anger for the people who caused it all, they laughed. They laughed and laughed. It was then that Jamie understood she would be ok. They hugged each other for a long time, rocking back and forth, simply being in the moment and supporting one another. When they let go, Jamie looked at Rachelle, grateful for her friendship and understanding.

"Thank you, Rachelle," Jamie said softly.

"Anytime, my friend. Anytime. Let's go get some sleep, huh?"

"Yeah. I think you're right. I was going to visit Park, but not like this. I heard Beamy is with him. I think I need to go home and sleep."

"She is. Jame, I mean no disrespect to you and your family. But where on earth did the name, 'Beamy' come from?"

Jamie chuckled. It wasn't the first time she had been asked that. It was a unique name. "Her given name is Beatrice Amy. I guess when she was little, she had trouble pronouncing it. What came out was 'Beamy,' and it stuck. It suits her. She is an absolute sweetheart. She beams and radiates warmth and kindness."

"Just like someone else," J.J. said as he came walking up to the women.

"Oh gawd, J.J., don't say things like that here. You'll ruin my reputation."

"We already know that about you, Jamie, my friend." Rachelle winked, squeezed Jamie's good arm, and walked away.

"So, uh, I don't think you should be alone right now. The kids and I were thinking that maybe you should stay with us for a couple of days. Unless you were going over to Pam or Bert's?" J.J. said hesitantly.

"No. I am not. Bertie is going through his own grief right now. And I don't have the energy to deal with Pam's onslaught of questions. If you and the kids don't mind, I would love to take you up on that offer."

"I wouldn't have said it if I didn't mean it. Come on, let's get out of here. I can put your bike in the back of my truck. We can stop by your place and pick up some things on the way. Dee

Dee is going to be stoked. She mentioned something about a movie night. Is that your doing?" JJ. asked, looking down at Jamie with a soft smile.

"It might be," Jamie said, smiling slightly.

Jamie bent down and picked up her things. JJ. grabbed her big old backpack, and they headed for the exit. As they neared the door and entered the waiting room, she heard something that made her stop in her tracks. Echoing through the room was the sound of a little girl giggling. She whipped around in a panic, her eyes wildly scanning the ER waiting room. In the corner of the room, sitting with what Jamie assumed were her parents, was a little girl. Jamie released the breath she had involuntarily held.

"Jame? You good?"

"Not by a long shot, dude. Not even a little bit. But I will be, eventually."

"We can talk about it on the ride home. Let's roll, shall we? Your chariot awaits."

"Why, thank you, kind sir," Jamie said, playing along. She looked at JJ. and said again, "I mean it, JJ., *thank you.*"

"That's what friends are for," JJ. said, looking down at her in a concerned but mostly caring way. "*That's what friends are for.*"

Together, Jamie and JJ. walked out of the hospital and into the parking garage, where her bike was chained. JJ. held her backpack as Jamie plopped her purse and other belongings into the basket on the bike. As she walked with her bike, she thought about what she and her coworkers and friends had been through. Each person went through something. Each person had their own horrific story from that night. As she continued walking with J.J. and pushing her bike, she started telling him her's.

Epilogue.

Ten months later, the town was starting to heal from that horrific fall night. The downfall of a small town was that everyone knew everyone's business. The upside was that everyone came together as a community, working together as a unit. So, the small town of Heatherwilde Falls did just that. They showed up for cleanups, held benefits, and did anything anyone needed. Powerlines were repaired. Tree branches were removed from streets, homes, and roads. The mess inside the hospital was cleaned up and processed. Too many funerals and memorials were held. Together, the town mourned and began to heal.

Jamie had graduated from college. She was now a nurse practitioner. After all that occurred, she felt a certain amount of responsibility and protectiveness for her friends and coworkers. She remained employed at Memorial Medical Center, but in a different capacity. She worked for an excellent doctor in one of the medical offices inside the hospital. She thoroughly loved her job. She was able to see patients in an entirely different capacity. It felt freeing to Jamie. She still saw her old coworkers, often meeting up for lunches and even hanging out with them. After bonding through the traumatic event, Jamie realized that it was ok to blend that line from coworker to friend.

Keith's parents got through the storm ok. So did his kids. And after hearing what Keith did for Tore, it strengthened his relationship with his kids, especially his daughter. Keith was still cranky and stern. But people saw him in a new light.

Charity left the hospital. She said she couldn't work in a place with so many reminders of all that they lost. She prioritized her family even more and got a job working at the local high school. Her kids didn't mind. They were glad to see her more.

Hugh also quit working at the hospital. He ended up inventing a lifesaving device, sparked by the events of that terrible night. He created an employee bracelet that, in the event of an emergency, could be pressed and would send an automatic response to central dispatch. It was also equipped with GPS, so no one's whereabouts would be unknown again. All the hospital staff were required to wear them while at work, and they were grateful for it, given what they had gone through. The invention was such a massive success that he was able to retire, spend most of his days with his kids, and help his wife at High Anxie-Tea. And he was finally able to go to a daddy-daughter dance with his youngest at their Spring Fling. He had the time of his life.

Milton, Kosina, River, and all the surviving ER nurses continued to work at the hospital. They felt that was where they could do the most good. Prue made a complete recovery and even returned to work after her injuries healed, although she transferred to the second floor and began working with OBGYN patients.

All the security guards that night received commendations from the police department. John retired and moved to a warmer climate. Glen went down to part-time and started a hostile environment training program for all current and future security guards. Bastian was offered jobs with both the local and state police forces. He said he felt that protecting the patients at the hospital was more important and chose to stay there. Robert and Eiler were also offered jobs by none other than Frankie. Both declined, citing similar sentiments to those of Bastian. Liatris and Wayne also stayed on. Tekonsha was on his way to a full recovery, albeit a slow one. He planned to come back to work as soon as he was cleared.

Tore was the one who was impacted the most. She was the youngest to go through such obscene terror. But instead of leaving nursing or the hospital, it made her more determined than ever to be the best nurse she could be. She decided to follow in the footsteps of the person she admired the most. She re-enrolled in college and joined the nurse practitioner program. Her family started paying attention to her after the shocking events and even told her how proud they were. Tore liked that, but found it didn't impact her much emotionally. She was grateful to be visible, sure, but Tore was proud of herself, and that felt better than anything her family could ever say to her.

The hospital hung plaques in memory of those they had lost. In a small space that had once been an unused closet, they displayed historical items from the old asylum, as well as printed stories from that time. That was in honor of Reid, who loved a good story as much as he loved history. A lovely photo of him sat there as well. Underneath the photo sat an engraving that read, "Big Red. Beloved son, wonderful brother, excellent nurse, all-around good guy, and the best storyteller around."

In the days following the events, the police did a sweep of the entire hospital. They noted all the tunnels that still needed to be boarded up. They found four that were still accessible. Before boarding them up permanently, the town officials went through them looking for any historical items. They also looked for more rotary phones. There was one on each floor of the hospital, one in the morgue, one in the mechanical room, and one in Myers Mental Health Clinic. None of them had been hooked up. They also found one at the school, one at Last Drop Coffee Shop, and one was found while they were renovating the local movie theater. (The same theater Jamie's parents had been in right before their accident.) Ten months later, Frankie still didn't understand their place in the events of that night. The community never learned about the phones.

Frankie had no idea how to explain something she herself didn't understand.

The little girl was never seen again. They went back and viewed the hospital security footage. Twice, they saw a little girl with long dark hair lead someone back toward the area where the mechanical room was located. One person was Dr. Kantivoric, the other was Benji. They couldn't see much of her or hear what the little girl was saying, but they did hear whistling as the girl walked with them. The investigation into the little girl remained open and active.

The most significant change that happened was in Jamie's life. After all that had happened and all they had gone through, she and Andy realized they wanted entirely different things. They ended things amicably. They both agreed they were better friends than anything else. He started seeing Tore, who was much closer to his own age, and they couldn't have been a cuter couple. Jamie was happy for them and thought they were a match made in heaven. Her friendship with J.J. slowly progressed and blossomed into something more. Neither had planned for it. Neither was looking for it. It just happened. He had been there every step of her healing journey. They spoke to Em, Dee Dee, and Rain about it before making it official. The girls, who had known Jamie their entire lives, were thrilled. Jamie moved out of her place and moved in with J.J. and the girls. J.J. did propose to Jamie, with the kids' blessing. But the couple decided they wouldn't rush it. A wedding would happen in good time.

Jamie was amazed at how her life had changed. She always thought she was content to be alone. She hadn't been looking for love. She enjoyed seeing Andy, but it had been very casual. Her relationship with J.J. was everything she didn't know she needed in her life. And she loved being a stepmom. It wasn't always easy, but it helped that she had known the girls all their lives and their mother had been Jamie's best friend. Her sister Pam was beyond thrilled and took every opportunity to give Jamie and "I told you so". She always knew Jamie would be a great mom. All of Jamie's nieces and nephews acclimated quite nicely to having new cousins. It was a wonderful, blended family.

One rainy summer day, Jamie awoke in a panic. She had been dreaming of darkness and weird sounds. She slowly opened her eyes and looked around for the source of the noise. A shadowy figure at the end of her bed slowly stood. It was tapping on the bedpost while whistling. Jamie blinked to clear her eyes as the figure came into full view. It climbed up onto the bed and crawled closer to Jamie. She was frozen in shock. There was Val, whistling and crawling toward her. She giggled and said, "Hi Jamie, did you miss me?" She smiled her abnormally large smile at Jamie and showed her rows of narrow, needle-like teeth. Blood was dripping off the top few. Just as Val got right up to Jamie, Jamie screamed. She screamed and screamed and screamed some more. She kicked and flailed, trying to get Val off the bed. Val giggled more. Her hand reached out and touched Jamie's shoulder. Off in the distance, she could hear a voice and felt someone else's touch. A familiar, calming voice said, "Jamie....Jamie, it's ok."

Jamie woke up with a start. J.J. was there next to her, holding her in his arms. He was telling her over and over that she was ok and that she was safe. He held her as she sobbed and shook. He held her until her heart rate normalized and she stopped shaking. He kissed the top of her head, repeating that it was just a nightmare, it was only a nightmare. He held her as she calmed down and fell back to sleep.

Later that day, Jamie and J.J. were over cleaning out Jamie's house. Even though Jamie had moved in with J.J. and the girls, she had resisted selling hers. She wasn't sure why. After several months of discussing it with J.J. and the girls, she decided it was finally the right time to sell. She and J.J. were slowly clearing out years of accumulated clutter.

"Ah, I am not saying you have a lot of junk, Beautiful. But I am not, *not* saying it either," J.J. said, laughing while carrying several boxes out to Jamie.

Jamie looked around for something to toss at J.J. To her left, she saw a balled-up pair of socks that had fallen out of one of the boxes. She picked them up and threw them at J.J. He batted them away, laughing harder. Jamie loved their playful times. She didn't realize how much she missed having that in her life. After her parents' deaths, her divorce, and re-enrolling in college, life became quite serious.

"I mean, look at this, Jame. What are you doing with an entire box of... what is this? Old technology?" J.J. said picking up old phones, pagers, and even an old PDA out of a big, broken-down box.

"Oh my god! I forgot all about these," she said excitedly. She picked them up one by one. "This is history right here. You can't find good quality like this anymore."

"Uh, yeah, no. No one uses that technology anymore. So 'quality' is insignificant, my dear woman."

"Yeah, ok. I know that. I just wanted to keep them out of the landfill, but I wasn't sure where to recycle them. So, the box just kept growing and growing.... You know how it is," Jamie said, shrugging and chuckling.

"Ok, well, figure out what you want done with your box of nostalgia while I run *this* box out to the truck, ok?"

"Yeah. Hey! I will search for tech recycling on this fancy new phone Dee Dee made me get."

"She would be so proud!" J.J. said, smiling widely, as he grabbed a box and went out the front door.

Jamie took the smartphone out of her purse. She knew that Tore was also thrilled that she had stepped into the current times. She started typing, *recycling old phones* when she heard a ringing. She stared at the phone in her hand, wondering why it was ringing. As she realized it wasn't the phone in her hands that was ringing, the hair on the back of her neck stood up. She looked down into the box, where, at the very bottom, she found her old neon light-up push-button phone. She hesitantly picked the phone up. Shaking like a leaf, she grabbed the handset and held it to her ear. Very cautiously, she said, "Hello?"

"Hello? Hello? Are you there?" asked a young voice. The voice then deepened slightly and said, "Are you there.... *Jamie?*"

Acknowledgment

I would like to begin by expressing my deepest gratitude to my loving and supportive husband. Your unwavering belief in me, your encouragement, and your endless patience have made this journey possible. Thank you for encouraging me to dream. I couldn't have done it without you.

To my son, thank you for being a sounding board and source of inspiration. Your creativity, positivity, and energy remind me daily of the importance of following my passion and pushing beyond my comfort zone. I am following my dreams because of you. I am also incredibly grateful to my nephews, whose encouragement and enthusiasm have never diminished. Your words of motivation have meant more to me than you could ever know.

A special thank you to Terri, Michael, E.F., and Heather for your invaluable input and thoughtful feedback. Your perspectives and insights have truly helped me.

Thank you all for your unwavering love, support, and belief in me-this journey would not have been the same without each of you.

About The Author

Tillie Coldwater is a multifaceted author whose passion for writing ignited in her youth and has only intensified over the years. As an outdoor enthusiast, she brings a unique perspective to her literary endeavors, blending her love for the natural world with her creative expressions. Tillie embraces life's beauty through hiking, kayaking, and gardening, and finds her bliss at the shores of Lake Michigan. She finds joy in family moments with her amazing husband, wonderful son, playful, gentle giant dog, and two spirited nephews. She draws inspiration from her vibrant family life, fostering a nurturing environment that encourages creativity and exploration.

Her creative spirit doesn't stop at nature; Tillie is also an avid knitter, photographer, and painter. A true autumn enthusiast, lover of dramatic storms, and spine-tingling horror books and films, Tillie infuses her writing with the same thrilling excitement. With a unique perspective, heart full of humor, and a spirit that embraces adventure, Tillie invites readers to journey into her world where the unknown is always lurking, and the line between reality and nightmare is never clear.